Terri Nixon was born in Plymouth, England, in 1965. At the age of nine she moved with her family to a small village on the fringe of Bodmin Moor, where she discovered a love of writing that has stayed with her ever since.

Since publishing in paperback (through independent small press BeWrite) in 2002, Terri has appeared in both print and online fiction collections, and published *Maid of Oaklands Manor* with Piatkus in 2013.

Penhaligon's Attic

Terri Nixon

piatkus

PIATKUS

First published in Great Britain in 2016 by Piatkus

1 3 5 7 9 10 8 6 4 2

A CIP catalogue record for this book
is available from the British Library.

ISBN 978-0-349-41265-8

Typeset in Caslon by M Rules
Printed and bound in Great Britain by
Clays Ltd, St Ives plc

Papers used by Piatkus are from well-managed forests
and other responsible sources.

MIX
Paper from
responsible sources
FSC® C104740
www.fsc.org

Piatkus
An imprint of
Little, Brown Book Group
Carmelite House
50 Victoria Embankment
London EC4Y 0DZ

An Hachette UK Company
www.hachette.co.uk

www.piatkus.co.uk

Part One

Chapter One

18 March 1899, Porthstennack

The weather was still winter-nasty. Clouds were building, almost purple in places, and the air was damp and heavy, with a stiff, chilly breeze that snapped at the hedgerows. The hill from beach to home seemed steeper than ever today, but Freya was smiling as she shifted her grip on the bucket, and ignored the rub of sand between her fingers; what did a little reddened skin matter when there was a birthday tea waiting?

Although it was nice to be special for the day at school, Saturday birthdays were so much more fun, and this one had been the best of days from the start. Papá had walked with her down to the sea after breakfast, as he usually did on Saturdays, but today his friends had greeted her as if she were already an adult: 'Good morning, Miss Pen'aligon!' 'Happiest of birthdays to you!' and 'Mornin', my lady,' and bowing and smiling ... It was lovely to be eight years old, and she shook her head pityingly for her seven-year-old self; such a baby, and she'd never realised it. Perhaps now she was even old enough to be a big sister, at last; her biggest wish might come true after all.

She huffed as she swapped her bucket from hand to hand. Wet fingers slipped on the handle, but once her grip was secure once more she turned her face towards the cottage, and made her legs go faster. Rare treats awaited, Papá had gone home early especially, although he'd pretended it was for something else. He might even have written her a new story for bedtime. That would be the best gift of all. And tomorrow the beach would be waiting, always waiting; each wave newly made and bringing any number of treasures tumbling onto the shore. Or none. That was the joy of it, to be the first to know.

She paid a visit to the privy before going into the house, and put the bucket against the door where she could look at it while she sat. Today's treasures were still covered in sand, and it looked as if something was moving in there too, but it was hard to tell with all the sliding and shifting of shell and stone, weed and wood. She must get a bigger bucket . . . but then how would she carry it? She frowned, kicking her dangling feet against the wooden front of the privy. Perhaps if she collected everything she wanted into a bag she could wear over her shoulder, instead? Or asked Papá's friend Mr Fry if he would look after it until Papá could bring it home each day?

She was still musing on this as she straightened her skirts over her chilled legs, grateful for the thick material even if it was damp. As she threw a handful of ash down the hole in the seat she had made up her mind to speak to Mr Fry, and by the time she reached the back door, and raised her hand to the latch, she had disregarded the problem and her thoughts moved forward to the tea that awaited just beyond. She heard voices, and habit froze her into a listening pose while she worked out which of the more troubling moods had taken her parents today. It took no more than a few seconds to find out.

'... was right,' Papá was saying, his voice low and tight, as if he was barely controlling his temper. Mama was the fiery one, but when Papá was roused he could be frightening too. 'I should never have re-named the *Julia* for you.'

'I never told you to!' Mama flashed back. Her accent always came out stronger when she was angry. If Freya closed her eyes she could imagine a lady like the ones in Granny Grace's Spanish books: dark-eyed beauties in bright colours, smiling ... but there was no smile in Mama's voice now. 'I *never* told you to do that, Matthew! You cannot blame me for what has happened.'

'I did it because of you!'

'Because you thought it would make me love you again?'

There was a silence and Freya held her breath. When Papá spoke again his voice was just tired. 'I didn't realise you'd stopped.'

'I ...' Mama hesitated. 'I was so young. But I did love you. I still do.'

'But you want more.'

'We *deserve* more, Matthew! Not just Freya and me, but you too ... where are you going?'

Freya's eyes widened and she picked up her bucket again, preparing to hide around the corner if she heard Papá coming to the door.

'To the Tinner's.'

'No! *Not* today! Freya will be home soon, and you will *not* spoil her birthday.'

'No,' Papá said, his voice dropping. 'Of course not. I was forgetting.'

Freya readied herself anyway, taking a step back just in case.

'Did you finish the story?' Mama wanted to know, and Freya was relieved, though not surprised, at the sudden change in her tone; everyone had learned to sway with the wind of her moods.

'Yes,' Papá said, 'I think she'll like it.'

Freya's heart settled a little; whenever Papá wrote something for her it meant he was happy, or at the very least not in a black despair. Some of his tales were hard to follow; filled with incredible creatures and troubled children, but the children always triumphed, and their adventures left her breathless. She hoped her special birthday tale would be a sea-story, those were always the best.

The arguing had fallen silent now; and Freya decided it was time to let them know she was home, so she pushed open the door. The smell of baking filled her nostrils, and she ignored the strained looks on her parents' faces, and beamed at them both. 'Cakes! Are they for me?'

'Of course for you, *mi tesoro*!' Mama stooped to hug her, heedless of her wet coat and her sandy hands and face. 'But first you must clean yourself, and Papá will give you his gift. *Then* the cakes will be cooled enough for you to eat.'

'Well,' Papá said, 'the important thing is what have *you* brought back for tea?' He examined the contents of the bucket, making slurping noises and licking his lips, which made Mama laugh, and the last of the tension in the room drained away.

Freya ran upstairs to change into dry clothes, shivering at the low rumble of thunder that rolled around the valley, trapped by the steep fields on either side. Thank goodness Papá was home tonight, not putting to sea in the *Isabel*. As she changed she pondered on what she'd heard; it was no secret that his boat was now named for Mama, but Freya had forgotten it had ever been anything else. Now she remembered it had once been *Julia*. She'd heard the sad story of Papá's little sister, who had died as a child from a simple chill ... Thunder sounded again, and Freya swallowed hard and removed her wet clothes faster. Changing the name of a boat was supposed to be a bad thing, even she knew that, but could it really be why Papá's catch was so low? Surely the fish didn't know he'd changed the name, and suddenly learned how to avoid his nets? Could fish even tell which nets belonged to which boat? They couldn't read, anyway.

No. It was what her Granny Grace would call 'a complete nonsense'. And now there were happier things to think on: Papá had written her a story, and that cost nothing so she needn't feel bad about it. And Mama's cakes ... Freya's mouth watered at the thought of them.

Downstairs again, dressed in rough but warm and dry clothing, Freya was glad to see her parents looking at one another without scowling.

'There you are.' Papá's fingers twitched over the cooling rack. 'You're just in time. You'd better hurry up, else I'll eat them all myself.'

Freya took one and bit into it. The warm sponge crumbled

7

on her lips, and she made a wordless sound of delight at the rush of sweetness and the tang of the hidden fruit. Her mother's face softened, and she heard her father's low chuckle behind her, and it was one of those perfect moments when she noticed all the good things around her. The kitchen was warm from cooking, and the smell of the fruity cakes still hung in the air, the sound of the rain just made it all seem cosier instead of making her shiver. Just this once it was nice to be the only child in the house; brothers and sisters might have stolen this moment.

'I have a gift for you,' Papá said.

'A story!' Freya forgot she wasn't supposed to know, but it didn't matter now.

He shook his head. 'Something else.' He raised an eyebrow as her face fell. 'Don't you want a birthday present? I can give it to someone—'

'Of course I do!' Freya spluttered bits of cake over her hand, and Mama clicked her tongue and gestured her over so she could clean her up. 'What is it? Liquorice?' Her favourite.

'No. Granny Grace and Grandpa have some of that for you though. Wait here a moment.'

While Mama wiped sticky fruit from Freya's mouth, Papá went into the pantry and came back with a large wooden box, which he placed on the table. Freya brushed away the last of the crumbs on her shirt-front, her eyes wide and fixed on the box, and then lifted the lid. Inside nestled a wooden boat – a Cornish lugger just like the *Isabel*, but with no name yet on its polished side.

'What do you think?' He sounded suddenly anxious, and Freya turned and wrapped her arms around him. She felt his hands shaking on her shoulders, as he returned her embrace. 'Does that mean you like it?'

'Yes!' She returned to the box, and carefully lifted the boat out and put it on the table where she could see all over it. It must have taken him months to make, since he was so rarely home; every detail was perfect. She couldn't wait to tell Juliet all about it in school on Monday. 'What's its name?'

'Her name,' he said. 'And it's whatever you want it to be.'

Freya pulled a face. 'Why does it have to be a girl boat?'

'Most are, it's good luck. So what will you call her?'

'I don't know yet.' With the echoes of their argument about re-naming the *Isabel* in her mind, Freya was determined to choose wisely. She brushed her finger over the polished wood, and peered more closely at the hand-stitched sails. 'Mama, did you make these?'

'No, that was your Grandmama Grace.'

Freya hoped she had imagined the tightening in her mother's voice. 'She can't make cakes as good as you can though.'

'As *well* as,' Papá corrected.

'As well as. Can I have another one?'

Mama smiled, then. 'Supper first, and then one more. And then you must go to bed.'

'But aren't I allowed to stay up later now I'm eight?' Freya made her eyes very wide; Mama usually found it hard to refuse her when she did that.

Mama laughed. 'Ah, but tomorrow you will not sleep later than you did when you were seven, will you? You will be out of bed just as early.'

'But if I promise to try?'

She saw her parents exchange a glance, then Mama

9

shrugged. 'Tonight only, since it is your special day, and Sunday tomorrow. You may stay up until nine o'clock, and not one minute later.'

Freya grinned. 'I'm going to wash my treasures, and dry them, and put them away, and eat my supper, and play with my boat, and—'

'You will have time for half that,' Papá pointed out. 'It's already almost eight o'clock.'

'Supper,' Mama said firmly. 'Sit now, and we will think about washing your treasures after we have eaten. Matthew, take the boat off the table and set the places.'

Supper was happy enough; there was no sliding back into those harsh voices and dark looks, and if Papá was worried about money, and Mama was cross with him for blaming her, they didn't show any of it. After Freya had helped clear the plates away, she and Papá emptied out her bucket and sorted through what she'd brought back. She'd been right, something *had* been moving in there; as she lifted one of the bigger stones off the pile a tiny crab came scuttling out.

Mama, passing the table with a jug of water, shuddered. 'Take that thing away!'

Papá winked at Freya and picked up the crab, and put it back in the bucket along with the stone and some seaweed for it to hide under. 'We'll take it back down to the beach tomorrow,' he promised. 'Now, you wash your hands and I'll go and find my book. I have a new story for you.'

'But I haven't played with my boat,' Freya protested. 'Please, Papá?'

'It's late, and anyway you can't play with her until you've named her.'

'I'll think of a name while I'm in bed,' Freya said. 'And then tomorrow, can I take her to the beach?'

'We'll see. Now go on, see you're clean and ready for bed when I get there.'

'Goodnight, Mama.' Freya picked up her boat, so she could look at it and find a name after Papá's story was over. 'Will you come to tuck me in?'

'After the story,' Mama promised. 'I must put your clothes to dry for tomorrow. And clean the rest of the plates. And the table needs to be scrubbed now you have emptied sand all over it.' Something about her tone made Freya look at her again, and she was certain she saw a glimmer of tears in Mama's beautiful dark eyes.

'I'm sorry we made a mess,' she stammered, her heart sinking. 'You work so hard.'

'We all do.' Mama sniffed and shook her hair back, making an effort to look cheerful. She smiled at Freya, but the smile slipped when she looked at Papá. 'I chose this life, after all.'

'You did,' he said tightly. 'And we're all together. That much we can be thankful for, can't we?'

Freya was dutifully pulling the covers to her chin when her Papá came into her bedroom, his journal in his hands. She felt the anticipation like a tingle in her tummy, and couldn't help bouncing on the bed a bit as she waited for him to settle into the chair next to her. Like a seven-year-old. She stopped quickly at that thought, but not before she had seen the smile tug at Papá's mouth.

'This story is called *The Scarecrow and the Whale*,' he said,

11

and when he opened his journal Freya could see lines and lines of close-packed writing, each one of those words written just for her, and it gave her a feeling of such happiness she wanted to hug him again. But she sat quietly and closed her eyes, and Papá began.

His voice was soothing and low as he read, and Freya left her room and went with her favourite group of children to a faraway island, where the whales played offshore and the mysterious Scarecrow made his appearance; a tall figure, gaunt and unsmiling, reading poetry printed in white on a bolt of black cloth. Freya worked with the children to build a fortress against the Scarecrow, helped them uncover the secret hidden in the poetry, but before she learned what role the whale was to play, Papá closed his journal.

'We've been longer than I promised your mama.' He sounded as regretful as Freya felt.

'Will we finish it tomorrow?' She was disappointed, but her voice was soft with fast-approaching sleep.

'Not tomorrow. I'm going out with Mr Fry and his crew.'

'But why?' Wide awake again now, Freya sat up straight. 'It's Sunday! Besides, you have your own boat.'

'A boat which isn't making any money,' Papá reminded her. 'And I know it's Sunday, but Roland – Mr Fry – has offered me a place on his night catch. Ned Scoble's been taken ill again. That'll mean money to buy you a bigger bucket,' he added, dropping his voice as if they shared a secret, 'so you can find a bigger crab to frighten your mama with.'

But Freya didn't smile back. 'I'm sorry I made a mess.'

'She wasn't cross about that.' Papá leaned forward to kiss her on the forehead. 'She just gets homesick sometimes, and misses her family. That doesn't mean she's not glad she's here with us. But, well, they have more money than we do, and I think your mama feels a little let down by the way things have been going . . .'

He seemed to catch himself then, perhaps he thought he shouldn't be telling her these things. But she wanted to hear them, and now she was older she was starting to understand why, more and more often, Mama's pretty face became clouded and sad. It sounded as though there was nothing she could do to help though, at least until she was big enough to leave school, and get a job gutting and scaling with the other girls.

Echoing the darker direction her thoughts had taken, the thunder growled outside the window once more and a splatter of rain hit the glass. Papá looked up, as if he could see through the curtains to the night beyond, and then smiled at her again.

'Don't worry about your ma, she'll be happier again when the spring comes. You know how she loves the sun. The catch will rise again, and we'll have money to buy nice things.'

Freya nodded, happy again. 'Will I see you in the morning, before you go?'

'I'll be leaving later than usual, so I'll take you to the beach,' he said. 'We can let Mama's new friend back into the salt water where he wants to be.'

He leaned over and turned the lamp to its lowest, leaving a faint glow which he would extinguish later, after she was asleep. By its dim light she could just make out the shape of the new boat on her dresser. She closed her eyes and wondered if she would dream its – *her* – name.

Papá kissed her again. 'Goodnight, Lady Penhaligon,' he whispered, and Freya smiled. No dreams needed.

The morning brought high winds, and Freya was forbidden to go to the beach after all. The roof of Hawthorn Cottage was rattling where the slates had loosened, and Mama kept glancing at the ceiling, as if she could work out where Papá would need to climb. She wanted him to stay home and fix it today, but he couldn't miss a chance to work, especially a night catch, where he would take on Ned Scoble's role as skipper. He left after a late breakfast of bread and dripping, taking Freya's bucket as promised.

Freya watched Mama's eyes following him through the small yard and out onto the lane. With his hat pulled down over his ears, and his collar up, he might have been anyone but for the way he carried himself; Freya would recognise that easy, long-striding walk anywhere. Her bucket looked so small in his large hands, and she felt again the disappointment of not carrying it herself. She didn't even mind running to keep up, as long as it was towards the sea. Her friends would be there; not one of them her own age, and all busy, but they always had time to say good day, and ask what she'd found.

'Come away from the window now,' Mama said. 'If the weather clears you may go down this afternoon. But now we have work to do.'

'Aren't we going to chapel today?'

'No. There is too much to do. The water is already on the fire, you can fetch the tub from the outhouse.'

Freya sighed, but waited until Papá had passed out of sight

before turning away from the window. She obediently fetched the big tin tub, and scrubbed it clean ready for the water Mama was heating. Then she scrubbed the big laundry stick too, and sat down with the suet grater to grate blue, mottled soap into the water. If only it were still her birthday! But she supposed Mama always worked on *her* birthday, so next year Freya decided she would do the same, it wasn't fair otherwise. It would be the grown-up thing to do.

Idly stirring the soap into the water, Freya pondered again the question of boats' names. She thought of Mr Fry's boat, the *Pride of Porthstennack*. That wasn't a girl's name. Or perhaps it was 'bride', and not 'pride'; she'd never taken any notice of the words painted on its side. Whatever it was called, it would have put out to sea by now, and Papá would be working alongside all the others. It wasn't the same as running his own boat, but at least Mr Fry was giving him a chance, and perhaps that would mean Papá wouldn't want to drink so much. It was puzzling; the less money he had, the more he wanted to spend it in the Tin Streamer's Arms up at Caernoweth. That didn't make any sense at all, as far as Freya could see, and just upset Mama even more.

Later, as she worked the small, upright mangle in the out-house, Freya kept looking hopefully out at the sky. It wasn't clearing, in fact it was getting worse. The outhouse door repeatedly banged closed so she pushed it as far open as it would go, and wedged a rock against it. Five minutes later the rock slid away and the door slammed shut again. Standing in the dark with her heart hammering, Freya felt the first tremor of real fear for her father. She went in search of her mother, who was stripping the sheets from hers and Papá's bed.

'Can I go to the beach?'

Mama shook her head. 'Everyone is too busy to watch out for you, and the rain is coming down harder now. Besides,' she straightened, and nodded to where Freya's coat was spread to dry on a rack. 'You've nothing to wear.'

'Will he be safe?'

'Of course he will, *mi tesoro*,' Mama said, more gently. 'Mr Fry is sensible, he would not let his skipper put to sea if he thought it was dangerous, and in any case Papá would soon turn back if things got worse.' She pulled the eiderdown straight, and adopted a brisker tone. 'Now listen. Tonight Grandmama Grace will be coming to stay with you. I'm going to meet a friend in Plymouth. She is all the way from London, and only staying a day or two. I'll return in the morning, but you will already be at school so I shall see you at dinnertime.'

Freya couldn't remember hearing about this friend, but that was no surprise; she often got bored when grown-ups were talking. 'Does Papá know you won't be here when he gets home?'

'I told him,' Mama said shortly, 'but whether or not he remembers, I cannot say.'

Granny Grace arrived just before teatime. She was Papá's mother, and had come from money a couple of generations ago, so she spoke almost like a toff but she had a tough streak in her that came out now and again – especially with Grandpa Robert. Her manner of speech had come down through Papá too; he didn't sound like most of the other fishermen. Freya was actually pleased whenever other children poked fun at her for talking the same as him, but when they saw their teasing was having the opposite effect to the one they hoped for, they soon stopped bothering with it.

Granny put her overnight bag in Mama and Papá's room, and saw Mama off with a wave. As soon as the door was closed, shutting out the wind that rattled the cupboard doors, she planted her stick firmly between her feet and leaned on it.

'Now then, Miss Freya, let's get the important matters out of the way.' She reached into her pocket and withdrew a paper bag. 'Liquorice, for the birthday girl!'

'Thank you!' Freya dipped into the bag and withdrew a piece of the sticky black sweet.

'Do you like your boat?' Granny asked.

'Oh yes, I love it ... her! Have you seen her with the sails on?'

'I have. Your pa showed it to me when it was all put together.'

Freya frowned. 'Mama doesn't like me to call him pa.'

'Well Mama's ...' Granny cleared her throat. 'It's not their way, where she comes from. But he's a Cornishman, and you're a true Cornish maid, for all you've got your mother's looks.'

'Have I?' Freya couldn't help but be pleased with that. Mama was like a painting, with her tiny waist and her clear skin, and her clothes fit her so well and made her look like a lady even though she was just a fisherman's wife.

'So, what's the name you've chosen?' Granny prompted.

'She's the *Lady Penhaligon*.'

Granny smiled. 'Well if that isn't perfect, I don't know what is. Grandpa Robert will paint the name on her for you, if you bring her up to the shop.' She looked out at the darkening night. 'Tomorrow will be soon enough for that, I think. You can come back with me after breakfast.'

'Granny?'

'Yes?' She was already bustling about the kitchen, and it was clear she was actually glad Mama had gone out and left her in charge.

'Why don't Papá's friends visit us now? They're nice to me at the beach, but they never come here no more.'

'Any more,' Granny corrected absently as she put two plates on the table. She didn't answer for a moment, but Freya waited and at last Granny sighed. 'Last year there was an accident, a bad one, you must have heard about it?'

'Mr Fry's accident?'

'Yes, that one. You remember his son, that used to be your pa's best friend?'

'James. I don't remember him, but I've heard Mama and Papá talk about him sometimes.' Those conversations had usually been short and sharp; James and Papá had stopped being friends a good while ago now.

Granny Grace nodded. 'Well, he was never a natural fisherman really, not like your pa. He left to become a stone mason's apprentice. Anyway, the *Isabel* wasn't doing too well, so Roland offered your pa James's place on the *Cousin Edith*. That was Mr Fry's other boat he had at the time, the mackerel seine boat. He hasn't got it anymore.'

'What happened?'

'Do you know those young lads they take out, the ones that swing the minices into the water to scare the fish into the nets?'

'Is that the rocks, on ropes?'

18

'That's the ones. Well one of the boys never heard Mr Fry shout for them to stop, so your pa went over to him. But he tripped, or ... stumbled somehow, right into the boy.'

'Did the boy fall in?'

'No, but the minice came around into the boat instead of into the water. Hit Mr Fry square on the knee and almost cost him his livelihood, as well as his life. As it was he had to sell the *Cousin Edith*, and came close to having to sell his cottage, too. It was only thanks to his crew, and the people he's helped over the years repaying his kindnesses, that he's kept his home and his trawler.'

Freya swallowed, feeling a little bit ill at the thought. Her own knees seemed to shrivel. 'I didn't know he was so badly hurt.'

'It was a dreadful business,' Granny Grace said. 'Doctor thought he was going to lose the leg, but he was lucky. He can walk again, with a stick, but he's still not right and can't work.

Dismay aside, Freya was still puzzled. 'But *he* still likes Papá, he's asked him to go out on his big boat tonight because Mr Scoble's not very well.'

'He's always had a soft spot for your pa. Always prepared to give him a chance. But the crew thought what happened was your pa's fault.'

'And was it?'

'No!' Granny pursed her lips and picked up the bread knife, then she shrugged. 'Well, maybe. And even if it wasn't completely his fault, trust is easy lost when men depend on each other.'

Freya took this in, feeling very grown-up now she knew a little bit more. 'Granny?'

19

'Yes?'

'Was Papá drunk?'

Granny didn't answer, but she began slicing bread with more vigour than usual. Freya decided it was best not to press for an answer, but she didn't think she needed to anyway.

'Granny?'

A heavy sigh. 'Yes?'

'When will Papá be home?'

'When the work's done. And before you ask, the work'll be done when it's done.'

Later Freya lay in bed, listening to the sounds of Granny Grace getting ready for sleep. Her footsteps along the creaking hallway were soothing, and even the door closing on Mama and Papá's room was a comforting sound – unlike the rain hitting the window, and the rising shriek of the wind. She looked over at the *Lady Penhaligon*, sitting safe and dry on the dresser, and tried not to think of Papá out there on the wild seas. Maybe he'd be on the beach by now though, unloading the catch, or separating the nets for mending from the ones that would survive another trip out.

She dozed, and drifted, remembering the Scarecrow and his poetry, and the children who battled him to escape the island. What could the whale possibly do? Maybe he would swim close enough to the island's shores for one of the children to swim to. They could climb on its back and he would take them to safety on the mainland where they could fetch help. She wondered if the brothers and sisters in that story ever argued, or if they were too happy to have each other, just like she would be to have a big family. She wondered too, if there were any whales off the Cornish coast . . .

A sharp crack of thunder brought her wide awake again, her eyes open but blind in the darkness. She must have slept longer than she'd realised; Granny Grace had come in and extinguished the lamp already. Or maybe Papá had come home and done it? He must have been very quiet. She slipped out of bed, and pulled the curtain aside and peered out; lightning stabbed at the side of the hill, and she barely had time to draw a breath before the thunder followed; a rumble that went on longer than ever before, growing much louder before it finally faded.

Freya listened for snoring from downstairs, where Papá would be sleeping on the couch, or for sounds of him changing into the dry clothes Granny had left for him in the kitchen. But there was nothing except the storm. She lit the waxy blob that was all that remained of her candle, pulled her dressing gown from the back of the door, and went out onto the landing. At the top of the stairs she listened again, but there was still nothing. Her toes curled against the cold, but she made them open out again, and went down to the front room. The couch was empty, the clock ticked, deep and impersonal as it marked the passing time, and a glance at it told Freya it was well past midnight. She went to the kitchen. There was the pile of dry clothes, just as Granny had left them, along with the hunk of bread and the butter dish, ready for Papá's supper.

Her heart was thudding painfully now. She looked at the door, as if hoping fiercely enough that it would open at any moment would make it happen. The door remained closed. The kitchen was a flickering confusion as lightning flared and

21

died, and flared again, and the thunder was almost constant. 'Papá,' she whispered to the empty room, 'where are you?'

The image returned, of her exhausted father making his way up the beach, dragging his feet in sodden boots, his bag weighted down with his portion of the catch Mr Fry shared out. That's if they had caught any; Mama said they would come home if the weather worsened, and it had certainly done that. She would go to meet him, then. Sleep would never come to her anyway, not until he was home and safe. The thought of telling Granny Grace came and went in a flash quicker than the lightning; she would refuse, and would insist on sleeping in Freya's bed too, to ensure she remained there.

Her coat was still in her parents' room, so, as quietly as she could manage, Freya took down Granny's coat from its hook by the back door, and found her own boots. They were still wet inside but it didn't matter. She pulled the enormous coat tightly around herself, over her dressing gown, and tied the belt. Then she blew out the candle and let herself out through the back door, and into the snapping teeth of the storm.

Chapter Two

The strength of the wind took Freya's breath away, until she learned to turn her head to the side and down. She waited until she was able to see a little better, and watched her own feet as they sloshed through puddles towards the gate of Hawthorn Cottage, and then onto the lane. Now she could hear the sea, and smell it too, that fresh, salt tang right off the water. She strained for the sound of someone coming up the hill, for voices, footsteps, even laboured breathing, but there was only the howling wind and the boom of the tide.

Within five minutes she was tasting sea-spray on her lips, and only then did she raise her face to stare forwards, into the driving rain. Lightning flickered, and left her with an imprint of the shoreline, but she could see no people in the lingering image. Boats had been dragged as high up the beach as they could go, turned upside-down and secured with ropes and weights, but in the dark she couldn't read the names. The bigger boats, including Papá's *Isabel*, would be anchored around the headland where the harbour provided some shelter.

The black sea rolled, looking like some huge, hump-backed monster, with white eyes that only opened when it struck rocks or the breakwater; the tide hissed its way halfway up the beach, but Freya couldn't remember how to work out if it was on its way in or out. She shouted, in case there was anyone there, but her voice was whipped away on the wind – she would find some shelter and wait.

For the first time in her life Freya felt a surge of anger towards Mr Fry; he shouldn't have sent his trawler out, he should have told them it was too dangerous. If he had done that, Papá would already be home, safe and dry and snoring. There was a sudden stinging in her nose and throat, and although she couldn't feel the tears she knew they were there. Shivering, she found the place where the breakwater met the sea wall, pulled Granny's coat straight and sat on it. She shoved her wet hands beneath her armpits and wished she'd thought to pick up gloves, then she lowered her head so her face was tucked into the little dry, quiet pocket formed by her arms and her raised knees, and waited.

After what might have been five minutes, but equally might have been an hour or more, she thought she heard something. A voice? She lifted her head, and turned it to lessen the noise of the wind. The storm was finally abating, and the sound had come from the other side of the breakwater ... Freya stood and brushed the sand off her chilled hands, then felt her way through the dark, up the steps and onto the breakwater. The wind was louder here, and gusted hard, but she heard the call again, coming from just ahead.

The thunder had gone from deafening shout to low grumble, and the swell of the sea was more rhythmic now, less fiercely unpredictable. Still, the water washed across the stone at her feet and she slipped more than once; it had been a dangerous idea to come out here, even if it meant she might find whoever was looking for her ... A gull's cry sounded, and Freya's heart skittered, then sank as she recognised the sound. There was no one here after all, just a hungry bird. Papá had told her gulls would sometimes even fly at night, in order to get at the smaller fish washed up by the incoming tide.

The disappointment was almost painful, but it told her one important thing: the tide was halfway in after all, which meant she would need to get back to the foot of the cliff, or perhaps even further, to remain safe while she waited. She turned to make her way back to the beach, but a fresh surge from the sea caused her to hurry and her foot went out from under her once again. Steadying herself on one hand and one knee, she started to rise, all her attention on the safety that waited at the other end of the breakwater, and a moment later she was slapped from head to boots from behind, thrown forwards, and then crushed flat by the weight of the wave. Dragging a ragged, shocked breath, she struggled to her knees, but the backwash stole her balance once more and sent her sliding towards the edge.

Her hands slapped around frantically, trying to find something to grip, but there was only smooth stone and the tug of the tide running back to the shoreline, pulling her with it. And then she was tumbling into empty air. Her scream was cut short, as she hit the water and it closed over her head, and

25

the roaring in her ears was everything until she realised she must take a breath. But if she did, she would die. Her dressing gown and Granny's coat pulled her down, and her boots were weights on the ends of her tired legs. The coat's sleeves unrolled, covering her hands and making her arms too heavy to lift, to try to swim, or at least struggle to the surface. Her dressing gown was a shroud.

In the terrifying blackness of her underwater world there was only one hope, and she made herself go still until she felt the pressure of the next wave. It was the only way she could tell which way was forward, and, with her heart pounding and her chest ready to burst, she felt something semi-solid beneath her outstretched boot. She scrabbled with both feet, but the sand shifted beneath her, making it impossible to find a grip, and every time she found the sea bed it vanished again, leaving her foot scraping only water. Her chest burned, and her feet cycled with increasing panic, until, finally, one more push from the sea urged her close enough to find her balance. She managed to raise her arms enough to push her hands behind her, helping herself to move forwards, but her head was growing light, and she had so little strength left ...

And then there was wind in her face, abruptly, without warning, and so unexpected it took a moment for Freya to realise, to trust it, and then to open her mouth and gasp in the air. She stumbled, knocked off her feet by another wave, and now she was crawling, the sea only rising as far as her aching shoulders while the sleeves of Grace's coat flapped and folded beneath her numb hands.

Breathing hurt, despite the unutterable relief at being

able to do it. Her elbows kept giving way and pitching her face-first into the sand, and as soon as she felt safe enough she stopped crawling, head down, with her hair hanging in front of her face like a dripping curtain. Relief gave way, surprisingly, to anger. More than anger. A deep, betrayed fury; she had loved the sea all her life. She had admired it, been in awe of its raw power, spoken to it like a friend even, and thanked it for the treasures it had given her. In return it had almost stolen her life. It smashed itself against the rocks behind her, and against the breakwater, expressing its own anger at losing her.

Another wave lifted her forward and she began to crawl again, over sand and pebbles, until she was as far up the beach as she could go. There was no question, now, of waiting for Papá; he would take a single look at her, and fear would make him so angry he might do anything. Forbidding her to come to the beach again would be no punishment at all, but even after his fury had died away he might not read her stories of sea adventures any more. So, she would get her breath back, and then she would go home, crawl into bed, and worry about explaining Granny's wet coat in the morning.

The sky was beginning to clear now, showing a thin slice of moon. The rain had stopped, and the wind had eased off until it was little more than a chilly tug on her wet hair. Freya settled into a gap between two rocks just above the high tide line, and wondered if she would ever stop shivering; it was making her ache all over, and that road was so steep she would only fall if she tried to walk it now. She closed her eyes, letting relief take away some of the anger and the discomfort. Papá would be home in the morning, and so would Mama, and Grandpa

Robert would paint the hull of the *Lady Penhaligon*. Everything would be the same ... except that Freya would never come to the beach again, not as long as she lived.

'Freya? Freya! She can't hear me ...'

'Let me try. Here, girl!' A hand, pushing her hair away from her face. A rough hand, but a gentle one. Until it started slapping at her. 'Come on, maid, wake up!'

Somehow she opened her eyes and looked into a pair of watery blue ones. She didn't know them. She closed her own again.

'Freya, love!' That was a voice she knew, and she prised her lids apart again, this time to see Granny Grace peering worriedly at her. A breeze lifted Granny's greying hair, and Freya wondered tiredly why she had opened the window when it wasn't summer ... She blinked as a spatter of rain caught her forehead, and only then did she feel the hard rock at her back and the soft sand beneath her, and reality returned to wrap her in its cold fist. She struggled to stand.

'Easy,' the rough-handed man said, and she recognised Brian Cornish, one of the few men who had remained true to her father. 'You've been here all night?'

Freya tried to speak, but coughed instead, making her Granny wince. She tried again. 'Not all night.' The effort of simply speaking made her feel nauseous and light-headed, and the further explanation she had been going to offer faded into a low mumble.

'We'll get her over to Roland's,' Mr Cornish said. 'Then I'll go and find Matthew.'

Freya slumped in relief; Papá was back. Nothing else mattered now.

'Is that my coat?' Granny said suddenly, and although she was still tight-faced and pale, she tried to sound stern. 'Well no wonder I couldn't find it this morning.'

'Sorry,' Freya muttered, and said no more as she gave herself over to the comforting sensation of a strong arm sliding beneath her knees, and another at her back, lifting her from the wet ground. She let her head fall against Mr Cornish's shoulder, and the gentle swaying sensation as he carried her through the hamlet lulled her thoughts and helped the shivers to subside. She was dimly aware of Grace walking at her side, and knew she was talking, but the words wouldn't settle into anything understandable so Freya gave up trying.

She coughed again, and Mr Cornish stopped, but it was only so he could knock at a door. Voices, some raised in alarm, others low and angry, and a hand on her forehead ...

'We'll take care of her here while you fetch her pa.'

There was no way of knowing how long it was before she heard Papá's voice, but the relief and happiness that washed over her made her want to cry. She twisted her head on the pillow, and saw him in the doorway. Unshaven and with his hair sticking up, and ... what was that? She frowned and peered more closely, but it wasn't until he had crossed the room and knelt by the side of her bed that she saw the welt, scored at the top with a nasty-looking cut, that coloured his jaw and split the edge of his lower lip. She had been right to worry, it had been dreadfully dangerous out there last night.

'All right, sweetheart?' he said, his voice shaking as much as the hand that cupped her cheek. There was a horrid smell hanging around him, familiar in a way, but she'd never known it like this: bitter and stale and strong. His hand, though, was as gentle as a breeze on her skin, and his eyes were a darker blue than usual, the brows furrowed ... he'd been as worried for her as she'd been for him, it seemed. The smell didn't matter; he was safe.

It was a good while later that she noticed Grandpa Robert's grazed knuckles. No one mentioned them.

After they moved her back up to Hawthorn Cottage, the days blurred and meshed; the curtains were always closed and it was hard to tell day from night. People came and went, sometimes sleepy, sometimes fired with a strange urgency; and strange smells were everywhere, even in the bed linen and in Freya's nightclothes. But not the same smell that had clung to Papá the morning after he'd been out at sea, that smell never came again. These were medicine-smells; pungent and ripe, they made her cough, and coughing hurt. But of all the bad things she could sense happening, none were as bad as the looks that passed between Mama and Papá whenever they found themselves in Freya's room at the same time.

They talked in low, accusing voices. Papá was tense, Mama was tight and snappish, and when they went out onto the landing and closed the door, Freya could hear them arguing, although the words were hard to make out. She heard them blame one another though, for Freya's decision to wait on the beach and help Papá home with his burden; he thought Mama shouldn't have gone to see her friend, she said something about it serving him right what had happened to his face, which had swollen and bruised badly over the days following the storm.

And then, a few days later, the worst thing of all happened. By now Freya was almost well again. She was beginning to eat properly, and was enjoying a warm vegetable soup for supper, when Mama came into her room with a large suitcase. She began to remove Freya's clothes from the wardrobe and place them in two piles on the foot of the bed.

Freya laid her spoon back on the tray. 'What are you doing, Mama?'

Mama picked up one of the piles of clothes and put it in the case. 'We're going to go away for a little while.' She sounded calm, but underneath it Freya could hear a tremble.

'Where?'

'To my friend's home in London. It will do you good.'

'Oh.' Freya thought for a moment, then frowned. 'Won't Papá lose too much money if he goes away from here?'

Mama stopped her packing, and came around to take Freya's hand. 'Papá is not coming with us, *mi tesoro*.'

'Because of the money?'

'Freya . . . ' Mama was struggling with something, and Freya went cold as she remembered those harsh conversations, blame igniting anger on both sides.

'Are we leaving forever?' she blurted. *Please, no . . . I don't want to . . .*

'I'm sorry, it will be difficult at first. For both of us. But you will have a new life, one that you deserve. As will I!' Mama's accent came out strongly in her agitation.

31

'But what about Juliet? And my other friends? What about school?'

'You will have a good schooling in London, better than you get at Priddy Lane. My ... my friend has good connections, he will find you a place.'

She drew Freya into her embrace, and kept talking about the same stupid things, and all Freya wanted to do was to pull away and shout: *you said your friend was a she! You don't care about Papá at all ... you don't even care about me, you just want to go back to a rich life that isn't yours anymore!* But she didn't do, or say, any of those things. She just sat, exhausted and drained, and too dismayed to argue.

Part of her felt a creeping relief that she would not be near the water any more, and her blank gaze came to life as she looked across the room at the *Lady Penhaligon* on the dresser. If Papá hadn't made it for her she wouldn't care if she never saw it again; the thought of the horrifying, heaving seas beneath something so delicate made her shudder inside. But he had made it, so she would take it to London, and think of him, and pray for him when the weather was bad.

Two days later, Papá lifted her into his arms and buried his face in her coat, and she heard the tears in his voice as he begged her forgiveness. But she didn't know what she was supposed to be forgiving him for, so, as before, she just stayed silent until Mama gently separated them.

'Come, Freya. London waits.' She turned to Papá, and reached up to kiss his cheek, and Freya heard her whisper, '*Que vaya bien, mi vikingo.*' Papá closed his eyes and his jaw went hard, and Freya understood his unspoken words: how could it *go well* now?

Mama took Freya's hand, and they splashed across the puddle-filled yard to where Grandpa Robert waited with his pony trap, the cases already loaded and tied down. He would take them up to Caernoweth, where the coach would carry them to Bodmin, and then on, on, on ... how far was London? And would she have the chance to say goodbye to Granny Grace?

Freya took a last look back at the cottage, at Papá standing in the doorway, his arms folded tight across his chest as if he were in pain, but trying hard to find a smile for her.

That desperate, bright-eyed smile would haunt her, she knew, until she was old enough to come home again. And in the meantime, as Mama said, London waited.

May 1899, Penhaligon's Attic, Caernoweth

My dear Matthew,

I hope this letter finds you in good health. I understand you to have stopped drinking now, which pleases me, of course, but I must tell you it is too late to hope it will bring me back to you. Our life is here now, and Henry (Mr Webb) is very fortunate in his situation, and will give Freya a good life. I know you would wish that, above all else.

Henry has kindly arranged, and paid the fees at, a very smart boarding school called St Catherine's, and Freya will surely do well there. She has settled in already, and is liked by the other students. She has your family's fascination with words and stories, and will write to you often, I am sure.

Take good care of yourself, mi amor (for I will love you always, in my heart). Our time together began well, did it not? We were a beautiful, accidental, but perfect union for a while, but I know you understand why I cannot remain in Cornwall with you, and no more can we expect our daughter to live that uncertain life.

Yours, in remembrance of happier times,
Isabel.

Matthew Penhaligon put the letter on the table and held out his hand, fingers spread, to check for shaking. Steady as the rocks that framed the coast. Steady as the floor beneath his booted feet. Steady as a man who no longer drinks. The letter sat there, rocking gently for a moment along its fold, before falling still. He stared at it. Nothing changed, the words did not suddenly rearrange themselves to tell him Isabel was coming home, that she was sorry for taking Freya away, that she knew how badly he hurt without them both.

Since Freya's near death not a drop had touched his lips, soured his breath, addled his head . . . each night he had withdrawn from the dwindling company of men who still spoke to him, and lain in his bed, his gut clenched so tight with guilt and despair that his muscles ached. He had somehow avoided looking at Freya's collecting bucket, her scribbles on whatever paper he could find for her, and what remained of her belongings, scattered around her room as if she were coming home at any minute.

He had gradually stopped staring at the empty chairs at the kitchen table, and imagining that last perfect moment, when they had been united in laughter on Freya's birthday. He prepared and ate his meals in silence. He realised he had never even finished reading Freya the story of the Scarecrow and the

Whale, and had posted it off, hoping Isabel wouldn't be too busy in her new life to read it aloud.

As his system cleaned itself, his mind played different kinds of tricks; he'd found himself thinking of Isabel as she'd been in the early days. Long before she had realised what kind of life she was accepting with him, and when she had begun to call him her Viking. He remembered the day they had met, the way she had looked, with the captain of the boat gripping her arm and looking around the busy Plymouth barbican for help with his young stowaway.

She had appeared every inch the indignant young lady, but Matthew was familiar with a little Spanish from his fellow sailors, and he hadn't been able to suppress a grin at some of the words that passed those sweet lips.

'You want her?' the captain had shouted, seeing his smile, and Matthew had shaken his head, but when the girl turned her face pleadingly to him, and her dark eyes had locked onto his, he realised that wasn't quite true. She flicked her thick hair back, letting him see the beauty of her cheekbones and her long, slender throat, and stretched out her free hand to him.

'Please, sir, this foolish man doesn't understand—'

'Who are you calling foolish?' the captain protested.

'If I go back to Spain my Papá will—'

'I know your father,' the captain interrupted. 'We do reg'lar business, how else would you know to hide on my boat? Your pa's a good man. Now, if I can't find someone here to take care of you, back you'll go, and this time you'll work your passage.'

'Please!' she called to Matthew again, ignoring her captor. 'I came here to look for my sister. Help me to find her?'

35

'Sister? Well why didn't you say so?' The captain let go of her arm. 'Mind, you still owe me for stowing away. If you can't pay me I'll see Señor Batista for it.'

'Then do so,' the girl said, with some satisfaction. 'I have no money, or I wouldn't have had to hide on your smelly old ship!'

'Right you are, I will. Then he'll know where you are, and come for you.'

'No ...' The girl looked panicked, and Matthew stepped forward.

'How much?'

The captain gave him a sly look. 'For her passage? Or to keep quiet when I see Señor Batista?'

'I'll pay steerage only,' Matthew said, in a deceptively calm voice, 'and if I hear her father, or anyone connected with him, has been asking questions, I'll know where to find you.' He made a point of checking the name painted on the boat's hull, and then smiled at the captain. 'So, how much?'

The captain glanced from Matthew to the stowaway and sighed. A few minutes later, and somewhat lighter in pocket, Matthew took the girl's arm and led her to the nearest bar, where he discovered, with no surprise whatsoever, that she had no sisters.

He looked at the letter on the table now, and realised a smile had found its way to his lips. Whatever had happened since that afternoon, those ten years when passion of one kind or another governed their lives, that first day was as fresh and clear in his memory as it had ever been. Without the alcohol to cloud his thoughts, he could recall perfectly, not only what had happened, but how it had felt. Maybe if he'd remembered it earlier, he wouldn't have let things slide into ruin.

But did he miss Isabel herself? Whenever he considered what he'd lost, his first thought was always Freya. Lively, intelligent, trusting child, blessed with her mother's eyes and thick dark hair, but his own easy-going nature ... she'd got the best of what each of them had to give. Her love of the sea had been his, too, and that felt like the deepest, surest bond of all. He'd always planned to one day introduce her to the joy of skipping over the waves, running with the wind in the sails, the cry of gulls overhead, getting louder as the nets filled ... he'd imagined her working alongside him, her face frowning in concentration, then smiling up at him as they set off home together at the end of the day ...

Those thoughts had sustained him through the worst of times as his business died, but it was impossible to not then be beaten low by the memory of the day he'd chosen drink, and the company of his crewmates, over easing Isabel's discontent. When Roland had decided not to put to sea that night after all, Matthew should have gone home, read the rest of the story to Freya, helped Isabel with whatever needed to be done, and then talked to her. Taken her to bed. Anything. Instead he had gone to the Tinner's Arms, and there he had stayed, left to sleep it off until he had felt a fist in his shirt-front, and then another in his face.

His own hand curled on the table as he pictured Freya, found wrapped in his mother's coat they'd said, shivering and terrified, wet from head to toe but no one knew if she'd just been hit by a wave, or had fallen into the sea. She herself had not told anyone. He'd lost count of the times he'd whispered, 'I'm sorry,' into an empty room, but he did it again now, in the kitchen of his parents' home. His home too, now.

'Don't torture yourself, boy,' his mother said softly from the doorway.

Matthew looked up. Grace came into the room and sat opposite him. He gestured to the letter. 'From Isabel,' he said, unnecessarily.

'What does she say?'

That she loves me still . . . 'That Freya has begun her schooling, and that they're settling in well.' *That she remembers our early days as I do* . . . 'That they're not coming back.'

Grace nodded. 'As we knew. You need to let them go, love.'

'There's some good news,' he went on. 'Freya is popular enough at school, and I daresay she'll be writing to me herself soon.' He drew a ragged breath. 'I'll be well in a minute, Ma. I just . . . ' he shrugged. 'I couldn't help hoping.'

'You wouldn't be human otherwise.' Grace had softened since that night, doubtless remembering Matthew's sister Julia, although she hadn't spoken of it. It was too terrifying to remember how quickly that other robust, healthy little girl had slipped away, and to see Freya lying in much the same state, shivering and convulsing; waking, screaming from terrible dreams . . . it had been the icy dash of water on Matthew's self-pity. He could only pray it had drowned it for good.

Matthew re-folded the letter. 'Where's Pa?'

'He'll be here d'rectly. You all sorted out in your room now?'

He nodded. 'Thank you for letting me move back in, Ma.'

'Where else would you go? Hawthorn Cottage is too big for you to be rattling around in, even if you could still afford the rent.' Grace patted his hand, and rose to begin preparing the evening meal. 'Roland still giving you work?'

'When he can. Ned's still not right, so I've got his place for a while.'

'Be a hard day for you when Roland's boy comes back.' It was a casual enough observation, but he noticed she'd stilled as she waited for his reaction. The bad blood between him and James Fry was public knowledge, and pointless to deny. He couldn't even blame James; he'd nearly killed the man's father after all.

'He might not come back.' But he didn't believe that; sooner or later James would have learned all he could from the architect he was working for, and be back to put it all into practice for himself. In the meantime he'd be wanting work, and Roland would have no choice but to give any vacant place on the crew to his son.

Matthew was saved from any further talk of James Fry by the arrival of his father. Robert grunted at them both and sat down with his pipe and tobacco. 'Got some mendin' to do tonight, maid,' he said to Grace. 'I'll not see you 'til bedtime, I don't reckon.'

'I'll help,' offered Matthew. 'Least I can do, you've put a roof over my—'

'Don't need your help.'

'Look, Pa, I—'

'I said . . .' Robert knocked the old tobacco out of his pipe onto the table, and fixed Matthew with a cool look, 'I don't need no help. You'd do better gettin' down the beach and sortin' out them nets for Brian Cornish while he still rates you worthwhile. Not many left who do.'

'Roland Fry does,' Matthew put in, unable to help himself. But if he'd hoped to sting his father into forgiveness he was disappointed. The blame for that fell on Matthew's shoulders too; Robert had been born in this town, lived here all his life, and now he could barely look his former friends in the eye thanks to his useless drunk of a son. Worse, the granddaughter on whom he'd unexpectedly doted, had been taken away. Even the shame was secondary to that loss, and until now no one had had any answers for his question: when would she be home? Matthew's fingers tightened on the letter he was about to put in his shirt pocket, and he caught his mother's eye. She shook her head minutely: *I know, but please . . . don't break his heart.*

Part Two

Chapter Three

Seven years later, Porthstennack harbour

The August sun was finally, blessedly, losing its strength. A welcome breeze stirred Matthew's sweat-damp hair, and he was just looking around for where he'd left his shirt, when he saw her. Isabel. Standing at the edge of the beach, as if to set foot on the sand would see her entangled once again in the life she had fought to escape. His heart lurched in sudden hope, and he looked beyond her, but she was alone. She waited, silent beneath her white parasol, clearly knowing he would come to her. She was right, of course.

'Where's Freya?' he asked, before she had a chance to say anything.

'And good afternoon to you, Matthew. I'm well, thank you.'

'Good. Where's Freya?'

Isabel relented. 'She is well. Can we talk? Civilly?'

'Wait here.' Matthew left her standing alone, and went to

find Roland. The skipper was waist deep in the calm sea, floating and checking a newly mended rowing boat with Ern Bolitho, and Matthew waded out to meet him, enjoying the cool water that plastered his trousers to his legs.

'Isabel's here,' he said. 'I'll be a few minutes, but I've not gone.'

Roland looked around, squinting against the setting sun. Then he glanced at the road. 'Not brought the little maid, then?' Matthew shook his head. 'Go on, boy,' Roland said. 'We can finish up here. Likely you'll have a lot to talk about, after all this time.'

'I don't know what she wants. It might be nothing.'

'She din't tell you she was coming?'

'No.'

'Likely it's not nothing, then. Go on.'

Matthew was about to argue, but Roland had already turned back to the boat, and instead he patted the old man's shoulder and sloshed back up the beach.

Isabel was watching him, her parasol lowered to rest on her shoulder now. She'd never felt the need to carry one when this had been her home, and she'd spent so much time out of doors; it was just another affectation, and underlined their differences all the more strongly.

His shirt was hanging off the breakwater to dry, and, acutely aware of her looking at him, he plucked it down. But it was too hot still to even think about putting it on so he tied it about his waist instead. Let her look away if it suddenly offended her to see him shirtless, he was a working man and this was his workplace.

'Right,' he said, drawing level, and then he continued on

44

past, without waiting to see if she followed. He called back over his shoulder, 'Tell me what you've come to say.'

After a moment he felt her presence at his side, and he glanced down at her. He didn't remember her being this small. Delicate. He looked at her wrists, and was struck with a sudden and unexpected guilt for her as well as for Freya; how could he have expected her to adapt to the life of a fisherman's wife? She was high-bred, a wealthy girl stowing away in search of romance and adventure, and what had he given her? Drudgery and thankless work.

He slowed his pace. 'Isabel,' he began, but she interrupted. 'Do you remember the letter I sent? The last one?'

'First and last,' he reminded her. 'Of course.'

'It was the truth. I loved you.' She wouldn't look at him, but he heard her voice catch, and he believed her. At least, he believed she meant it.

'Why are you here?'

'I'm going away. To America.'

Matthew said nothing. He didn't trust himself. America? He swallowed hard, his throat tight, suddenly, and found the question that was burning through him. The only question that mattered. 'And Freya?'

Now Isabel did look at him, a fierce and direct stare that examined far more than the colour of his eyes, or the way his eyebrows always told of his mood. She searched his face, and then her eyes took in every exposed inch of him. He couldn't think why, until she spoke again.

'You are healthy now. You no longer drink.' It was not a question, and she had known it before, but perhaps she was worried he might have fallen into his old ways.

45

'Not in eight years,' he confirmed.

'And you have steady work?'

Matthew's eyes narrowed at the questions. Was she looking to return? More to the point, did he still want her to? He answered carefully, 'Roland is skippering again, but he gave me Ned's place. Just temporary, 'til I save enough to get the *Isabel* re-fitted and working again.'

'Ned's place?'

'Ned Scoble. He died, what, three years ago?'

She nodded slowly, her eyes back on his again. 'Then Freya will come back to you.'

The breath went out of him, and he sagged onto the low wall beside him, his head lowered. From some distance he felt her gentle hand on his bare shoulder, her thumb rubbing absently at his collar bone, while he composed himself, then she sat beside him on the wall .

'You were always a good father, Matthew,' she said, her voice soft. 'Freya adores you. Will you take her back?'

'Will I . . .' Matthew lifted his head and stared at her. '*Will* I?' How could she doubt it?

'I am engaged to be married.' She lowered her hand to her lap again and moved slightly away from him. She had never enjoyed the smell of his work, but he no longer cared. Freya was coming home.

'She hasn't told me any of this,' he said, when he could think straight again. 'She sent me a birthday letter just last month, but she hasn't said anything about coming home, not for years.'

'This is because she does not yet know that Henry and I are planning to leave England. She believed, as I did, that her time here in Cornwall was over.'

'Why are you going?' He didn't really care, but felt obliged to ask anyway. 'I thought your Mr Webb was hoping to put himself forward in the next general election?'

Isabel raised an eyebrow. 'Freya seems to have kept you well informed.'

'All she's told me is that the Unionists are hoping to make a good showing, and that he's one of them.'

'Politics,' Isabel waved her hand. 'Bores me silly.'

'That doesn't bode well for a politician's wife. Will you go back now, and tell her? Will she be pleased?'

'Pleased? She will think Christmas has come early. Yes, I will tell her, and then I will write to you when I know more. No doubt she will write immediately.' Her smile fell away as she stood up. 'She will be here by the end of the summer.'

Matthew stood with her. 'Thank you,' he said quietly. 'I know it will be hard for you.'

'I will miss her,' she admitted, blinking hard. 'I miss you as well, but—'

'I know. We were never the real thing, though, were we?'

To his surprise she gave a little laugh. 'No, I suppose not. Who knows if that even exists? You rescued me though, and we had a lot of fun at the start.' She lifted her hand and placed it over his heart, then traced a line down his chest. 'And you were always, *always*, my beautiful Viking.'

'Don't.'

'Why not?' She glanced around. 'Is anyone looking?'

'No, but—'

'I know every inch of you,' she said, in a musing tone, and opened her hand out, splaying it over his stomach. 'But you're still a mystery, and not mine to solve. I hope you find your *real*

47

thing, Matthew Penhaligon.' With a sigh of regret she stepped away, but he could still feel the path of her finger on his skin, and the heat of her hand.

'I will write again with the arrangements.' She made her way back to the road, and Matthew remained behind, watching her. He placed his own hand over the phantom warmth of hers. There had always been that heat, that fire between them, but it had never been enough to hold her, to make her let go of what she had run away from before. And when a fire died, what was left?

February 1910, Bodmin, Cornwall

There was no going back now. Secrets, lies, call them what you will, she had spun them until she hardly knew the truth herself any more. Anna Garvey glanced at her daughter, looking pinched and worried, and far older than her seventeen years, and the doubts she had so far suppressed began to rise again: what had she been thinking? To leave everything behind and come here, grasping at the one flimsy line that might, just *might*, draw them into calmer, safer waters ... she must have lost her senses. But what choice had there been, in the end?

Aunt Oonagh might have helped. She'd certainly have wanted to. But it would have put her in the worst position possible. Uncle Colm would have spared less than a minute's thought before turning Anna away, and telling her to straighten her own affairs; he couldn't risk becoming embroiled in this terrifying mess, and she couldn't ask him to. Cousin Maeve was married, and had her own concerns, and as for cousin Keir ... he'd have been the one person she could have relied on, but the money Anna had scraped together had barely got her and Mairead as far as England, let alone New Zealand.

Anna's breath hitched in a surge of sorrow as she realised she might never see any of these, her only true family, again. She couldn't write and explain, even once she was settled, only to drag their undeserving lives through something too dark to contemplate. Better they should believe her sordid story of falling for a man who wasn't her husband, than they should be burdened with the terrible truth. They would feel betrayed and angry, and they might even miss her, but their lives would remain untouched in every other way.

They had finally reached the last leg of this exhausting journey, and Anna seized her case in one hand, and her daughter's hand in the other, and walked across the road to where the coach waited. It felt like a lifetime ago that she had last been comfortable, and in familiar surroundings, but even if comfort waited at the end of this journey, the familiarity would have to be built afresh, in a new country and with new people. What would they make of her and Mairead? Especially poor Mairead ... The girl was a bundle of nervous energy, chattering like a magpie one minute, silent and withdrawn, even sullen-looking, the next. Small wonder.

The coach journey, after the relative luxury of the train from Plymouth, was a form of jolting, slow torture. The roads were not as bad as she'd feared – deepest Cornwall was perhaps not so far beyond what she knew, after all – but it seemed to take forever to cover just a few miles, and the day was dark-ening already. Anna pulled her scarf further up her chin, and saw Mairead do the same.

'Won't be long now.' How many times had she said that in the past two days?

Mairead nodded, and returned to staring out of the window, at the lowering sky and the heavy drops of rain that blatted across the glass. Not so different from home, perhaps, but hardly weather to lift the spirits. The other occupants of the coach were similarly inward-thinking, and Anna relaxed into her seat, reasonably sure no one was interested enough in her and Mairead to strike up a conversation.

Her thoughts turned once again to what she had left behind, but now the first flush of panic had settled there was a new, gnawing worry; that someone would piece together what had happened, or that she or Mairead would say the wrong thing and bring their world to a crashing halt. It was likely they would be forever running away, but at least they had this place to run to. For now.

'Are you sure Doctor Bartholomew got the telegram?' Mairead asked suddenly, cutting through the gentle snores and heavy, head-cold laden breathing of the other travellers.

'It was sent in good time. He should have received it.'

'And he won't mind?'

'Mind?'

'Well, that he's been renting the place off you for all these years, and now you're just going to take it off him and move in?'

Anna frowned. As much as it pleased her that Mairead had given some thought to their reception in Caernoweth, and its effect on other people, she didn't want to admit the same thought had been niggling at her own already cluttered mind. 'I don't want to upset anyone, of course,' she said carefully, 'but I do own the property. And it isn't his main livelihood, he only takes the profits after the rent is paid, and that can hardly cover the costs of running the place.'

'Well, I just hope he got the letter,' Mairead said doubtfully, and Anna had to bite back an irritable reply, after all Mairead was right to be concerned. What *would* they do if her erstwhile tenant proved difficult? Her lawyer had wired to inform him of her intention to move into the Tin Streamer's Arms, and that she would be arriving soon, but there had been no time to await a reply. Because he was a doctor she assumed him to be a man of some refinement, or at least good manners, but what if he turned out to be nothing more than a country quack with a raw temper?

She tried to spend the remainder of the journey practising her persuasiveness, and silently rehearsing the words she would use to oust the gentleman, but all she could think about was how good it would feel to lay her head on a pillow and close her eyes. The jolting of the carriage actually proved quite soporific, once she became accustomed to it, and her head began to droop, only to be brought up sharply again each time the wind blew the rain against the window.

At last they arrived in Caernoweth. The coach pulled in at an hotel with a generously sized yard, and Anna climbed down and retrieved their cases from the rack. Mairead alighted and stared at the huge building, her eyes wide.

'Is this it?'

'No,' Anna said, with some regret. 'It would be nice, wouldn't it? But this is a proper hotel, the place we're looking for is just a pub.'

'Where is it?'

'I've no idea,' Anna admitted. She led the way out of the hotel's yard, and Mairead followed, and they found themselves standing at the top of a steep hill that appeared to be the town's main street. There was only moorland at their back, so at least that meant there was only one direction to go in, and Anna took a fresh grip on the handle of her case.

'Right, *ma mhuirnín*, let's find this place before we fall asleep on our feet.'

There were few people about, but dotted among the dark shops they passed were houses with warmly lit windows, and sparsely placed gas lamps flickered above their heads; it looked as if this town was going to be similar to the one they had left behind, by sight at least.

Despite the discomfort of the weather and the heavy case, Anna felt a flicker of hope that it wouldn't be so terrible here after all. Her optimism was strengthened when she glanced at one of the shops they were passing; like many of the shop fronts they'd passed it was an ordinary house that had been converted to a business, and although the front window was dark there was the unmistakably steady glow of electric light from a room beyond, that spilled across racks and racks of books, piled haphazardly and seemingly at random. She looked at the sign above her head; *Penhaligon's Attic. Curators: Robert and Grace Penhaligon.*

All her beloved books were back in Ireland. There had been neither time nor room to consider packing any to bring away with her, and she was already missing them. As Mairead had grown older and more independent they had become the perfect escape from an increasingly dull existence. Dull, that was, until the violence . . .

'Mother, come on!' Mairead's voice cut into her thoughts. 'We're already nearly halfway down the hill, it must be here somewhere.'

'Right. Let's see . . . ah. Look, there, on the other side of the road.' Anna pointed to a plain door with a sign hanging above it, and although she couldn't read it she knew what it would say. Her heart began to pick up pace, and she took a deep breath. Now she would discover whether or not this Doctor Bartholomew would be the source of more trouble, or if he would simply accept her and Mairead into his home. Then there was the question of how on earth she was supposed to run a pub when she'd had no experience, had rarely even been inside one. But one hurdle at a time.

'Is it not open yet?' Mairead said when they'd drawn close enough to see. The windows were dark, but, as in Penhaligon's Attic, there was light in the rooms beyond. 'It seems as if it must be quite late.'

'Not really. It's just dark early because of the weather, and the time of year.' Anna pressed her face against the window, and cupped her hands around her eyes to cut the reflection from the nearby gas light. 'I can see someone moving around in one of the back rooms. We'll go around that way, come on.'

There was a small yard at the back, with a low wall running around it and a battered-looking gate that hung off one hinge. Anna lifted it with her foot as she pushed, and manoeuvred it creakily back until it hit a clump of overgrown grass. She left it there, not sure it would survive the return trip, and led the way towards the door that loomed into view at the end of the roughly laid path. She tried the handle, prepared to leave it and walk to the nearest window to knock, if necessary, but the handle turned and the door swung inwards. Anna could see a little better now her eyes had adjusted, and she found herself at the lower end of a narrow passageway with a gentle upwards slope and what looked like an earthen floor.

Halfway along the passage, a door stood ajar to her right. There was only darkness beyond it, but curiosity led Anna to push the door wider, and a second later her heart leapt and staggered as a shape flashed by her, a lighter shadow in a roomful of dark ones, and vanished through the door to the garden.

'Mother of God!' Mairead breathed. 'What in the world was that?'

'I think it was a cat,' Anna said, hoping she was right. 'It was too big to be a rat.'

'Are you sure?'

'No.'

There was a silence, and then Mairead giggled. It was a rare and much-missed sound, and Anna smiled in the darkness and reached back for her daughter's hand. 'Come on, let's go and find this Doctor Bartholomew before we talk ourselves back out into the rain.'

The passage ended with two doors standing at right angles to one another, and beyond them both lay their future. The one in front would probably lead into the bar, the one on the right to the house. Anna's insides tightened for a moment, and she felt the flutter of sick fear once again, but there was no alternative beyond returning to her home and facing what awaited there. She grasped the handle of the door on her right and pressed down the latch, and then she was standing in the back kitchen of her own pub.

For a moment she and Mairead stood in silence, then Mairead spoke. 'I was expecting something a bit ... grander.'

'I'm sure I don't know why,' Anna said. 'I told you from the start it would just be a little place. And old.' But she couldn't deny the sinking sense of disappointment at the squalor of the room. She coughed as the tickle of dust and soot stroked the back of her throat, and discovered the taste had already settled on the back of her tongue. She fought the urge to spit.

'How old is it?' Mairead put her case down and started to walk around the kitchen, touching the crooked cupboard doors, and running her fingers along the cluttered worktop, dancing them over pots and pans, and grubby-looking utensils.

'Well if it belonged to Malcolm Penworthy it must date back at least to the Civil War, so that's the middle of the seventeenth century. Probably before that.' She nudged a blackened coal scuttle with her foot. 'I don't think it's seen a wash cloth since.'

'And it's been in your family all this time?'

'Yes. Don't mess with those things until they've been cleaned.'

'Why didn't you tell Father about it, when you knew it was yours?'

'Not now, Mairead.' Anna longed more than ever for her own room, and time to think. 'I'm going to find Doctor Bartholomew,' she said, to discourage any more questions. 'You can stay, or come with me, as you wish.'

'I'll stay.' Mairead looked fearfully at the door that led to the rest of the house. 'I won't touch anything, I promise.'

'See that you don't. We don't want to upset him or his wife any further than we already have.'

Mairead sat in the chair by the range and gave a sigh of bliss, and for a second Anna envied her the ability to close her mind to the difficulties of life. Then the feeling faded, and her heart contracted for the struggles that lay ahead for her daughter.

As she stepped back out into the passage she readied her greeting, composing one to fit whatever type of man Doctor Bartholomew turned out to be, but when she pushed open the door to the pub, she found herself in a dark, presumably empty room. She stood a moment, torn between the need to find the doctor, and the natural curiosity about her new home, but before she'd had the chance to decide which was more important she heard a scuffle behind her in the passage, and then a low-pitched mumble.

'You'll be she, then.'

'I suppose I would be.' Anna studied the newcomer, surprised and disappointed. He was short in stature, and his clothes ill-fitting. His hair – such as remained – was wispy and white, and floated around a lined face like mist. His overall appearance seemed to have been assembled entirely by accident. His manner left a great deal to be desired, too, and when he unfolded his arms and thrust out his hand she was mortified to find herself hesitating. But she shook it, hoping he hadn't noticed.

'It's nice to meet you, Doctor Bartholomew,' she said, trying to sound as if she meant it. 'I'm Anna Garvey. But,' she added, as the ghost of her old humour surfaced, 'you may call me "she".' The joke fell flat, but the man had clearly found his amusement elsewhere.

'You'm mistaken, miss. I'm not the doctor. My name's Joe Trevellick.'

'Oh. Then you are . . . ?'

'Me and the wife works for 'im.' Trevellick gave a little huff of laughter and shook his head. 'Doctor. Me! Lord save us!'

Anna blew out a relieved breath. 'I'm sorry, I had no idea he hired staff. Where will I find him?'

'He do work from his own house. Bottom o' the 'ill.'

'Oh.' When it became clear Mr Trevellick was going to volunteer no further information, she went on, 'I gather he's told you who I am?'

'You'm 'ere to take back your place, I reckon?'

Before Anna could reply, a stout, red-faced woman emerged from the door to the kitchen.

'The wife,' Joe said. 'Esther, this 'ere's Mrs Garvey.'

Anna held out her hand. 'It's good to meet you, Mrs Tre—'

'Saw the girl in the kitchen.' Mrs Trevellick was evidently as blunt-spoken as her husband, and even more disapproving. 'Young girl like that did'n ought to be dozin' as if there's nothin' t'be done.'

'Mairead has had a very long journey,' Anna said, trying not to sound nettled, and failing. She found a more conciliatory tone. 'Of course I understand this is your home, and we couldn't just go and search for our room, so I came to find . . . well, the two of you, as it turned out.'

'We only 'eard about all this yester morn,' Mrs Trevellick went on, as if she hadn't spoken. 'Poor business, if you d'ask me, when 'ard workin' folk is put on the road at the whim of ... ' She looked Anna up and down, plainly unsure what she was. 'At the whim of folk who should know better,' she finished. She met Anna's stare with a defiant one of her own, and Joe, arms folded, coughed into the crook of his elbow.

'I'm putting no one on the road, Mrs Trevellick,' Anna said, in her most soothing voice. God knows she'd had to use that enough in the past. Exhaustion was setting in now though, and she had to struggle not to simply dismiss everything for the day and ask where she could sleep. 'I was actually hoping you and Mr Trevellick might stay on. I'd like to learn the trade myself, of course, but I'd as soon learn from you.'

Joe and his wife exchanged glances. 'What about livin' arrangements?'

'That's something we'd have to think about. It's all been something of a rush.'

'You'm right there,' Mrs Trevellick observed drily.

'How long have you been here?'

'Good twen'y year.'

'Where did you live before that?'

'We got Joe's parents' house give to us. Built it theirselves, they did.'

'But 'tis rented out,' Joe added quickly. 'And it's all the way down t'Porthstennack.'

'I don't know where Por ... where that is,' Anna said. 'But if you agreed to stay on a while to help me learn, you'd be able to give appropriate notice to your tenants. You'd stay here for, say, a month, and Mairead and myself would share a room. After a time, if we work well together, you'd continue working for me, but with a better wage instead of lodgings.' Anna fought to

58

keep her voice authoritative and decisive, but her jaws tightened with an incipient yawn. Oh, just to fling herself onto a bed, *any* bed, and close her eyes . . .

'What sort of a wage?' Mrs Trevellick was asking.

'We'll discuss that when I see how you work,' Anna replied, when she was certain the yawn had been subdued. 'Are we agreed?'

Joe and his wife looked at one another again, and it was clear in which direction the question was passing. Mrs Trevellick gave a barely perceptible nod, and Joe cleared his throat again.

'Right you are, then.'

'Good. And I'll watch and learn from you.'

'Starting tonight?'

'No.' Just the thought of it made her want to run away again. 'Tonight you'll carry on as normal. As I said, it's been a very long journey, and both Mairead and I are dead on our feet. Where is our room?'

'Joe'll put yer bags in the back room,' Mrs Trevellick said. 'Nearly fell over 'em in the kitchen, we did. Dangerous.'

'I'm sorry,' Anna said, more meekly than she would have liked. But now that the promise of sleep was within reach she was fighting just to stay awake. 'I'll take Mairead up now, and I'll see you in the morning.'

'I'll have breakfast for you at seven.' The woman paused in the doorway. 'I do s'pose you ought to call me Esther, then.'

'Thank you, Esther.' Anna was finally able to give her a smile. It was not returned, but Esther nodded and left, and Anna felt as though she'd negotiated a white water river, and emerged, still spinning and not knowing which way she was facing, but at least now in possession of a paddle.

A little later, having forced herself to undress and change into nightwear, Anna finally slid into bed. The sheets were musty-smelling – she couldn't tell if they were actually damp or just freezing cold – and the pillow was hard and lumpy, but she couldn't remember ever feeling so grateful, and contented to be exactly where she was. She was under no illusion that she would feel the same way in the morning, but for now it was a necessary acceptance.

Mairead was already asleep beside her, and after a moment of listening to the noises rising through the house from the now-opened pub, Anna felt her limbs growing blissfully heavy and she drifted towards sleep. Tomorrow would begin a day of careful negotiation, and even more careful exchanging of information, with the Trevellicks. She and Mairead would be seen by the people of Caernoweth, and judged in the same instant, and she would know if they had made a terrible mistake in coming here.

Chapter Four

The first of Anna's problems became obvious even before breakfast. After the briefest possible wash, she dressed and arrived, still shivering, in the kitchen of the Tin Streamer's Arms. Maircad was so close behind her that Anna suspected she hadn't bothered to wash at all. Not that she could be blamed; when you climbed from your bed and saw the curtain frozen to the window, and your breath condensing in the air in front of you, the last thing you wanted to do was strip down to your chemise and beyond to splash yourself with cold water.

Joe Trevellick was in the yard, they were informed, taking the barrels to the gate, to await collection by the brewery; Anna remembered leaving that gate wedged in the tall grass, and hoped she wasn't about to be torn off a strip for it. Then she shook herself and reminded herself it was her gate. Her grass. Her pub.

She smiled at Esther. 'And what will you be doing this morning?' She'd intended it as a polite question, even as her first lesson in the running of an English country pub, but Esther had obviously decided she was going to take it as a personal attack.

'Don't you worry, Miz Garvey, I'll be workin' some 'ard! There's tables to clean, *and* floors; there's laundry to do; there's glasses and tankards to wash and polish; that bar won't shine itself, neither. Then there's dinner to get ready, and—'

'I wasn't questioning your job, Mrs ... Esther. I was just curious.'

The woman looked at her steadily for a moment, then nodded. 'Fair enough. Now you know.'

'Yes. I wonder if you'll excuse me? I would like to look around outside in the daylight, and see what needs fixing. If anything,' she added hurriedly, seeing a defensive shutter come down. 'I seem to remember the gate might be a little bit ... loose.'

Anna left Mairead to her breakfast porridge, and stepped out into the cold passageway to the yard. Yesterday it had seemed to go on forever, but in daylight, and with a good night's sleep behind her, she could see it was much shorter than she'd thought. She peeked in at the room they'd passed last night, and saw a storeroom, with barrels and boxes piled every bit as untidily as the books at Penhaligon's Attic, but without the same allure.

There was an awful lot of work to be done, and Anna made an effort to quash the familiar, rising resentment. Being forced to leave her home was one thing, being unable to contact her family another, but to add to it the crushing realisation that her life was going to become an unrecognisable cycle of cleaning, mending, and making do, was enough to make her want to cry. She sniffed, and let out a breath that only shook a little.

She was safe here. And so was Mairead. Everything else would have to follow as it would.

Blinking at the bright, watery sunlight in the yard, she took one or two steps down the path, and gave a startled yelp as a cat leapt off the roof of the lean-to, and dashed across her path. Presumably it was the same animal as last night, although it was impossible to tell; still, it *was* definitely a cat, so that was something.

Joe appeared from around the side of the building. 'Don't mind 'im, Miz Garvey. I just chased him out from the hen-houses.'

'We keep hens?' That was an unexpected bonus.

'Good layers, when they'm left to it. The bleddy cat do keep pesterin' them though, puts 'em off. We'll 'ave to kill 'em soon, to make 'em pay.'

Anna grimaced. She hoped she wouldn't be expected to participate in that. 'Does the cat live here?'

'Much as any cat, I s'pose. I found 'im as a young'n, when I was up to Trethkellis back along.'

'Found him?' This was the most she'd heard Joe talk so far, and she wanted to encourage him.

'Just sittin' by the side of the road, he was, lookin' at me all pathetic. Started following me, so I picked him up to keep him out of the road.' Given the number of stray cats, and the nuisance they often caused, this display of tenderness was a welcome, if surprising, revelation.

'Did you give him a name, as well as a home?'

'I just calls him Arric.'

'Is that Cornish for something?'

Joe shrugged. 'Not so far as I know. The name just popped into my 'ead while I was up the coast.'

Arric appeared to have recovered from his eviction from the hen-houses, and sat with one paw in the air, licking along the length of his leg. He paused and looked directly at Anna, then resumed his leisurely cleaning routine. With the atmosphere still pleasant between herself and Joe, Anna decided against mentioning the repairs, and returned to the house and opened her case. Inside lay the paperwork for Doctor Bartholomew's signature – she could only hope he would sign it without making life too difficult.

Freya consulted her list, and mentally crossed off at least four items; Grandpa Robert truly had no notion of the cost of things and he seemed determined for them to eat like kings, even though her birthday wasn't for another month yet, and Papá's not until June. The shop's plummeting fortunes were a source of dismay she kept to herself, but with Papá's boat in such a state of disrepair it was hardly likely he would be skippering again for a very long time. If ever. That meant Penhaligon's Attic inhabited very shaky ground, and if Mr Fry had to lay Papá off from *his* boat, it would be the only income they had.

Robert looked up from where he was twisting a newly mended book into his vice. 'You'll be all right carryin' that, maid?'

'Of course.' *Half of it will stay on the grocer's shelf after all.*

She took down her coat and shrugged it on, then set off towards the grocer's shop. As she went she took a shilling and some pennies from her right coat pocket and transferred them to her left, muttering, 'Eggs, potatoes, carrots, bread, tea—'

'Freya!'

She turned to see Juliet Carne hurrying down the hill behind her, and waited. When Juliet had caught up, Freya gestured to the laden basket over her arm. 'Shopping? Or cooking for Mrs Packem?'

'Cooking. As ever. One of these days she'll have to admit to her friends that she can't bake a loaf to save her soul.'

'Well don't be late for work whatever you do,' Freya warned. 'Mrs Bone will have your hide.' The housekeeper at the Caernoweth Hotel already had her beady eye on the two of them, apparently convinced they spent their entire afternoon shifts doing nothing at all despite evidence to the contrary.

'If Mrs Bone tears any more strips off me there'll be nothing left,' Juliet said glumly. 'Anyway, the reason I wanted to talk to you was to ask if you'd seen the new girl yet?'

'New girl?'

'Someone's taking over the Tinner's. A widow-woman and her grown-up daughter, they do say.'

'Who says?'

'Esther Trevellick, for one. Susan Gale, for another. She was there when the doctor got the telegram, and she told Esther. She reckons they'll come today if they're not here already. Doctor isn't best pleased.'

Freya looked ahead to where the pub sat, blending seamlessly in the middle of the row; unidentifiable but for the ancient-looking sign above the door. 'No, I shouldn't think he is. Not that he's ever best pleased about anything. And what about the Trevellicks?'

'Out, I suppose. Back to 'Stennack. That means David and Ginny'll need to find a new place to live. It'll be Furzy Row for them, most likely. David'll hate that.'

But Freya was more interested in the newcomers than in the fate of the Trevellicks' tenants. 'How old is the daughter?'

'I don't know. That's why I'm asking. Grown-up's all I heard.'

Freya grinned. 'I bet she's really pretty. What if David Donithorn or James Rowe, or even any of the lads our own age,' she added pointedly, 'take a fancy to *her* instead of you?'

Juliet gave a snort that reminded Freya of when they'd been little girls at the school down the road. She drew herself taller. 'I'm not worried about them.' She gave Freya a knowing little smile. 'They know where to come when the fever's on 'em, that's what matters.'

Freya gave her a half-smile in return, but couldn't help looking over her shoulder in case someone had overheard. At school, until Freya had left Caernoweth, they'd both enjoyed pushing into the boys' marbles games – it made sense, since the boys' marbles were so much better than theirs – and they'd even regularly joined in with 'fox and hounds', again, with the boys, who didn't mind as long as the girls agreed to be the foxes. At the time, this fascination Juliet had with the boys' games had been worthy of little comment, but now Freya wondered if, during the time they'd spent apart, Juliet had ever moved towards spending time with other girls instead. Perhaps not.

She was aware of the way people spoke of Juliet around town; shaking heads, and mutters of, *she's no better'n she ought to be*, but it didn't seem to bother Juliet, so Freya tried not to let it bother her either. Besides, Juliet was a local girl in a town that valued its own; people could shake their heads from here to Truro and they'd still offer their home, help and friendship, should they be needed.

Mrs Bone, however, housekeeper of the Caernoweth Hotel where they both worked each afternoon except Sunday, kept a very sharp eye indeed on Miss Juliet Carne, and made no effort to hide the fact.

'You'd better get off to Mrs Packem's,' Freya said, 'or you won't be finished before shift starts.'

Juliet shrugged. 'I've only to bake a few things this morning, she's going away for a few days. I won't be late.' She prepared to cross over to the lane leading to Mrs Packem's house. 'Keep a watch going, and tell me if you see the new people!'

'I will.' When Juliet had gone Freya glanced towards the pub again, and shrugged. No doubt she would hear soon enough what everyone thought of the new owner; Caernoweth usually went one of two ways when someone moved in, and once its mind was made up it took a great deal to change it, for good or ill.

She pushed open the door to the bakery, and tried not to let her gaze dwell too long on the shining, golden rolls with their honey glazes, and the delicious-looking knobbly cottage loaves and plaits. Instead she bought a single white loaf, and Mrs Kessel, the baker's wife, passed over her change with a sympathetic smile.

'You wait, maid. Soon as the tourists come back to your shop, you'm gunna be leaving here weighed down with fancy breads.'

Freya gave a polite little laugh, but privately doubted it; tourists didn't want to buy books. Not for the first time, she wondered whether to broach the subject of widening Penhaligon's Attic's appeal. Mrs Kessel's shop didn't carry much in the way of sweet, baked goods, she provided bread and pies, but that was largely all. But Freya could bake quite well, thanks to Granny Grace, so perhaps she could begin to offer buns or biscuits as well. She found a sad smile for the memory of the stern woman, made soft only by her family and her beloved books. Gone almost a year now, Granny Grace had left the three of them anchorless; they each mourned her alone, and in their own ways, and sometimes Freya could almost hear the no-nonsense voice chastising them for it.

Now though, she heard Grace telling her to pick up her feet and stop dawdling. *There's work to be done, girl, and no one'll do it but you, so look lively.* She said goodbye to Mrs Kessel, and carried on thinking about ways to turn Penhaligon's Attic's fortune to the good. Two doors up, Mr Watts provided her with the vegetables she needed to make a stew, and the eggs. With the leftover change she bought some tea, and began eyeing the liquorice strips on the counter. Ought she?

Her mouth already watering, she turned the last shilling over in her grocery pocket, and, with a sigh of mild regret, she left it there. In her other pocket jingled the money she had set aside for the butcher, and she wandered slowly up the hill past the civic office, with her thoughts moving on to what she could afford to fatten the stew. A shilling would buy two pounds of mutton, and then maybe she would go back and look again at the liquorice strips.

Her attention occupied in this way, she was almost knocked off her feet by a hurrying figure bounding down the steps. Startled and dizzy, she stumbled to the edge of the pavement and was only saved from falling into the road by a hand gripping her arm and dragging her back.

'Hellfire! That was a close call. Are you all right?'

Still shocked, Freya looked up to see a vaguely familiar young man, studying her with a concerned expression. Recognition came slowly, but when it slipped into place she immediately stood straighter. The Battens of Pencarrack had seldom been seen in the town until quite recently, and Freya resisted the urge to look around, to see if anyone was watching while the richest man in Caernoweth – or who would one day be, since he was the elder son – stood in the street apologising to *her*.

'I'm so sorry, Mr Batten. I should have been looking where I was going.'

'But you *were* looking,' he pointed out. 'It was my fault. I'm afraid I'm in quite a sour temper, but that's no excuse. Please accept my apologies.'

'That's quite all right,' Freya said, embarrassed, and had to stop herself from asking what had put him in such a poor humour; if Hugh Batten was anything like his father, then reputation said his mood was apt to turn even more unpleasant without a flicker of a warning. Mr Batten, however, was looking at her now in a way that suggested that was unlikely. He even smiled.

'You have very nice manners. What's your name?'

'Freya Penhaligon, sir.'

'From the book shop?'

'Yes, sir.'

'My nephew Harry keeps asking his mother to take him in there, but she ... well, she's very busy.'

'Oh, I wouldn't expect a Batten to spare our little shop the time of day,' Freya said, politely enough, but making it quite clear she knew what he'd been going to say.

Mr Batten surprised her by smiling instead of denying it. 'Well perhaps I shall bring him myself,' he said. He paused. 'You sound ...' he frowned, thinking. 'Not *entirely* different, but have you always lived here?'

'I spent some time in London, sir. I was schooled there, at St Catherine's in Chelsea.'

'Gracious! That's a coincidence, my elder sister Dorothy attended there for a short time.' He lowered his voice and winked. 'It seems they did a jolly good job on you, if not on her.'

Freya tried not to laugh, and concentrated on straightening her gloves. 'Also,' she volunteered without really knowing why, 'my mother is Spanish.'

He started, and peered at her more closely. 'She was the ... Of course, I remember her.'

'Really, sir?' Freya wasn't sure what to make of his reaction. Her mother had attracted all kinds of attention, she knew that, but she hadn't realised her fame had spread as far as Pencarrack.

'I'll be damned.' Mr Batten's hazel eyes roved over her with a discomfiting boldness. 'Yes, you have a look of her about you, now you mention it.' He studied her a moment longer, then pulled himself together. 'Well, this encounter seems to have quite put my temper to bed. I apologise once again for my clumsiness, and I'll see young Harry gets his wish.'

He touched the brim of his hat, and walked away, leaving Freya staring after him in bemused curiosity; he was only in his early twenties, yet he remembered someone who had left here eight years ago and had only returned, as far as Freya knew, once in all that time ... Either her mother's exotic appeal had exceeded even Freya's own fond, and probably biased, memory, or Mama had led a more complicated life than any of them had ever imagined.

Anna pulled the front door closed behind her, glad to see the back of that dingy little bar room already. Daylight had shown it to be as unwelcoming as the rest of the house. A few tables, in a poor state of repair; a stone-flagged floor, covered with sawdust that might have come from the Ark soaking up last night's spills; the bar itself sticky and unwashed; and the small window grimy. Esther's assertion that she was ready to begin an energetic cleaning of the place had apparently not included starting before lunch.

The town was different in daylight, too. Last night it had felt closed-in, the gas lights few and far between, and the houses looming overhead, sparsely lit and almost sinister. This morning Anna could see the road was much wider than she had thought, with decently made pavements, and the houses well cared for. Not a particularly prosperous town, perhaps, but one where its inhabitants took pride in their homes. She glanced behind her and gave a small sigh. Most of its inhabitants, at least.

Before turning towards the doctor's house she glanced up the road to see if the book shop appeared to be open. She couldn't tell, but was struck by the way people were moving around each other, with the familiarity and purpose of people who were used to sharing a space, and who had too much to do to stand idle. At home she'd rarely gone into town, preferring to spend her days reading in the garden, or walking along the cliffs with Mairead, but she'd always imagined it to be a chaotic kind of hustle and better left alone. Now she wondered if perhaps she hadn't shied away just that little bit too much, and missed out on something more invigorating.

At the foot of the deep, wide steps of an important-looking building, a young couple stood in conversation ... Then Anna peered closer and decided that in fact it was unlikely they were a couple after all. The gentleman was evidently just that, his clothing marked him out as such, but the girl was dressed very plainly, and clutched a basket. A girl who ran errands was hardly likely to be spending more time than she should with a gentleman of means.

Anna turned away, dismissing the thought as soon as it crossed her mind. How was she to know how things were done here? How the gentry conducted themselves? Simply because life and station at home had been very clear-cut did not mean Cornwall was the same. Besides, she had more important things to do now than concern herself with such trivialities.

She folded the papers she carried, which were under threat of being tugged out of her hand by the wind, and tucked them inside her pocket; one last formality before the running of the Tin Streamer's Arms reverted entirely to her. She could only hope she hadn't alienated the Trevellicks entirely – if they left she would have no one at all.

Doctor Bartholomew's house was easy to find: a squat, square house, at the bottom of the town's main road. In the centre of the junction stood a memorial of some kind: a male figure on a tall plinth, without a horse or any other embellishment, but, like most of the rest of the town, kept beautifully clean. She peered closer and read the small brass plaque, and her eyes widened: Malcolm Penworthy. Her ancestor. Evidently he was a man of some note in the town, not just the landowner and publican she'd believed him to be.

To the left of the monument was a narrow, unnamed lane with a few houses dotted along its length, and straight ahead the main road wound away downhill, twisting out of sight after only fifty yards or so. The beach most likely lay that way. Mairead and the beach had always been like two sides of the same coin, and a walk later would do them good after being cramped in train and coach for so long.

Another plaque caught her eye, this time beside the door of the doctor's house, and Anna took a deep breath and went up the path. She knocked on the yellow door, and before her hand had fallen away from the knocker the door opened, and a pleasant-featured woman of indeterminate age peered up at her. She seemed friendly enough, but her voice was rough, and pitched almost too low to hear.

'Ev 'ee gotfee?'

Anna stared at her, baffled, her mind trying furiously to unscramble what her ears had heard, to try and make sense of it in case she gave offence.

'I'm sorry, heavy ... heavy what?' she said at last.

The pleasant expression vanished, to be replaced with a distinctly cooler one. 'Hev 'ee got yer fee? Money!'

'Oh! I'm so sorry. No. That is, I'm not here for medical reasons. My name is Mrs Garvey, I own the Tin Streamer's Arms.' She held out a hand, but the woman just looked at her. 'Is the doctor at home?' Anna went on, feeling foolish as she withdrew her hand.

'He'm in back.'

'Oh.' When it became clear that was all, Anna added, 'Might I see him?'

'He'll be ready d'rectly.'

'Sorry, he'll be ready when?'

'D'rectly he'm finished with the boy. Boy've got bad rash.'

'Ah. Thank you.'

As silence fell Anna could hear murmuring in a room beyond the hallway, and the housekeeper stood aside and gestured her across the threshold. 'You'm lettin' cold in,' she observed, as though it were Anna's fault. Indeed such was the force of her personality, Anna even murmured a low 'sorry' as she crossed into the hallway and the housekeeper shut the door with a solid thump.

After a minute or two, a woman and a boy of about twelve emerged from 'in back', and as the boy passed the house-keeper he gave her a bright smile and the woman visibly softened.

'Be 'ee all right then?' she said to the boy's mother.

'Right as a trivet, little monkey. No more'n a nettle rash to get out of school! Doctor's furious.'

The housekeeper startled Anna by laughing. 'Monkey's about right, then. Get on with 'ee, Bobby Gale, and don't give your ma no more trouble.'

Bobby scratched at his reddened arm. 'I won't.'

'See you don't go teachin' the young 'uns none o' your tricks, neither!'

'I won't!' The boy ran off down the path, and his mother followed, and then to Anna's relief the doctor appeared. He looked at her without expression for a moment, probably

74

waiting for his housekeeper to announce her as a new patient, but before anyone spoke he clearly realised who she was. His brow lowered slightly, and Anna could see exactly how things would progress, and her heart sank.

Doctor Bartholomew spoke to his housekeeper without taking his eyes off Anna. 'Mrs Gale, I imagine you have jobs yet undone.'

Mrs Gale. Now the softening of her attitude towards little Bobby made sense, and Anna was about to ask how many more grandchildren she had, but Mrs Gale had resumed her earlier cool expression, and now she vanished down the hall to the kitchen.

'Mrs Garvey?' The doctor stood aside and gestured for her to precede him into his office. She did so, and stood waiting while he followed her and settled himself behind his desk. He nodded to the chair opposite, and Anna sat, hoping she appeared calm, confident and at ease in her right to reclaim her own property. Inside she was squirming.

She kept her voice as steady as she could. 'Doctor Bartholomew, I appreciate this must seem—'

'It does.'

'Excuse me?'

'This is my business you're taking away.' The doctor's lean, bearded face was tight, and his voice lost all pretence at politeness. 'How on earth do you suppose it feels to be ousted from your property without so much as a month's notice?'

'I will give you that month's notice, of course,' Anna said, more firmly. 'However, you cannot possibly object to myself and my daughter moving into the room above it, since we have nowhere else to go. You don't live there yourself, after all.'

'The Trevellicks do.'

'And that's another thing. I was never informed you were hiring staff, which was most remiss of you. As a businessman.'

'It's an informal arrangement. I don't pay them a wage, they work for room and board.'

'You don't *pay* them?'

'Not that it's any concern of yours, their pay comes from the ability to let out their own property. Which they couldn't do if they were living in it.'

'And in the meantime you reap the profits of the pub, pay me the rent, and keep the rest?'

'Profits!' Now the doctor laughed, but it was a harsh sound. 'Mrs Garvey, once the rent is paid I can barely afford to keep the place in coal, let alone ale, and as for profits? Well.'

Anna shook her head, in a mixture of dismay at this news, and bewilderment. 'I don't understand. If that's the case what is your objection to having it taken off your hands?'

'I have no objection. I'll happily sign your paperwork.'

'Then why—'

'The point is, Mrs Garvey, the way you've gone about it!' The doctor rose, and his chair scraped on the wooden floor, then rocked on its back legs, settling back into place with a slam that made Anna wince. 'I will need a witness to this farce, of course.'

'Mrs Gale?'

'Of course not! I'll call into the Tinner's Arms later today, and bring my solicitor. He might have something to say about the way this disgraceful affair has been conducted.'

'I have offered you a month's notice.' Anna rose too, not enjoying the discomfiting feeling of being seated while the doctor glowered at her. She was not a child being reprimanded by a teacher. 'My circumstances required me to come here immediately. But,' somehow she found a bright smile, 'you are more than welcome to pay rent for another month. *I* have no objections to *that*.'

The doctor stared at her. Anna had read of a thunderous expression, but it was the first time she could honestly say she understood it. The brows were drawn down, casting mid-blue eyes into shadow, the muscles in the jaw jumping, the upper lip almost swallowed up in the turbulent trembling of the lower. There was an explosion waiting to happen inside that mouth, and Anna found herself utterly fascinated by the prospect; after everything that had happened, all the helpless feeling of being trapped and terrified, this was something she could cope with, and even triumph in. She would welcome the chance to engage in a full-blown battle of words, if it came to that.

But the explosion died in a heavy rush of wordless sound, and the doctor shook his head. 'Mrs Garvey, you have made a very poor choice in crossing me.'

'I'm sure I don't know what you mean by that. I am simply claiming my property.'

'I am a leading citizen in this town.'

'And I'm glad to have met you.' Anna held out her hand, and kept her voice pleasant. 'I hope we can be good neighbours, Doctor Bartholomew.'

His hand remained by his side for a moment, and just when Anna thought she would have to lower hers, he reluctantly took it. The handshake was brief, and his expression still grim. 'I will call in later today,' he repeated. 'Mrs Gale will show you out.'

Out in the hallway, Mrs Gale was oddly keen to talk, all of a sudden. 'Got a daughter, the doctor d'say?'

'Yes. Mairead.'

'How old?'

'Seventeen.' The door remained closed, and Anna waited, with growing impatience, but Mrs Gale did not open it.

'She've had schoolin'?'

'Of course.'

'Ah.'

'She looking for work?'

Perhaps she was concerned for her own job, or Esther's. Anna relented, and gave her a reassuring smile. 'Not yet. Mrs Gale, would you—'

'She be livin' with you a long time, or lookin' to wed, do 'ee think?'

'She ... won't be looking to wed for quite some time. Forgive me, but I don't feel it's right to be standing here discussing my daughter with you.'

Mrs Gale was undeterred. 'What about you, then? Widowed, I und'stand. *You* lookin' to wed?'

'No!'

'You'm not bad lookin', for an Irish.' Mrs Gale sniffed.

'Well, um, thank you, Mrs—'

'What brings you 'ere so sudden, like?'

'Circumstances.' The reply was short enough that Anna hoped it would stem the flow of questions, but Mrs Gale was not to be thwarted.

'Bit suspicious, if you d'ask me.'

'Well no one did.' The sharp, defensive words had dropped out before Anna could bite them back, and she saw the woman's eyes widen, and a small, satisfied smile flicker at the corner of her mouth. Anna could have bitten her tongue out. Who did this woman think she was, to interrogate her like this? She'd evidently been looking for a chink in Anna's armour, and she'd found it.

'Well, if you'll excuse me, I've work to do.' Anna tried to sound polite, and even conciliatory, but it was too late.

'People around here mind their manners.' Mrs Gale pulled open the door. 'Just a word to the wise, like. Secrets don't stay secrets long.'

'I have no secrets,' Anna lied smoothly.

'If you say so.'

The door shut behind Anna, and a weak February sun fell on her face, and she had to fight the sudden sting of tears. Why was she being punished like this? Was it a judgement because she had lapsed from her faith? Questioned everything from the moment her first child had lost its tenuous grip on life and left her body in a rush of blood and pain? Surely she'd been entitled to call on her God, and demand to know why? The more so when her second and third children had followed the same short, brutal path, but at last there had been Mairead. Red-faced, squalling . . . a long, difficult and agonising delivery had left them both in the same state, she recalled, able to do so now with a faint smile that eased her despair a little. But her faith had already been broken, and so this – she looked up at the memorial – was both her punishment and her salvation. Which of those would prove the strongest in the months and years to come? No one could know.

She almost turned towards home, but despite her assertion that she had work to do, she decided on a walk instead; it would be not only a relief but a necessity to clear her head before she faced Esther Trevellick again. So she walked towards the beach, and after following the winding road for a while she found herself passing through the tiny village of Porthstennack, little more than a huddle of fishermen's cottages and narrow lanes that crawled along the edge of the shore. The harbour and the beach, such as it was, were separated by a breakwater that jutted out into the sea, and there were boats tied up at the harbour wall, bumping and scraping against the stone as the swell lifted them.

Sharp and salty-fresh, the wind coming off the water whipped her hair in all directions, and stung her skin, but gradually the familiarity of the smells, and of hearing the roar of the grey-green sea, wove a new calm through her and she began to relax. They were on the wrong part of the coast to even pretend she could see home from here, but this was almost as good as being back there; it was shingle and shale rather than golden sands for strolling, and the sound of the water rushing over it was both exhilarating and deeply soothing.

Women worked on early catches, gutting, salting and storing, while the men cleaned their decks and prepared for the next trip. She'd see many of these people soon, no doubt, looking at her across the bar with raised eyebrows, and she tried to put Mrs Gale's warning out of her head, but she couldn't. She could almost hear the questions that would be running through people's heads: *what kind of widow runs away from her own home and family just when she's needed the most?* And *Your daughter don't look too distressed at losin' her father.* And the coldest one of all: *What are you hiding, Mrs Garvey?*

Until she gritted her teeth and made an effort to integrate herself, those eyebrows would stay raised, and the questions would only get louder. Sooner or later she would have to find some answers.

It was almost teatime when the doctor made his appearance. True to his word he introduced his companion, a man of a similar age: mid-fifties, Anna guessed. He too exhibited deep disapproval, but there was nothing they could protest, and the paperwork was duly signed and witnessed.

'Are you sure you're not wanting the extra month?' Anna asked, knowing the answer even as she asked. Still, if she offered it in the presence of his solicitor he would have no grounds for complaint later.

Doctor Bartholomew looked around the still-grimy bar room with ill-concealed distaste. 'I had no idea they'd let it become such an eyesore,' he admitted. 'I think you've done me a service, in fact.'

'Then we'll be amenable neighbours after all,' Anna said. The doctor didn't reply, but at the door he proffered his hand for another of his quickly dropped handshakes. 'Good luck to you, Mrs Garvey, you will most assuredly need it.'

When the two men had gone Anna gazed around her, trying to dismiss the creeping despondency his words had fostered. There wasn't another pub that she'd seen in the town, and there certainly wasn't one in Porthstennack. There wasn't even a church there, which would make it a hamlet, she mused rather than a village. But working men and women were thirsty people – this might be a new town for her, a new country even, and she might be surrounded by strangers, but that at least was a solid truth no matter where you were.

She sat on one of the rickety chairs, and gave it an experimental wobble. It bore her weight easily enough, it was just crooked. That could be fixed. She ran a hand across the table, and grimaced at the smears of coal dust on her fingers. A good scrub would brighten the place a bit. Next, she went behind the bar. They had a beer engine, which meant they had a cellar. And there were free-standing barrels, which indicated a choice of beers, and therefore a relationship of some sort with a brewery, rather than relying on home-brewed ale. It wasn't just a converted front room, the bar room might be small, but it was purpose-built, and the bar itself made of a good quality wood. Solid and unblemished, except by dirt.

Some of her despondency abated. It seemed that leaving the running of the place to the Trevellicks, who had no vested interest in profits, had been the doctor's biggest mistake, and anyway, it couldn't be as bad as it appeared; once people were in and drinking, it would be a different story. Any pub during the day must seem a bleak and lifeless place, but then anywhere that only came alive at night would certainly present a different face when empty and quiet. The reverse of the street outside.

Today was Saturday. Tonight she would remain downstairs and get a feel for the kind of customers the pub attracted on a pay day, but there was a great deal of work to be done first. Work with which she had no idea where to begin. She went through to the kitchen to find Esther, but instead found Mairead, standing at the sink and scrubbing potatoes ready for their evening meal. Her fingers were reddened by the cold water, and Anna could see them shaking as they gripped the potato.

'Where's Esther?' she asked, wishing she could rip the potato from her daughter's hand and replace it with a book, or a pen, or even a basket of shells.

Mairead didn't turn. 'I don't know.'

'Are you all right, love?'

There was a pause, then Mairead said simply, 'I miss home. I know we can't be there, but I still miss it.'

'I know,' Anna said. 'But listen, there's a beach just down the road. It's a nice one, I've seen it. Lots of stones.'

'Oh!' Mairead twisted to look at her, and some of the tightness in her face melted away, as if it had been Anna's hand on her cheek, instead of simply words in the air. 'Can we go now?'

Anna shook her head regretfully. 'It's almost dark, love. Besides, I've work to do, and so has Esther.' She looked around. 'If I can find her.'

'What time does the pub open?'

'I've no idea.' There were so many things Anna would have to learn. But it would be a start to put a pan of water to boil, so she did that, and Mairead seemed happier now she was there, and some of her old chatter came back as Anna searched for a pile of rags to begin cleaning the bar.

By the time Esther showed her face the bar room was looking a little brighter. The tables were clean, the old sawdust swept away, and the rugs beaten and laid back down. The floor was still filthy, however, and Esther's sigh indicated she sensed an order winging her way.

'I've got some water ready,' Anna said. 'If you help me move the tables, I can throw it down and start scrubbing.' Her fingers were already aching from cleaning the tables, but she was ready to do what must be done, and keen that Esther shouldn't feel too put-upon; she was too important to Anna's learning.

'No, Miz Garvey.' There was relief in Esther's voice, no doubt that Anna had not asked her to do the job. 'Don't do it like that, you'll drown your clothin' and it bain't so easy to dry this time of year. Pick a square,' she indicated the stone flags. 'Do one at a time. Wash it, dry it, and then move on.'

'But that will take hours!'

Esther eyed her, and then the door through which she clearly wished to escape. Then she sighed again. 'I'll start that end, you start this. We'll 'ave it done d'rectly.'

After an hour Anna sat back, and gave a little gasp of pain. She'd never imagined scrubbing would make so many different muscles ache; her shoulders and her back, her hips and her knees, all throbbed to one degree or another, and her hands felt as if they would never uncurl from the scrubbing brush again. But it was done, and the floor was clean and dry.

A bigger triumph though, was that despite having their easy life upended, her unofficial tenants had actually unbent in her direction, just a little. Esther had worked in grim silence at first, but gradually Anna's deliberately subservient approach turned her replies from grunts, to short sentences, and finally to useful instruction.

Joe Trevellick brought in more coal and lit the fire. Judging from the smoke that belched out of the cracks in the chimney it had been a good long while since it had been lit, which meant the dark dust that had covered every surface had been there just as long. Anna bit her tongue against the rebuke that sprang to mind, and simply thanked Joe, and asked him to ensure the chimney was cleaned the next day. He nodded, and she saw a glance flicker between him and his wife that wasn't altogether disapproving.

Esther then wiped down the bar, under Anna's watchful eye, and Mairead rinsed out the tankards and glasses that had been piled beneath it. With no time to spare they were ready to open, and Mairead hurried nervously back into the house, leaving Anna and the Trevellicks to welcome the evening's customers. Anna realised she had missed her evening meal after all, but at least Mairead would have a chance to eat hers, albeit alone.

She braced herself for the swarm of thirsty men and women, and readied her mind to take in everything she saw, the quicker to learn the trade and take over the running of this, her very own business. But that swarm did not happen. During the course of the entire evening she counted only seven customers, and two of those did not stay any longer than it took to swallow one pint of ale each. None of the customers were women. Each of them sat away from the bar, at one of the newly cleaned tables, but no one seemed to notice they left with unmarked sleeves, and that the glasses they drank from were grease-free.

If this was pay day it was no wonder Doctor Bartholomew was making no profit. It would cost more to replenish the fuel they had burned than they had sold in ale, so it was something of a miracle he'd been able to pay the rent. Anna went to bed exhausted and despondent, and lay wide awake in the darkness, listening to Mairead's soft breathing in the bed beside her. When she finally slipped towards sleep, one, clear thought followed her down: they had no choice but to stay, so she had to turn the pub into a profitable business. Somehow.

Chapter Five

Penhaligon's Attic, Caernoweth

Freya listened for her grandfather's heavy tread on the stairs, but he was sleeping late again; he'd finally begun to realise the business was in decline, and worry was taking its toll. The strain that existed between him and Papá was a frustrating and saddening thing too, and was likely to continue as long as Papá was working for Mr Fry instead of running his own boat. But all Papá's wages went into keeping the shop and the house, so where was he to find the money to repair the *Isabel*? It was the saddest of circles to be caught in, but both men turned to Freya to provide a smiling countenance and a cheerful word, just to make life bearable for them all. So, as always, she determinedly steered her thoughts towards happier things, in order to present that smiling face to Grandpa when he rose to begin his day.

Today it was easy to do; she re-read the letter she'd

received this morning from fourteen-year-old Emily Parker, who lived in Plymouth. They'd met a while ago during a day trip Emily had taken with her father and, despite the age difference, Emily had proven to be such a bookworm they had become firm friends, and wrote regularly. Emily came from a family with four children, an older sister and twin baby brothers – Freya had never lost her longing for siblings, and so a visit from Emily was the next best thing. Perhaps next time she would bring her sister, who was closer to Freya's age.

She glanced at the clock, and gave an irritated click of her tongue. There was no sound from upstairs, and in another hour she would have to leave for work at the hotel. That meant she would have to close, and although customers were few and far between it still rankled to have to lock the door and turn the sign. Just in case.

She ran a critical gaze around the small, crowded shop, her eye picking out every book that lay crooked, and her fingers itched to straighten them. But Granny Grace had always stayed her hand. *Make it too neat, and people will be afraid to browse. A little higgledy-piggledy lets people know it's all right to pick the books out and look through them.* Grandpa Robert had smiled at his wife, and echoed the sentiment. *Old books is different, maid. They call to the heart, not to the eye.*

But Grandpa rarely smiled any more, and he still turned to Granny's empty kitchen chair now and again, his mouth already open to speak, before memory slapped the animation from his face and he looked down at his plate again. Papá had changed too, trying less often to breach the barrier between them, as if he'd given up all hope of real reconciliation. But he was hardly home nowadays anyway; the boats kept him at Porthstennack from before daybreak to after nightfall, and when he was home he often fell asleep in his chair, exhausted and still smelling of the catch.

He had left early this morning, his tired stumbling around downstairs bringing Freya awake and listening for the slam of the door as he left. She could hear his boots on the road for a moment, even over the rising shriek of the February wind that caught the edge of the building next door and was cut into thin ribbons of sound. Resisting the temptation to pull the covers over her head and go back to sleep, Freya had instead risen in the dark to begin another pointless and solitary morning in the book shop.

It was hard to remember a life that wasn't this; her London years might as well have happened to someone else. Boarding school had come as the biggest shock of all; St Catherine's wasn't a bad place, but as a new girl, and from a rural town, she had certainly struggled to settle in, and it hadn't helped that school holidays had always fallen at a time when Mama and her friend Mr Webb were entertaining in Mr Webb's country house. She had barely seen Mama for the first year, but, unable to bear the thought of worrying her mother, she insisted she had made plenty of friends and was happy.

Mr Webb himself had been unlike anyone she'd ever encountered. She was used to honesty, to a debatable degree in some people, it was true, but certainly the raw honesty of spirit she'd known all her life. Mr Webb was well off for money, seemingly popular, and full of smiles of which very few seemed real. He'd provided her and Mama with a home in the city, and paid for her tuition at St Catherine's, but he did not live with them. It had something to do with his career ... Mama had been very vague about that in her letters. He'd spent his days closeted in his own town house, with his politician friends, and Mama had never had any problems attracting people, and quickly made a set of friends of her own. It wasn't that she was bad, or cruel, but as if she had rediscovered a life of privilege she'd thought she hated, and had only now realised how well it had suited her.

She didn't even seem to mind that she hardly ever saw her husband-to-be. Freya remembered Mama and Papá during happier times; warmth and laughter, touches, smiles, secret looks when they thought Freya's attention was elsewhere. Wasn't *that* what marriage was supposed to be about? When Freya married that would be all she wanted.

A movement caught her eye; someone outside the shop peering in. Two people, actually, one a little shorter than the other, but it was impossible to see who it was through the misty glass. Freya instinctively drew herself up and pulled her dress straight, a smile of welcome ready. *Old books call to the heart* ... yes, but if the face is met with a scowl like yours, Grandpa, the heart won't be listening.

For a moment she thought the visitors would just pass by after all, but the door clicked open, setting the bell jangling, and two women came in ... Freya recognised the mother and daughter who'd inherited the Tin Streamer's Arms, and her mind moved quickly, seeking an excuse to turn the woman away. But it was too late to pretend the shop was shut now, she would just have to be civil.

Grandpa Robert had plenty to say about Mrs Garvey and her simple-minded daughter in the two weeks since they had moved in, but none of it good. According to his good friend Brian Cornish, who'd heard from the doctor's housekeeper Mrs Gale, the two of them had either been cast out of Ireland for witchcraft, as if it was still the Middle Ages; were stealers of children for money – just like that awful Amelia Dyer and *her* daughter – or the widow was searching for a rich husband to do away with. You could have your pick of tales, but not one of them made you want to put out your hand and have this woman shake it.

Mrs Garvey was hatless despite the weather, which gave her a wild appearance, and her expression was taut, apprehensive even, as she approached the counter. 'Good morning, Miss . . . Penhaligon?'

Freya nodded, keeping her right hand firmly below the level of the counter, her fingers curled. 'Mrs Garvey.'

'Ah, my fame precedes me,' Mrs Garvey said with a wry smile, and Freya blushed, but could think of nothing to say that wasn't either a lie or insulting.

'I'm Mairead,' the girl offered, thrusting her own hand out. Freya blinked in surprise, but reluctantly unclenched her fingers and shook it. Mairead was around her own age, perhaps a year or two younger, but had the exuberance of a child; a wide smile on a pixie-like face, flushed from the wind and from walking, and eyes of a mossy sort of green, like her mother's.

'I'm Freya.'

'Sure, that's a pretty name. Like a Viking queen. But why do you have a name like that? You're too dark to be a Viking.'

'Um, yes, I suppose I am,' Freya said, taken aback by the bluntness of the questioning. 'My mother chose the name.'

Mairead peered beyond Freya as if she expected to see Mama standing there. 'She doesn't live here anymore,' Freya added. Keen to avoid being pulled into the questions she could see coming, she spoke to Mrs Garvey instead, gesturing at the laden shelves.

'Do you enjoy reading, Mrs Garvey?'

'Where *is* your mother?' Mairead persisted. 'Does your father still live with you?'

'I do enjoy reading, yes.' Mrs Garvey put a hand on her daughter's arm, hushing her without words. 'I had a great many books at home. I was sorry to leave them.'

Freya ignored the prodding of her own curiosity and remained polite. 'Well, perhaps you might find something here to replace them.'

'I'm sure I will.' The woman looked around. 'You've certainly a great many here. But that's for another time, I just wanted to call in and introduce myself properly today. Put a few rumours to rest.'

'Rumours?' Freya cleared her throat and tried to hide her embarrassment, but Mrs Garvey gave her a look that suggested she hadn't succeeded.

'Oh, I'm aware there has been ... talk, and we expected that. But we've nothing to hide, I promise. We've just taken a little while to settle in.' She smiled again, and Freya realised she was actually quite pretty when she lost her pinched, nervous look. 'I won't trouble you any longer, but I'll certainly come back and—'

A thump from overheard made them all look up.

'That's just my grandpa,' Freya said. 'He's been sleeping more lately, he's ...' she caught herself about to explain his worry for the shop, and bit back the words. What in the world was she thinking, to unburden herself to a stranger? 'He's not as young as he was,' she finished, rather lamely.

'Ah, now. Who among us is?' Mrs Garvey smiled.

The clock ticked away an awkward silence. Freya listened for the bedroom door opening, but there were no more sounds from upstairs. 'I think I'll just go and check,' she said, when it became obvious the woman was not leaving as quickly as she'd indicated she might.

It only occurred to her as she was halfway up the stairs that if Papá discovered she'd left the shop unattended, let alone in the company of a woman no one trusted, she would feel his hand across the back of her head. And rightly so. But something about that thump . . . She hurried on.

'Grandpa?' She tapped gently at the door, but there was no answer and she knocked again, harder, her heart pounding more heavily now. 'Can you hear me?' She took a deep breath and pressed the latch. The click echoed all along the landing and she paused, hoping to hear her grandfather's terse, *Go away, girl, I'll be down d'rectly!*

But there was no sound, and when Freya pushed the door open she saw, with a nasty jolt, an empty bed and one foot, still clad in its woollen bed sock, sticking out from the other side of it. Her insides lurched, and she crossed the room in a few steps and rounded the bed. Grandpa lay half on his side, his eyes closed, and Freya dropped to her knees beside him and put a hand on his chest. She closed her eyes briefly in relief; he was breathing. Grandpa was a burly man, rough-featured and with a reputation, like his late wife, for sternness, but in his rucked-up bed shirt and socks he looked helpless, and suddenly much older. Freya rolled him gently onto his back, hoping she wouldn't startle him.

'Grandpa! Wake up, you've had a fall from your bed.'

'Is he all right?' Mrs Garvey stood in the doorway, her face shadowed with concern.

'I don't know,' Freya muttered, turning her attention back to Grandpa. 'I can't wake him. I think he was asleep when he fell, but he might have knocked himself out.'

'Is it all right if I come in?'

Freya nodded, grateful. 'Where's Mairead?'

'She's still downstairs, she'll keep a watch on your shop for you.'

'That's very kind of you both.' Freya looked at where Grandpa's head lay on the thin carpet, but there was nothing close by that he might have hit it on, and there was no blood. Mrs Garvey came around the bed and knelt beside Freya. She reached out, and turned Grandpa's face towards her, and Freya flinched.

'His mouth! What's happened?'

'He needs help, urgently. I'll go for the doctor.'

Freya started to ask if it was serious, then saw the look on Mrs Garvey's face, and swallowed a new lurch of fear. 'He lives at the bottom of the hill. I'll—'

'No, I'll go for him. You stay here in case your grandda wakes. He won't want to see a stranger.'

'It's the house with the yellow door, by the memorial statue.' Freya's lips felt numb, and she heard her own words as a mumble, but they must have been clear enough because Mrs Garvey stood and brushed down her skirt.

'I know it. I'll be as quick as I can. Don't let him move.'

Freya nodded, her eyes still on Grandpa. It was as if invisible fingers had hooked themselves onto his lip and his lower eyelid, and were pulling the right side of his face downwards. A thin dribble of drool rolled down his chin, and then both his eyes twitched, and the left one opened. The right remained closed and in the grip of those awful, tugging fingers.

Freya laid a hand on his forehead, hoping he couldn't feel her shaking. His good eye swivelled to meet hers, his brow creased in sudden panic, and he got his left arm beneath himself and tried to rise. Tears sprang to his eye and he tried to speak, but could manage only a mumble, and more drool which Freya blotted with the hem of her skirt.

'Hush, Grandpa.' Her words were forced out of a throat tight with dismay. 'Doctor Bartholomew is on his way.' She tried on a confident smile, but could feel it wavering and instead pretended to look out of the window. She could see nothing through her blurred eyes but a bright square, and she could feel Grandpa's fear through her fingers. Keeping one hand on his, she talked to him. Nonsense, mostly, about the weather, the hotel, and Mrs Bone, who ruled the cleaning staff with a rod of iron and a personality to match.

She didn't know what she'd have done if he'd slipped under again, but her own worry started to subside as time went on and he remained conscious. Finally, with a leap of relief, she heard the bell on the door downstairs. Grandpa had heard it too, and he looked at her with frightened hope.

She nodded. 'That'll be him.' She folded her fingers around his limp ones, but she had no idea if he was trying to squeeze back.

Doctor Bartholomew gestured for her help to lift Grandpa

back onto his bed, then ushered her from the room with a few
sharp words. After waiting outside for a while, straining unsuc-
cessfully to hear anything, she re-joined Mrs Garvey and her
daughter downstairs.

'It was kind of you to stay,' she said. 'And to fetch the doctor.
Thank you.'

Mrs Garvey turned to Mairead and opened her mouth, but
then closed it again and Freya saw that the girl was staring at
her mother with a blank look on her face. Mrs Garvey didn't
try to snap her out of it, and Freya's patience stretched until,
after what seemed an age, Mairead blinked and returned to a
more wakeful state.

Mrs Garvey touched her cheek and spoke gently. 'Run and
tell Mrs Trevellick I'll be late this morning. And stay and help
her. I'll wait here with Miss Penhaligon.'

Freya shook her head. 'There's no need, really.'

'There's every need. You've had a shock. Run on, Mairead,
or Mrs Trevellick'll be after giving me a proper telling off.'

When the door had shut behind her daughter, Mrs Garvey
guided Freya to a chair and sat her down, then took off her
own coat and hung it on the back of the door. 'Now, where's
the tea kept?'

'Tea?'

'Strong, sweet tea. What the doctor would have ordered, if
he'd thought about it.'

'Mrs Garvey—'

'Please.' The woman touched her hand. 'Let me take care
of you. And you must call me Anna.'

'Anna. The kitchen is through there.' She listened to the
homely, comforting sounds of someone moving about a kitchen,

and the doctor above tending to Grandpa, but fear was creeping through her. What if he didn't get better? She couldn't bear it, not so soon after Granny Grace ... No. It couldn't happen, so it wouldn't. She shut her eyes tight and felt like a child again, warding off bad thoughts, but she shouldn't be doing that. She had the running of the household, and the family, and she *must* draw herself back upright and prepare herself to cope with whatever happened next.

She became aware of a presence at her side, and when she opened her eyes again Anna was standing there with a tray holding two cups and a teapot, and Granny Grace's best milk jug.

She blinked at it, certain she should be doing something other than drinking tea. Then she sat bolt upright. 'Oh! I have to get word to Papá.'

'Where does he work?'

'Porthstennack. He's a fisherman.'

'Will he not be out at sea then?'

'He might be working on the shore today, it depends on what Mr Fry wants him to do, since he's not permanent crew. I must go and find him.' But the thought struck her cold. Since she'd returned to Caernoweth she had always found some excuse not to venture near the sea, but it would have to happen sometime.

'And what could he do if we told him?' Anna said gently. 'Worry, and lose a day's pay on top of it?' She put the tray on the counter and poured Freya's tea. 'Why don't we just sit tight, and try to talk of something else? At least until the doctor comes down. Then you can go and find your father, and I'll watch over your grandda.' She gave Freya her cup. 'Now, what shall we talk about?'

'I don't know.' How could she even think about anything else?

'Well, to start us off, that's a lovely toy boat on the shelf, there.'

To her own surprise, Freya smiled. 'Papá made it for my eighth birthday.'

'It's beautiful. I'm not an expert but it looks like skilled workmanship.'

'Thank you. I'll tell him you said so.' She paused, searching for more. 'He'll be pleased.'

They sat in silence for a few minutes and Freya sipped her tea, half her attention on the stairs, and straining for sounds of the doctor's return.

'Would you like to know why myself and Mairead are really here?' Anna said at last.

Freya's eyes widened. 'I'd never presume to ask, but ... it does seem odd. You being all the way from Ireland and all, and not having family here.'

'I suppose so, although I did have family here at one time. It's nothing sinister, or even exciting, I'm sorry to say. It goes back as far as a man called Penworthy. He was apparently some sort of ... man of note, around this area. Have you heard of him?'

'Malcolm Penworthy? The man on the memorial?'

'Yes, that's him.'

'He was definitely a man of note, he founded the whole town.'

'Really?' Anna raised an eyebrow. 'Anyway, he was my ...' she counted off on her fingers '... eight or nine times great-grandfather. Or something.'

'That will stop people in their tracks,' Freya said. 'Once everyone realises you're descended from him they'll be falling over themselves to be nice to you, and you won't be able to move for invitations to supper.'

'Do you think?' Anna didn't seem as pleased as Freya had expected her to be. 'Anyway, Malcolm's daughter, who inherited the Tin Streamer's Arms when Malcolm died, met an Irishman and moved to Clonakilty. She let the Tinner's to her younger brother, and it stayed in the English side of the family until there was no one left.'

'Except you.'

Anna nodded. 'They tried to find my father, but he disappeared when I was a baby. So they wrote to me, and asked me where they might find him. I didn't know, and eventually the inheritance passed to me instead. I'd no idea about the place, to be honest, so I decided to leave it with Doctor Bartholomew and just take the rent, like everyone else had done. Then ...' she paused, then shrugged. 'Then I changed my mind, and here we are.'

'I heard you're a widow. I'm sorry for your loss.' Freya was about to ask why the bereavement necessitated a move to England, but Anna spoke first.

'Thank you. Now it's your turn. I've noticed some of the fishermen stop in at the Tinner's, which one is your father? I might know him.'

'He doesn't drink,' Freya said, too quickly, perhaps. She glanced at the ceiling. 'Is that the doctor?'

Anna's expression was far too shrewd for Freya's liking, but she pretended to listen carefully. 'I don't think so.' She put her cup back on the tray. 'So. Why not tell me about this shop.

How did your family come to run a second-hand book sellers, of all things, in this out of the way place?'

Freya accepted Anna's polite, but feigned, interest for the distraction it was. 'It was Granny Grace's family, the Yorkes. They were quite wealthy, years ago. They had a successful shop in Truro, called Yorkes' Emporium, but it caught fire one night.'

'Oh, how dreadful! Was anyone hurt?'

'No, they were a few doors down, visiting friends when it happened. The fire didn't reach beyond the main shop, so the rest of the house was saved. But almost everything in the shop was either burned or damaged by smoke.'

Anna shook her head. 'Those poor people . . . what did they do?'

'They couldn't bring themselves to try and re-build the business, so they gave what they'd salvaged to my great-grand-parents. Most of it was old books from their cellar, which my great-grandfather put away. He'd no love for books, but Granny Grace did, and when she married Grandpa Robert she took them with her. That was the start of Penhaligon's Attic.'

'It's a grand name.'

'She said it was like a treasure-trove of memories.'

'She's right.' Anna looked around the cramped shop appreciatively. 'And you bind and mend the books here, too?'

Freya nodded. 'When I have time. Grandpa taught me when I came to live here. He tried to teach me the books too, the tally, I mean, but I could never work it out right.' She stopped, listening, again, but this time she really had heard something. She rose, feeling sick. 'The doctor's coming.'

*

Doctor Bartholomew ignored Anna and spoke to Freya, his voice brisk. 'It's a stroke, Miss Penhaligon. Your grandfather's a very sick man.'

Freya swallowed and her voice trembled. 'What can we do?'

'Well, I could give him a treatment with salt and soapsuds but it would do little good, and would only make him uncomfortable. There is no evidence it will help.'

'Doctor,' Anna put in, 'Freya has asked you what she *can* do, not what you're *not* going to do.'

Freya blinked at the hardness of her tone, and wished she could tell her not to be rude. Doctor Bartholomew might not be the most amenable man, but he was learned, and he was here to help. The doctor's face had frozen in response to the sharp retort, and Freya held her breath in case he chose to simply leave. Instead his eyes narrowed and he inclined his head slightly towards Anna, grudgingly accepting her admonition. But he still directed his words only to Freya.

'All you can do, Miss Penhaligon, is to remain vigilant, in case of a further attack, and be ready to help him with everyday functions for a good while. He might regain the use of his right side, but we must be prepared to accept that he likewise might not.'

'Will he get better?'

He pursed his lips, and, catching another glare from Anna, he spoke more gently. 'Well, from speaking to him, and carrying out a short investigation, I've reason to believe it was a mild occurrence. Though it's perhaps best not to expect a full recovery. He is awake and aware, which is a good sign.'

Freya thanked him, and paid him five shillings from the till. Poor Grandpa ... He'd be mortified to think his own illness had left them even shorter of funds. She wouldn't mention the cost to him, but that didn't change the reality of it.

'I'll call again,' the doctor said, and Freya watched the money disappear into his waistcoat pocket. She couldn't help a little wince at the thought of paying out even more.

'There's no need, doctor, thank you. We'll follow your advice.'

Anna put a hand on her arm. 'I'm sure the doctor won't charge another five shillings just to look in on his way past the shop.'

'My fee is my fee.' Bartholomew sounded more like his usual self, now. 'If the girl doesn't need my help, she needn't have it.'

'Then I'll pay,' Anna said.

'No!' Freya looked at her in alarm. 'I can't ask you to do that.'

'You're not, love. He is.' Anna jerked her head at the doctor, whose lips tightened.

'I don't have any preference as to where the money comes from,' he said bluntly. 'You must sort it out amongst your-selves.' He picked up his hat and gave each of them a brisk nod. 'Call on me if you have need, you won't find my medical knowledge wanting. Good day to you both.'

When he'd gone Freya sank into her chair again. 'What will we do?'

'Well, for today at least, you're going to let me help,' Anna said. 'Do you want to go and find your father now?'

Freya considered, but decided against it. 'No, you're right. There's nothing he could do, and we can't afford to lose his pay. Bad enough I'll have to stop working at the hotel.'

'Oh, that looks like a nice place. The coach dropped us there but it was late and I've not been inside. Is it grand?'

'Very.'

'Do you like working there?'

'Not really, but it's better than nothing. I do the rooms, just from lunchtime 'til teatime.'

'Then you must go there today,' Anna said firmly. 'I'll run down and explain to the Trevellicks, and be back in time for you to go off to work. Tonight you'll be able to talk things through with your father and decide what's to be done.' She lifted her coat from the back of the door. 'Will you be all right until I get back?'

Freya nodded. 'I'll give Grandpa something to bang the floor with if he needs me, then I needn't shut the shop to sit with him.' She peered out into the rain-swept street and managed a wry smile. 'With all those people out there, queuing to get in, I don't want to be closing, do I?'

Anna followed her gaze and smiled back. 'I'm sure they're all just waiting around the corner, to give you time to see to your grandpa.'

She slipped out, and Freya looked after her thoughtfully as the door closed. Who'd have thought the woman everyone viewed with such closed, suspicious minds would be so nice? And descended from Malcolm Penworthy, no less. She was almost royalty. Some people would certainly not like that.

Chapter Six

Mairead had carried the message about Robert Penhaligon to Esther Trevellick, and when Anna arrived to break the further news that she would not return until supper time, the reaction was predictably sniffy.

'I don't know as how you plan to learn everything that needs to be done, if you're never 'ere.'

'It's one afternoon,' Anna pointed out, keeping her tone reasonable. 'And it's for a good reason. Mr Penhaligon *is* very sick.'

'And I'm sorry to hear it,' Esther said. 'But young Freya should be with him, not you.'

'She has to go to her other job, or she might lose it to someone else.'

'We can't all have exactly what we want.' Esther lifted the bowl of soapy water from the sink, and Anna was sure she was making it look deliberately heavy and awkward; she managed perfectly well normally. Now she grunted, and sighed, and some of the water sloshed onto the floor. 'That'll be a danger,' she muttered.

Anna seized the nearest towel and dropped it over the tiny puddle. She placed her foot on it and wiped it briskly back and forth, then bent to finish the job. 'There, that's fine. I'll see you at supper time.'

'That was clean,' Esther said in aggrieved tones, staring at the crumpled and now dirty towel that Anna tossed onto the drainer. 'I'll have to wash it all over again.'

'I'll do it tonight.' She couldn't resist adding acidly, 'Along with anything else you'd prefer to leave for me to do. But I *will* be caring for the shop, and for Mr Penhaligon senior, this afternoon.'

Despite her strong words she felt a faint flush of guilt on her cheeks as she walked out of the pub and up the road. Offering to help had obviously been the right thing to do, but she couldn't deny it had been fuelled by self-interest; this was a perfect chance to ingratiate herself into the community. The doctor might even speak less harshly of Anna at home, which in turn might perhaps silence some of the gossip with which she herself had provided his housekeeper. Although, in Anna's experience, people were always quicker to share the unpleasant than the pleasant, still it shouldn't be long before Mrs Gale's flapping tongue reversed some of the damage it had done.

But Freya's relief at her return quashed those cynical thoughts, and Anna was surprised to discover she was genuinely glad to be doing what any good neighbour should do. Back home, in her isolation, it would never have occurred to her that people were helping each other in this way, but they would have been, she realised now. And no doubt with equal enthusiasm.

Freya was waiting to leave, and gave her an old walking stick she'd unearthed. 'It was Granny Grace's,' she said. 'Grandpa might want it so he can bang on the floor if he needs help. Thank you so much, Mrs Garv— Anna. I'm that grateful, honest I am.'

After she had gone, Anna went upstairs to check on Mr Penhaligon senior. He was sleeping now; the doctor had given him some kind of draught, and he was not disturbed as Anna placed the walking stick beneath his left hand. It was all she could do, beyond keeping the shop open. She went back down the dark, narrow stairs, her shoes clunking on the wood that showed in places through the thin carpet, and tried not to compare it unfavourably with the thickly carpeted comfort of her former home. But the simmering resentment was still there and, despite knowing she was helping both herself and the Penhaligons, there was a tightness in her throat as she went into the empty shop and took her place at the counter.

The shop remained empty all afternoon, but for a scholarly young man who came in looking for a history of Caernoweth Fort.

'I'll see what we have.' Anna crossed her fingers beneath the counter; any sale, no matter how small, would help.

'Of course, you know,' the customer said, with a self-conscious little frown, 'strictly speaking you're calling it *New Fort Fort*. Caernoweth, you see?'

'No,' Anna said, puzzled but smiling. He was affable enough, a little earnest, but not at all pompous.

'Well. Caer – fort. Noweth – new. Not new *now*, of course. Built by Henry to keep out the Spanish, you see. New Fort Fort.'

'Ah. It does sound a little silly, when you say it like that.' Anna went over to the history section. After a few minutes she found something that seemed to fit, and brought it back to the counter where he began flicking through it. 'What about Porthstennack then?' she asked at length.

He blinked his way back from wherever the book had taken him. 'Ah, yes. Now. Yes. The entrance – porth, you see? Stennack would refer to tin lands. Lands where tin is *mined*, of course, not lands *made* of tin.' He gave a little laugh, then looked at her with an enquiring lift of his eyebrow. 'But you are not Cornish, Mrs . . . ?'

'No.' Anna chose to ignore the unspoken part of the question. 'I'm from Ireland. I've only been here a short while.'

'Well, you have a veritable cave of wonders here.' He gestured at the over-stacked shelves. 'I have a very good friend in Plymouth who would gain much from a visit, I think.'

'Ah, Plymouth,' Anna smiled. 'Mouth of the Plym?'

'Yes!' He beamed, and she felt like a child praised by a teacher. 'The river Plym, of course.'

'Of course. And your friend is a scholar, like yourself?'

'Oh, Tristan . . . that is, Mr MacKenzie, is an author, and an historian too. I'm merely his friend and research assistant.'

'Well I hope you visit again, and bring Mr MacKenzie.' She waited, but he showed no sign of closing the book. 'Will you be buying it then, sir?'

'Oh!' He folded it shut, with obvious reluctance. 'Of course. How much is it?'

'It's a very valuable book,' Anna said, carefully noting the way his coat fit, and the good quality material of the suit beneath. 'I'm not sure you'll want—'

'Oh, I've no doubt of its value,' the young man said. 'But it's exactly what we're looking for, you see.' He took out his wallet, and waited to hear the price.

Anna only hesitated a moment. 'Two shillings and six-pence.' That was half the doctor's fee paid.

He smiled. 'I thought you were going to say five, at least!'

'Ah, no, of course not.' Anna tried not to let frustration seep into her voice. After all, a lower price would bring him back far more quickly. 'It was lovely to meet you, Mr ...?' Now it was her turn, but he was more obliging.

'Kempton. Edward. Teddy.' He tucked the book beneath his arm and glanced out at the rain with a grimace. 'Shocking weather.' He lifted his hat to Anna. 'Very nice boat on the shelf, there. Good workmanship. Lovely. Cheerio.'

And then he was gone, leaving Anna slightly bemused. But she had enjoyed the company, however brief. She looked at the boat Freya's father had made; not out of place in a town so close to the sea, but its gleaming, polished beauty was strikingly at odds with its dusty surroundings. It was evidently well cared for, and quite rightly, but perhaps the shop might benefit from some of the same loving attention. Anna decided she should offer to help, especially now she was getting used to cleaning and dusting, and her muscles no longer protested quite so loudly when she used them.

After Mr Kempton's visit the afternoon crawled by. There was no sound from Mr Penhaligon, and twice Anna crept wor-riedly into his room to find him unmoved, but still breathing steadily.

Freya returned, smelling of carbolic soap, and she hugged Anna briefly in gratitude before she went upstairs, still in her outdoor clothes, to see her grandpa. Startled and touched by the embrace, Anna began to tidy some of the books, instead of fetching her coat to leave; she wanted to see the relief on Freya's face when she heard about Mr Kempton's purchase.

She was crouching by the stacks at the back of the shop when she heard heavy footsteps outside. Although the door sign had yet to be turned to 'closed', it was fully dark and the rain had been coming down in sheets for the best part of the afternoon. Not a time for the browsing public, it must be Freya's father.

Anna had time to wonder if they had made the right decision after all, not to tell Mr Penhaligon about his father, before the door opened with a jangle, to admit a tall man with wet, dark blond hair. He glanced quickly at the counter and, seeing the shop was empty, he yanked his pullover upwards to reveal a greasy-looking shirt beneath. His voice, raised to call through to the house, was muffled behind the wet wool as he peeled it over his head.

'House door's locked again, Pa! I've told you I don't like coming in through the shop.' Anna stood, and, emerging from the depths of his clothing, Mr Penhaligon saw her and frowned. 'Who're you? Where's my father?'

She ignored the bluntness of the questioning, since it must have come as a shock to see a stranger in place of his family. 'I'm Anna Garvey,' she said. 'Mr Penhaligon, I'm so sorry to have to tell you, but your father is ill.'

'Ill? How ill?' He frowned and came closer. His blue eyes were shadowed and tired, the brows above them darker than his hair and very straight. She couldn't imagine him smiling. 'Where is he?'

'He's upstairs. Freya is with him. The doctor's been, and says to keep your father calm and comfortable.'

'What's wrong with him, is it his heart?' He started for the door, but it opened before he could reach it, and Freya came in, her cap askew, her eyes red.

She wrapped her arms around her father. 'Oh, Papá, it's horrible to see him looking so old. The doctor said it's a stroke.'

'Christ!' He put her at arm's length, and his voice shook. 'I'm going up to him.'

Freya shook her head. 'He's just gone off to sleep again. Have your wash, and I'll fetch your supper.'

Mr Penhaligon looked at her for a moment and appeared about to argue, but then the tension went out of his rigid frame, and he kissed her crooked cap and squeezed her shoulder. Anna couldn't say why she was surprised to see the easy affection between these two, perhaps it was simply because of the hard set of his jaw, and those straight, fierce-looking eyebrows. Perhaps it was just that, in her limited experience, fathers normally left all that kind of thing to mothers. Uncle Colm had certainly never publicly bestowed such affection on Maeve. Whatever the reason, it spoke of a real bond between these two, and she wished she'd seen more of it between Mairead and Finn.

'Will you stay to supper, Anna?' Freya broke into her thoughts.

Anna smiled her thanks. 'Thank you, but I ought to go back home.' Then she added, in a deliberately dry tone, 'Mairead will be furious with me for leaving her with the Trevellicks.'

For a second she thought Mr Penhaligon was going to smile too, but then his gaze went to the door to the main house.

'Thank you for staying today,' he said instead. His voice had lost the hard edge of surprise and worry, and now she could hear the tiredness she had seen in his face. 'It was good of you to give up your time.'

'Not at all. I was glad to have been of help, and for the chance to get to know Freya. She's a credit to you, Mr Penhaligon.'

He did smile then, showing surprisingly good teeth and a deepening of the lines around his eyes. It changed him completely, and Anna couldn't help smiling back. 'I mean it,' she said. 'She's well-mannered, and very pleasant company.'

He looked at his daughter, who seemed embarrassed, but pleased. 'She is,' he agreed, 'but I can't take the credit for that.' He wiped his hands on his shirt and held one out to her. 'Thank you again, Mrs Garvey.'

'Since Freya calls me Anna, perhaps you should, too.'

'I'd prefer Mrs Garvey.' His face closed again, as if he blamed her presumption on his unguarded smile, and had just remembered she was not to be trusted. Anna felt more than a little foolish; it seemed she had plenty of work to do to win the town over, after all. She picked up her gloves and coat, and smiled at Freya.

'I'm just down the road if you need any help. You can call in anytime.'

Freya nodded. 'Thank you, Anna.' There an unmistakable emphasis on the word, to accompany the quick glance at her father, and it did not escape his notice. He raised one eyebrow, just slightly, and Freya cleared her throat and had the grace to flush as she went to open the door. 'I hope to see you again soon.'

'I'll call in tomorrow,' Anna promised. Looking back through the window as the door closed behind her, she saw Matthew drop his hand onto his daughter's shoulder and move past her into the hallway beyond the shop.

She knew she ought to have been feeling the relief of duty discharged, but walking down the rain-drenched street she could not easily dismiss the Penhaligons from her thoughts. Freya would have to give up working at the hotel, and they would lose a good wage. She realised she'd forgotten to tell them about the book, but it would be discovered when they totalled the takings that evening, assuming they did it each day. Perhaps they didn't, though. Freya had already said her grandda was worried about their plummeting profit . . . an idea clicked into place, and she picked up her pace.

The Tinner's Arms was open, but you wouldn't know it except for two men sitting at a corner table. It would cost more to heat and light the bar tonight, than they would take in profits, but Anna had done all she could for now; the place was warmer, as spotless as she could make it, and much more comfortable, and clean pumps also meant better-tasting ale, which ought to do the trick once word got around. It was only a matter of time, surely?

She searched for Mairead, eventually finding her in the back room, armed with a cloth and an expression of trapped misery. 'Come back into the house,' she called, risking the wrath of Esther Trevellick, who frowned at her.

'She'm helpin' out. They tables won't wipe theirselves.'

'This won't take a moment,' Anna assured her with a bright smile. 'And then we'll *both* help.' She drew her daughter into the kitchen and shut the door, before explaining her idea.

'I'm to work at the shop?' Mairead said doubtfully. 'For nothing? For how long?'

'Just until Mr Penhaligon senior is fit to take up the job again. The Trevellicks don't need us both, and to be honest they don't really want either of us, do they?'

'Well no, but—'

'It'll be nice for you too, getting out of this dark old place. I know Mrs Trevellick takes advantage of you when I'm not here to keep her in check.'

'She thinks I'm ...' Mairead's voice trailed away, but Anna heard the unspoken word, *simple*. It was a word they'd lived with for so long now, but still stung them both. And it was untrue.

'You'll be helping out Freya,' she went on, 'so she won't have to give up her job at the hotel. You'd start on Monday.'

'I won't be able to go to the beach.'

'Of course you will. Just not so much. But you're not a child, Mairead. Not anymore. You shouldn't be ...' She nearly said *escaping*, because that's what it was, but she saw a shadow cross Mairead's face and bit the word back. '... playing your days away,' she said instead. Then she had an idea. 'Maybe the Penhaligons will even let you look through their financial books. Freya's not good with numbers, she's told me as much. '

'That would be fun.' Mairead sounded a little happier. 'But how will I be able to look after the shop *and* Mr Penhaligon? I can't just leave the shop and run up and down the stairs after him, can I?'

Anna sighed. 'I can't imagine that would be a problem, to be honest, even Freya knows it. She just doesn't say it aloud.

There was only one customer today, and he was from out of town. So, if you hear Mr Penhaligon knocking for help, you'll just turn the shop sign over. Perhaps put a note on it or something, to say it's just for a minute.'

Mairead thought it over, then nodded. 'All right, then.'

Anna glanced quickly at the door to ensure it was shut, and lowered her voice. 'But you'll be careful, won't you? Remember what we've talked about. And what depends upon it.'

Mairead's expression fell again. 'How long do we have to keep telling these stories?'

'Hush, sweetheart.' Anna took her hand and squeezed it. 'Try not to think of it as stories.'

'Is this really going to be us now?' Mairead gazed around the large, still-messy kitchen, and Anna could see her comparing it unfavourably with the one they had left behind.

'It's all we have, and if we lose it . . . ' Anna shook her head, and could only repeat, 'It's all we have.'

Caernoweth Hotel

Freya straightened her cap and hurried after the other girls. She was not exactly late, but not really in good time either, and the housekeeper was favouring her with a look of warning. Freya fumbled with the ties on her apron and caught up with Juliet, who had also slipped in at the last minute under the frustrated eye of Mrs Bone.

'How's your grandpa?' Juliet asked, stopping at the first of their allocated rooms on the ground floor. 'Is he better yet?'

'He's fair, but it's only been a week.' Freya followed her into the room and clicked her tongue. 'Are people really incapable of straightening an eiderdown, at least?'

'That's what *we're* for,' Juliet pointed out. 'You London types are all the same.' Freya shot her a look, and Juliet grinned. 'I take it back, you *used-to-be-London* types.'

'I've lived here longer than I lived in London,' Freya pointed out, but it was an old argument. 'Anyway, why are *you* late?'

Juliet glanced behind her, then crossed to the door and pushed it as closed as she dared; doors were to remain open while cleaning was taking place. 'I didn't go home last night,' she whispered.

Freya's eyes widened. 'You weren't with David Donithorn again?'

'No.'

'Who, then?'

'James.' Juliet sounded half-proud, half embarrassed.

'Rowe? Well at least he's not married.'

Juliet didn't answer immediately. She began pulling the coverings from the bed and Freya helped, wondering at her friend's unusual reticence. Eventually Juliet stopped, and sat down, patting the bed beside her.

Freya looked nervously at the door, then sat too, half her attention on the corridor, as if she'd be able to hear Mrs Bone approach, which, of course, she wouldn't. The housekeeper always made sure of that.

'Not James Rowe, neither,' Juliet said in a low voice.

'Well? Who was it?'

'James Fry.'

'He's back?' Freya thought immediately of her father, and her insides did a nervous roll.

'Well I 'aven't just run all the way back from Dorset,' Juliet said, a little waspishly. 'Of course he's back. He's stayin' in this very hotel, as it goes.'

'Why hasn't he gone to Roland?'

Juliet eyed her shrewdly. 'You know why. And so does most of the town.'

'He surely can't still be angry with him, after all this time?'

'He should be angry with your pa, not his own,' Juliet agreed. 'But James is ... ' A tiny smile flickered around her eyes. 'He's a passionate man. He feels things deeper than you'd think.'

Freya shrugged, unimpressed. 'Well if Roland finds out James is back and hasn't gone to see him, it'll just hurt him. And he doesn't deserve that.' Another thought occurred, then. 'If you were with James, and he's staying here, how did you still manage to be late?'

Juliet's smile broadened, and she glanced at the rumpled bed. 'Like I said, he's a passionate man.'

Freya leapt up. 'This isn't his room, is it?'

'No, don't worry,' Juliet grinned. 'But his bed will be just as messy.'

'Oh, stop it!' More than a touch embarrassed, Freya straightened her apron. At that moment the door opened wide, and Mrs Bone fixed them both with a glare they recognised immediately. Juliet had stood too, but not quickly enough, and the housekeeper pointed to the rug in the centre of the floor. Juliet moved to the spot, and stood with her eyes cast down while Mrs Bone's words sliced her from crown to toe.

When the housekeeper had left, Juliet let out a huge breath and turned to Freya with a scowl. 'That was your fault.'

'How so? Anyway, you're used to it. How many times has she done that to you?'

'I can't count them,' Juliet admitted. 'All right, since you don't want to talk about James Fry, tell me about Mrs Garvey and the idiot girl.'

'Don't call her that! She's helping out, and I think it's kind of her.'

'I thought they said she was simple. How can she look after a whole shop by herself?'

'She's done a brave job so far. Anyway, I don't think she's as bad as they say.' Freya began rolling the discarded bedding ready to take to the laundry. 'She seems sweet, just a bit of a daydreamer. Other than that she's very direct, a bit like you. Although,' she added, with a little smile, 'I have no idea if she's as popular with the gentlemen as you.'

'Gentlemen?' Juliet laughed and unfolded fresh bedding. 'James Fry is the only one 'round who's ever come close to that. Apart from them up at Pencarrack, of course.' She gave Freya a sidelong look as she opened out the new sheet and flapped it loose over the bed. 'Is she pretty then?'

'Quite.' Freya considered. 'No, actually very. In an odd, unusual sort of a way.'

'I hate her already.'

'Don't be mean,' Freya grinned, as she helped tug the sheet straight. 'I think you'll get along famously once you meet.'

'What of her mother? Is she as suspicious as they're all saying?'

'By "all", I assume you mean Mrs Gale?'

'And around town,' Juliet pointed out, 'you've heard them.' She plumped the pillow, and together they lifted the heavy

116

eiderdown back onto the bed. 'Mrs Gale reckons she's got a dark secret, and it's to do with the girl. She reckons the people of Ireland have sent her away for ... ' she shrugged. 'Well, some say she's a witch.'

'Ridiculous!' Freya laughed. 'The Tinner's would be a good place for her though, if she was. They say Esther Trevellick's descended from a long line of witches, going back to the Middle Ages.'

'Gossip! Again?' Mrs Bone's silent feet had brought her into the room without either of the girls noticing, and Freya's hands trembled as she straightened the antimacassar on the back of the chair. Making fun of the rules was one thing, but if Mrs Bone saw fit to dismiss her they would lose the last steady wage they had. And over something so silly ...

'The two of you will not work together again,' Mrs Bone decided. 'I shall put each of you with someone who can be trusted to get here in good time, and to work in silence.'

It was disappointing to be separated, but a relief, nevertheless, to have kept her job. Despite her gratitude Freya crossed her fingers against being sent to work in the laundry, a job she had despised all her life, but Mrs Bone sent her to find Fiona Tremar, the supervisor, who rolled her eyes and threw her a pile of pillowcases without a word. Juliet was sent to the laundry, and sullen Miss Pawley.

By the end of her shift Freya had had time to think about the unwelcome news Juliet had brought to work. If James Fry had returned from Dorset, Papá would probably lose his work with Roland. He would have to give up his dream of saving enough to get the *Isabel* seaworthy again, and they would probably lose their home and—

'The *girl's* in the shop this time!' Miss Pawley was saying, in tones of disbelief. 'Juliet Carne told me. *Alone*, if you ever did, and her not capable!'

'With the old man sick? What's the maid thinkin' of?'

Freya saw the two women looking questioningly at her, and stared back, drawing on all the confidence she'd learned in London. She kept her voice even. 'Miss Garvey very kindly offered to watch the shop, so I could come to work.'

'Much good she'll do. Everyone knows she's simple.'

Freya's composure snapped. 'She is not! And her mother was a great help too.'

'Well, now,' Miss Pawley said, with some satisfaction, 'there we have it. Her mother's ... well. She've come here, and put Mr and Mrs Trevellick on the road. What right's a furriner got to turn 'em out, when *they've* been there these twenty years or more?'

'She hasn't turned them out, they've still got their home in Porthstennack. And anyway, it was Doctor Bartholomew who lost the most from it, and he's not spreading horrible rumours so why should you care?'

'We dunno nuthin' about her,' Miss Pawley persisted. 'She could be there now, robbin' your shop!'

'And she *could* be cooking Grandpa's meal, sweeping the floor, or selling a hundred books.' If only that last one could have been true. 'Besides,' she added hotly, 'we do know something about her. She's a direct descendant of Malcolm Penworthy.'

The two maids blinked. It might have been funny if Freya hadn't been so cross. 'Malcolm Penworthy?'

'That's why she's inherited the pub,' Freya said. 'It's always been in the Penworthy family. And you should mind your gossip.' How easy it was to pretend she hadn't had the same doubts, heard and believed the same suspicions, and been just as ready to turn the woman away from the shop. She could almost feel the urgency in the two girls to be away, so they could be among the first to share the news.

Then she remembered Mrs Garvey's oddly flat reaction to the news that her well-respected name would earn her a good deal of interest, and she wondered if she'd done the right thing sharing it after all.

Chapter Seven

'Come on, Pen'aligon, it's pay day. One drink!'

'Let 'un be, Ern. If he says he don't want to come in, he don't 'ave to bleddy come!' Roland Fry scowled, and laid a cautionary hand on Matthew's arm. 'Besides, the little maid'll be waiting supper.'

Matthew forced a smile. 'Hardly "little" anymore.' He and Roland watched the men filing into the Tinner's, but Roland didn't follow immediately. He kept hold of Matthew's arm, preventing him from continuing his walk up the hill, and when the last of the crew had gone into the pub, letting the door swing shut behind him, he turned a shrewd eye back on Matthew.

'How is it?'

'It?'

'Come on, boy, 'tis cold enough standin' around here without you playin' coy.'

Matthew smiled. '*It's* fine. Thank you.'

'You're going to have to forgive yourself one day,' Roland

said, in a conversational tone that belied his complaint about getting in out of the weather. 'You paid for what happened. Several times over.'

'You could have died!' The words came from somewhere Matthew had thought buried and forgotten, and his throat went tight with remembered fear and shame.

'I wasn't talking about that,' Roland said. 'Anyway, you was hardly more'n a tacker back then.' His faded eyes searched Matthew's. 'Look, skippering a lugger at eighteen ... you had a right to be proud.'

Proud. Yes, he'd been that all right, until he'd made his biggest mistake, and then pride hadn't stopped his crew starting to drift, to find better paying boats ... and sober skippers.

'You all told me,' Matthew said dully. It was as if Roland had lifted the lid on that long-buried memory, and it crawled out now, black and slimy, to remind him of all he had lost, and what he no longer deserved. The rain helped; it hissed against the road, and the rooftops, and made everything seem as if it were happening somewhere else. He shook his head, feeling the rain flying off his hair in tiny droplets. 'You all said it: "You don't want to go changing the name of your boat, Pen'aligon. Bad luck, that." And I didn't listen, did I?'

'You was in love,' Roland said simply.

'No. I wasn't.'

'Well,' Roland shrugged, and casually blew rainwater off the end of his nose, as if he were happy to stand there and talk all day. 'Your Spanish beauty turned your head, anyway. Question is, did the drink ever help?'

Matthew faced him square on; the old man knew the answer to that one. No point lying. 'Yes,' he said. 'Sometimes.'

'Helped you forget you had a lonely wife at home, eh? And a daughter.'

Matthew's stomach twisted with self-loathing. 'Why are you talking about this now? You know I hate what I did.'

'Because I seen the way you was lookin' at that door, just then.' Roland jerked his head towards the pub door. 'Like you was thinkin' *just one drink*, like Ern said.'

'No, you're wrong. I know what's waiting for me at home, and how lucky I am to have it.'

'You sure?'

'I won't ever drink again, I—'

'I know you won't. I just want you to remember why.'

Matthew nodded. He'd thought he was hiding it so well. 'I'll remember,' he said quietly. 'You gave me back my livelihood, after I cost you yours.'

'That's not what I want you to remember,' Roland said again. He pointed his pipe towards Penhaligon's Attic. 'You lost her once, and you was lucky to get her back. She's old enough now that she won't need to be dragged off to London by her mother, she's just as likely to take herself off there.' He tapped Matthew's arm. 'I watch you, boy. I watch you carefully. I don't like to see that thirsty look, not when the cost is so high.'

'I appreciate it, Roley. Honest. But you don't have to worry.'

Roland nodded. 'There's something else. Your boat.'

'What about her?'

'She'll never run again, we both know that.'

'She might,' Matthew said, but he pictured the *Isabel*, and all that needed fixing just to make her seaworthy, never mind efficient. He was fooling no one, least of all himself.

'Sell her,' Roland urged. 'Get what you can before she falls apart for good.'

'And then what? No, it'll take a while, but—'

'Take your place on my crew.'

Matthew's hands curled at his sides. This should have been all his prayers answered, especially after all this time, but instead it just felt like the end of his dreams.

'I've been 'oldin' it open,' Roland said. 'It's been a now-and-again arrangement for too long, but why do you think I never took on a permanent after Ned died?' He shook his head. 'Look, I didn't say nothin' before, 'cause I know what it means. It's 'ard decision.'

'Don't think I'm not grateful, it's just—'

'You're a skipper,' Roland said. 'I know how that is, it's in your blood. But think about it. For the sake of the little maid.'

Matthew took a deep breath, and willed the sense of finality to the back of his mind; Roland was right. Everything had to be for Freya now. He'd had his chance and thrown it away. 'I'll take it,' he muttered, painfully aware of the ingratitude in his voice. 'I'm sorry. And thank you.'

They looked at one another for a moment, and there was understanding on Roland's lined face. He nodded. 'All right. Give yer pa my best. And the little maid.'

'Will do.'

Roland was silent for a moment. Then he squinted through the rain, fixing Matthew's eyes with his. 'I trust you, you know, boy. I wouldn't give you the job if I didn't.'

'I won't let you down.'

'I know. Now get on home.'

Matthew raised a hand, and waited until the old man

had gone in to join the rest of the crew. With a week's wage burning against his thigh, and the thought of cool ale and companionship just the other side of that heavy door, it took a huge effort to turn away and take his dry mouth, his pounding heart, and his lies, up the hill towards home.

At least the door at the side was open this time, so he didn't have to go through the shop. He stood shivering in the cold hallway and peeled off his wet outer clothes, dropping them at the foot of the stairs, and then went to his room to wash. Even the torrential rain hadn't taken the stench from his hair, and he called down the stairs to Freya to bring some hot water; he deserved to wash in luxury today, in honour of Roland's offer. The more he thought about it, the more he knew it was the only thing he could do, now; it might even allow them to hold onto his mother's beloved shop, and build it into something Freya could one day be proud of.

While he waited for the water, clad in his trousers and dirty vest, he knocked on his father's bedroom door. 'Pa? You awake?'

A grunt from the other side told him it was all right to go in, and he found Robert sitting up against his pillows. A tray was balanced on his lap, holding a book in the familiar stages of repair, and he clutched a glue brush in his left hand. His right was curled on the bed, but as Matthew watched he saw the fingers twitch slightly. Out of habit he touched his jaw, remembering how it had felt to feel that fist smash into it, and how he'd known, even before he'd learned why, that he'd deserved it.

He took the chair at his father's side. 'How are you? Are you getting any more feeling back?'

'A lickle bit.' Robert spoke slowly, deliberately, and Matthew realised, with a jolt of pleasure, that he was hearing every word clearly instead of guessing what Robert was trying to say. 'Freya' – it came out as 'Fwaya' – 'said the doctor might ... wisit again soon,' Robert finished, with a little nod of triumph, and Matthew blinked back tears. He looked away; the old man usually showed little patience with displays of emotion. But when he turned back he saw the glisten in Robert's eyes too, and, moved by instinct he grasped his father's hand, glue brush and all, and raised it to his lips.

'Mr Penhaligon?' Mrs Garvey stood in the doorway, holding a bowl of steaming water. 'Which room should I put this in?'

'Where's Freya?'

'She's still at work, I assume. Mairead spent the day here, and I was just collecting her to bring her home. Which room, then?' She nodded a little impatiently at the bowl, and he realised it must be heavy.

'The next one along. Thank you.' He cleared his throat and replaced Robert's hand on the covers. 'Thank you for lending us Mar ... rayd, did you say?'

She nodded, with a little smile at his clumsy attempt. 'It's an Irish form of Margaret.'

'It's, uh, a very nice name.' He rose to his feet. Her eyes went to his filthy vest, and he shrugged an apology and gestured to the hot water. 'I'll be presentable soon. And Freya will probably ask you to stay to supper when she gets back. I just want you to know that if she does, you're welcome.'

Mrs Garvey regarded him frankly. 'That's very kind of you, Mr Penhaligon.'

There was the slightest of pauses before she said his name, and he felt his lips twitch. 'Please,' he said, with exaggerated politeness, 'do call me Matthew.'

'And I'm Mrs Garvey.'

He couldn't help a grin at that, but as he lifted the bowl out of her hands he caught the strong scent of ale in her hair, and almost dropped it again. His smile died and his insides twisted painfully. 'Thank you again, for this,' he said, his voice suddenly rough. 'I'll be down for supper shortly.'

As he pushed past her he was aware of her looking after him, clearly puzzled by his abrupt change of manner. The smell lingered in his memory long after he had closed his bedroom door against it, and he put the bowl down hurriedly on the dresser, before sinking onto his bed and letting his head fall forward into his hands. Roland's words came back to him: *you was thinkin' 'just one drink'*.

'I was,' Matthew whispered. 'God help me, I was.' His fingers sank into his hair and clutched hard, tugging at it as if he could punish himself for his thoughts. If he'd gone into the Tinner's it wouldn't have been just one. It had never been just one, no matter what he'd always promised Isabel, and then himself. And if he'd broken his promise tonight he'd have missed speaking to Robert, missed that careful, painfully formed sentence, missed the chance to remember who this man had once been, and could be again. He remembered his father's tears, and the feel of the papery thin skin beneath his lips, and he felt some of the agony of temptation fall away.

He was tired, and had been sorely tested, but Roland had saved him once again. The gratitude for that was immeasurable.

Freya did ask Anna to stay to supper, but Anna made her excuses and left, taking a reluctant Mairead with her. The two girls had apparently found common ground in the past few days, and Anna was torn between relief and pleasure for Mairead, and worry that an easy friendship might result in confidences shared.

'Are you working tonight?' Mairead cut into her thoughts. 'I thought you told Mrs Trevellick not to expect you.'

'No, I'm not working.'

'Then why the rush?' Mairead was almost running to keep up, and now her voice took on a worried note. 'Have I done something wrong? Given something away? I promise, I think *everything* through before I—'

'No.' Anna slowed her pace, and spared her daughter a glance before looking back at her feet, moving easily along a pavement that had been quite unfamiliar just yesterday. She made an effort to soften her voice. 'It's nothing. I just have a bit of a headache. I'm away for a lie-down when we get in.'

'Why don't you go for a walk instead? To the beach, maybe?'

Because I want to be on my own ... because I'm feeling ... because I shouldn't ... 'Because it's nearly dark.'

Alone in their room, she still couldn't settle. She crossed the floor to pull the heavy, slightly damp-feeling curtain closed, and instead remained there, staring out at the night. Her chest still felt tight; it had not loosened from the minute she had seen Matthew Penhaligon kissing his father's hand, with tears standing out in his eyes. When he had stood up she had found her eyes drawn to the outline of his frame beneath his dirty vest; strong in the chest and shoulder from the hard physical work he did every day, but almost hollow in the belly. Too thin, and his eyes so tired . . .

The smile, that had vanished so quickly when he'd moved closer, had been a momentary light that was answered by a flare deep inside her, one she had thought long-since dimmed forever; she still felt its warmth, surely it must show in her face? Curious, she adjusted her focus so she could see her own reflection in the window, but there was no sign of the sudden and ridiculous longing that had taken her so much by surprise. Just messy dark hair, a lived-in face she knew too well, and unreadable eyes. She closed them and took a deep breath, trying to forget how it had felt to stand so close to him, but it was all there in her traitorous memory: his hard jaw, relaxed by relief and amusement, the smell of hard work lingering around him, his height, his voice . . . And something about the way he had almost snatched the bowl from her, made her wonder if he hadn't been swept up in the same moment.

Anna's eyes flew open again. 'No, no, no,' she whispered, seeing her breath form on the cold window. 'Stop it, now!' She wiped furiously at the glass, and turned away from the black night. What was she thinking? He was just a fisherman, working someone else's boat out of a nondescript little hamlet, in a country that wasn't her own. That he seemed more than physically attractive to her was nothing more than an extension of her pleasure at witnessing the touching moment he'd shared with his father.

Her thoughts moved to Finn. They'd married young, and liked each other well enough, and even if they hadn't been in love they'd both been contented with the knowledge that they had time to let affection grow between them. They would grow old together, and be comfortable. But time – and violence – had shown them a different plan, and the fear and sorrow had faded into little more than irregular pangs of regret. She missed her aunt and uncle, and her cousins, far more, but they were every bit as lost to her now. Still, she'd been happy and hopeful all through her childhood and her early married life, and that was more than an awful lot of people could claim. If that was the last taste of happiness she would have then she had already learned to do without it.

Caernoweth Hotel

James Fry let his gaze rove slowly over the walls, across the ceiling – marking the ready-cast plaster stucco with distaste – and back down again, past the carved dado and then across the basketweave parquet floor. It was becoming a curse, really, that he could not simply sit in a room and enjoy his surroundings without wondering who on earth had thought that particular ceiling rose went with that frieze. That's what came of spending your youth in grander houses than you could afford; it all took on a somewhat sour aspect, associating décor with the feeling of inadequacy.

There were too few people around, not enough of interest to draw the eye away from the appalling mish-mash of different styles. The hotel served the town well in the summer, but it was February now and holiday-makers were few and far between. The people James had seen since his arrival two days ago had consisted mainly of those visiting Polworra Quarry in some official capacity – perhaps land or business interest was being auctioned off, but since it was quarry land, not premises in town, it held no interest for James. However, he was smartly dressed and well-spoken, and so invited attention whether he liked it or not.

On the inevitable occasions he'd been engaged in conversation, he had quickly sought escape to his own room, and it was during one of these hurried retreats that he had literally bumped into Juliet, the sharp-tongued but refreshingly willing chambermaid. He had rounded the corner, checking over his shoulder, and Juliet had been backing out of his room, pulling the door closed. The collision had not been a gentle one, and she had given him a rough ride about it, but he had soon soothed her bruises. He smiled, remembering how quickly her scolding had turned into laughter, and then into that frankly inviting look he had been unable to resist.

'Sir? Another drink?'

James looked at the waiter, then back at his whisky glass. 'No. Thank you.' It was all well and good sitting here, silently picking the décor to pieces and reminiscing over a brief, though satisfying, liaison, but sooner or later he was going to have to visit his father. His heart fluttered at the thought, and he re-considered the offer of another drink, but rejected it again; a clear head was a must. Not only because he had some serious talking to do, but he could hardly start spouting about how Matthew Penhaligon was a drunken liability, if he himself wafted in on a cloud of Scotch fumes. He took a deep breath and consulted his pocket watch; it was time to face his own failures, and stop tying himself in knots thinking of Penhaligon's.

He picked up his hat, and frowned, examining it. Did he look too much the city gent? It had been a long time since he'd felt part of his home town, if he ever really had, but that was no reason to present himself as a stranger – to his father, of all people. Then he looked out of the window, at the rain that swept the driveway and battered the hedges that flanked it; bad enough he had no recourse to a vehicle, or even a trap, but he'd be damned if he was going to catch pneumonia simply to prove a point. He put the hat on.

The road to Porthstennack seemed longer than he remembered, and in the dark he kept walking into the hedges and tripping over the uneven ground. He passed Hawthorn Cottage, the place Penhaligon had rented for his family. Gas light shone unsteadily from the front room, but there was no way to tell if the Penhaligons lived there now. It didn't matter; he wouldn't have called in if they did.

Finally the hamlet loomed ahead, and the lights in those houses set up a flickering echo in his memory. A sudden and wholly unexpected rush of nostalgia swept over him; he'd returned only once since he'd left to begin his apprenticeship at the age of twenty-four, and that had been a strange and difficult time for everyone. No time for rebuilding relationships, either with his father or with his childhood home. He'd been gone again within two days, and vividly remembered the relief of climbing aboard the coach in Caernoweth and not looking back.

His feet took him, without conscious guidance, down Paddle Lane to the house in which he'd grown up. Just beyond the row of fishermen's cottages, the steep shale bank gave way to shingle, that sloped sharply to the sea, and the sound the water made as it rushed over the stones enhanced that unnerving sense of time slipping back.

He paused by the front door, his hand raised to knock, but his stomach twisted into a tight knot of apprehension and suddenly he was sure he'd be unable to speak. A gust of wind from the side, and the discomfort of the rain seeping beneath his collar, urged him on. He knocked. He waited. Eventually he heard the bolt being drawn back, and the door swung inward. A barely recognisable old man stood there. Stooped, hesitant, seemingly half the man he'd been.

'Pa.' James tried not to show his dismay, and forced a smile onto his face. He knew it was a weak and hopeful one, but better that than appear brash. Roland stared at him. Wordless, he reached out a hand and brushed it across James's coat, as if testing an old and familiar illusion. When he withdrew the hand he curled his fingers over the wetness, and raised his eyes to James's.

'You'm back,' he said, in slow, wondering tones.

'Pa, I'm so—'

'Don't tell me you're sorry, son. Don't.' Roland stepped aside. 'Come in out of the rain. We'll talk. You'll stay?'

James felt a stinging at the back of his throat. 'Yes,' he said. 'If you'll have me.'

He stepped into the dim hallway, and was immediately assaulted by the familiar smells: a supper not long finished, coal dust from the fire in the front room, and, underlying it all as always, the tang of salt and fresh fish. He heard the door close behind him, and the bolt slide into place, and his heart gave a fresh jolt; he had spent so long imagining how this reunion would be, what he would say, and now here he was.

He sat on the edge of the lumpy settee, his hat in his hands, his coat and trousers sticking uncomfortably to the backs of his legs. Roland sat opposite, and now he didn't seem the old, frail man in the doorway; in his own chair, his composure regained, he was once again the strong, hard-working man James remembered. He gestured for James to take off his coat, and waited in silence while he did so.

'Tea?' he asked, when at last James had freed himself of the drenched coat.

'That would be nice, thank you.'

'Ring for the maid, shall I?'

James looked at him, baffled, and Roland let out a great bark of a laugh. 'There, now you look more like the boy I know.' He waved at the kitchen door. 'Go on, then. And let it stew a while.'

James waited for the water to boil, and gazed around the familiar kitchen. If he half-closed his eyes he could picture his mother standing at the table, his father sitting by the fire, himself kneeling on the floor with his precious drawing pad and ruler ... but when his memory showed him a twelve-year-old Matthew Penhaligon sitting opposite and grinning at him, with a mischievous spark in his eyes, he shut it down, fast. He rummaged in the pantry, noting its sparse but sensible contents, and, to his pleased surprise, found a crumbling cherry cake.

When the water had boiled he poured it over the tea in the pot, and took it into the front room along with cups, plates and the cake. 'Who made this?'

Roland shrugged. 'Dunno, now. People still seem certain I live on potatoes and fish.'

'I remember them bringing food for a long time after Ma passed, too,' James said.

As a boy of fourteen he'd sullenly watched as the procession of neighbours brought parcels and covered bowls, and soft words of sympathy, and he'd wished them all away, wanting only his mother. But when they'd inevitably eased off he found he'd missed them. Not the food, but the feeling of being cared for. Since the accident the hamlet would have rallied again, and especially since James had left again so soon. There would have been a similar outpouring of support then, and just because the *Pride of Porthstennack* was once again thriving didn't mean her skipper's popularity had waned.

Aware this was the moment, James cut a generous slice of cake and passed it to Roland, then took his own plate back to the settee, where he picked at the cherries, wondering how to start. Eventually he put the plate down, his appetite hampered by the knot in his stomach.

'Pa, I stopped writing to you because—'

'Because you were too busy. I understand.'

James closed his eyes briefly. 'No. Because I was angry.'

'Angry with me? For taking *your* best friend under my wing and givin' him a chance?' Roland sounded sharper now, and there was a familiar darkness in his expression.

'He hadn't been my friend for a long time. You know that.' James heard his own voice picking up the strong Cornish accent he had worked so hard to lose, and that made him angry all over again. 'After what he did to you, how could he be?'

'Was it what happened to me,' Roland asked shrewdly, 'or what that meant for our business, sellin' the *Cousin Edith*?'

'Both!' James stood and began to pace, nervous energy sending him from window to door, his hands clenching and unclenching, his mind searching for all the reasons that had been so clear ... until now. Until he had to try and articulate them to a man he'd let down, abandoned, and who now sounded like a stranger even if he no longer looked like one.

'You left long before that accident.' Roland put his own plate aside, the cake barely touched. 'A good five, six years.'

'But I came back when I heard! You're the one who sent me away again.'

'You was just one year off finishin' that 'prenticeship! Your place wasn't here, it was up there, learnin' your trade.'

'I'd have stayed, if you'd wanted me.' James heard a slight emphasis on the last word and wondered if it was as evident to his father, what he'd meant. The old pain of jealousy and anger had not eased.

But Roland appeared not to have noticed. 'Learned a lot then,' he said, 'about stone masoning, and building posh 'ouses.'

'Yes. Why was that so wrong?'

'It wasn't.' Roland looked at him squarely for the first time. 'I was so proud of you. That's why I sent you back. But I missed you too. I gave young Penhaligon a chance back in '97, when his catch fell off, just like that Richard Shaw fella gave you.'

'It's nothing like the same.' James's head was pounding already, and he rubbed his temples. 'Matthew's business went bad because he didn't listen to advice. He only thought about keeping his wife happy, not about his boat, or his baby daughter and how he would provide for her.'

'He made a mistake, boy.'

'And he was paying for it! He'd have learned, eventually. We all know the Porthstennack folk wouldn't have let them starve, any more than they'd let us, after Ma passed. But *you* had to go and give him a job, teaching him it was all right to go drinking his wages away because the mighty Roland Fry, king of Porthstennack, would pay the bill!'

Roland stared, his mouth slack with shock. 'It wasn't like that,' he stammered. 'I wanted to help him *because* of the little maid.'

'And look how he repaid you!'

'It was a bloody *accident*!' Roland thumped the arms of his chair, setting his tea cup rattling.

'An accident caused by being drunk,' James pointed out in a tight voice. 'On *your* boat, at your invitation. An accident that nearly killed you, and left your – our – business in ruins. An accident, Pa, that wouldn't have happened if you'd left him ashore the minute you realised he was a risk to you all.'

A silence fell between them then, broken only by the wind blowing down Paddle Lane, between the two rows of tightly packed houses, and by the ever-present pounding of the waves on the shore. James couldn't look at his father, but he knew Roland would still be staring at him, stunned by the accusations.

The painful thing was, James knew it had all been done with the best of intentions. And he himself was partly to blame.

But Roland was an experienced sailor, a respected skipper of long standing, and when Matthew Penhaligon had rolled up that day, stinking of ale, Roland should have put him aside. Gone out under-manned if necessary ... When he thought of what would have happened if the boy had been swinging his minice at head height he went cold. Why couldn't Roland see it was fear that made him so angry?

'Did you stop to think about how the lad felt?' he asked, returning to his seat. He was right, his father's eyes were still on him, and still filled with hurt astonishment.

'Lad?'

'The boy who was working for you. The one swinging the stone.'

Roland swallowed and looked at his knee, misshapen and weakened these past twelve years. He smoothed his trousers over the lump. 'I don't even know which boy it was,' he muttered. 'Could have been any of 'em. But he'd have been all right.'

'Would he? How?' James gestured at the cake. 'Maybe it was his wife, or his mother, who made that. Still paying for what Matthew Penhaligon did. You think he found more work that season?'

'Stop it,' Roland said tiredly. 'Please, boy. I know you feel I've let you down. Selling *Cousin Edith* wasn't something that came easy, and you've lost a good half of your inheritance. And I'm sorry for that. But can't we just be grateful you're doing all right now? That you're going to make your mark in some other way?'

James took a deep breath. 'We're both at fault, Pa, that's what I wanted you to understand. That I didn't just bugger off to Dorset and forget about everything that was happening here. I wasn't too busy to write. I wanted to. Started to, so many times. But I was scared of what I'd say.'

'Well now you've said it.'

James ran his fingers through his hair. 'Yes. And we understand each other?'

'Ar, I think we do.' Roland leaned forward, and startled James by patting his hand. 'I'm glad you came back, boy.'

'So am I.' James felt absurdly like crying.

'How long are you back for?'

'I'm ...' He couldn't tell Roland he'd lost everything. Not yet. 'Dorset's served its purpose. I want to move back in here, properly. If that's all right.'

Roland appeared as relieved as James that all the bile had been spilled between them now. It was time to clear up and move along. 'That'd be 'andsome.' Just like him not to make a song and dance over it, but the quiet pleasure in his voice was enough. 'Tell me about Dorset, about the business. Doin' well?'

James picked up his now-cold tea and took a mouthful. This was where things might get sticky again ... 'I want to start my own. Business, that is. Here. Or rather, in Caernoweth.'

'Stone mason?'

'No. Architect. But I'd need offices. So before I can look into leasing some I'll need to work, and earn some capital.'

'As a stone mason?'

'No one's hiring, I've asked. Not even at Polworra.'

'Where, then?'

James looked at him, mildly exasperated. 'Well, on the *Pride*!'

'Back on the boats, eh?' Roland stared into his tea cup, swirling it and showing an inordinate interest in the leaves.

James frowned, suddenly unsure. 'Why not on the boats? It's what I know best, after building work. I've been asking around, ever since Ned Scoble died you've had an opening for a permanent crew member. And I'm a hard-worker, you know—'

'It's not that.' Roland put his cup down and linked his hands. The look on his face was that of someone who knows a pleasant interchange has suddenly become very short-lived. 'I don't have an opening.'

'But I was talking to Ern Bolitho, he—'

'It don't matter who you were talking to. Place was filled as of tonight.'

James fixed his eyes on the dark window, hardly trusting himself to speak. He cleared his throat, but it still came out as a croak. 'Matthew.'

'He's different now. Never drinks no more, not since what happened with the little maid.'

'What?' James turned back to his father. 'What happened?'

'It's done. Past.'

'What happened, Pa?'

'Are you still staying?' Roland's face took on an expression of half-hope, half-defiance.

James sighed. He would find out about Freya from some other source; in the meantime the last of his savings was tinkling into the coffers of the Caernoweth Hotel. He wanted to accept his father's hopeful gesture with grace, and with the gratitude he felt, but some deep, and very old, childish part of him spoke first: 'If you haven't let my room out to Matthew Penhaligon.'

Roland's expression said it all.

Chapter Eight

Penhaligon's Attic

Anna closed the door behind Freya and Matthew, making sure her smile was fixed in place until they could no longer see it. Only then, as she went back into the kitchen, did she allow the smile to fall away.

'Dear God, what possessed me?' She stared at the package on the table, as if by sheer force of will she could change it from its current state into the promised Sunday lunch she'd so casually offered. Why had she suggested it? Offering to care for Robert while they went to church was one thing, she could have left it at that and still had their gratitude. But now, having never cooked a pie before in her life, she had sent a hard-working man and his daughter out into the rainy morning, with the promise of good, hot food upon their return.

She poked the package, and the raw chicken, killed by Joe and grudgingly chopped by Esther, squidged beneath her fingers. Ought she to cook it before it went in the pie? Perhaps being sealed in pastry and put in the oven would do the job? Pastry! That was another thing!

'Cookery book,' she murmured, eyeing the cupboards. 'There must be one *somewhere*.' She glanced at the clock on the mantel; she likely had a little under two hours, maybe longer if Matthew and Freya stayed to talk after the service. If Grace had not possessed such a thing as a cookery book, there was always the shop; there would doubtless be one there that would tell her how to proceed. But a quick search of the shelves in the pantry revealed a small red Century notebook, and she gave an exclamation of relief to see neat handwriting on its first page.

'Recipes collected and shared,' she read aloud. 'Oh, Grace Penhaligon you are a treasure.'

She seized Freya's apron, and tied it, then picked up the book. It fell open at a page with a scrap of paper in it, and a recipe that included a great deal of vegetables. She peered more closely at the paper, yellowed with age, and gave an involuntary shout of laughter. Scrawled in a surprisingly neat, but evidently still a child's writing, was a short poem. She read it aloud, in tones of delight:

'Dear Ma,
I'll eat up all my carrots,
Though I hope there are not many.
But cabbages I will not eat,
Not even for a penny!'

In Grace's own handwriting, was added: *Matthew, aged 10*.

*

141

'I'll see you eat your vegetables, my lad.' Still smiling, Anna began to flip through the book, looking for instructions to make pastry. Of course, Grace had likely not needed such basic instruction, and might not have taken the time to note it down ... 'Come on, come on, pastry ... ah! Chicken and ham pie. Well we'll just have to make do without the ham.'

She put the book open on the table, and studied the list of ingredients. When she'd assembled them all on the table she allowed herself a little moment of pleasure; soon the room would be filled with the smell of hot chicken pie, made by her own hand, and from one of her own chickens. It would be such a rewarding feeling. Still smiling, she moved the canister of flour to one side, and her eye lit on the package of chicken again.

'I'm fairly certain I should be cooking you,' she told it, with narrowed eyes. She opened the range, blinking against the sooty flakes that blew out, and then bent down to see further into its interior. There was plenty of heat coming off it, that was for sure. She took a shallow pan off the wall and rinsed it under the tap, then opened the package of chicken and emptied the lumps into the pan. When she put the pan on the hot plate, and poked at the chicken with a spatula, it hissed a couple of times, then settled to a slow sizzle. That sounded right. Now for the pastry.

Five minutes later Anna was staring at her fingers in dismay. Every finger was coated in a gluey mixture that looked more like off-white mud than anything you'd want to put into your mouth. She peered at the book again, and at the bowl in front of her. More flour, perhaps? She upended the canister, and coughed as the white dust flew up into her face, and only just stopped herself in time from wiping it away with her sticky hands.

'This isn't how it's supposed to look. Not at all.' She plunged her hands once more into the bowl, and pushed her fingers through the mess as the book described, but it wasn't 'coming together in a paste' of any kind. More flour, then. She'd be using their entire week's supply at this rate.

She reached for the canister once more, and almost dropped it in shock at a loud rapping sound just above her head. 'Mother of God . . .' she muttered. She'd almost forgotten she was there to look after Robert Penhaligon. She seized a cloth and wiped her hands as best she could, lifting the chicken off the hot plate before running up the stairs. Who knew how long she would be? It would be just like fate to set fire to the kitchen while she had her back turned.

She knocked at Robert's bedroom door. 'Mr Penhaligon?' A low grunt came from inside the room, and she took that as permission to enter. 'What can I do for you?' she asked, going in. The curtains were open, Freya had seen to that before she left for church, but the room was still dim; the clouds were glowering at the windows, and promised a great deal of rain before long.

Robert was frowning in much the same manner. 'Who're you?'

'I'm Anna Garvey, didn't Freya tell you I'd be here today?'

'Oh, ar.' His expression remained closed and unwelcoming. 'Don't need you.'

'Then why did you knock?' She nodded at the stick he still clutched in his good left hand.

'Changed my mind.' He laid the stick back on his bed. 'Go on, now.'

'Mr Penhaligon, I'm here to—'

'I know what you're here for. You're here for if I need you, an' I don't. So bugger off.'

'There's no call for that,' Anna said, somewhat stiffly. 'I could have broken my neck running to see what you wanted.'

'You'm not wanted here!' he said, suddenly sharp. 'I've 'eard about you, an' I'm not wantin' you in my house, but I've got no choice. The maid'll have who she likes in.'

'You've heard what about me?' Anna's instinct was to leave the room immediately, before he could see how his harsh words had affected her, made her throat close up and her eyes sting. But she remained, and even moved closer to the bed. 'Go on, what is it you think I'll be doing, while your son and his daughter attend prayers?'

He didn't reply, but his eyes slid from her gaze. 'Mrs Gale says you'm hidin' somethin'. Says you'm here under a pretence.'

'Does she now? And since you've not been three feet from your bed these past days, how is it you've heard *what* she's saying?'

'Brian Cornish tell'd me. He keeps his ear to the ground.'

'And does this Mr Cornish agree with her?'

Robert cleared his throat. 'As it goes, he don't know what to think.'

'Well then, perhaps you'd do me the same courtesy as your friend? You might at least reserve judgement until you've cause to form one for yourself.'

'No smoke without fire,' he muttered. 'Mrs Gale've stopped talking to Freya over it, and won't have nothin' to do with anyone who drinks at your place.'

Anna chose to ignore him, but her insides churned; already she had divided the town, and she'd barely spoken to anyone yet. 'Why did you call for help, Mr Penhaligon?' she asked again, but he shook his head.

'It don't matter. Go back to your bakin'.' He gestured at her floury apron, but she saw his face twist in discomfort.

'Are you in pain?' she asked, more gently. The man was ill, after all; no matter how cantankerous he was, he didn't deserve the sharp side of her tongue.

'No.' He shifted on the bed, and grimaced again. 'Go on, and send the maid soon as she gets back.'

'Mr Pen—'

'No!' He bit his lip, and as Anna watched a parade of varying expressions cross his face, she began to recognise them. Sympathy welled up in her, but she couldn't help also feeling a little stab of amusement, largely brought on by relief.

'Do you need your chamber pot?' she asked, as deferentially as such a question would allow. The face he turned on her confirmed she had been correct, but he shook his head.

'I do not. I'll thank you to leave now.'

'I can help you.'

He sighed, accepting a measure of defeat. 'Just get the pot for me, then go.'

'You'll need help.' She tried to sound matter-of-fact. 'Which ... uh, what do you need to do?' He looked at her, appalled by the question, and she shrugged. 'Mr Penhaligon, this is what I'm here for!'

'You bain't gettin' your hands on my nethers,' he said. Then his manner shifted to something faintly conciliatory, though his voice was still gruff. 'Look, fact is, I might not be sure yet

145

what you are, Mrs Garvey, but you'm a lady. Of sorts. This is no task for you.'

'Nonsense. I was a nurse until I left Ireland. I've helped men, women and children alike to do what nature calls for. Now will you let me help you?'

'A nurse?' He eyed her doubtfully.

'A nurse. Now, where's the pot?'

Robert sagged, accepting the inevitable. 'Under that end,' he pointed to the bottom of the bed. 'Do 'ee wash your hands first though, I don't want no flour where it'll do least good.'

Anna went to the wash basin, and when her hands were duly cleaned she took out the porcelain pot, folded back the blankets, and helped Robert to swing his legs off the bed.

Robert paused, his hands grasping the bottom of his nightshirt. 'A nurse, you say?'

'In a hospital.'

He nodded, and sighed. 'Well, just watch what you'm about.'

As he squatted over the pot she knelt behind him, supporting his back. He accepted her presence without further demur, but still she obligingly looked away, in case it made a difference. After a few minutes he indicated he had finished, and she told him to lie on his side. She dampened a cloth at the basin, and her hands were gentle as she cleaned him, but she saw a tear trickle from one eye, though he quickly twisted his head so it was absorbed by the pillow.

When he was ready to turn again she eased him to a sitting position and helped him straighten his nightshirt. He pulled the eiderdown up around his chest, as if to try and regain a dignity he had never lost, and fixed her with a slightly defiant look, which she ignored and bent to pick up the chamber pot.

'I'll just see to this. I won't be a moment.'

'The boy got indoor plumbing put in a few years back. Grace ... Mrs Penhaligon, was sore proud, I tell 'ee.'

'I'm not surprised,' Anna said. 'He looks after the house well, doesn't he? Matthew, I mean?'

'He does.' Robert's eyes met hers fully, for the first time since before she'd laid hands on him. 'Downstairs, off the kitchen.'

'What?'

He jerked his head at the chamber pot. 'Privy.'

When she returned, she slid the cleaned pot beneath the bed and she moved about the room for a minute or two, straightening and tidying and trying to regain that sense of trust. 'Are you comfortable now?' she asked at length.

'I am.'

'And will you let me help you again, if you need it?'

He gave her a faint, embarrassed smile. It changed his face completely, and she saw echoes of Matthew in the deep lines at his mouth. 'I will, nurse. And thank you.'

'Not at all. I told you, I'm used to it.' She tweaked the eider-down so it fell more neatly across his feet.

'Why are you here?' The question was sudden, but Anna was ready for it. She sat on the bed.

'I inherited the pub a good while ago, and I'd never intended to move here. But recently I found myself needing a new home.'

'Freya said you'm a Penworthy.'

'She's correct.'

'That might make a difference.' Robert looked at her a

long while, as if judging the truth of it, and he finally seemed satisfied. 'Matthew's a good 'un. He's done right for the girl.'

'I don't know him very well,' Anna said, glad of the chance to talk about him. 'But he seems very solid. And Freya dotes on him, doesn't she?'

'He's had his troubles,' Robert said. 'Do 'ee know of them?'

'No, it's not my business.'

'I think it is, given the circumstances.' Robert thought for a moment. 'He struggles, or he did, with the need for drink.'

Anna tried not to let her disappointment show. She didn't have wide experience of alcohol, but still she'd known one or two men in the past with that problem, and it saddened her to learn that Matthew was flawed in such a way. She wondered how long ago Robert was talking about, and if the worst of that struggle was past.

'I'm not sure it's something you should be telling me,' she said carefully. 'That's Matthew's business, surely?'

Robert tipped his head on one side, and his eyebrows came together. 'I'm tellin' you because you own a pub. And so's you can decide how comfortable you'd be, gettin' involved with this household.' His eyes held hers; he was reading her like a sheet of music, and the song was one he was familiar with. Of course it was likely Matthew had several women looking to claim a part of his life.

Anna rose and patted his hand. 'Thank you for your concern. I ought to be going back down now, but do let me know if you need anything more.'

'I will.' He lifted the stick briefly. When Anna was halfway across the room he spoke again. 'Nurse Garvey?' She turned back, and he sighed. 'Matt's had his dark times, but you're right, he does good for this place. For his family.' A flush crept up his neck, and he looked away. 'I've not been all I should be. I'll make it right with him.'

Anna smiled. 'I'm sure there's blame on both sides. Rest, now, you need to get some sleep.'

She left the room, and started down the stairs, the smell wafting through the house reminding her of the mess she'd left behind in the kitchen. She grimaced. Well, if she could successfully pretend to be a nurse, there was no reason she couldn't also pretend she could cook.

The chapel had been less than a quarter full, for which Matthew was guiltily thankful; much as he appreciated the town's concern for his father, he was tired of replying with the same words, over and again: *yes, he's doing well, thank you. Sends his best regards.* But it had taken a good nine years to win back the favour of these people, and it was only really with Freya's return that they had begun to accept him again, so he nodded to everyone who caught his eye, glanced apologetically at the heavy clouds above as if to explain his hurried disappearance, and took Freya's arm.

'Best get back and let Mrs Garvey go back to the . . . to her home.'

'It was so nice of her to offer,' Freya said, one hand atop her hat to keep the stiff wind from sending it down the hill. 'But wouldn't she have wanted to come to chapel herself?'

'I assume she's Catholic, if she practises at all.' Matthew realised he hadn't even thought to ask. 'I'm sure she'd have said.'

They were met with a wave of warmth, and a delicious smell, as they removed their coats and boots in the hall. The kitchen door was ajar, and Matthew went in. Anna turned, her face flushed from the oven, breaking into a smile. She seemed embarrassed by its suddenness and spontaneity, and concentrated on hanging her oven cloth over the rail.

'That smells good,' Matthew said, to cover the faintly awkward silence. 'It's kind of you to cook.'

'It's just a small pie,' Anna assured him. 'Absolutely no trouble. None at all.'

Matthew blinked. 'Um. Good. How's Pa?' He moved towards the door. 'Not asleep, is he?'

'He wasn't the last time I looked in on him. We had a . . .' she paused, then gave a tiny shrug, 'a little chat, while you were out.'

'Chat?' Matthew's eyes narrowed. 'Has he been giving you a rough ride?'

'He shouldn't listen to gossip,' Freya said crossly. 'Brian Cornish ought to know better, I'm sure he's been filling Grandpa's head with all kinds of rubbish when he visits.'

Anna placed a water jug on the table and Matthew noted how she surreptitiously tried to press heat-blisters on her palm against its cool sides. 'Well I'm sure everyone can make up their own minds.'

Freya looked at them in turn. 'Grandpa's being nicer to Papá now,' she ventured. 'We thought perhaps it was because of what happened. Because he was frightened.'

'Perhaps that was part of it,' Anna agreed, 'but from our little talk I'd say he's not going to slip back again.' She turned to Matthew again. 'I think he wants to talk to you, but best leave it a while, he was a bit . . . emotional.' She smiled at them both, and began untying her apron. 'Right, well the pie will be five minutes, not much more. I'll leave you to enjoy it.'

'Won't you stay?' Freya asked, predictably enough and quite forgetting to ask her father first. But Matthew wanted to know more about what his father had said; his heart had picked up at the news he wanted to talk. Anna was looking at him, unsure whether to accept, and he smiled.

'How big's the pie?'

She smiled back. 'Well actually it's quite big.'

'Good. Freya, run to the Tinner's and fetch Miss Garvey to join us.'

'Oh, thank you, Papá!'

'Yes, thank you,' Anna said. 'It's very kind.'

'Not at all. It'll be nice for Freya to have the company, and your daughter's been a great help. I'll just go and wash my hands.'

He went upstairs to change, and as he passed his father's bedroom door he couldn't resist tapping gently. 'Pa?'

Robert's voice was still weak, but held a note of its old brusqueness. 'Come in, boy, don't stand there.'

Matthew went in. 'How're you feeling now?'

'Fair. You look smart, lad.' His speech was almost normal again, only slightly slurred, and slow with constant tiredness.

'Just come from church,' Matthew said.

'Yes, so the Garvey woman tells me.'

Matthew slid a tentative hand beneath his father's weakened right one, and his insides leapt as he felt a faint pressure against his palm. 'The vicar asked us to pray for you,' he said. 'The whole congregation.'

'I don't deserve it,' Robert muttered. There was a long pause, then he said, even more quietly, 'I been a right bastard to you, boy.'

'You were right to be,' Matthew managed. 'After what I did.'

'Your ma never condemned you like I did. She was right, you was drowning, and you needed our help.'

'Pa—'

'I was no kind of father,' Robert insisted. 'True enough, you deserved that thump I gave you, but once you'd tried to make amends I should have done different by you. We lost our baby girl, should've seen we was losin' you too.'

'We'll talk,' Matthew promised, his throat tight. 'This afternoon, when you've had a rest.'

'And I was a right bastard about her an' all,' Robert went on, as if he hadn't heard. 'That Garvey woman. I'd no right to be. She's descended from Penworthy, did you know? Freya told me.'

'Yes, I know. Get some sleep, Pa. We'll talk later.' Matthew's voice was soft; he could scarcely trust himself to speak in his normal tone. He left Robert dozing against his pillow, and went to his room, unbuttoning the stiffly starched collar as he went. As he changed into more comfortable clothing for the afternoon's work ahead, his thoughts were preoccupied with his father's words. A warmth crept through him, and as he plucked his old blue waistcoat from the back of the chair, he wondered how much of an influence Anna had been in turning Robert's thoughts. Likely more than she claimed. Maybe more than she even knew herself.

By the time he'd descended the stairs again, he could see through the half-open kitchen door that Freya and Mairead had returned and were setting the table. Anna was straining carrots, and the room was a buzz of chatter and warm smells. Matthew stayed in the hallway for a moment longer, feeling his chest loosen and his brow smooth out. For the first time since he could remember, he was approaching a mealtime with nothing but pleasant anticipation and a gurgling stomach.

'What's Juliet like?' Mairead was asking.

'Terrible,' Freya said. 'But you can't help liking her, all the same.'

'Have you known her long?'

'All my life. We went to the same school until I moved to London. She was a holy terror at times, and got into all sorts of mischief. Mr Ogden, our teacher, said she was the only maid he'd ever consider caning, and he did, too. Just on the hands though.'

'She sounds like one to watch,' Anna observed, shaking carrots onto a plate. 'Freya, how hungry's your da likely to be?'

'Give him lots, he doesn't eat nearly enough.'

'I thought he looked a little thin—' Anna stopped quickly, and, out in the hall, Matthew glanced down at his midriff and pressed his shirt flat. *Thin?* Well perhaps ... But he couldn't remember being hungry very often, and where was the sense in eating if you weren't hungry? It was just a waste of good food. He buttoned his waistcoat, noting for the first time how it hung loose everywhere but his shoulders.

'Shall I fetch him?' Freya was asking.

'No, let him be,' Anna said. 'He might have gone in to talk to your grandda. I don't want to rush that.'

Touched, Matthew pushed the door wider and went in. Freya looked up from where she was pouring water from the

153

jug into four tumblers. 'I was forgetting, you haven't even met each other yet. Mairead, this is my father, Mr Matthew Penhaligon. Papá, Miss Mairead Garvey.'

Matthew shook the hand he found thrust at him. 'Pleasure to meet you, miss.'

Mairead was a year or two younger than Freya by the looks, with her mother's mossy green eyes and frank way of looking right at you. There was an easily bandied opinion around town that she was simple-minded, but he already knew otherwise; this girl was no simpleton.

'I understand we've you to thank for sorting through our books,' he said, with a smile of appreciation. 'Freya tells me you've a gift.'

'I enjoy it.'

Further conversation was cut short by the squeak of hinges, and the waft of heat, as Anna opened the oven. She bent to take out the pie, and gave a little exclamation.

'What is it?' Freya asked.

Anna straightened, and looked over her shoulder at them all. She was biting her lip, and for a moment Matthew thought she was upset about something, but the look melted into a giggle and when she turned and put the pie on the table they saw why. His gaze rose to meet hers, and as the pastry monstrosity in the pie dish bubbled and sank between them like an unenthusiastic volcano, his grin became a snort of laughter.

'I'm sure it'll taste fine.' He picked up a knife and prodded the pie, which spat once more before subsiding into a half-collapsed pile of lumpy pastry and spilled gravy. Amid a combination of embarrassed groans, and assurances that everything would be delicious, the pie was divided between five plates, one on a tray for Robert, and despite the look of it, the smell made Matthew's mouth water.

'Anna called you my da,' Freya told Matthew, eyeing her lunch with undisguised suspicion. 'I like it better than Pa, don't you?'

Anna put a loaded plate in front of Matthew, and his eyes widened. 'I'll never eat all that!'

'Ah sure, just leave what you can't manage. Your own da will be wanting—'

'See?' Freya interrupted. 'Mairead, do you call your ...' She stopped, a blush staining her cheeks, and she looked so mortified that Matthew was sure she didn't notice the look that flashed between Mairead and her mother. But the conversation was moving too quickly to explore the reason behind it.

'Don't fret, love,' Anna told Freya. 'That is what Mairead called her father, though, yes. I'm sorry, Matthew, I didn't mean to start something.'

'Don't pay it any mind.' He was just relieved she seemed at ease with the casual discussion of her deceased husband. Perhaps he'd died longer ago than everyone thought. Or maybe he'd been something of a bully, and less to be mourned than forgotten. That was an all-too-frequent tale, he knew.

'Mama always made me call him Papá,' Freya said, recovering, with an apologetic look at Mairead, 'but I'm not sure I'll always do it.'

'Call me whatever you like.' Matthew dug his knife into the slice of pie and watched the steam roll out.

'But don't call me late for dinner,' Anna finished for him.

He looked at her again; she was covering her mouth with

her napkin, but her eyes met his over the top, and lengthened as her hidden smile widened.

He turned to Freya, glad of the distraction, suddenly. 'You really don't want to call me Papá anymore?'

'I don't know. Maybe for now, but I think it sounds a little bit ... childish.' She frowned. 'You're not too upset, are you?'

'I never took to it,' he admitted. 'Your mother used it from when you were a baby, but when you started to say it I never got half the thrill as when you would come out with "da da", even though it didn't mean me.'

'What did it mean?'

He grinned. 'Anything from "walk" to "bread" to "I don't like whatever it is you're trying to do to my hair, Mama".'

Freya looked embarrassed, but smiled back. 'Well if I use it now it won't mean any of those things.'

'Where is your mother?' Mairead asked. Anna gave her a sharp look, but Mairead took no notice. 'Is she dead?'

'Mairead!'

'Well, is she?'

Freya was about to answer, but stopped, and when Matthew followed her look he saw that it would have been pointless saying anything; Mairead was staring into space, and although her eyes were open the lids were fluttering, as if she slept and was dreaming. After a moment Anna's hand closed gently on her arm, and Mairead blinked.

'What were you saying, Mother?'

'Nothing, *ma mhuirnín*. Eat your meal.'

Freya exchanged a glance with Matthew, and bent her head to her own plate. Matthew felt compelled to answer Mairead's question anyway. 'Freya's mother, Isabel, wasn't happy in Cornwall.'

'Oh?' Anna said. 'I can't think why anyone would want to leave, I think it's a lovely place.' But her voice held the ring of politeness only, and Matthew could sense the sympathy with another outsider, even one she'd never met.

'She came from a wealthy family.' He tried not to sound resentful, because, in truth, he wasn't. But he was aware that was the popular impression of the way things had ended for the Penhaligons. 'She tried to settle in, and the people here took to her quite well, but she was made for that other life really. She's gone back to it now.'

'It must have been hard for you both.' Anna sounded even more sympathetic, to Isabel's plight. 'Still, as long as you're all happy now, that's the important thing.'

Conversation flowed more easily then, mostly between the two girls. Listening to them talking about Freya's job, and her dubious friend Juliet, it was as if they'd been friends for years. Freya no longer seemed surprised or discomfited by Mairead's blunt questions, and if she chose not to answer them the Irish girl would happily move on to other subjects.

'I lived near the beach at my old house,' Mairead volunteered. 'I used to go collecting things. Shells and suchlike.'

'Freya used to do that, too, when she was little and we lived closer to Porthstennack.' Matthew smiled at his daughter. 'She used to call the things she found her "treasures", whether they were or not. Found some good stuff though ... in amongst the crabs.'

Freya returned his smile, but it was a little tight around the edges. 'I did.'

'Perhaps we might go together one day?' Mairead said eagerly.

Freya frowned. 'Perhaps. If we can find the time.'

'Seems you two have a little more in common than we thought,' Anna said. 'But you must both want to go, mind.' She too seemed to have noticed Freya's reluctance, but Mairead just looked pleased.

'It'll be a lot of fun to see who can find the most perfect shell, or the smoothest piece of driftwood, won't it, Freya?'

Freya agreed, but she soon turned the conversation back onto her school days. Matthew noted she spoke more of her early days with Juliet, than her time at St Catherine's, in London. For the first time he realised she hardly ever brought that subject up, although it would be more easily remembered, and almost certainly as rich in anecdotes, if not more so, than her days at Priddy Lane.

His attention was pulled, with increasing frequency, to Anna. She ate with an elegance somewhat at odds with her slightly wild appearance, a delicacy, even, and once he'd noticed it became harder and harder to look away. She began preparing each forkful only when she had completely finished the last, and he realised he was slowing down to match her speed, and enjoying the meal all the more for it. He found too, that he was anticipating her rare comments with pleasure, and wondered why it was that word had flown around town that she was not to be trusted.

Mrs Gale seemed to have been the sole instigator of this gossip, and must have taken a violent dislike to her from the outset, but again, why? Anna was generous, with both her time and her larder, she was unfailingly polite, undoubtedly intelligent ... His eyes were drawn to the angle of her jaw, her thick eyelashes, and her long neck and the way her hair curled against it. She was an unusually appealing woman, but Mrs Gale's dislike couldn't all be based on jealousy; Anna was not the only good-looking woman in town, most of them had pleasant manners, and hardly any of them had trouble holding a conversation. Besides, Susan Gale was too old to feel the presence of a younger woman as some kind of bar to her own happiness.

Anna laughed at something Freya had said – a proper laugh this time, no hiding behind a napkin. She gave herself over to it whole-heartedly, putting down her fork to rest a slender hand at her breastbone and glancing over at him to see if he was laughing too. He wasn't, of course, but then he hadn't heard a thing Freya had said for a good ten minutes. Anna's smile died as her eyes met his, and he didn't know whether to feign humour to bring it back, or just to accept that he had broken this fragile moment. Then, as their gaze held, he realised with a pleasurable jolt that she too was in danger of forgetting their daughters were sitting there. He cleared his throat, and they both shifted their concentration to Freya once more, but for the remainder of the meal he was aware of the gentle weight of Anna's presence on his heart. It felt as if it belonged there.

Anna and Mairead prepared to leave soon after the meal was cleared away, and as Mairead went to fetch their coats Matthew drew Anna into the small porch at the back of the kitchen. 'I just want to say something. About before.'

'Before?' But she knew, he could see it in the way her eyes skipped from his face to her shoes, to her hands, to the kitchen behind him.

'I can't ignore it,' he said, with quiet urgency. 'I understand it's wrong, but I can't help it.'

It took a great deal of effort not to touch her face when she finally stilled and looked at him, but he kept his hands at his sides and waited for her to speak.

'Matthew . . . ' Her voice was little more than a whisper, as if it had taken all her strength to form that one word, and now she could say nothing else.

'Don't worry.' His hand disobeyed him, staying low but reaching blindly for hers. 'It's nothing. It'll pass. I'm sorry.'

'Are you?' She looked down, seeming a little dazed, and surprised to see their fingers touching, and withdrew her hand.

He took a deep breath, wondering if he'd imagined it after all. He searched for a more formal tone. 'Will you, and Mairead of course, visit us again?' She didn't answer, and he took a step back, but her hand flashed out and caught his wrist and he felt a flicker of hope.

'I want to.' She lifted her eyes to his again and he saw her fine dark eyebrows pulled down in an expression that was almost pain. 'I do want to, but I'm afraid.'

'Don't be. I can control myself, I'll keep my distance.'

'That's not what I'm afraid of.'

'What, then?'

'What if . . . if it's not nothing?'

His heart faltered, and he lowered his voice again. 'Would that be so terrible?'

'That's the problem. It wouldn't be terrible at all.'

Matthew quashed the surge of elation that roared through him, but Anna searched his eyes and must have seen it anyway because when she spoke again there was a note of caution in her voice.

'It's too soon.'

'I know. You're in mourning.'

'Yes.'

He blew out a breath. It stirred her hair, and she did not flinch away the way Isabel had, when the drink had soured him. 'The girls like each other,' he said, 'and I hope we've become friends too. Would that be enough to bring you back? If I swear to keep my distance?'

'People will talk.'

He smiled, and her expression cleared, but she raised a questioning eyebrow and he shrugged. 'I think we're both used to that, aren't we?'

She seemed to realise then that she was still gripping his wrist, and she let go. But some of the light had come back into her eyes. 'Well I certainly am. I've heard next to nothing about you though.'

'You can't have been listening very hard.'

'Oh, but I have.' She looked surprised at her own boldness. Now the words had been spoken, the tension had eased and he was passionately relieved that he hadn't just let her go home without examining what had passed between them.

Freya and Mairead came over, and Anna stepped away from Matthew, leaving him feeling a little bit breathless and adrift. After a minute or so of farewells she and her daughter left, Freya went back into the kitchen, and Matthew was left staring at the closed door, wondering if he had imagined the whole thing. Only the lingering sensation of her hand on his wrist convinced him he had not.

*

Late that afternoon, as he and Freya worked in companionable silence on their usual Sunday book repairs, he acknowledged that his mind had been anywhere but where it should have been in the actual moment of Anna's leaving. He experienced a moment's cold panic as he realised he couldn't even remember if he'd given himself away in front of their two daughters; how could he be sure that the dream that was playing in his head, of taking her face between his hands and kissing her full on those laughing lips, had not actually happened?

He frowned, thinking hard: he had thanked them for their visit; then thanked Anna for preparing the meal; Anna had returned the compliment, thanking him for his hospitality. Then – he grinned – hadn't she said he was a good boy for eating all his greens? She had.

His laugh, quiet though it was, cut across the shop, and Freya glanced up from her glue brush with a puzzled smile, although she looked as though she didn't care what he'd been laughing at and was just glad to hear it. He shook his head, and she returned to her work without question. But after a moment she put down her brush, and came to sit beside him.

'Papá?'

'Still calling me that, then?'

'For now.' She paused, and he waited without comment. 'I don't know if you already know,' she went on, 'and I don't want to spoil the day, but I heard something yesterday. From Juliet.'

'Oh?' Matthew pressed the cover on his book shut, and clamped it while he waited again for Freya to continue. He was tempted to tell her to leave it, if it was bad news, but tomorrow would be an early start and he'd be away for two days, maybe three. Whatever she had to tell him, it would have to be now. Besides, it would take a lot to spoil this day.

'James Fry is back.'

He stilled, letting the slow roll in his gut settle. That was a hell of a lot, all right. He wondered if Freya realised the implications, but one look at her face told him the answer to that. Of course she did; she wasn't a child. Thank God he hadn't told her about Roland's now pointless offer – she'd be spared disappointment at least.

'And Juliet told you this?'

'Yes. She . . . um, she saw him. He's staying at the hotel.'

'Why would he be staying there?' He was musing aloud and didn't expect an answer, but Freya had one anyway.

'Because he's still furious with Roland over giving you a job after what happened.'

She must have been wrestling all afternoon with the decision of whether or not to tell him, it was the only thing that kept him from snapping at her, *that won't stop him from getting me kicked off his place on Roland's crew!*

His mouth was dry, and he felt the beginnings of a headache. Numbers started thundering through his mind, and none of them added up; the shop, food, fuel for heating, his own boat and the repairs it would need after all . . . Freya's part-time job just wouldn't do it.

She touched his arm, and he realised she already knew that, too. 'I can ask for more hours,' she said, her voice timid. 'Papá, I'm so sorry.'

'It's not your fault, is it?' He was thinking fast. If James was at the hotel he hadn't yet gone to Roland. Perhaps if he got there first, begged him . . . but that would mean driving the wedge even harder between father and son. He remembered the way it had felt to hear his own father's words of regret, his wish to put things right, and he shook his head; he couldn't do that to Roland. Or even to James.

'I'll think of something. I'll get the boat mended. I always knew I couldn't rely on Roland's generosity forever.'

'I'll do anything I can to help,' Freya promised.

Matthew nodded. 'Talk to Mrs Bone tomorrow.' He saw her stiffen slightly. 'Freya? What's to do?'

'Nothing. I'll speak to Mrs Bone.'

Through narrowed eyes he watched her go back to her table. He had the feeling he knew exactly what was to do, and that Mrs Bone might well not be the best person to speak to after all. He sighed, and looked at the book he had just clamped. When he'd done that, his heart had still been light, the memory of Anna's smile danced behind his eyes, and her words: *It wouldn't be terrible at all*, still whispering in his blood. How quickly things change. He wanted a drink.

Chapter Nine

The temperatures plummeted overnight. Early on Monday morning Matthew closed the door behind him, leaving his father and Freya sleeping away the rest of the dark hours. He pulled the neck of his pullover higher, sinking his chin into its meagre warmth, and took note of the wet roads ... at least they had not frozen.

His insides were in tight knots as he began walking; would he be back within an hour, or would Roland give him this promised two-day catch before breaking the news about James? Hands thrust deep into his pockets, he concentrated on the soothing sound of his boots on the otherwise silent road, and rehearsed what he would say to ease his old friend's burden.

He's your son, of course I understand. He deserves this more than me. You have to take this chance to re-build your relationship.

The Tin Streamer's Arms lay to his left, across the road. He found his gaze dragged to its closed door as he passed, and was surprised, and deeply relieved, to find his first thought was not for the barrels and bottles on the other side of that door. Instead he pictured a pair of green eyes, laughing at him over the top of a hastily seized napkin, and a slender, heat-blistered hand holding a glass of water as if it was fine wine. His hands unclenched in his pockets, and a sense of calm crept over him; whatever Anna Garvey brought to the town in the way of gossip and suspicion, she had shown his family only kindness and generosity of spirit. If they must be merely friends to preserve that, it would have to be enough.

He hoped it could be, because God knows he wanted to touch her again, and his breath caught with the intensity of it. His pace had slowed, but now he picked it up again and soon drew close to the memorial to Sir Malcolm Penworthy. Civil war hero, squire ... his likeness stood tall and imperious, an example to them all. Penworthy ... such an apt name.

Matthew gave a short laugh. What was so different in their make-up, that changed the way their lives were destined to go? He himself was loyal, honest and not afraid of a day's work, yet look at the weakness he'd discovered; the foolish belief that a temporarily numbed mind would ease the pain of failure. Well he'd learned different. Life was what it was.

The town gave way to the long, winding lane to the beach, and as he drew level with his old cottage he stopped to look a while, if only to put off the moment when he must hear his fate in the reluctant words of his skipper. Whatever the reason, he rested his arms on the top of the gate and stared through the dark at the squat, lumpen silhouette of the cottage, at the yard, filled with puddles still touched with moonlight, at the rough walls, and the window-frames that had always been in need of paint when he'd lived there.

If he closed his eyes, he could picture it in summer. The early days, when Freya was just a few months old and Isabel had sat with her in the small garden, looking at him with sleepy bliss. 'She is so beautiful, do you not think so, my Viking prince?' His heart had been full of them both then, Isabel and their tiny, perfect daughter, but it had been less than a year later that he had noticed the first signs of sadness in Isabel. That had soon melted into discontent, which became anger, and from there, when she realised she was truly trapped, into the tired, hopeless acceptance that hurt most of all.

A gust of wind brought him back to the present, and he straightened. A woman was looking out of the window, where Freya had so often stood waiting for him to return in the evening; Nancy Gilbert, another widow, and a recent one. She had four young children, all under eight, the poor girl. Generally considered a beauty, she was at least likely to wed again and her life would settle once more. But during this period of mourning she would certainly be struggling with the rent on Hawthorn Cottage, not to mention feeding her little ones.

He raised a hand in a mixture of polite greeting and apology, and moved on, wondering again what lay ahead for the day. He was fortunate enough, compared to Nancy; if the worst happened he could at least get a job in the tin mine at Wheal Furzy. He'd be spending his days in choking blackness and dust, instead of with the sharp tang of salt, and the wind snapping the sail above him, but he'd do it, if it became necessary. To save his home, and Freya's future. In the meantime, provided Roland was prepared to offer a day's work today, all Matthew could do was make the best of it.

'All right, boy?' Roland was working with Ern Bolitho, securing nets on the *Pride of Porthstennack*. The trawler bobbed on the choppy water, bumping the harbour wall, and Roland's former mackerel seine boat, *Cousin Edith*, was high and dry, awaiting its own season in the summer. Matthew still had trouble even looking at that one, after what had happened on it, and he knew it was hard for Roland to see it run by someone else.

'All right, Roley?' he returned, fixing an easy smile on his face. 'Colder today, then.'

'Ar.' Roland clambered stiffly back onto the harbour wall, one hand as ever on his twisted knee, and picked up his leather bag. He checked inside it and flung it onto the trawler's deck. 'Cod'll be good 'n' sluggish.'

The rest of the crew were ready, but Roland took Matthew aside. 'Listen, boy. I've got to tell you—'

'I know, James is back.' Matthew managed a smile. 'I'm that glad. Really.'

'He's taken it bad,' Roland said. 'That I gave you the job, I mean.' He shook his head. 'Timing's all, eh?'

'He must know I won't take it. I've been thinking, I can get a job at Wheal Furzy.'

'The mines? You?' Roland pushed back his hat to scratch his head. 'No offence, boy, but you wouldn't last a day.'

'I'm strong enough,' Matthew protested. 'And it's manual work, not much to learn.'

'Exactly. You'd be that bored, you'd be halfway back down the road 'fore crib time.' Roland gave him a faint smile. 'No, you're a fisherman through and through. James i'nt. Job's yours.' He started to limp away, but hesitated and looked back, sounding less sure now. 'If you're still all right with not bein' your own boss.'

Matthew made a helpless gesture. 'Of course I am, Roley, but—'

'Right then. Cod's waiting.' Roland climbed aboard, and Matthew watched him for a moment, bemused and relieved. Then he bent and untied the rope that secured the boat, and threw it ahead of him before following. The roll of the deck beneath his boots calmed each taut nerve, soothed every chaotic thought, and brought a cooling mist of peace over him. Conflict awaited, there was no doubt of that, but for now there was just this sensation, these smells, the creaking and snapping of deck and sail, and the shouts of his fellow crew-members as they got under way. There was only this.

The Tin Streamer's Arms

Trade was finally picking up. The number of customers had grown noticeably over the past weeks, curiosity had given way to a general approval of the newly cleaned premises, and, with the chimney cleaned, the fire was kept well stoked and the pub was no longer choked with what Esther called 'smeech'. There were still no women to be seen, besides Esther and Anna, but it was a start.

Monday promised to be a busy night after the general

169

abstinence of Sunday. Anna's conscience was starting to prickle at her; this morning she had seen Mairead off to Penhaligon's Attic, squinting against the watery sunlight reflecting off the wet road; Freya had worked in the shop all morning, then made her way to the Caernoweth Hotel at lunchtime; Matthew – she couldn't help a tiny, secret smile – would have set off to Porthstennack before the sun was up.

Shop doors were opening and closing, from the bottom of town to the top. Younger children had wound their way down to the little school at Priddy Lane, older ones had left their beds early for long shifts at mine and quarry, and in various apprenticeships. In the Tinner's back yard even Mr Trevellick was swapping barrels, and Mrs Trevellick grumpily pegging out towels on the line while the rain held off ... Anna was struck by the realisation that she was the only one still drifting, still aimless, still pretending this was a temporary situation. Beyond the back-breaking work of cleaning ancient grime off the furniture and fittings, she had played very little part in the actual running of the pub. A mixture of nerves and reluctance to expose herself to more gossip had persuaded her to leave the customers to the Trevellicks.

But now it was time to take the helm, as terrifying as the prospect was, so she spent the remainder of the day learning how to use the beer engine without creating a mess, and likewise how to draw a drinkable ale from the casks in the bar. While she did so she practised her confident smile, her path from bar to table, her mental arithmetic, and, most of all, her answers.

By nine o'clock she was wilting on her feet, but no longer viewed the serving of drinks with such trepidation. There were fewer dark looks now she had come forward, and even one or two nods of greeting, and it soon became clear that it wasn't only the warm cleanliness of the Tinner's, and the sharp, fresh-tasting ale from clean pumps, that had changed things.

'You was all the talk after chapel yesterday.' This from one of the fishermen from Porthstennack, who usually sat at Roland Fry's table. 'Is it true you'm a Penworthy?'

'I am,' Anna said, silently thanking Freya. 'I believe I'm the last of them.'

'But you'm Irish?'

'Yes, from his daughter Jane. She moved to Ireland late in the 1600s. Can I get you another drink?'

He nodded, and Anna turned to re-fill his tankard. From the corner of her eye she saw the door open, and her heart stopped beating just for a moment as she saw the light reflect off fair hair. But it wasn't Matthew, it was someone she'd never seen before. He came towards the bar, somewhat hesitantly, but clearly recognising the fisherman who'd spoken.

'Brian Cornish! It's good to see you.' He held out his hand. Anna gave a wry smile; so this was Robert's friend, he of the wagging tongue. Well, he seemed harmless enough, and now he knew why she'd moved here perhaps he would be good enough to spread that word, too.

Mr Cornish automatically took the stranger's hand, but Anna saw his previously friendly expression close down, and the handshake was very brief. 'I 'eard you was back, Fry.'

'I'm living with Pa,' the newcomer said, somewhat pointedly, before belatedly noticing Anna. He smiled, and put out his hand to her too. 'Well, I don't know. Go to Dorset for a mere eighteen years and everything changes.'

Anna shook his hand, smiling back. 'I'm Anna Garvey.'

'Ah, a beautiful colleen.' James converted the handshake to an elegant brush of his lips on the back of her hand, making her blush. 'James Fry. Architect.'

'Pleased to meet you.'

'Likewise. Where's Mrs Trevellick? Still in the land of the living, I hope.'

'She's still here. At least,' Anna glanced behind her, 'I *hope* she's still here and not run off and left me on my first proper night.'

He laughed. 'And what brings you to our shores?' he asked, glancing around the pub, as if looking for someone in particular.

'This pub. It might be my first night, but the pub's belonged to me a good few years.'

'So she says,' a voice behind Brian muttered, and Anna's heart sank. It was one of the coldest of her patrons, a black-haired young man named Donithorn.

'And why shouldn't it be the truth?' James queried, his eyes narrowing.

Donithorn shrugged. 'Where's her proof? Could be anyone. And she looks a bit chipper for a widow, dun't she?'

'A widow?' James's smile slipped. 'I'm so sorry, I've been a bit crass, haven't I?'

'Not at all.' Anna shifted her attention to Donithorn, and her voice rose slightly. 'I apologise if my demeanour doesn't fit your expectation, Mr Donithorn, but I have a duty to my customers.' She became aware of conversation falling off all around her, but she went on, 'If you prefer, I'll sit in the corner and weep into the dregs. I'm sure that'll satisfy anyone who thinks I'm being too *chipper*.'

'Bravo,' James said quietly into the silence that followed, and Brian Cornish's snort echoed in his tankard. Anna let out her breath. At least she had two allies, even if there did seem to be a difficulty between them. This James Fry certainly didn't fit the usual expectation of a Tinner's customer, and Anna's curiosity was piqued – the irony was not lost on her that she was exhibiting exactly the kind of reaction she'd so resented in the Caernoweth inhabitants. And with that in mind, was it really a good idea to antagonise someone like David Donithorn, even when she felt justified in her annoyance? She was supposed to be building bridges instead of burning them.

She cleared her throat. 'Mr Donithorn, I appreciate none of you knows anything about me, but—'

'Nor do we want to.' Donithorn finished his drink in one gulp and put it on the bar. 'You're keeping bad comp'ny, *Mrs* Garvey.'

Anna glared after him, no longer bothering to hide her annoyance, as he pulled the door open and went out into the night. 'Well, how rude! I was trying to apologise, after all.'

'Bad company?' James enquired. 'Who would that be?'

'Don't pay him no mind,' Brian said. 'He's bitter.'

'About what?'

Brian looked at him as if he were simple. 'About what? About what happened to your pa, and his part in it!'

There was a pause, then James said flatly, '*He* was the boy on the boat. The one swinging the stone.'

'You didn't know, then?'

'How could I? Pa sent me back to Dorset before I could find out anything. What happened to Donithorn afterwards?'

Brian shrugged. 'He never worked on the boats again. No one would have him.'

'But it wasn't his fault, it was—'

'Penhaligon. I know.'

'And he got away with it,' James said, in a bitter voice. 'Made a new start, thanks to my gullible father.'

'Now, lad—'

'Don't "now, lad" me! Matthew was a selfish, dangerous drunk, and he proved it. Pa will never be right again, and losing *Cousin Edith* more than halved our income.' He frowned, evidently remembering something else. 'And what happened to the daughter?'

'What?'

'Pa said something happened to the child. What was it? What was bad enough that *finally* stopped Matt drinking?'

Anna looked from one man to the other. She wasn't at all sure she wanted to hear this.

'Storm of '99, it was.' Brian's voice was low, as if the telling of it hurt him, too. As he described how eight-year-old Freya had been found half-frozen on the beach Anna closed her eyes, picturing it all with rising horror. When she opened them again James's expression was dark, his lips tight.

'And you still believe Penhaligon deserves a helping hand? He could have killed her. His own daughter!'

Brian scowled. 'He lost the maid for years over that. I'd say he paid dear enough. Be half the man your pa is, Fry, and learn to forgive.'

Anna jumped as a glass banged onto the bar at the far end, and she went to fill it, but the need to know everything about Matthew was biting at her concentration. Had he really stopped drinking? Or was her inheritance the real reason behind his sudden interest? An unattached man, not yet forty, fit and healthy – not to mention handsome – he must have his choice in such a small town, so why would he suddenly find a ragged Irish widow so appealing?

And she *was* ragged; Anna looked at her stained apron, plain dress and old shoes. So different from the way she had been . . . She shook off the memory; what she'd once been was not the issue, this was what she was now. What she had. This life, this pub, and Mairead. She remembered Matthew's low, only half-amused voice telling her she hadn't been listening hard enough to hear the townspeople's talk. Well, she had now.

Chapter Ten

Freya had not even finished her breakfast when she heard the shop door rattle in its frame. She glanced at the kitchen clock in surprise; who would be looking for books this early? A knock sounded, and she dropped her spoon back in her porridge, and wiped her mouth while she hurried in to the shop. Early or not, they could not afford to lose a sale.

She didn't know whether to be disappointed or pleased to see Mairead, her hands cupping her eyes as she peered through the locked door, but she couldn't help smiling to see her jump as she belatedly realised Freya was already staring back at her.

Freya slid back the bolt and opened the door. 'What are you doing here so early?'

Mairead came in, blowing on her hands. 'We've a job of work to do, and I mean to get a good deal of it done before you go off to the hotel.'

'What job?' The books were neat enough, although still

not properly square in their places. Freya was about to pass on Granny Grace's wisdom about that, but Mairead was already walking to the counter.

'I need ink. As many colours as you have. And at least one ledger. Two, if you have them.'

'What job?' Freya repeated, but she rummaged in the box beneath the counter and came out with three half-used ink bottles – two were black, but the third left a green smudge on her fingers.

'I'm going to help you get this place in order,' Mairead said. 'Mother doesn't need me getting under her feet now she's taken charge, so what better time?' She paused in her search for a blank ledger. 'I'm sorry, she said I shouldn't forget to ask: how is your grandda?'

Although the thought had not been her own, she did look genuinely concerned, and Freya found she didn't mind at all that she'd had to be prompted.

'He's still tired,' she said, 'but it's getting harder to make him stay in his bed. He's getting back to his old self very quickly, and as dearly as I love him, that's not necessarily good news.'

'Isn't he happier with your da now, though?'

'That's one of the good parts. As for the rest,' Freya produced an old book and passed it over, 'all I can say is, I hope whatever you have planned for this place works, and quickly.'

Mairead opened the book, studied the few lines of figures that had been entered, and then ripped the pages out. 'No need to bother with those, they were old when Noah was a lad. Time to start fresh, what do you think?'

'But you've been through the books already.'

'They're a mess, Freya. You need to keep better records or

you'll find yourself in deep water one day.' She smoothed the blank pages and let out a deep sigh of satisfaction. 'Look at that. Was there ever a prettier sight?'

'And you're going to mess it all up,' Freya pointed out with a smile. 'Do you really like doing this? Numbers and things?'

Mairead's face took on a distant expression, but this time she was fully aware, and her eyelids didn't flutter. 'Numbers are perfect. They don't change what they are, and you can't argue with them.'

'*I* can,' Freya said, somewhat glumly. 'They never do what I want them to.'

'That's because you're scared of them. I'm going to teach you not to be.'

'And you younger than me!' Freya sighed. 'Right then. Show me. And while you're at it, see if you can make *that* column,' she laid her finger where the profit would go, 'tell a prettier story than the one it's been telling for the past few years.'

'Pass me the book you're using now,' Mairead said. 'And then, yes please.' She flashed Freya a grin. 'I'd love a cup of tea.'

When Freya returned with two cups and the teapot, Mairead was no longer behind the counter. She was nowhere to be seen, in fact. Anna put the cups down. 'Mairead?'

'Here!' The girl's voice came from one of the darker corners, and Freya went around the free-standing shelves to find Mairead on her knees, a pile of books beside her on the floor.

'What are you doing?'

'What kind of books do you sell?'

Freya gestured vaguely. 'These. All sorts. Second-hand.'

'No, you don't. You sell a select and sought-after collection of local interest and history books, research material, and novels.'

Freya blinked. 'Do we?'

'Of course you do.'

'And is that different?'

'We'll soon find out.' Mairead stood, clutching the books she'd selected. 'These need to go on the counter, they're beautiful.'

Freya eyed them doubtfully. 'I suppose they are. Or were.'

'Will be again, once we've finished with them. They shouldn't be tucked away back here.'

'Well *you* found them,' Freya said, a little defensively. She wasn't sure she liked being told what a poor job she was making of the family business.

'I knew where to look, because Mother saw them when she was serving that gentleman from Plymouth the other day.'

'What gentleman?'

'The one who paid half a crown for the book about the fort.'

'Half a crown?' Freya stared. 'Who would pay that for an old book?'

'Historians. Scholars. I found the transaction when I was sorting through your books, and I asked my mother about it last night. She told me she'd seen a lot more books like it, but that they were tucked away.'

'We don't really get many historians in.'

'That's because they don't know what you've got.' Mairead went back to her dusty corner. 'If we could afford a small advertisement somewhere, it would pay for itself in no time, I'm sure of it.'

It was hard to ignore Mairead's certainty, and Freya felt a tingle of excitement. She applied her mind to how they might raise enough money to place an advertisement, but Mairead broke into her thoughts, with a bluntness that was no longer surprising.

'You're not very good at keeping things tidy, are you?'

'Well, I—'

'We'll need to get this place ship-shape. And then we'll need an inventory.'

'That would take weeks,' Freya said, aghast.

'Then we'll start today. How on earth are you supposed to tell others what you have, when you don't know yourself? I'll come every day, good and early, and in the meantime we'll set our minds to placing an advertisement as soon as we're ready.' Mairead put down another armful of books, and pushed her hair away from her eyes with her sleeve. 'What do you think?'

Freya smiled. 'Let's make a start.'

Around mid-morning they stopped for a break and a piece of honeyed bread. The shop remained open, and after Freya had checked on her grandpa, she and Mairead sat behind the counter, glad of the rest. It was short-lived, however, and when the door opened and Hugh Batten came in, Freya quickly shoved her piece of bread beneath the counter and surreptitiously wiped her sticky fingers in her skirts. Just in case.

Mr Batten had brought his nephew Harry with him, and Freya nodded politely at them both. 'Good morning, Mr Batten, Master Harry.'

'Good morning, Miss Penhaligon.' Ushered forward, Harry

held out his hand, and Freya shook it, biting her lip against a grin as she saw his face falter. He looked at his fingers as he withdrew them.

'It's quite all right, it's only honey,' Mairead said. 'She's hidden her bread under the counter so you can't tell she's eating.'

Freya rolled her eyes. Mr Batten saw it, and his mouth twitched. His eyes lengthened in a smile as he very deliberately held out his hand to shake Freya's. Cringing, she shook it, trying to make as little contact as possible, but when he withdrew his hand he made a great show of examining his fingers.

'Now that we've completed the ancient Cornish ritual of honey-smearing,' he said with a grin, 'I think you're allowed to call me Hugh.'

Freya couldn't help laughing, despite her acute embarrassment, and she nodded. 'Hugh it is, then.'

Harry had already wandered off to explore among the shelves, and Hugh shook Mairead's hand too, but his attention immediately swung back to Freya. 'What do you have that might interest a boy of ten, Miss Penhaligon?'

'We have a copy of *Peter Pan in Kensington Gardens*.' Freya moved from behind the counter to help him find it. 'It's the story about a boy who never grows up. What do you think of that, Master Harry?'

'I should hate to never grow up,' Harry said, appalled. 'I want to be old enough to ride my pony on my own, without Uncle Hugh, *or* Mother, coming with me.'

'But Peter Pan gets to do something much more exciting than ride.' Freya found the book and handed it first to Hugh, in case he should think it unsuitable. 'He gets to *fly*!'

Harry turned rounded eyes on her, then looked eagerly at the book in his uncle's hand. 'Can I have it, Uncle Hugh?'

'Wait, wait,' Hugh murmured, flicking through the book. He met Freya's eyes across the top of it, and winked. 'Oh, I don't know . . . this seems awfully grown-up to me.'

'Uncle Hugh! Don't be mean!'

'See here . . . there are all kinds of dangerous adventures – I think you might have to wait a year or so.'

'Please!'

'Maybe until you're twenty.'

'Mr Batten, I do believe you enjoy torturing the boy,' Freya remonstrated, but she was smiling. It was difficult not to; Hugh was smiling at her again, wider than ever. As he looked back at the book, and freed her own gaze, Freya let it travel over his smartly tailored clothes, and clean shoes. His hands were long-fingered and elegant, flicking the pages with one hand, the other cradling the book, and she blinked away the image of them wrapped around her own.

At last he relented, and handed over the money. 'But I'm going to read it to you,' he told Harry. 'No use letting your mother loose on it, she'd get all the voices wrong.'

'She would,' the boy agreed, outwardly gloomy, but with an excited shine in his brown eyes. The boy must have everything his heart desired at Pencarrack, but here he was getting caught up with delight over a second-hand book. It was impossible not to respond with real pleasure to that.

'Well then, it seems our business here is done,' Hugh said. 'More's the pity. I'd expected to spend longer searching.'

'Well, we do have a lot more books.' Freya hoped she wasn't blushing as deeply as she felt sure she was.

'Another day then, without a doubt.' Hugh tipped his hat to her, gave Mairead a tiny bow, and took Harry's hand.

The boy swung around in a wide circle, dragging his uncle with him. 'Goodbye, Miss Penhaligon! Goodbye, Miss Garvey!'

'Goodbye, Master Harry,' they chorused, and when the shop door shut behind them Freya sat down, and avoided Mairead's eye.

'Well, that young man has a thumping crush on you,' Mairead observed archly. 'You know it's out of the question, of course?'

'Of course.' But the words stung, nevertheless; Hugh had been playing a growing role in Freya's private thoughts of late. 'But it doesn't hurt to be on good terms with them up at Pencarrack.'

'The little boy seems pleasant enough. Not full of airs and graces.'

'I thought that, too. I'm surprised, with Dorothy Batten as his mother.'

'Who's his father?'

'Ah.' Freya finished chewing, taking her time and enjoying watching Mairead grow more and more impatient. 'Nobody knows. Dorothy was well known as a bit of a gadabout in the old days, but then she went away, and came back with a baby boy. Her father made her go out into the town though, and not hide away at Pencarrack, so the scandal died down quite quickly in the end.'

'And how true is it?' Mairead sounded doubtful.

'Oh, quite true, I think. I know she went to London; she was on the same coach as Mama and me until we got to the train. Then she went first class, of course. She must have met someone quite soon after we arrived. Either that or they already knew each other and planned the whole thing.' Freya wiped her sticky mouth with the back of her hand, drawing a disapproving look. 'Did you ever want brothers or sisters?'

'No, they'd only get in the way.'

'In the way of what?'

'Well, me. What I want to do. Older ones would have been too bossy, and younger ones would just steal everyone's time. I'm glad I'm an only child.'

'But doesn't it make you wish, sometimes, when you see other children holding hands?' Freya heard the wistfulness in her own voice, but Mairead looked at her as though she had suggested cutting each other's hair off.

'Holding hands? Why in the world would you want that?'

Freya shrugged, feeling a little foolish; she was the older girl here, yet sounding the most childish. 'Never mind. I just . . . sometimes I think it'd have been nice, that's all. To have that closeness.'

'Did your mother not hold your hand?' Mairead sounded surprised.

'She wasn't very fond of walking anywhere, so there was no need.'

'Your father?'

'Sometimes, when I was very little. But he was usually carrying something when we walked.'

'And you think a brother or sister hanging off your arm would make things feel . . . nice?'

Freya laughed. 'When you put it like that, I'm not so sure.' Mairead didn't seem to be the kind of girl given to what-ifs, and she suspected if they walked anywhere together and Freya offered a friendly hand, Mairead would be quite horrified. Freya felt an odd rush of affection for her nevertheless.

'Papá used to read to me when I was little,' she said, to change the subject. 'He grew up with storytellers, and booklovers. He even wrote stories himself, but he hasn't done that for years. No reason to now, I suppose.'

'What kind of stories?' Mairead picked up her pen once more.

'Sea stories. Adventures. I'm sure he still has some in his journal, but I haven't seen it for a long time.'

'Why doesn't he send them to a publisher? Or are they not very good?'

Freya gave a surprised laugh. 'Well of course *I* think they're good! But I don't think he's ever thought of it.' She pondered, her interest piqued. 'Do you think he should?'

'He'd have nothing to lose, and maybe a lot to gain.' Mairead shook her head. 'I can't believe you've not even considered it, working in a book shop. And everyone saying you're so clever!'

'I'll talk to him about it,' Freya said, still amused. 'Your ma said she left a lot of books back at your other home. Will she have them sent?'

'No.'

Mairead's answer was so abrupt, Freya didn't say anything for a moment. Then curiosity prodded again. 'Did you leave a lot of things behind?'

'Everything.' Mairead's voice had gone from bold and direct, to barely audible, and Freya waited to see if she would elaborate, but she didn't.

'Why?' she ventured at last. 'It can't have been *so* sudden, your leaving, surely?' Mairead didn't answer. 'If your da hadn't ... died, would you have stayed?' Freya couldn't imagine the pain of losing her own father. But perhaps Mairead hadn't been as close to hers. She never mentioned him. 'Mairead?'

'Let's talk about something else.'

'I'm sorry.'

'No.' Mairead put down her pen. 'It's all right. I asked you about your family, you've every right to ask about mine. It's just ... ' She chewed her lip for a moment and glanced at the door that led into the house. 'I'm not supposed to talk about it. Not even to you.'

Freya raised an eyebrow. 'Not talk about your *family*?'

'It's so hard!' It was as if Freya's question had chipped away a stone in the wall Mairead had built around her private thoughts. 'I have to think everything through before I speak, and ... ' she managed a little laugh, 'Mother will tell you that's not something I'm fond of.'

'All right, I won't ask what it is you mustn't tell, but why must you keep it from us?'

Mairead sighed. 'We gave up everything to come here. And you're right; we had a good deal to give up, just like your own mother.'

At last Freya was beginning to understand. 'Did you lose your fortune when your father died?'

Mairead looked hopelessly torn. 'Please, don't.'

'I'm sorry,' Freya said again, and lifted the stack of books to begin re-arranging them on the counter.

Mairead worked silently from that moment on, and Freya began wishing the minutes away until it was time to leave.

After another hour of trying not to ask the wrong questions she untied her dusty apron.

'I ought to change my shoes and go to work; Mrs Bone has promised me extra hours if I can get there on time for the rest of the week. I'd rather be early.'

'Best hurry on then,' Mairead advised, also sounding relieved. 'Freya?'

'Yes?' Freya paused, with one hand on the door handle.

'Will you promise not to tell anyone what I said?'

'Of course.'

It wasn't until she was walking to the Caernoweth Hotel that she remembered one of those rumours about Anna; *a widow looking for a rich man to do away with.* Well it was a good thing Papá was by no means rich, or she might have felt distinctly less pleased when she'd seen the looks that had passed between him and Anna on Sunday afternoon.

Porthstennack Harbour

James pulled his coat closer around himself, and watched his father's boat manoeuvring skilfully into its allotted place. Even before the *Pride* bumped to a gentle stop, men were jumping ashore. Some he recognised, others were new, and then there was the one who made his fingers twitch and a band of iron clamp his forehead.

As children, the two-year age difference between himself and Matthew Penhaligon should have been an unbridgeable gap, but James's love of learning had carried him into Matthew's parents' shop day after day, where Robert and Grace had turned an indulgent blind eye to his reading without buying, and would often invite him to stay for supper.

Those days … James shook his head now, watching Penhaligon throw the coiled rope onto the jetty and jump after it. It hardly seemed possible that this was the same smiling boy he'd known for so long; the hair was a darker blond now, and the distinctive straight eyebrows darker still, and just as stern-looking. His hands moved easily along the rope, and his face was set in concentration, stubbled from a night at sea and frowning with effort as he pulled the *Pride* closer and secured it to the harbour wall.

James waited, leaning against the breakwater, and listened to his father and the others shouting to each other. His head ached, it had been grinding steadily away since he'd returned to the hotel on Sunday night to pay his final bill. The confident smile he'd flashed as he'd passed over the money had felt as if it were pulling his face to pieces, but it was as much a necessary tool as his pencils and his rulers. Now the very last of his savings were gone, and where would he earn the capital to start up his business? Wheal Furzy? Polworra Quarry? The bloody *markets*? At least working the stone at Polworra might have been a start.

Penhaligon deserved nothing Roland had given him, not the second chance after the accident, not the admittedly spo-radic work since Isabel had left, and certainly not the place in *Pride*'s permanent crew.

James levered himself off the wall and made his way across the beach. Matthew worked on with the others, his coat loosened in the heat of hard graft, despite the chilly wind. It seemed all had been forgiven, or forgotten, by Pa's crew during the past few years, such was the force of their skipper's popularity. *If Roley Fry's prepared to give the man a chance, he's all right by us.* Christ.

Matthew turned, mid-laugh, and saw him. The laughter died. 'James. I heard you were back.'

'Matthew. I heard you'd stolen my job.'

'Look—'

'No, *you* look!' James took a step closer, his throat tight with anger. '*I'm* not the one who smashed my father's knee and nearly ruined him. I'm not the one who couldn't steer a straight bloody line for the drink! I'm not the one who nearly let my daughter die, because I couldn't keep out of the pub! And yet I *am* the one who's pushed aside and left with no income.'

'You could have come back sooner,' Matthew said, his voice low and hard. 'Your pa only asked me on Saturday if I wanted this.' He wheeled, preparing to walk away, then swung back and repeated, through gritted teeth, 'You could have come back *sooner*!'

'Unlike you, I was doing something worthwhile,' James said. 'Learning my craft.'

'Ignoring your father.'

'As if you care!' James's voice crept higher again, and he lowered it, reluctant for Roland to witness this. 'He's *my* father, not yours. Yours did the right thing the night you abandoned your child to the sea. He should have done it more often, and harder.'

'Is that your answer too, then?' Matthew demanded. 'Just hit out? No wonder your pa doesn't want you on his boat.'

'It was *my* place, you bastard!'

'He didn't think you were ever coming back! That's why he offered it to me. He waited long enough.'

'He offered it because he felt sorry for you!'

Matthew pushed his damp hair from his eyes. 'And he felt nothing for you.'

James took the deepest breath he could manage, which still left his lungs almost empty, but he found enough air to say, in little more than a whisper, 'You haven't won. He'll see what you are, what you *still* are, and he'll cut you loose.'

'Maybe so.' Matthew's eyes glinted in the cold afternoon light. 'But until that day this job is mine.'

James watched him return to *Pride of Porthstennack*, feeling sick. He'd liked Matthew once. They'd stood apart from the rest of the lads, but always together; two blond boys, one tall and square-shouldered, one slender and a head shorter, both more interested in books than in trolley racing and football games. Rivalry had never reared its head between them. Not once, even when Matthew had returned from a trip to Plymouth with a beautiful Spanish bride in tow. James had truly been glad for him.

Isabel Penhaligon was exciting and passionately unpredictable, but Matthew had seemed both worthy of her, and more than a match. They were always either shouting at one another, banging doors and throwing things ... or wrapped together so tightly you couldn't tell where one ended and the other began.

James shook his head now, uttering a short, pained laugh. He had never thought about Isabel in a romantic way, she was too hot-headed for his taste. But such was his and Matthew's closeness, that when their daughter was born and he had seen the couple's relationship soften into something real, he had been surprised by an unexpectedly fierce envy. The perfect child completed the couple as a family, and what had Matthew done? Left her to die.

And *still* Roland offered him the hand of friendship.

James felt the bitter envy rising again, while Matthew resumed his work as if he had not just delivered the most cruel cut possible to a man. He watched only until he saw his father approach the little working group, and the sounds of men working in companionship and trust followed him as he trudged back across the beach.

The sun was dipping, such as it was. Matthew picked up his discarded coat and went to say goodnight to Roland, still trying to banish the sight of James's face from his mind; if he could have turned back time and caught the words before they'd flown from his lips he would have. But it was too late.

'Thanks again, Roley. I'll see you in the morning.'

'Stocker.' Roland pointed at the bag of extra fish on the breakwater. 'Don't be forgettin' that, now.'

'I won't.'

'Get on then, boy. See you 'morra.'

Muscles aching, Matthew heaved his share of the stocker over his shoulder and set off towards town. The climb was steady, relentless. It wouldn't level out until it reached the top of Caernoweth itself, where the hotel gazed down over the town like a stern schoolmaster. He didn't have to walk quite that far, but by the time he reached Penhaligon's Attic he was always ready to sink into a chair and not move for a week.

He pushed open the side door, and as he peeled off his damp jumper in the hallway he realised there was still someone working in the shop, despite the lateness of the hour. He glanced at the peg where Freya kept her coat – his mother's old one, which she had refused to give away – but it was not there, and his heartbeat picked up as he pushed open the door.

'Ah. Good evening, Mairead,' he said, trying not to let his disappointment show.

'I'm sorry it's only me, not my mother,' she said, and Matthew blinked.

'Um, I'm not sure what—'

'I expect you'll see her soon, though.' She was sitting on the floor surrounded by books and ink pots, and writing in a ledger. 'I hope you don't mind,' she went on, before he could think of anything to say. 'I waited until the shop was closed.'

'Waited for what?' Relieved at the change of subject, he came further into the room. 'What are you doing?'

'I'm marking each title with a colour. Well, a colour or a symbol, since you only have two colours. To show what kind of book they are.'

'You're writing down every book we have?' He looked around the cluttered room.

'No, just the most important ones.'

'Why note them at all?'

Mairead sat back and regarded him frankly. 'Because you've a lot of books that are worth a good deal of money to certain people, and you ought to be able to keep them to hand.'

'Really?' Matthew crouched beside her and picked up the nearest book. 'And is this one of them?'

'Do you think it is?'

Sensing a test, he considered it carefully. He found himself remembering things his parents had told him, things he'd barely taken notice of at the time, since they had nothing to do with getting his first boat. But now he studied the date of publication, the publisher, the spine ... 'I'd say no,' he said at last.

'Why not?'

'Because it's a recent date, the publisher is still very much in business, and it's not a subject a lot of people ask about.'

'Very good.' She removed it from his grasp. He couldn't help grinning at her prim manner. 'I wouldn't bother cataloguing this one. This one, however,' she handed him a heavy, leather-bound volume, and before he even opened it he knew it would be a draw for any book-lover. 'You could charge five shillings and upwards for this, and someone would pay it.'

'Five?'

'And up,' she confirmed. 'Freya and I worked on this all morning. I'll let her tell you what we discussed, about how we might help the shop.'

'You know a lot about this business then?'

'No. But I know a lot about numbers. And how to make them work.'

'Yes, so I see.' Matthew rose as he first heard the door shut, then Freya's footsteps in the hall. He cleared his throat, making an effort to sound casual, although he knew now it was pointless. 'Is your mother coming to meet you again?'

'No, she's working now, so she won't get a lot of time off.'

Again, he swallowed disappointment, but with a little smile this time; there was something liberating about accepting his attraction to Anna Garvey. The anticipation of seeing her again filled him with a sweet kind of hopelessness, like a child looking in at a shop window filled with things he could not touch.

Further conversation was halted as Freya came into the shop. 'You're still here, Mairead? You must have something to eat before you go home.'

'No, thank you.' Mairead climbed to her feet. 'I'll be back in the morning though, we've done a grand job today.'

'*You* have,' Freya said politely. 'You did most of it. Thank you.'

'Well, that's true, but you helped a little.' Mairead nodded, and Matthew had to bite his lip against a grin when he saw Freya's mouth drop open, then close again.

Mairead slipped her coat on and said her goodbyes, and Matthew caught a look that flew between the girls; a single raised eyebrow from Mairead, a barely perceptible nod from Freya. His curiosity was piqued, but he would wait until later to ask. There was something more important to discuss now.

When Mairead had gone, he jerked his head towards the door. 'Come upstairs, I need to talk to you and Grandpa for a minute.'

Freya's face tightened. 'Is everything all right?' She drew a short, sharp breath, as she remembered. 'What did Roland say? Are you going to lose your place on the *Pride*?'

'No.' He smiled at her look of immense relief, re-living it for himself. 'Come on, we've got some decisions to make, but I don't feel like going through it all twice.'

*

In his father's room, Matthew told them what Roland had offered, and what he had decided. There was a silence from Robert, but he was nodding slowly.

'You'm right to accept, I won't say otherwise. But what about the *Isabel*?'

'That's what I need to talk about.' His voice caught, but he swallowed, and went on, 'I'm going to sell her. Won't get much, but I'll get something.'

Robert spoke in a low voice, but his eyes were fixed on Matthew's, seeing right into him. 'Your last chance of being your own skipper. Are you sure that's what you want?'

'It's Roland's job or Wheal Furzy,' Matthew said. 'Yes, I'm sure.'

'And what about James?' Freya wanted to know. 'What if he makes things difficult?'

'Don't pay him no mind,' Robert said dismissively. 'He won't be back.'

Matthew exchanged a look with Freya and shook his head minutely; Robert was tired, and still unwell. No need to worry him just yet. 'Did you speak to Mrs Bone?' he asked instead.

Freya nodded. 'She said I could have extra hours if I'm on time all week.'

'Good. See that you are, then. Things will be different for a little while, and it'll be hard work for us all, but, my beauties,' he looked at them both in turn, and found a smile that fitted surprisingly well. 'Things are finally looking up for Penhaligon's Attic.'

*

195

Later Matthew nursed a cup of tea alone. Freya had long since gone to bed, but he couldn't settle. He sat in the kitchen, what passed for a sitting room since the front of the house had been converted, and turned over in his mind the confrontation on the beach that afternoon. James had every right to mistrust him, but then he hadn't been around to see how he'd tried to make amends over the years. Maybe he'd eventually learn to accept Roland's judgement, but in the meantime the seas were going to be very rough indeed.

He thought back to his boyhood, to James with his precise drawings, and him with his reading; his mother's love of books had been ingrained in him from the start. James had accepted that in a way none of the other lads had, just as Matthew had provided James with paper and rulers, and sharp pencils when he could.

He remembered James's excitement at being accepted for a valuable apprenticeship; learning how to cut and dress stone would go a long way towards his dream of becoming an architect, but his friend's actual leaving had gone barely noticed, by himself at least. He'd been too wrapped up in trying to keep Isabel happy, and his boat in profit.

'God, Matthew Penhaligon you're a bloody fool,' he whispered into the empty kitchen. He wished he could find the courage to go back to Porthstennack now, and tell James how wretched he felt, but it would do no good. He wiped the back of his hand across his mouth, and made himself take another gulp of tea, but it wasn't what he wanted.

He'd thought sharing tonight's good news would finally put the craving to bed, but there was only one thing that would banish the memory of James's hurt betrayal. He closed his eyes and pictured Anna instead, but all he could think of was how she would be standing behind the bar right now. He could smell the malty, pungent scent of hops and barley, hear the laughter of his crewmates ... he could taste the cool, bitter flavour as the beer ran down his throat.

With a groan he swept his tea cup aside, hardly hearing the crash, and pulled open the back door to stand in the freezing night, clad only in his shirt and trousers. The wind whipped his hair and sliced through his clothes to numb the skin beneath. He lifted his face to the sky, letting the cold air creep inside his open collar and tug at the front of his shirt, and took a deep breath as if it were the liquid salvation his body craved.

After an unknowable time he felt the tide roll back, and he gradually became aware of the cold. His realised his arms were clutched tight across his chest, and his bared toes were curled into the wet grass, and he made himself relax. Unfolding his arms, he opened out his hands, spreading his fingers wide, and stared at them in the thin moonlight. Steady. He let out a shuddering breath and turned to go back indoors; another demon battled and subdued. For now.

Chapter Eleven

The Tin Streamer's Arms

The Trevellicks had begun to pack their things away into boxes, preparing to move back into their own home in the hamlet by the sea. They'd made a great show of reluctance, but Anna had overheard Joe remark to his wife how it would be nice to be, 'set in me own chair of a night-time, with no thought that the youngster might come a-trippin' in and find me in me bleddy drawers'. She'd had to back away, chewing her knuckles, and when she told Mairead, the girl's look of horror was almost enough to set her off laughing again.

She glanced at the clock, and tried not to think about her aching feet, which would be at least another three hours trapped in their tight, heavy shoes. Word had finally spread that the Tinner's was once again becoming a pleasant place to spend the evening, and although that was gratifying, it meant long, long shifts, and each day felt like a week. Keeping on top of the cleaning was a little easier now the initial assault had been made, but it still took the entire day, from a six o'clock start until she fell into bed well after midnight.

But the work, though hard, was at least coming more naturally. Anna was learning to feel the difference in the pump when the barrel in the cellar was about to run empty, and to know which of her customers would sit quiet with an empty glass, and which ones would be shouting for a new drink before they'd drained the one they had. She moved quietly about the room, ignored by almost everyone now, clearing empties and picking up useful local knowledge like sand off the beach.

Brian Cornish was a mine of such information. Porthstennack born and bred, he kept largely to himself, but was popular enough that people would call him over to their table most evenings, to drink and talk. His mackerel business was not yet coming into its best season, and he spent the days in the meantime working over the vegetable plots allotted by the church, which meant he had no need to rise as early as most of his group, and when they left he usually came back to the bar. There he would sit in contented silence for the most part, but now and again his tongue would loosen, and he'd share news from the hamlet with Anna, and sometimes warn her if someone was having a bad time presently and might benefit from being left alone to stare into their drink.

Tonight the only men left at the corner table were Brian Cornish and James Fry, and since the two of them were still uncomfortable in one another's company it was little surprise when Brian brought his drink across early, and settled into his seat.

'All right then, maid?'

Anna was getting used to the Cornish use of the word now, but it still made her smile. 'I am, Brian, thank you.'

'Joe not about?' He peered about for Mr Trevellick.

'He's busy in the back. Packing, I think.'

'Ah, 'course. Young Donithorn's goin' to be mazed for a bit.'

'Amazed about what?'

'Not a-mazed. Mazed.' He saw her baffled look, and shrugged. 'Not best pleased.'

'I've never seen him anything but ... mazed,' Anna observed. 'But why in particular?'

'When Joe and Esther take back their cottage.'

'I'm still not with you.'

'Well, him and Ginny's going to have to find new lodgings. Back with his ma, no doubt.'

'Oh no ... ' Anna's heart sank. Had she really dared to hope things were slipping into place? 'Doctor Bartholomew said they were letting out, but I had no idea it was David and his wife.'

'Not your fault, girl,' Brian said quickly. 'Alice'll be glad to have her boy and his wife stay for a bit, and they got no kids.'

'He can't live with her forever, though, surely?'

'He'll go up Furzy Row, I should think. The miners' cottages, top o'town,' he clarified, seeing her blank look. 'Lad on the end'll be able to move in with the Thomases in a bit – old Muggy Thomas won't see out another winter.' He determinedly changed the subject to something more pleasant. 'How's the young miss getting on up t'Penhaligon's?'

'Oh, she loves it.' Anna smiled. 'They're finding an awful lot of wonderful books hidden away, and Mairead is busy working out their worth, and planning how they can find new customers.'

'Clever maid,' Brian nodded. 'And young Freya will be glad of the company. She's a good 'un.'

'She is. I hear Robert is improving too. So if the shop does pick up new business he'll be happy.'

'Matthew'll be mighty relieved. He was proper close to his ma, and if they had to close down her shop it'd break his 'eart.'

Anna felt the usual lurch in the pit of her stomach at the thought of Matthew. She wished she had a clearer memory of the expression on his face as they'd said their goodbyes on Sunday last, but all she could remember was reaching for his arm as he moved away. She felt the lean strength of his wrist now, as if she still held it, and remembered the way her skin had reacted, sending a flicker of warmth through her ... but she couldn't remember anything else except the way his breath had stirred her hair as he'd sighed.

Brian's voice cut through her thoughts. 'Speak of the devil, you'll soon see his horns.'

'What?' Anna looked up, her heart thudding. The door was swinging shut, and Matthew was already making his way across the room to James's table, moving with an urgency that drew the eyes of the other customers. Those eyes widened when they realised who it was and registered the fact that he was here at all.

James rose, but he didn't share their curiosity; instead he looked worried. 'Pa?'

'He's come over bad,' Matthew said, his voice low. 'At the boat. Doctor's gone to him.'

He put a hand on James's arm, but James pushed him aside and moved towards the door.

'Stay away. I mean it.'

'Here, boy.' Brian gestured Matthew over. 'Sit down, you're lookin' done in.'

Matthew sat on the stool Brian indicated, his face blank with shock. 'It was so sudden. We were just scrubbing the decks. Nothing different. He went over, like ... ' He shook his head, and Anna saw him take a ragged breath. 'I ran for Doctor Bartholomew, he told me to fetch James.' He looked at Brian, his brow creased. 'What do you think? Shouldn't I be there with Roley?'

Anna spoke, keeping her voice gentle to take the sting from her words. 'Not if James doesn't want you there. It will only upset Roland. Neither of you wants that.'

'Go on home, boy,' Brian advised. 'I'll come and find you if I hear anything.'

'I'm not finished on the *Pride*,' Matthew said, rising again. 'There's still—'

'Leave it. You're in no fit state.'

Brian was right, Matthew was sweating with the exertion of running, but he was pale. His eyes were dark with worry, and his long fingers were working, agitated, at a button on his coat. Abruptly he seemed to realise where he was, and he stilled. His eyes went to the row of pumps on the bar, and then behind Anna, to where the bottles lined up, variously full, and temptingly close.

'Come through to the back,' Anna said quickly. 'Just until you've had a chance to get your breath back.'

He seemed to notice her properly for the first time, and as

his face relaxed, and his hand dropped away from his coat, she felt a rush of protectiveness towards him. Something about the grateful, trusting way he followed her wordlessly through to the house made her feel strong and capable ... and obliged to be the anchor he seemed to think she might be.

She led him through to the sitting room. It was hardly used, and smelling musty because of it, but he took a deep breath and she realised even that smell was preferable to the heady scents out in the bar. She called up the stairs for Joe or Esther to mind the bar, then showed Matthew to a chair while she perched on the very edge of the settee. He sank into the chair as if his legs had suddenly run out of strength, and leaned forward, his elbows on his knees and his forehead supported by his hands. Anna waited, saying nothing, while he gathered himself.

'So soon after Pa,' he said at last. 'I didn't think I'd be so scared again.'

'Your father's doing well.'

Matthew nodded. 'And Roland's a tough old bugger.' He said no more for a moment, and Anna found herself desperate to fill the silence, to block out the sounds that drifted through from the bar: glasses clinking, chairs scraping back, and the last few calls of farewell between friends and publican. But she remained silent, while Matthew bowed his head again.

His hands were clean from scrubbing, but the rest of him was filthy; caked in mud and sand, and stained with fish guts and oil and the Lord only knew what else. He hunched forward, helpless and frightened for his friend, his shoulders straining at the seams of his coat as his fingers kneaded at his temples.

'Can I get you a cup of tea?' she asked, hesitating to break into his thoughts, as dark as they might be.

He shook his head without lifting it. 'No. But thank you.'

'I'll leave you to rest, then.' She rose, but as she passed his chair on her way to the door it was his turn to reach out blindly, and to grasp her hand. His face, raised to hers, was filled with anguish, and she knelt beside the chair.

'He's going to die, Anna,' he managed, in a broken voice. 'I know it.'

'Hush,' she whispered, and put her hand to his cheek. 'The doctor seems a good—'

'Roley knew it, too,' Matthew said. 'He looked scared at first, and then he just became so ... empty. Like he was already gone.'

'Oh, Matthew.' Anna slipped her hand around the back of his head and pulled him closer. They remained still, Matthew's forehead pressed against her shoulder, his hand still clutching hers as he struggled to regain his composure, but he made no attempt to move away. Even the pain in her constantly bruised knees ceased to matter as she held him, desperately wishing he was wrong, but he would not have mistaken such a look.

'I just hope he held on until the doctor got there,' Matthew said, when he at last shifted out of her embrace. 'I'd hate to think of him being alone. We were late finishing. We were ... talking, a good while, before we started to clean.'

Anna didn't ask what they were talking about, but it would have been something important, Roland Fry was not one to waste his words on nonsense. She rose to her feet, trying not to seize on the moment that had just passed between them, in order to answer her doubts; Matthew was already grieving, if he had clung to her with anything other than despair then she would learn it in time. He stood too, and seemed as awkward as she felt. But he did not move away, and when she looked at him his face was unreadable.

'Will you go back down to the beach?' she asked.

He nodded. 'I'll have to. But I don't want to.'

'I'm sure Brian would come and help you.'

'It's not that.' He sighed. 'I just can't face the thought of seeing him. Not yet.'

'Then let me make you that tea.' She rested her hand on his forearm feeling the tension there, and squeezed gently. 'And then we'll both go.'

He glanced at her hand, seemingly surprised to see it there, then he laid his own over it. It was cold, but comforting nevertheless. 'Don't be daft,' he said, and he sounded almost normal again, but she could see he was touched.

'I'll have the tea, though,' he said, and now there was gratitude in his voice, and he gave her a smile that, although faint and sad, sat well on his face. It deepened the lines by his mouth, and curved his lips, so that suddenly all she could think of was how they would feel pressed to hers. She was appalled, but she couldn't help it. She realised she was staring, but before she could find the words of apology, he had cupped his hands around her face and drawn her closer, and then she no longer had to wonder.

His lips moved over hers, and she both felt and heard him breathe her name, her mouth tingling where his breath touched. She could do no more than utter a wordless reply, a tiny sound that escaped and was swallowed instantly as he claimed her lips with his. His hands dropped to rest lightly on her waist, hers rose so that her thumbs brushed his jaw, her fingertips pushing into the short hair at the back of his neck. When they parted they were both breathing hard. Anna looked down at where one of her hands now rested over his heart, rising and falling with his breathing. 'This isn't the time.' The words found their way out, despite her wishing she could bite them back.

'No.' He released her, and she stumbled, then held herself steady. He rubbed his face, hard, as if waking from a deep sleep. 'I'm just a bit . . . I'm—'

'Don't. If you're going to say you're sorry, please don't.' She still couldn't look at his face, in case she saw regret there. Why now? When his emotions were tangled, when his world was about to crumble at the edges and he wouldn't know which way was up? When the drink would be calling him louder than ever, and she owned a pub?

'I ought to be going,' he said, stepping away.

She swallowed hard, fighting the mess of feelings that twisted inside her. 'Do you want me to come and help?'

He seemed ready to accept, then glanced at the window and shook his head. 'It's pitch dark, and besides you have work here.'

'Then you leave it too, there's no need to do it tonight.'

He nodded, then turned to leave, but Anna stopped him with a hand on his shoulder and he looked back. His eyes caught the light and she saw how the darkness of his eyelashes made them look almost purple in the centre. They were glistening, and she knew he would be glad to be alone with his grief, so she only said, very quietly, 'You repaid him a hundred times over, you know.'

He closed his eyes briefly, and let out a heavy breath. 'I hope so. And I'm not.'

'Not what?'

'I'm not sorry. We'll talk.'

Her chest loosened with relief. 'When you're ready.'

He studied her in silence, and as the moments ticked away, she sensed that he too had stopped trying to deny the intensity of their feelings, and the inevitable fusing of them.

He leaned in and pressed his lips to her forehead. 'Soon.'

March 1910, Truro

James Fry stepped out of the solicitor's office onto the wet pavement, and let out his deeply held breath slowly, feeling his heartbeat settle more with each second that passed. The words of his father's will rattled around in his head for a moment, jumbled and tripping over one another, but the main message stood apart, glowing.

> To my son James Harold Fry I also leave my trawler, the *Pride of Porthstennack*. This to be bequeathed on the understanding that no crewman is to be left without income as a result, and that said boat shall not be sold for profit.

'Oh, Pa,' James breathed, 'you have no notion ... thank you.' He became aware that passers-by were looking at him oddly, and he straightened his coat and settled his hat more firmly before finding the nearest pub, and drinking a toast: to his late father and the lifeline he had thrown. He'd been so certain the *Pride* would be given to Matthew, it was only now that he allowed himself to acknowledge what a disaster that would have been for his own prospects. But now he had the business, even halved as it was since the accident, he could relax a little, and work out how best to use it to raise money for the future he really wanted.

Later, travelling back to Caernoweth by coach, he found himself thinking about Roland properly, for perhaps the first time since he'd made his decision to return to Porthstennack. He put aside the jealous pain he'd felt at the way his father had built Matthew Penhaligon into the son he wished James had been, and instead he remembered the days immediately following his mother's death, when Roland had not been ashamed to show his grief. That had marked the beginning of his determination to see James had every chance to make a good future for himself. Roland's pleasure when James had at first hidden his true feelings, and agreed to crew the *Pride* and learn the trade, had been both moving and a little saddening. It really had been a simple thing to make him happy, after all.

His eyes fixed on the window but seeing none of the scenery, he let his memories carry him forward, to that astonishing day when renowned architect Richard Norman Shaw had agreed to take him on at Bryanston House in Dorset. Roland had told everyone who would listen that James was going to be a rich architect too, one day ... James had been at pains to point out that he was being taken on as a stone mason's apprentice, but that hadn't made a jot of difference to Roland, although sadly that was where his proud prophecy ended; James's own attempt to set up in business had used every last scrap of his savings, before collapsing anyway.

No matter; James might be broke, but his dreams were still intact, and now he had a foothold in the town. No one of any note would travel to Porthstennack for anything other than the supposed health benefits of the sea air, and to gawp at the boats, but Caernoweth was a different prospect. Wheal Furzy was producing good tin, at a time when tin was in decline elsewhere, people were coming to appreciate the chance to get out of the grime and dust of growing towns, and the old fort overlooking the sea was crying out to be restored.

Even the pub was improving daily, but it was still a men-only meeting place, and had no rooms to offer, so the Caernoweth Hotel had little competition closer than Bodmin. But if James could persuade some of the local businesses to buy into the fort with him, to sponsor its restoration ... James felt a smile cross his face, and saw it echoed in the interested eyes of the young lady opposite, who'd been looking at him often over the top of her book.

He recognised her, vaguely, as the younger daughter of Charles Batten, from Pencarrack. Louise? No, Lucy. A pretty girl, and clearly enjoying what she saw as she watched him. For once, though, he did not strike up a conversation. He had other things on his mind, such as how soon he might be able to remove Matthew Penhaligon from the payroll of the *Pride of Porthstennack*. The terms of the will were clearly skewed in Matthew's favour, but if he were persuaded to leave after, say, a month, then surely that could not be interpreted as James putting him out of a job? Besides, the solicitor would have stopped keeping a watchful eye by then, and James would be free to do whatever he wished.

He felt a twinge of unease at the way his own mind was working, but he only had to remember Matthew's words on the beach for his heart to harden again. If he hadn't let his life go to such ruin, and almost destroyed the woman and child he claimed to love, their friendship might even have survived Roland's blind affection for the older boy.

As it was, that affection had remained a barrier between them until the very last; Roland's decision to linger behind with Matthew after work had been what killed him; instead of coming to the pub, with his son and his crew, he'd died on the deck of his own trawler, surrounded by fish guts and slime. James felt a stinging at the back of his eyes and blinked quickly, trying to banish the image of his father's still form, and Doctor Bartholomew's unusually sympathetic expression as he rose to greet him. Roland was gone, may God bless him, but James was here, and the remaining boat belonged to him now. A means to an end. A living to be made. And, if he squinted into the future far enough, it would be his first step on the way to achieving his real goal.

Settled in his mind now, he turned his attention back to Miss Batten, and kept it there. When she felt the weight of his steady gaze, she lowered her book and smiled.

Chapter Twelve

Penhaligon's Attic

Freya ran her finger down the list of figures in the right-hand column, and when she raised her face to Mairead, she was smiling. 'You made it look very pretty indeed.'

'It's not as bad as we feared, is it?' Mairead had the look of someone well pleased with her work, and Freya thought she looked more relaxed now than she'd ever seen her.

'Not even nearly,' she said. 'Even if this one school follows through on their order, and actually comes to collect the ones they've chosen, we can ink those figures in. Oh, and if they do . . . ' Freya's heart was singing as she imagined telling her father and grandpa. 'It will turn everything around!'

'Thanks to that one visitor, with his half-crown book,' Mairead said. 'And my mother's sharp eye.'

'And to your idea of cataloguing everything! They'd never

come all this way on the off-chance, so if you hadn't made that list they'd never have known what we had.'

'You wrote the letter,' Mairead reminded her. 'That was your idea.'

Freya accepted that, with a little twinge of pride. She had scrimped on groceries as far as she'd dared; if Grandpa had found out he'd have been furious, and as soon as the cataloguing had been complete she had spent almost all her remaining wages at the printer's shop. Nauseous and apprehensive, she handed over the money, but receiving the printed lists, and professional-looking headed paper, she had felt a thrumming sensation in her blood. She'd sent the first letter just last week, enclosing one of the lists, and the school had replied immediately, expressing interest and starring all the titles they intended to purchase.

'Right then,' Mairead said, 'when you send the next one out to the next school, cross through the purchased titles but make sure they're still readable.' She grinned. 'That way they'll see what they've missed out on.'

Freya nodded. 'We mustn't tell anyone about this yet, not until the school sends their man to collect the books. It would be awful if I got everyone's hopes up and it came to nothing.'

'I'll find a box,' Mairead said. 'You get the books out, and we'll have them packaged ready. Because they will come for them,' she added firmly. 'You'll see. This is just the start.'

'Should we perhaps hand-write a note and attach it to the letter, to explain their choice might be sold already?' Freya suggested.

Mairead nodded thoughtfully. 'We could. That might make them order more quickly.'

'All right. 'How about: "Please be aware these titles are on general sale, and are only confirmed as available at this time of writing. However ..."' she trailed off, frowning. 'Um, "however ..."'

'"However, every effort will be made to replace any item sold between the time of writing, and receipt of your order."'

'Perfect. I'll write the next letter tonight, but I must go to work now, or Mrs Bone will regret giving me those extra hours.'

'You won't need them for long,' Mairead pointed out. Her smile slipped, and Freya realised it wouldn't be long before she herself was no longer needed, since Grandpa was almost ready to be up and about. Of course, that was the best possible news, but what would Mairead do then? Freya wanted to reassure her that she wouldn't be simply cast aside when he came back to work, but that was not her decision, and Grandpa had only slightly unbent towards the Garveys since his chat with Anna. She could only hope there would be room for them all to work together when Penhaligon's Attic became the success she'd always known it could be.

On her arrival at the Caernoweth Hotel she went to the laundry for a fresh apron and was surprised to see Juliet Carne sitting alone.

'Where's Miss Pawley?'

Juliet shrugged. 'Don't know. Care even less.'

'What's wrong?' Freya plucked a clean apron from the pile. 'You look terrible.'

'Thank you.' Juliet sniffed. 'That's exactly what a girl needs to hear when she's been put aside for someone else.'

'Oh, no. James Fry?'

'No. He's been seen walking out with Lucy Batten. He met her in the coach from Truro on Friday, on his way back from the reading of Roland's will.'

'It's no great loss,' Freya said. 'He's much older than you, anyway. He's only two years younger than Papá! Who, then?'

Juliet stood and tugged her uniform skirt straight. 'It doesn't matter.'

'Not David Donithorn?' Freya groaned. 'It's hardly being "put aside for someone else" if it's his wife!'

Juliet shot her a dark look. 'I said it doesn't matter. You'd better go or Miss Pawley'll have both our hides. Then Mrs Bone'll come looking for what's left.'

Freya clicked her tongue. 'I do feel sorry for you, but there are some good men around, who'd give anything to catch your eye. You don't have to go throwing yourself away on married and old ones.'

'I'm not throwing myself away on no one.'

'You know what I mean.'

'I suppose. Anyway,' a smile broke on Juliet's face at last, I've finished with all that. I'm gunna save all me wages, and move to Plymouth. Get wed to a rich bloke with his own house.'

'Find one for me too.' Freya smiled back, and slipped her apron over her head. She knew she was forgiven, when Juliet poked her tongue out.

'Find your own, Penhaligon!'

Freya went back into the hotel, still smiling, but as she put her hand on the door of the first of her rooms, Juliet's words clicked into place, and she stopped, a sinking feeling creeping through her. *The reading of Roland's will.* Papá hadn't been summoned to that, which could only mean one thing: he had not been named.

It had been just over a week now since Roland's death, and in the first few days the *Pride of Porthstennack* sat skipperless in the harbour. After Papá's shock had eased into a gentler, quiet kind of sorrow, he had realised no one was working her, and spent more time than ever at the beach, fixing, cleaning, and finally guiding her crew when they put to sea again. Now, despite all that hard work, James would take the chance he'd been waiting for, and put him off for good, and Papá would waste no time in looking to Wheal Furzy for employment.

Freya shuddered at the idea, and moved through the rest of her day impatient for the end of it. No matter that she'd intended to present the upturn in Penhaligon's Attic's prospects as a *fait accompli*, it would surely go some way towards easing Papá's burden if he knew all was not as hopeless as he thought. She pictured him trudging home, already thinking of how it would be to spend his days beneath the ground, and the more she thought about it, the more she imagined him breaking his walk at the Tinner's Arms.

With that thought burning in her mind she didn't wait for Juliet after work as normal. Instead, as soon as she left the hotel, she hurried past Penhaligon's Attic towards the bottom of town. There was no clear thought behind it, except to share the news of the book orders as soon as possible, before he either did or said something he could not take back. Or he sought solace in the heft of a tankard.

But as she neared the bottom of town her throat closed tight and her mouth dried. There was still a good way to go, but the thought of stepping onto the sand and shingle, so close to the unpredictable and soulless sea ... Her footsteps slowed, and then stopped. Her stomach roiled, and she really thought she might be ill. She closed her eyes and felt again the dark terror of the water closing over her head, cutting off her breath, the pressure crushing her chest, and her own traitorous clothing dragging her down. And then the frightened voices calling to her ...

'Freya!'

She opened her eyes again. The voice was coming from behind her, where the town still offered safety and peace, and she turned, glad of the glowing lamps that spilled their light across the pavement. Anna had come out into the yard behind the Tinner's, and she hurried through the gate and down to where Freya stood.

'Where are you off to in the dark?' She peered closer. 'Are you quite all right? You look like a ghost in these lights.'

'I'm well, thank you,' Freya managed. 'I just wanted to see Papá.'

'He'll be home soon, won't he?'

'I know, it's just ... I think Mr Fry will put him off the boat today and I just wanted to tell him it wouldn't matter so much.' How could she say she was scared he might not come straight home, but instead call in to the very place Anna called home?

'Surely James wouldn't do that,' Anna said. 'Your da's been working on that boat all the hours God sends.'

'Mr Fry hates him.' Freya made herself stop there, not knowing how much Anna knew of the history between the two men. 'But Mairead must have told you about the shop? How things might be working out for the best now?'

'I've not seen her since breakfast, but I'll come back with you now and fetch her home. You can tell me then. Just let me speak to Mrs Trevellick a moment.'

Freya watched her as she crossed the road, and thought about that quiet moment in the doorway between her and Papá that they thought she hadn't seen, and about how Papá's manner that afternoon had been different. Perhaps if she could make sure Anna was still there when he came home, that light would come back into his eyes.

'Miss Penhaligon?'

She jumped. Hugh Batten stood on the pavement behind her. He held the arm of a smartly dressed woman, and it took a moment for Freya to recognise her as his older sister Dorothy. On her hand swung young Harry, evidently bored with his evening walk. Harry grinned at Freya now, with the openness of familiarity, but he knew better than to speak up in the company of adults.

'Are you unwell, miss?' Hugh asked, concern in his face.

'A little,' she said. It was easier than trying to explain. 'I thought perhaps a walk to the beach might help.'

'In the dark?' He drew closer, and let go of his sister's arm. 'You seem a little distressed. Are you all right?' His face was very close to Freya's now, and she found herself searching for some flaw in his features, and finding none. She looked away, disturbed by her own curiosity and the satisfaction it had found.

'I'm not at all distressed. Mrs Garvey will walk me back in a moment.'

'If you're sure?'

'She's sure, Hugh, for heaven's sake!' Dorothy looked at her younger brother with a shrewdness that made Freya uncomfortable. 'Her friend will see her home. Come along, it's time for Harry's nightcap.' She gave Freya a hard look as she drew her son away, but Harry waved. Freya waved back and was rewarded with a big smile before the little boy trotted away with his mother.

'I'm sure Harry will be asking to visit the shop again soon,' Hugh murmured, and his eyes held hers for a disconcertingly long moment before he touched his hat, and turned to follow his sister and nephew home to Pencarrack.

Anna walked her to the shop, but was as reluctant to leave as Freya was to let her. When Papá came in and saw her still there, his tiredness seemed to simply fall away; neither of them was even pretending any more that they felt only friendship for one another. They moved to stand closer together, as if each was feeling the tug of the other and could not ignore it. Freya's heart swelled to see it, and even the excitement about the book orders felt a poor second place.

But as she and Mairead explained what they had done, and set out their plan for continuing with the venture, she was aware of something even more wonderful happening. Just like a real family, they began to talk over one another, disagreeing, shouting one another down, and sharing ideas, as if the shop belonged to all of them equally. The noise rose, and so it wasn't until they heard the voice in the doorway that they realised Robert had come downstairs.

'What's to do then?'

Papá rose to his feet. 'You shouldn't be down yet, Pa. Go back to bed, Freya will bring your supper.'

'I don't think so,' Grandpa Robert said. 'Sounds like you'm talking about the shop. *My* shop. I'll just sit 'ere in my own kitchen, if you don't object.'

Despite his words, Freya noted he didn't sound particularly cross. He leaned heavily on Granny Grace's cane as he walked, but his eyes were clear, and his hand hardly shook as he hooked the cane on the end of the table and lowered himself into his seat.

'Mr Penhaligon, it's good to see you up and about,' Anna said. 'Can I fetch you a cup of tea?'

'Can do, if you like.'

As Anna passed Papá's chair, Freya's sharp eyes caught a smile flickering between them, and her own mouth twitched. 'Grandpa, you're looking very well,' she said. 'We've exciting news, but you'll know that. How much have you heard?'

'Enough. Things picking up then, are they?'

'We hope so.'

'And it's a good thing too.' Papá sat back in his chair and fixed his eyes on his father. 'Because James Fry has inherited Roland's boat. And we know what that means.'

Grandpa chewed at his knuckle for a moment and then said, 'He's put you off?'

'Not yet. I only heard today, from Brian. James hasn't spoken to any of us yet, but we all know he won't have me on the crew.'

'So what will you do, boy?'

'He can come back to the shop,' Freya put in quickly. 'With this new project, we—'

'I said what will you do?' Grandpa cut across her, and she fell silent. She looked at Papá, whose expression was darker again now.

'Wheal Furzy. I'll go as soon as James is finished with me.'

'Papá, no!'

'You won't last,' Grandpa said. 'Not you, not down that mine.'

'That's what Roland thought.' Papá had a sad little twist to his mouth. 'Pity he's not here to see me prove you both wrong.'

'But the shop will be all right now,' Freya protested. She turned to Anna for support. 'Won't it?'

'Grandpa's right, Freya,' Papá said, in a flat voice. 'You and Mairead have done a brave job, but we can't rely on it. It might never be repeated, you know that as well as I do.'

'But we were talking about it just now! You never said anything about still having to go to the mine!'

'I got all caught up in it,' he admitted. 'I even forgot it wasn't my shop, for a minute. Fact is I can't afford to lose a steady wage, not if we want to keep the house and the shop.'

'Perhaps James won't want to lose an experienced crewman,' Anna ventured.

Papá shook his head. 'He can have his pick. Plenty of us about. But I'll talk to him before I go to the office at Furzy. Put my case.' He gave a brittle-sounding laugh. 'Throw myself on his mercy, I reckon.'

Grandpa nodded. 'He's not stupid. And he knows Roland rated you high.'

'That's the problem.'

'He was a good lad, when me and your ma knew him.'

'Eighteen years is a long time, Pa. Lot of water's passed under the bridge since then.'

Grandpa fixed him with a look. 'Thing about water under the bridge, boy, is that it's gone.' He rose, a little unsteadily now, as if the discussion had wearied him more than he wanted to admit. 'I think I'll 'ave that tea upstairs, miss, if you don't mind.'

'I'll bring it.' Papá took the cup from Anna, and went to help his father. To Freya's relief, Grandpa let him.

When they had gone, Anna sat back down. 'Don't let anything they've said put you off.' She brushed her hand over Mairead's cheek. 'It's a wonderful idea, and might just be the saving of the place. But Matthew's right, too. He needs to be working.'

'The mine will destroy him,' Freya said, fighting tears. 'He won't be the same. He loves the sea so much.'

'He loves you more,' Anna said gently. 'He knows what's to be done to provide for you.' She took Freya's hand. 'Try not to make it even harder for him, if you can help it.'

'I won't.' Freya looked closely at Anna, and decided it was time. 'Are you and Papá becoming close?'

Anna flushed; it gave her skin a delicate rosy glow, and she seemed much younger suddenly. 'I think a lot of your father,' she said at last, glancing at the door to make sure he hadn't returned. 'But it's ... there are certain ... difficulties.' From the corner of her eye Freya saw Mairead's fingers curl into her palm. Naturally she'd be thinking of her own father, and Freya could have pinched herself for being so thoughtless.

'This is the first time I've seen him since the night Roland died,' Anna went on. 'It's been an emotional time.'

'Of course. I'm sorry,' Freya mumbled.

'No apologies needed.' Anna sat up straighter as she heard Papá's tread on the stair. 'Now, let's talk more about these people you're hoping to attract to the shop here.'

*

When Anna and Mairead left, Freya washed the supper plates and then went into the back yard to find her father. He was standing in his usual spot by the wall, watching the distant horizon, and although the sea was not visible, she knew he was seeing it anyway.

'Will you really have to give it up?' she asked, in a small voice.

'I hope not, Lady Penhaligon. But I can't afford to re-fit the *Isabel*. And what else is there?'

'You promise you'll talk to James first, though?'

'I promise.'

'Mairead said something about sending your stories away, to see if someone would publish them.'

He gave a soft laugh. 'That would be something, eh?'

'Won't you try?'

He looked at her, and she saw the half-smile playing at the corners of his mouth. 'I didn't realise you were being serious. No one wants children's stories. Except children.'

'Do you still have your book?'

'You remember that?'

Freya thought about those close-packed lines of neat writing, and what they had meant to her as a child. 'I'll never forget it,' she said. 'It made me happy to know you were writing.'

He turned back to face the distant sea. 'It might not, if you knew that I wrote those stories in a fog of drink.'

'I did find some of them confusing,' she admitted. 'But the stories still came from inside you.'

'They were for you, no one else.'

'So you won't do it?'

He shook his head. 'I sent the book to your mother when I

realised I hadn't finished reading you that last one. She can't have read it to you, if you didn't know that.'

'Then I'll write to her,' Freya said. 'She must still have it.'

'I wouldn't be so sure. She won't have wanted to bother with taking it all the way to America with her.'

'Still. I'll write.'

He smiled. 'If you want.'

'I do.'

'Right then.' He spun her to face the house again, and gave her a little push. 'Go on to bed, Lady P, or you'll have Mrs Bone to answer to in the morning.'

'Are you coming in?'

'In a little while.' He faced the empty night again, with the sea in its black distance. 'I have some thinking to do first.'

Freya let herself in through the back door, and as she turned to close it again she saw her father brace his hands on the waist-high wall and lower his head. His shoulders rose and fell as he took a very deep breath, and when he stood straight again his head was held a little higher than before. She closed the door as quietly as she could, and went to bed. Tomorrow would see their world change, and she could only hope it would be for the better.

Chapter Thirteen

James let the curtain fall back, hiding the shingle slope and the beach beyond it. Word that the most profitable boat out of Porthstennack was now his had helped him gain some ground in his quest for re-acceptance by his father's crew, but he had some way to go yet. This morning would, hopefully, take him further along that path.

He pulled his coat from the hook by the door, and tugged his hat down over his ears. He could almost hear his father's grunt echo through the hallway: *Cover up proper, boy, 'tis brave cold out there.* He allowed himself a small smile of remembrance, and followed it with a silent apology for what he was about to do, then went out into the chilly morning.

The crew were already at work, Matthew Penhaligon among them, and James went over to them. He nodded a greeting, accepted their half-hearted nods in return, then gestured for Matthew to follow, and led him back up the beach until they were standing beneath an overhang at the bottom of the cliff.

Matthew had a wary look, not yet defeated, and prepared to fight. 'Before you say anything, I—'

'Just listen.' James waited until Matthew's stance had relaxed and he looked less likely to strike out, and went on, 'I'm not putting you off. All right? You can stay.'

Matthew stared, his lips parted to speak, but no words emerged. Eventually he blew out a heavy breath, and with it came a kind of half-relieved, half-disbelieving laugh. 'You mean it?'

'Look, I'm not going to cut off my nose to spite my face. I need experienced men. Pa wouldn't have taken you on if he didn't trust you. And besides that I've seen how you've worked for his business, while I've been ignoring my duty to him.' James felt oddly emotional as he saw the tension fade from Matthew's face. He was saying the words he'd prepared, but he hadn't expected to feel the truth of them. He tried to make himself remember his pain and anger at what Matthew had said, and what he had done, but to his frustration all he could think about was his regret that their friendship had fallen so far.

Matthew pulled his hat off and worked at it, clearly struggling for words. 'James, about what I—'

'It's passed and gone. I've said some regrettable things too.'

'I didn't mean it,' Matthew's voice was low. 'I know Roley thought of you all the time.'

'And there's the proof,' James couldn't resist saying, and indicated to where the *Pride* rose and dipped with the tidal swell.

Matthew followed his gesture, and smiled ruefully. 'I

knew it even before he left her to you. I was just . . . hitting out.'

'Well, I won't deny you hit hard,' James admitted. 'Look, don't read too much into this, it's a job offer. Business. Nothing more.'

'You won't regret it. I don't touch a drop now.'

'So Pa said.'

'I'll work hard for you, Jimmy.'

'Skipper will do, Penhaligon.'

Matthew studied him for a moment, his blue eyes keen. Then he nodded. 'Skipper it is. And thank you.'

'Right. Well, you're in charge today, at least. I have business in town. I'll be back by noon.' He could see common sense at work in Matthew, who'd refrained from questioning this early disappearance, or asking how often it was likely to recur. This arrangement might work out well after all. But if all went to plan this morning in Caernoweth, it wouldn't matter whether it did or not.

He left Matthew to re-join the crew, and heard the muted cheers of celebration as they heard the news. It gave him an isolated feeling, knowing they had all been discussing him and the inevitable, and unpopular, prospect of Matthew's departure. Where was the justice? He himself had done nothing but learn a trade, and then return to take over his father's beloved business, yet he was instantly the one to be mistrusted.

Penhaligon on the other hand . . . well. James shook off the tired frustration of all that Penhaligon had been forgiven for. As he splashed through the rivulet that ran down the beach his boots crunched on wet shingle, and he felt the day's first icy leak of water through them. How much longer before heavy,

226

wet socks and blistered feet would be a thing of the past? It all depended on the next hour or so.

Penhaligon's Attic sat two-thirds of the way up the town. Not one of the biggest houses, but the generously sized front window lent itself well to displaying wares. James stopped outside and let his critical and practised gaze rove over the front of the house, from the brickwork at the bottom, to the round attic window in the Cornish slate roof. He examined it as closely as he could, and saw no obvious structural failings; there were no cracks around the windows that he could see, and the chimney looked solid. The roof, too, appeared well cared for. Despite Penhaligon's money worries, he had clearly spent what he did have very wisely. Something he could never have done if he was still throwing his wage into the pub's coffers.

James pushed open the door and was immediately, and unexpectedly, assaulted by memories. He stopped still, only vaguely aware of the figure at the counter, and let those memories have their way, just for a moment. The smell made his chest tight, the combination of dust and ink, glue and paper. He closed his eyes and saw Grace and Robert Penhaligon, their faces kind as they gestured to the child he'd been, standing awestruck in the doorway, scared to come in. Matthew lived in Paradise, he'd thought then. And before long this very shop had been a second home, and Grace and Robert his honorary aunt and uncle.

There was electric light here now, replacing the gas he remembered. Likely an indoor privy as well; most of these houses had been modified to include those, unlike the cottages in Paddle Lane. The steady light lent itself well to the browsing of books, it fell evenly and brightly along the spines, and James found himself drawn to the titles nearest to him.

'Excuse me?'

James turned, to see a very pretty, dark-haired girl at the counter. 'Miss Penhaligon?'

'No, I'm Mairead. Freya's gone to work early.'

'Ah, of course.' The accent came through clearly now. This must be Anna Garvey's daughter. She didn't fit his expectations at all; no vacant stare, no constant fidgeting, no sign of the idiot people were saying she was. 'My name is James Fry.'

Mairead had evidently heard of him, and her expression hardened. 'I'm afraid the younger Mr Penhaligon's also at work.'

'Yes, I've seen him this morning.' He smiled at her look of worry. 'Don't fret, Miss Garvey, he's still got his job.'

'Oh!' Mairead visibly relaxed. 'That's good of you, Mr Fry.'

'Please, call me James.' She must be at least seventeen, but the arch of her eyebrows gave her a look of perpetual, childlike curiosity. He wondered what Freya looked like now, and if she took for her mother or her father. 'I wonder if I might speak to Mr Penhaligon senior, if he's well enough?'

'I'll have to check.' Mairead kept looking at him as if she expected him to turn into a snapping wolf, so he gave her his friendliest smile.

'Thank you.'

There followed a brief silence, where neither of them moved, then Mairead sighed.

'Well, I'm not leaving you in here by yourself!' She gestured to the door, and James was unsure he'd heard correctly;

she'd gone from timid and grateful to schoolteacher-sharp in the blink of an eye. He stared at her for a moment, and although she wouldn't meet his gaze, neither did she subside. She merely held her arm out to indicate that he should step outside.

'It's quite all right,' he said. 'You can trust me, I assure you.'

'Well you would say that,' Mairead pointed out. 'But I'll not be responsible for you in here alone, so ... if you wouldn't mind?' She came out from behind the counter, and crossed to open the door to the street. Faintly amused, he obediently crossed the threshold to the street and the door banged shut. He heard her draw the bolt, and he spent the next five minutes pretending to be looking at the window display; people were throwing him curious glances, and, amused or not, he had no wish to make it appear as if he'd been forcibly ejected from his childhood haven.

Just when he was starting to wonder if the girl hadn't left the house by the side entrance, he saw movement beyond the glass and she came back into the shop. She pulled open the door again, and stepped back.

'Mr Penhaligon's ready for visitors now.'

'Thank you.'

'It's the room on the—'

'On the right, at the top of the stairs,' James said. 'Yes, I know.'

As he mounted the first stair those memories washed over him again. He and Matthew thundering up and down the narrow hallway, pushing each other and yelling, only to receive a thwack on the back of the head from Robert's open hand, or a look from Grace that could wither granite. He heard the ghost of Matthew's giggle, and his own, as the boys looked at each other after each remonstration, both silently daring the other one to speak first. The recollection of those days nearly made him change his mind, but there was more at stake than a thick ear now.

He knocked at the door of Robert's bedroom, and pushed it open, then he faltered, feeling the same shock of dismayed recognition as when his own father had opened the door to him in Porthstennack. Robert sat up in bed, his formerly rounded face now gaunt and spare, but his eyes glinted with sharp intelligence as he gestured James closer.

When he spoke, the years fell away. 'Well if it in't young Mr Fry. Come in, boy, don't be dawdling in the doorway, you're causin' a draught.'

James closed the door behind him, and crossed to the bed. He shook Robert's hand. 'You're looking better than I expected,' he said. 'I was so sorry to hear about Grace.'

'She's missed,' Robert said simply. 'The Irish lass tells me you're wanting to speak to me about summat?'

'Straight to the point, as always.' James dragged the chair away from the dressing table, and towards the bed. 'May I?'

'Goin' to be here a while, eh? Yes, go on.'

'I imagine the Iri— uh, Miss Garvey, has also told you I've kept Matthew on the crew?'

'You imagine c'rect. Don't think I'd be so accommodatin' otherwise, do you?'

'No, I should think not.' James shifted in his seat, and searched for the words that had made so much sense on his walk up the hill. 'Mr Penhaligon, you know how close I was to my father these past months, since I came back.'

'So Brian said.' Robert softened a little. 'Your pa was a good 'un, lad. My condolences. You must miss him sore.'

'I ... yes.' James swallowed past an unexpected lump in his throat. *A good 'un.* Roland had surely been that. Another apology found its way from his heart to his father's memory as he went on.

'Before he died, we talked a lot. About Matthew, about what had happened, and about how it had affected the two of you. As father and son.'

Robert closed off a little then, James could see it. He reached out and laid his hand over the older man's. 'Pa hated to think of that. And so do I. Matthew and I have made our peace, I hope you and he have done the same?'

'To a point,' Robert said gruffly. 'Not sure I like the thought of being gossiped about, though.'

'No gossip,' James assured him. 'Just concern.'

'Well you needn't.'

'He's worked hard for you. For this place.' James indicated the room around them. 'It seems all his wages have gone into maintaining it, when they could have—'

'Gone into fixing his boat.' Robert snatched his hand away. 'I know! I don't need no pipsqueak coming in here and telling me what I know.'

'He'll inherit the shop one day though,' James said, hiding his embarrassment. 'There's that.'

'He will. And Freya after him.'

'That's something, at least.'

Robert's eyes narrowed. 'What are you pushin' at, boy?'

'Nothing. I just ...' James rose and went to the window, affecting great interest in the weather. 'Pa told me about the

231

will, and said he wished he'd left me the boat earlier. So he could watch me getting to know the job, and to love the *Pride* like he did. Before it was too late.'

Robert's voice was blunt. 'You think I should hand the shop over to Matthew now.'

'Of course not, it's not my place to suggest such a thing.' James struggled to hide his surprise at the speed with which Robert had caught on; he'd been prepared for a far more difficult job. 'I mean,' he went on, turning back, 'not unless it's what *you* want. I just wanted to pass on my father's regrets, so you can decide.'

'But Matthew's got his job on your boat, he don't need this place.'

'He doesn't need it, no. But it would provide him and Freya with security. A solid future. And ... ' This time James's silent apology was directed at Matthew himself. 'With that security he'd certainly find it easier to avoid the temptation of drink.'

Robert stiffened. 'That was low.'

'I didn't mean it to be.' James sat back down, and looked Robert directly in the eyes, those eyes he remembered lit with secret laughter even while they'd pretended fierceness, and softened with affection when he grumbled about Grace's exacting standards. 'Mr Penhaligon, I owe you so much. I practically lived here after Ma went, and Pa was at sea. When I heard you'd been taken ill, and then especially when I lost Pa, I didn't want either you or Matthew to feel the same regrets we felt. That it was too late.' He sat back. There was nothing more he could say now, it was up to Robert.

'You and Matthew proper fixed now, are you?'

'We are.'

232

Robert sighed. 'I should have thanked you for keeping him on. I'm grateful, boy. And I'll think on what you've said.'

'You're looking tired. I'll come again when you're up and about.'

'Good.' Robert's expression was one of remembered affection, and he even gave James a small, wry smile. 'Just don't leave it eighteen years next time.'

Making his way back downstairs, James tried to fight off the sickening feeling of having twisted people's lives out of shape. He hadn't forced anything, Robert had reached his conclusion all by himself. It would all work out. It had to. He sat on the bottom stair for a moment, composing himself and straightening his thoughts. As he did so he looked around him, at the narrow hallway; spare boots, coats and scarves for three. A house filled with memories, bedrooms above his head for Matthew, Freya and Robert, rooms that held their own secrets and their own sadnesses. Their own private joys and whispered dreams. This was a family home.

But he didn't have a family.

Anna stood in front of the Penworthy memorial, staring upwards until her neck ached. So, this was the man everyone admired so deeply? The sculptor had certainly made him look straight, tall and undeniably heroic, with a full head of wavy hair and a direct stare out over the town, as if still keeping a watchful eye on the goings-on of his people. Anna wondered what he'd think of her, and what had brought her here.

She looked back down, and, feeling a bit dizzy, she sat on the step at the foot of the statue. It was getting dark, and she could already see the sparkle of frost on the road, picked up by the gas lamps and turned from hazardous to magical. The pub would need opening in a few minutes, and she told herself she was simply enjoying the fresh air, not waiting to hear the footsteps and voices of the fishermen coming up the hill. She was not waiting to see the dark blond hair of one of them gleaming in those same street lights. She was not waiting to hear his voice, to fathom whether it held despondency or contentment.

But when she did hear them at last, she could not ignore the flicker of pleasure and anticipation that ran through her. She should have opened the pub by now, but Joe would be happy enough to do that. Instead she melted back into the shadow of the statue, and waited, her breath shortening as she strove to pick that one voice out of the general murmur of conversation and laughter.

'Comin' in, Pen'aligon? Celebrate young Fry's change of heart?'

Anna let out a relieved sigh, but it froze in her throat as she heard Matthew say, 'Why not?'

She stood quickly. 'Mr Penhaligon!'

The voices fell silent, and Anna squared her shoulders and walked towards the little group.

Matthew stepped away from them. 'Mrs Garvey. What can I do for you?'

'I wonder if I might have a quick word. It's about the shop. A message, from Mairead.'

'Oh. Go on, lads, I'll see you in a bit.'

The crew carried on to the Tinner's Arms, leaving Matthew

standing in the road, and Anna stopped a few feet away, suddenly unsure what to say. She hadn't planned this far ahead.

But Matthew spoke first. 'I wouldn't have had a drink, you know.'

'It's not for me to—'

'Yes, it is.' He closed the distance between them and took her hand, and led her around the back of the memorial. Only the faintest light touched his face here, and showed her what he was thinking. He dropped his bag on the ground at his feet. 'I just wanted to see you.'

'And you'd not have touched the drink?'

'I didn't last time, did I?' he reminded her. That memory brought with it another, and her lips tingled. His face was very close to hers. 'Can we stop dancing around this now, Anna?'

The smell of sweat and raw fish came off his clothes, and it might have repulsed her on anyone else, but on Matthew it seemed perfect and right. She could feel his breath on her chilled skin, and then his hand was on her waist, the other brushing her jaw. She leaned into his palm, and he used the gentle pressure to raise her face until their eyes met. His hand slipped around to the small of her back and pulled her closer, and then his silently questioning lips were on hers, and she gave them the only possible answer.

The warmth of his touch seemed to burn through her coat, and she lifted her arms to encircle his waist, fighting the urge to slide them beneath his coat instead, to feel the solid strength of him beneath her own fingers. His mouth was firm, his lips cool, and as his tongue brushed hers with gentle curiosity she heard his breath catch. All sensible thought fled, and she gave herself completely to sensation.

235

At last the kiss broke, and he drew her head onto his chest. She felt him sigh, and tightened her hold on him. 'I could stay here all night,' she murmured. 'Can we?'

He gave a little grunt of laughter. 'You're just trying to avoid facing Esther Trevellick.'

'You know me too well.'

'I'm starting to.' He pulled back, his hands still linked behind her. 'I'd say this has been a pretty good day, when all's said.'

'Well it's just improved a good deal from my point of view.'

He smiled and kissed her forehead. 'I don't know if it matters to you, but there's been no one since Isabel. No one I've wanted the way I want to be with you.'

'She's a hard one to live up to,' Anna confessed. She was abruptly aware of her shabby coat, her messy, hatless hair, and her flat, unstylish work shoes.

He stepped back, spreading his hands wide, and bowed deeply. 'Well as you can see, I'm quite the catch myself.'

She let her eyes explore the frayed turtle-neck sweater, the oily coat and filthy trousers, and she laughed. 'Then it seems we're a good fit.'

'I'd say so.' His grin faded, and his eyes softened on hers. 'Look, I don't know what's proper when someone's in mourning. Just tell me if it's ... impolite, or—'

'It's not.'

'Good,' he breathed, and bent to kiss her again. This time the flicker of heat travelled from her lips right through her body, and she thanked the stars above that she and Matthew stood exposed to any passers-by, clothed, and chilled by the

236

night air. Had they been in the private warmth of her home, or his, she knew very well how it might have ended, and, worse, that she would regret nothing.

After they had made their reluctant goodbyes, she watched him walking backwards up the hill, blowing kisses at her through the chilly night air. At length he turned and walked past the pub, to Penhaligon's Attic, and although she felt his departure like stolen warmth, she couldn't keep the smile from her face as she began the short walk to the Tinner's.

'He *is* a catch, if you don't mind my sayin'.'

Anna's heart leapt and stuttered. A woman sat, half-hidden in shadow, on the low wall that ran around the garden of the lowest house in Caernoweth. Her features were hard to make out, but when she stood up Anna could see she was smiling, at least.

'You'll be the widow Garvey then?'

'Yes.' Anna looked around her in trepidation, half-expecting to see a great mass of the town's women all moving towards her, wearing the expressions of suspicion and mistrust she had come to recognise all too well. But this woman was alone. She moved into the light, and Anna could see her breath condense in the chilly air.

'I'm Ellen Scoble.' She held out her hand, and Anna shook it, still thinking furiously; how much had the woman heard? Then genuine curiosity overtook that particular concern.

'Why are you sitting out here in the cold?'

Ellen shrugged. 'On my way home,' she gestured vaguely in the direction of Porthstennack. 'Only it's my foot, see? Givin' it a bit of a rest while I can.'

Anna squinted. 'What's wrong with it?'

'Blisters. Be 'ard to find somewhere t'sit once I start on the beach road.'

'Come into the pub,' Anna said. 'Let me find something to pad your boots.'

'That'd be kind. Thank you.'

Anna led the way through the back gate of the Tinner's Arms. All the way up the narrow passageway, past the store-room and into the house itself, she wondered how apologetic she really ought to be; Matthew was married, certainly, but his wife had long since left the town. Did this woman have designs on him herself? As she led Ellen into the sitting room she tried to sneak a glance at the woman's left hand, but saw only worn leather gloves.

Ellen began unlacing her sturdy boots, while Anna hunted about until she found a clean white handkerchief. When she produced her scissors and began to cut it into two, Ellen gasped.

'Don't be doin' that!'

'Why not? It'll help, won't it? Here, tuck this inside your stocking, wrap one half around your heel, the other half over your foot to keep it in place.'

After a few minutes, and with some half-hearted protests, Ellen stood, her boots once again laced tightly, and the relief on her face obvious. 'So kind, Miz Garvey, thank you.'

'Call me Anna. And you're most welcome.' She hesitated. 'Can I ask, how much did you hear or see? I mean—'

'Oh,' Ellen waved a hand. 'Don't you worry none, Miz Garv – Anna. It's hard bein' alone after you've had knowledge of a husband. No one'll think the worse of you for seekin' some solace.' Her friendly face clouded a little, and Anna was about to ask, but Ellen saved her the need.

'My own husband, Ned, used to work on Roley Fry's boats. He died some years back.'

'Oh ...' Anna touched Ellen's arm. 'I'm so sorry. Are there children?'

'Only one. Edward. He's seven, and the image of his pa. Ned would've been burstin' with pride.' Ellen gave her a little smile, but Anna's heart contracted at the sorrow in it.

'Where were you walking from?' she asked, following Ellen through the passage, and watching her feet carefully. The boots were ill-fitting and slid up and down the young woman's heels; hardly surprising she'd raised blisters.

'Wheal Furzy.'

'You work down the *mine*?'

'Naw! Surface work.' Ellen flexed her right hand. 'Spalling, mostly.' She saw Anna's questioning look. 'Breaking the rocks and ore. It's 'ard work, but it's regular. It don't pay too bad, neither.' She pulled open the door, peered out into the night, and shivered.

'Who cares for Edward while you're doing that all day?' Anna asked, feeling very spoilt, despite what she'd previously considered the hard work of the pub.

'Depends. The guild takes it in turn with the little ones.'

'Guild?'

Ellen stopped in the open doorway. 'You should join! We meet once a month.' She closed the door, still on the inside of it. 'Next meeting's a week on Sunday, after church. That's when most of us are free. Only takes half an hour or so out of the day – can't afford more, what with the 'ousework to do an' that.'

'But what is it?'

'Come along to the school on Sunday week,' Ellen said. 'End of Priddy Lane, near to twelve o'clock as you can manage. I'll meet you outside and take you in.' She opened the door again, and this time she stepped out into the cold night. 'It'll be good, you'll see. And people will get to know you, and stop bein' so suspectin' of you. I'll tell 'em how kind you are!' She gestured at her newly padded foot, and then gave a little wave, and a moment later Anna was standing in the doorway wondering what had just happened, and what on earth would happen next.

Chapter Fourteen

Matthew dragged off his wet coat, and hung it on the hook by the door. Freya and Mairead were talking together in the shop, and the low murmur of their voices sounded familiar already; so much so that it took a moment for him to register it as relatively new. He smiled, then looked up at the sound of a heavy, uncertain step on the stairs.

'Pa?'

'Need to talk to you, boy.' Robert paused on the narrow staircase, one hand on the rail, the other rubbing at his forehead.

'Go back,' Matthew said. 'I'll be up d'rectly. I'll just wash.'

'No. In the shop.'

'But you—'

'In the shop,' Robert insisted.

Matthew subsided. 'All right. Let me help you, at least.' Robert regarded him steadily for a moment, and Matthew had the unsettling feeling that his father's eyes were seeing more than he usually did. 'You look tired, Pa,' he said, more gently.

'I'm tired enough,' Robert admitted, 'but I'm able to find my way into my own shop.'

Matthew shrugged, and went back to removing his outer work clothes. He deliberately didn't watch his father's slow progress down the stairs, but there was a new tension in his muscles, ready for the slightest sound of a stumble.

Robert pushed open the door to the shop and as Matthew moved past him to climb to his room to wash and change Robert gave him that oddly penetrating look again, and Matthew frowned. What was on the old man's mind? Well, he would find out soon enough.

By the time he re-joined his family, Mairead had gone, and Freya and Robert were sitting at either end of the kitchen table. Freya had made tea already, and Robert poured his into his saucer, and slurped it noisily. There was no sense pushing him, so Matthew picked up his cup told them his own news.

'I've still got my place on the *Pride*.'

'Mairead told me.' Freya smiled. 'It's such wonderful news!'

'Isn't it just?' Word got around town quickly enough when it was bad news, so it was nice to know the grapevine worked for good, too, wherever the news had come from. 'I'm still having trouble believing it. I really think he's on the road to forgiving me.'

'I think so too,' Robert said.

'He's said it's just a business decision, but I have hopes.'

Robert nodded. 'You was close, once. Reckon you could be again.' He put his saucer down and linked his hands on the table in front of him, studying the threadbare cloth. Matthew replaced his own cup, wondering if he was going to like what he was about to hear.

'Between your ma and me, some 'appy memories was made here.' Robert blinked rapidly. 'And then there are some that still make me weep, to this day.'

'Little Julia, God rest her soul,' Matthew said quietly. 'Pa—'

'James came up 'ere today.'

Matthew blinked. Whatever he'd expected, this certainly wasn't it. 'Here? What for?'

'We talked about Roland, a bit. About how he was sorry he'd not given over the boats sooner. So's he could, you know, enjoy watching James learning them. Help him if need be.'

'I see.' Matthew exchanged a puzzled look with Freya, but her eyes widened at the same moment he too realised what was happening. He didn't say anything more, but waited, his heartbeat picking up.

'Made me think,' Robert said. 'The shop's going to be yours someday, might as well be sooner as later.' He raised his eyes from the table-top to Matthew, and they were watery, but steady. 'I want your promise you'll tend it well until it's your own girl's turn.' He nodded at Freya.

Matthew didn't know what to say, and if he had, he wasn't sure he'd have been able to say it; his throat had closed, and he couldn't remember when he had felt more like putting his arms around his father and whispering heartfelt thanks into his roughly clothed shoulder. It had nothing to do with the shop, or even with the relief of security in his home and his future. But this, finally, was where the chasm that had opened between them eleven years ago was bridged.

*

Later that evening, Matthew once again stood out in his yard, but this time there was no siren call from bottle and cask. There was cold starlight, and there was an ache in his bones and muscles from the hardest day's work he could remember – his efforts to prove to James he was worthy of the faith placed in him – but there was also the memory of Anna's smile, her lips parting beneath his, her cold hands on the back of his neck. And now there was the feel of Robert's hand on his shoulder as he'd accepted Matthew's silent gratitude, and gone back to his room. Freya had watched him go, then exchanged a smile with Matthew; Robert would have been deeply relieved at the lack of gushing thanks, and keen to make an exit in order to stave them off.

Matthew looked towards the Tin Streamer's Arms, and felt his heart expand, even as his shoulders loosened and his hands relaxed. The future of the Penhaligons was shaping into something solid and hopeful, and if the future of the Garveys became entwined with it, it could only strengthen them both. And there would be no one happier.

*

Anna pulled her coat tighter. Priddy Lane wound ahead of her, a rough, muddy track with grass pushing up through its centre, the edges worn away by carriage wheels and possibly even the odd agricultural motor making its wheezing way to the fields farther down. Anna picked her way carefully, and decided the children must all arrive at school with terribly dirty shoes. It was odd to think of a very young Freya, walking this way with her friends in all weathers.

As she came closer to the school she couldn't help wondering

244

if she'd imagined the entire conversation with Ellen Scoble. She'd not seen her since that odd meeting over a week ago, and the more time had gone on, the more she doubted the woman had really meant what she'd said. Surely it had only been a spur of the moment utterance, out of politeness?

Raised voices, but no discernible words, drifted down the lane, and Anna's footsteps slowed. Did she really want to join some gossipy women's guild? What if she let something slip that caused more questions than she had answers for?

She rounded a corner and saw the school, and a cluster of perhaps ten or twelve women clutching baskets and boxes, and packets of all shapes and sizes, The same women Anna had seen around the town, and who had looked at her and Mairead with varying levels of curiosity. Some of them had relaxed a little, once they'd got talking, but today Anna's wary gaze met a disturbing number of stony faces, tightened lips and drawn-down brows, and an expectant silence that felt like a physical weight. Her heart sank as she recognised Susan Gale, Doctor Bartholomew's housekeeper, and she stopped, suddenly more nervous than ever.

'There you are!' Ellen's voice was bright enough as she broke away from the group, but in the harsh daylight, Anna could see the tiredness that the low light in the sitting room at the Tinner's had softened. 'Come on, 'tis cold enough to freeze the spit in yer mouth.'

Anna joined her, surprised, but not displeased when Ellen swapped her basket to the other side, and seized Anna's arm as if they were already old friends.

'Anna Garvey, welcome to the Caernoweth Widows' Guild.' Ellen spoke with a shy kind of pride, and Anna finally understood why she'd been invited.

'It's kind of you to ask me.' She smiled around at the other women, some of whom smiled back, more of whom didn't. She took a deep breath and kept her expression open and pleasant. There was no question of following the itch in her feet that wanted to take her back up that mucky lane and back into the seclusion and warmth of the Tinner's Arms; this was an important step forward in becoming a real part of this town, and given the pure chance of her meeting with Ellen, it was not one that was likely to be repeated.

It became clear that the raised voices had been in argument with one another, before Anna had arrived to provide a distraction, and the disagreement soon reclaimed their attention.

'Door's locked,' Ellen told her. 'Big Alice reckons we ought to force a window and climb in anyway!'

'Who'd lock it?'

Ellen shrugged. 'Caretaker, most like. Was bound to happen sometime, I suppose. I'm all for doin' that thing with the window, but I reckon we'd 'ave to actually break one, and that'd cost us dear. Tuppence each in the kitty goes to pay for the hire of the room – we 'aven't got enough put by to pay for a smashed window.'

'Where will you go if you can't use the school?' Anna asked. Someone was rattling the door as if their frustration alone would be enough to persuade it open. 'The town hall?'

'Blimey, no! We couldn't afford that. Hard enough to find the two shillin' the school takes, and we're only here an hour a month.'

Anna looked at the women, who had started to shiver now they had cooled from their walk and were simply standing there. She wondered again what was in their baskets; sewing projects, maybe? She had no idea what went on at a meeting such as this, but one thing was abundantly clear; there was real disappointment passing between them all.

'Ladies!' She raised her voice, just a little but it cut through the muttering. 'Why not come back to the Tinner's Arms with me? You can use the bar for your meeting. Free of charge.'

After a brief silence, during which most of the women seemed to look to Mrs Gale for guidance, Ellen spoke up.

'That's a kind offer, Anna. Thank you.'

'The *pub*?' Mrs Gale sniffed. 'I should think not!'

'Just a moment.' A diminutive woman stepped out of the throng. 'Mrs Gale, I'll thank you to remember this is still a meetin', even if we are outdoors. Things will be conducted proper.' She turned back to Anna. 'You're offerin' us your pub, and in return you're askin' what?'

'Asking? Nothing.'

'She's offerin' out of kindness,' Ellen said. 'Just like she cut up her own good handkerchief to put in my boot and stop the blisters rubbin'.'

'Did she now?'

'Don't matter,' Mrs Gale insisted. 'She'm not one of us. Never will be.'

'She's a widow, and she lives in our town,' Ellen said crossly. 'That's what we're about, isn't it? I say we take up her offer, and get in out of the cold.'

'Into that grimy, smelly place? That's for the men. Women don't go in there!'

'I don't know when you last came into the Tinner's,' Anna said, 'but it's cleaner now.'

'Women and men don't mix.'

'There won't be anyone else there this afternoon. We don't open until six.'

'It's full of drink!'

'I can make you all tea.' She did a quick count in her head. 'Provided you don't mind taking it in turns for the cups.' Her patience was wearing thin now, and the cold was getting to her. 'Look, whoever would like to continue with whatever it is you do, follow me. You're welcome to whatever warmth and comfort I can give you.'

'I'm for it,' Ellen said, predictably enough, and Anna smiled at her.

Another voice chimed in, 'Me an' all,' and another agreed, and eventually Anna led all but Mrs Gale and three others back to the pub.

Halfway along the passage, she met Joe Trevellick coming out of the store room. He stopped dead still and stared, his scant eyebrows disappearing into the brim of his hat.

'What's to do, Miz Garvey? What're all these ... these ...' he gestured at the women, all of whom he'd have known in some capacity or other, but who seemed to have taken on a new and terrifying identity once assembled in a large group. Anna understood how he felt.

'We're having a little meeting, Joe. Would you be so good as to ask Esther to boil plenty of water for tea?'

'No time for tea, thank you all the same,' came a voice from somewhere behind in the group.

Joe peered past Anna. 'Meetin'? What kind of meetin'?'

It was on the tip of Anna's tongue to tell him it was none

248

of his business, but instead something made her clasp the old man's shoulders and smile. 'I have absolutely no idea.'

In the bar, the women looked around them with undisguised interest. Most of them would have seen the inside of a pub before, Anna knew, but perhaps only on high days and holidays; she'd certainly never seen one of them here in the few months since her arrival. One or two remarked on the brightness and the cleanliness, which apparently went against all expectation or former experience of this particular pub, and it took a firm coaxing from the tiny woman who'd spoken up at the school, before the women shed their coats and began moving chairs and tables to form a rough circle.

Anna looked at those coats, which they'd draped over the bar. There were all of a kind: warm, sensible, torn here and there, but mended with care and skill for the most part. Pockets bulged with gloves, scarves and handkerchiefs, and Anna noted that her own coat, alongside them, looked markedly out of place in its neatness and relative newness.

Ellen prodded her in the back. 'Time's precious, maid. Can't be wastin' it. Come and sit down, you can meet everyone proper then, 'stead of standing here like you was a prize cow at a fair!"

The analogy was a good one, and Anna felt sure she was being judged by many of the same criteria as she found an empty chair and moved towards it. She held herself as upright as she could, and walked calmly, but was acutely aware she carried no basket or package to place on the table before her, as the others now had. The chair scraped horribly against the stone floor as she pulled it away from the table, and the noise echoed around a pub that suddenly felt a lot less like the warm, familiar home it had become.

'This is Mrs Alice Packem, she's in charge just now.' Ellen gestured at the small-boned woman, who nodded.

'This is good of you, Miz Garvey.'

'Please, call me Anna.'

'All in good time, Miz Garvey.' Mrs Packem waited until Anna was settled, then rapped on the table. 'Let's go around clockwise and introduce ourselves.' Anna nodded to each person in turn as they gave their names, knowing she had little hope of remembering any of them. Except one.

The generously sized woman nodded. 'Alice Donithorn.'

'Known as Big Alice,' Ellen added. Anna flushed at this apparent rudeness, but Ellen grinned. 'It's all right, she don't mind. It's only our way of tellin' the Alices apart. And besides, she's my ma.'

'Well, it's lovely to meet you,' Anna said. Big Alice and her daughter were much alike: round of feature, with curly hair and an open, friendly expression – both could hardly have been less like the man who was presumably a son and a brother to them.

The other names flickered for a moment while Anna tried to find some way of connecting them to their owners, but she quickly gave up and decided to speak to each woman separately later, instead. She couldn't help wishing Mrs Gale had seen fit to join them; this might have been the perfect time to break through her icy suspicion and instigate some kind of thaw.

'Now, to business,' Little Alice's knuckles hit the table

again, as conversation swelled. Silence fell, and Anna felt as if she had returned to her school days. She gazed around at the various packages people had brought, and eyed the conspicuously empty table in front of her.

'Don't worry,' whispered Ellen, 'Next time you'll be—'

'Hush please, Ellen,' Little Alice said, but her voice gentled as she spoke to the younger woman. 'Now. Martha. Would you like to start us off today?'

The woman to Alice's left stood and picked up her basket. She went to the bar, where she pushed aside the coats and, into the empty space, she put three jars of jam and a pile of neatly finished wash cloths, to nods of approval. Then the woman next to her rose and took two small loaves of bread from a box, and put those alongside Martha's things. More nods, as the woman returned to her seat.

When it was Ellen's turn she laid out a small pile of freshly laundered clothes – outgrown by little Edward, no doubt – and half a fruit cake. Anna watched, with a growing sense of humility, as each of the women emptied their baskets and boxes, and placed wrapped packages of food, clean clothing, and other items on the table.

Some of the things that appeared were more unusual: a box of broken clock parts, a pile of old newspapers, and one woman – who might or might not have been called Betsy-something – carefully placed a box, containing a pair of fierce green eyes that glared balefully out at them through the several holes. The hissing sound from within made it quite clear this was no cosy domestic pet.

Anna glanced at Ellen and raised an eyebrow. Ellen grinned. 'Mice is a problem, sometimes you just needs a catcher for a week or so. That there cat gets passed around every now and again, and while he's bein' fed he's happy to stay put. We calls 'im Ripper. You know, for—'

'Yes! Yes, I know. Does this happen every month? The food and suchlike?'

Ellen nodded. 'If some of us has a glut of fruit, we makes jam. Edward grows out of his clothes, I knows Martha's grandson will be of an age to be wearing them soon. Same goes for all of this other stuff.' She pointed at the cake. 'I know with just two of us, me an' Eddie won't eat all that, so I cuts it in half. We'll have it while it's fresh, and someone who've not had cake for a good while will take the rest. And they'll enjoy it more than the mice would've.'

'It's wonderful.' Anna was awed by the simplicity of it. 'How did it all start?'

'The guild've been goin' over a hundred year, I do b'lieve, maybe more. I forget the year, but back along Wheal Furzy was hit by a flood, washed out the lower levels and took most of the town's men. The widows came together to support each other then, and to share what they had in exchange for somethin' else, that they might never see otherwise.'

Anna couldn't think of anything to say; the solidarity of the town suddenly seemed less threatening and more comforting, yet she felt more an outsider than ever.

'We'm not all widows,' Ellen went on, 'since some've 'ad the good fortune to wed again. Like Martha Rodda there. They'll sometimes bring extra stocker. That don't 'appen a lot, but now and again, you know.'

'Stocker?'

'When a catch've been sorted for the stuff that can be sold

252

on, the skippers share the rest out among the crew, and some of the wives'll salt it and bring a bit of it to the meetin.'

'And what if you have nothing?'

'Oh, we've all got something. What seems useless to one might make a deal of difference to another.' Ellen gave a little laugh. 'Couple months back, I was 'avin' a bit of a panic, on account of I couldn't find nothin' I thought people'd want. Then Ma comes by, to walk to the meeting with me, and spies a broken fence post lyin' on the ground. "That'd be 'andsome for the 'ole in my shed roof," she says. And blow me if it din't fit exact once we sawed it up! With a little shovin' that is.'

Anna smiled. 'Well if it's broken things you want, my daughter has a wealth of sea-shells at home. She only likes to look at the perfect ones but can't bear to throw anything away once it's broken.'

'Nothin's useless. Get her to make a picture with 'em, make an 'andsome birthday gift, wouldn't it?' Ellen shrugged. 'I couldn't afford to buy no works of art, but if someone was to gift it me I'd 'ave it up on my wall in two shakes of a lamb's tail.'

Anna looked at her in dawning wonder. 'I never even thought of it like that,' she admitted. 'I was on the verge of telling her to throw them back onto the beach.'

Ellen winked. 'Next time you'll be bringin' a little some-thin' then, won't you?'

Before Anna could reply Little Alice was on her feet again, and knocking on the table. Her knuckles must themselves be made of wood. Anna hid a tiny smile, and felt more than ever as if she were in the presence of a stern schoolteacher.

'The pledge,' Little Alice instructed, and the rising tide of voices was drowned out by the scrape of chairs as the women rose to their feet and spoke in unison:

Where there is need, there I will be.
Where there is sorrow, there I will be.
Where there is fear, there I will be.
I give my solemn vow, that all I have to spare shall be shared without question,
And that I shall abide by this solemn pledge of the Caernoweth Widows' Guild.

It was simple, and heartfelt, and Anna's faint smile had vanished from the moment the first words were uttered. There was need in this room, but there was also pride, and it was an emotional moment for someone who'd never really encountered either to such a degree.

'Other business, then,' Alice said, when they had settled back into their seats. 'Has anyone managed to persuade Nancy Gilbert to come along?'

'Who's Nancy Gilbert?' Anna whispered.

Ellen leaned closer, keeping one eye on Alice. 'She was married to John Gilbert, but he died not three months since.'

'Oh, the poor woman.'

Ellen shrugged. 'Maybe, maybe not. He was no great shakes, everyone knows she wed him out of spite to her da. She've got a family to feed, but her landlord've waived her rent for the time.'

'That's generous of—'

'Ladies, please!' Alice knocked on the table again, and

Anna fell silent, but the faintly cynical glance Ellen gave her made her wonder about Mrs Gilbert's landlord's motives. 'Now,' Little Alice continued, 'whether Mrs Gilbert chooses to join us or not, she's still our concern. Martha, come to me afterwards. You can take a couple of things down to her on your way home. Anything else?'

'I got a tree blockin' the stream bottom of the house,' maybe-Betsy said, her voice timid. 'Can't shift it, and the pony's gone lame so he can't pull.'

'Can anyone help?' Little Alice's gaze drifted over the group, and Martha spoke but she sounded doubtful.

'I could ask John, but his back's none too clever just now. I can't let 'im risk too much, or we'll be out of pocket.'

'Ask him if you please, Martha.'

'My chimney's smeechin' again. Think it's cracked.'

'Wheel fell off the cart last Tuesday.'

'If anyone can spare the time I've got a gate off and it needs another pair of hands to 'elp fix it.'

Each problem was greeted by hesitant suggestions, and promises of help where possible, but Anna began to see some of the problems faced by these women. Hard-working, every one of them, and many of them physically strong, and more than capable, but many others were in their later years, and a lifetime of smashing rocks at mine and quarry, and of salting fish on the shore, had left their bones aching and weak. It was all very well to share what they had like this, but they really needed strong hands and good tools, not bread and jam. She offered her own help to fix the broken gate, and her offer was accepted with a gratitude that made her feel even worse for not understanding before.

After a brief discussion of who was entitled to take Ripper home, and which of the elderly and needy residents of town and hamlet would benefit from a visit from a guild member, Alice shared out the collected items as fairly as possible. What was left over was put into a box and given to Martha Rodda to take to Mrs Gilbert.

'Now, this business about the school,' Alice said, and Anna raised her hand.

'Why not have your meetings here, from now on?'

A few voices joined in murmur, and on the whole it seemed an approving sound, but Alice pursed her lips. 'How much would you charge next time?'

'No charge at all. You can all keep your tuppence per month, or carry on paying into the pot, as you like. But you'll not be paying me.'

'That's ...' Alice looked around at her ladies, and saw the hope on their faces. A few pennies saved would make a difference, however small. '... That's very kind of you, Miz Garvey.' There was still some reservation in her tone, but Anna sensed, with a cautious relief, that she had finally begun to chip through the protective barrier behind which the town and hamlet sheltered; these women, while not her customers, would be their way in. And once they were in, they'd be safe.

The entire meeting had taken less than twenty minutes once they had started, but there was Sunday work to be done and Anna had no opportunity to talk to any of the guild members, but they each gave her a grateful smile as they left. Finally Alice Packem too vanished into the chilly afternoon, leaving Anna and Ellen alone.

'I just want to say, thank you so much for introducing me to everyone today,' Anna said.

'That's all right.' Ellen shrugged her coat over one shoulder. 'I'm glad you came out. Us less fortunate ones 'ave to stick together.'

'Let me hold that for you.' Anna took the bread so Ellen could manoeuvre her way into her coat properly. 'Will Edward mind swapping cake for bread?'

'Blimey, no!' Ellen laughed, and took back the bread. 'He loves a thick piece of this with some butter, an' Ma made some fresh yesterday. He'll be proper 'appy.'

'Who's he with today?'

'My neighbour.' She faced Anna, shy again now. 'I 'ope we can be proper friends, Anna.'

'I feel as if we already are.' Anna smiled. 'Do I have to sign a membership list for this guild, or anything?'

'Naw! You say the pledge, like the rest of us, and that's good enough. Next time I'll let you in on the people. Who's a good 'un and who's best avoided.' Ellen winked.

'I think I've already met a few of the latter,' Anna said, a little glumly, and Ellen laughed.

'No doubt. Most folk are all right though.'

'What's the priest like?' Anna asked, as she led the way through the passage to the yard.

'You're a Catholic?'

'Lapsed, regrettably,' Anna admitted. 'But it'd be good to know if there's someone who will hear confession.'

'You'd have to go farther afield to find one of yours, I'm afraid. Local preacher's a Methodist. He's all right, but no one's confession would be safe with him.'

'Oh?'

'He's got an old woman's likin' for gossip.' Ellen shook her head. 'No, unless you're wantin' him singin' your name from the pulpit, you'd best not to trust 'im with yer darkest secrets.'

Anna's insides twisted, although she knew it was a figure of speech and nothing more. Still, it served to remind her she was on the brink of becoming too relaxed in the unexpected pleasure of Ellen's company.

'I ought to go in,' she said, partly with reluctance, but mostly in relief that she'd been brought up sharp by reality; she couldn't afford to become unguarded, not for a minute. It was one thing to want to integrate herself into the life of the town, and win the trust of its inhabitants, but a single wrong word could bring everything crashing down. Perhaps in time it wouldn't matter so much, but just now everything was too uncertain.

She would continue to host the guild meetings, free of charge; she would help fix a gate here, or a wheel there; she would take note of those who would always, *always* look on her with suspicious eyes, and she would learn from them. Because they would be right.

Chapter Fifteen

June 1910

Just over one month after the accession of King George V, Anna removed the last of the bunting from the walls of the Tinner's Arms, and packed it away; it felt strange to have been celebrating the succession to the throne of one man while mourning the loss of his father, but such was the way of things ... the king is dead, long live the king.

On Thursday 16 June, the day Matthew turned thirty-eight years old, Penhaligon's Attic saw its own form of coronation: the deed of gift was drawn up that transferred ownership of it from father to son. Eager to congratulate the new owner, Anna slipped away from the Tinner's Arms, and hurried to the hotel to await the arrival of the Truro coach.

It had taken some time for Matthew to be sure enough of Robert's health to allow him to travel, and he had still been less than sure, but finally allowed himself to be persuaded. As he climbed from the coach, all his attention was on helping Robert down after him, and only when his father's feet were firmly set on the road did he turn, with a hopeful expression that melted into a smile as he caught sight of Anna.

'Did everything go well?' Anna stepped forward to take Robert's arm.

'Shop and house. All Matthew's now.' Robert had begun to walk straighter lately, but after the long drive cooped up in the coach, he had stiffened considerably. The horses moved away, and the other travellers dispersed, most of them to the Caernoweth Hotel just a few yards away. Anna gave Robert time to settle himself ready for the short walk to the shop he no longer owned, and tried to see past his fixed expression to the emotion beneath. She couldn't.

Over the top of his head, she raised a questioning eyebrow to Matthew, who shook his head and shrugged minutely; it was impossible to know what was going through Robert's mind, and the old man wasn't one to volunteer the information. All they could do was respect the fact that today he had made the boldest, most loving gesture he could have made, and had placed himself wholly in the hands of his only living child.

Outside Penhaligon's Attic, Robert looked at the newly painted sign above the shop's name, *Proprietor: M. Penhaligon.* He gently removed his hand from Anna's arm. 'Go on in,' he said in a gruff voice. 'I'll be in d'rectly.'

Anna followed his gaze, then exchanged another glance with Matthew and followed him inside. Mairead was studying one of the large ledgers that lay on the counter, and Freya, home early from work in honour of the dual occasion of the day, was carefully dusting the beautifully crafted model boat by the cash drawer.

'Is it done?' Freya looked beyond them towards the door. 'Where's Grandpa?'

'Just outside,' Matthew said. 'He's well enough, but it's a big thing he's done today. We should remember that.'

'Does he seem sad?'

Anna put an arm around her. 'Just thoughtful. It's to be expected.'

'It's so odd to think James Fry's the one who put the idea in his head,' Matthew said, not for the first time. 'I still can't fully believe that.'

'And he's being all right with you? On the boat?' Anna asked.

'Rarely see him, to be honest. He seems to be forever off having meetings. No idea what for. Tea, Freya?'

Freya suppressed a sudden smile, and lifted the *Lady Penhaligon* back onto its shelf. 'I've made some sandwiches, they're in the kitchen.' She and Mairead seemed full of secret anticipation, but Matthew was too distracted watching his father through the window to notice.

Anna slipped her hand in his. 'Come on. Let's leave him to his thoughts awhile.'

Some of the tension went out of him. His face relaxed, and a smile creased the corners of his eyes. 'We'll go for a walk later?'

'We will.'

He squeezed her hand, and she leaned against him briefly, enjoying the rare, clean smell that clung to his freshly laundered suit. They followed the two girls into the kitchen, and Anna let go of his hand and stepped back.

'Happy birthday!' Freya lifted the linen cloth off a plate that stood in the centre of the table, and revealed a large fruit cake. No decoration adorned its top, but the bumps and swells of the beautifully darkened cake were enough to show it was densely packed. Freya must have been saving all her money for a good while to have made this. Matthew stood stunned, he'd clearly forgotten.

Anna smiled and gestured for him to sit. 'We'll wait until your da comes in, then we'll all have a piece of cake and celebrate your day properly.'

'Happy birthday,' Mairead added, and, to Anna's astonishment, came over and put her arms hesitantly around Matthew's neck. The hug was brief, but Matthew was visibly moved. They all jumped as they heard the shop door shut loudly, and the bell jingled.

'It's all right,' Anna said. 'The sign's turned, it'll just be Robert.'

Robert came into the kitchen and saw the cake, and his own expression of surprise mirrored Matthew's. 'What's this?'

There was an awkward pause, and Anna couldn't think of a single thing to say.

'It's for you,' Matthew said, surprising everyone. 'Freya made it to thank you for what you've done today.'

'I hope you like it, Grandpa.' Freya acknowledged her father's apologetic look with a smile. It didn't matter now, after all – why shouldn't they share the pleasure, just as they would share the cake?

'Well, what are you waiting for?' Robert said. 'Get the knife, boy.'

The evening passed in companionable chatter, and even Robert joined in, instead of hurrying away, as he normally did, the minute the meal was over. Matthew told them about the new cathedral in Truro, and how they'd lost track of time gazing at it and nearly missed their appointment with the solicitor.

'It's some 'andsome,' Robert agreed. 'Got three spires.'

Anna's interest was piqued. 'I'd love to see it sometime. Is it Catholic?'

'Anglican,' Matthew said. 'Taken them thirty years to build it.'

Freya laughed. 'So you'd have been *eight* when they started! I remember my own eighth birthday. That's when Papá made me the *Lady Penhaligon*,' she added to Mairead, but her face clouded as the less joyful memory of that time surfaced, and she fell silent and looked down, tugging at the edge of the table cloth.

'Birthday,' Robert said, in a musing tone. He glanced at Matthew, then at the remains of the cake, of which very little was left but a small wedge and a lot of crumbs. No one spoke for a long moment, and Anna wondered if Robert would acknowledge out loud that he had forgotten; Matthew would hate it, and be embarrassed, and poor Freya would be put in an awful position, having to choose between the two men's feelings.

At last, Robert leaned over and picked up the wedge of cake. 'Half for you, half for me?' He broke it into two pieces and dropped the larger piece onto Matthew's plate. 'Happy birthday, boy.'

The two of them saluted each other with their crumbling cake, and Anna's mouth stretched into a wide smile as she popped the last piece of her own slice into it. She looked up as she felt the weight of Matthew's gaze on her, and suddenly had difficulty swallowing. She hurriedly swigged her tea, and stood to begin clearing the plates.

'Leave them,' Freya said. 'You and Mairead are guests. I'll tidy these away.'

'Well, if you're sure,' Anna said. 'I suppose we ought to be going home.'

Matthew saw her to the door, draping her coat about her shoulders, and she was left in no doubt that he was every bit as reluctant to part company as she was. He tugged her collar, pulling her towards him, and spoke against her temple. 'About that walk?'

'Yes?'

'I'll call for you in an hour, if that's all right?'

Anna adopted a formal tone that made him smile. 'That will be perfect, sir.'

'Will Esther mind?'

'Oh, I do hope so.' She grinned, and stretched on tip-toe to kiss him. He caught her as she moved away, and she felt his amusement in the press of his lips on her forehead. 'She's finally worked out you're the boss, has she?'

'She's learning.' Anna wrapped her arms around him, her fingers tracing the groove of his spine. She felt the low vibration in his chest as he laughed.

'I'm not surprised. I'm learning too.'

'Good.' Anna straightened and patted his shoulder. 'I'll even let you choose whether we walk up the hill or down.'

'Very kind of you, milady.' He tugged an imaginary forelock. 'I'll see you in an hour. Wear sturdy shoes.'

'I've no other kind.'

That much was true, but in the event she was glad she'd chosen boots over shoes. Matthew met her at the back gate, and both of them ignored Joe Trevellick's rolled eyes as he'd come out to fetch a new barrel; putting aside jokes of being in charge, Anna had barely had a night off since the night she'd taken the reins. A rare, warm evening such as this was to be enjoyed, and what better day to choose freedom than Matthew's birthday, and the day he became the owner of Penhaligon's Attic?

'Ah. Up the hill. I approve.' She took his arm, and together they meandered slowly through the town, taking their time, enjoying the closeness. 'Why do I need sturdy shoes?'

He glanced at her feet. He was wearing his work boots, having changed out of his good suit now that the business with the solicitor was done, and was wearing rough trousers and his old blue waistcoat over his clean shirt. 'I'm taking you to see the old fort. It can get a bit soggy underfoot, even in summer.' He smiled. 'I'm that glad you came tonight, Anna.'

'I am too. Happy birthday.'

He hugged her arm tighter to his side. 'When's yours, by the by?'

'January the third. And don't ask me what year,' she warned, and he huffed a laugh.

'As if I'd dare. Those boots look set to bruise.'

'They are, should they be pressed into service in that capacity.' Anna looked up as he stopped, a quizzical look on his face. 'What is it?'

'You. Sometimes you're as down to earth as they come, ready to muck in with the rest of us ... but now and again you say something that makes me think ...' He shook his head. 'No matter.'

'No. What?' She kept her tone light, but thought furiously back over what she'd just said, trying to work out if something had slipped out that shouldn't have.

265

'Just ... properly well educated, I suppose. Like you ought to be a teacher, or something.'

'Well I didn't do a terrible job with Mairead,' she mused. 'Even though she can run rings around me when it comes to numbers.'

'Well, maybe one day you'll think about becoming a real teacher.' Matthew put an arm around her, and she was glad to be held against him, not only for the pleasure of feeling his movement, his breathing, his strength, but also because he couldn't see her face when they walked like this. Things were going so well, but one slip of the tongue might ruin everything. She had to keep her guard up ... but how much longer could she do it?

The fort was something quite extraordinary. Anna had seen the tips of its two main towers from the road, as they'd drawn closer the evening they'd arrived, but it had been dark by the time they'd got here, and they'd not been back since. There was a rough path that led away from the hotel, past the mine and its ugly row of miners' cottages, and out onto the moor. They followed it over the next rise, and as the land fell away again ahead of them she saw the crumbling perimeter walls, and the steep slope leading to the fort itself. Those walls still stood strong against the fierce winds that whipped off the sea, the perfect lookout over both land and water.

'Caernoweth Fort,' Matthew said. 'Quite something, don't you think?'

'Gorgeous. Though, of course,' Anna added, remembering Teddy Kempton's words, 'that would make it New Fort Fort.'

Matthew chuckled. 'I suppose it would, come to that. We used to come up here when we were tackers.'

'Tackers?'

'Kids. Me and James. The others went down to Porthstennack, chasing cats and what have you, and we did that too. But we liked it here best.'

'Even though you'd always wanted to go out on the boats?'

He shrugged. 'Oh, we spent plenty of time at the beach too, but off-season James and I would come here and play soldiers.'

Anna watched him striding alongside her, his long legs covering the ground with ease and familiarity, and she tried to imagine what he'd been like as a boy. She couldn't do it; he was too tall, too assured in his movements, his shoulders too square and his hands too strong. 'I think you were born at the age of thirty, at least,' she said at length.

He laughed. 'Where on earth did that come from?'

'Never mind. How are things now, with James?'

He slowed his pace, and thrust his hands into his jacket pockets. 'I can't work him out, to be truthful. I don't see that much of him, but when I do he's all over the place. One minute nice as pie, the next he's giving me this look.'

'What kind of look?'

Matthew shrugged. 'I don't know. He's trying to make a new start here, and he's got every reason to hate me. It's like he's reaching out, but against his will. Like he *wants* to patch things over, but he doesn't *want* to want it. You see?'

'Like he keeps catching himself forgiving you, but he knows, or rather thinks,' she amended hurriedly, 'that you don't deserve it.'

'No, you were right the first time. He knows I don't.'

'I didn't mean—'

'Anna, listen.' He stopped. 'You know what happened, you know my part in it, and you know how it nearly destroyed everything. I've no secrets from you, and you don't have to tip-toe around me. James is the bigger of us. I've said some … truly nasty things to him since he's been back, and yet he's still keeping me on the *Pride*.' He let her go, and turned away. 'He's the bigger of us,' he repeated, so quietly Anna barely heard him.

She fought a rising guilt at his declaration of complete openness between them, and took his hand. 'I'm glad things are easier between you now. But if he can find it in him to forgive you, I think you ought to meet him halfway, don't you?'

'He's done nothing wrong.'

'No, silly.' She shook at their linked hands. 'I mean forgive *yourself*.'

'That'll take longer,' he admitted. 'But I'm trying.'

They walked in easy silence until they reached the lower perimeter wall. Matthew climbed onto it and began to walk along it, his arms held out to the sides like a tightrope walker. 'This is what we did when we were kids.'

'Tackers!' Anna grinned. She watched him wavering on the top of the uneven wall, his open waistcoat blown back by the stiff wind, his hair likewise. Now, finally, she could see the child in him, in his laughter as he almost unbalanced.

'Wait,' she called, and lifted her skirt out of the way. 'I'm coming up too.'

'Wait there.' Matthew made his way back to where she waited, and took her outstretched hand. The loose rocks slipped under her feet, and one or two fell away, leaving her scrabbling for purchase, but a moment later she was standing next to him, the wind stealing her breath as she faced into it. From where he now stood behind her, Matthew slipped his arms around her waist and she leaned back into him.

His breath grazed her skin as he lowered his head and kissed her neck, and she held his arms firmly around her, tilting her head to allow his lips the freedom of every exposed inch of skin. Bizarrely, out here in the wide open, in bold silhouette on top of this wall, she felt more safely alone with him than in the sitting room at the Tinner's Arms, or in any of the other places they had stolen moments like this over the past few months.

Suddenly needing more, she twisted in his arms, and raised her hands to his shoulders. She looked at him for a long, silent moment, taking in everything from the way the late evening sunlight accentuated the blue of his eyes, and the silver-grey rings around the irises; the creases at the sides of his mouth; the surprising darkness of his eyelashes and brows. Then she brought his mouth closer, with the tiniest amount of pressure on the back of his neck.

She slipped her hands into his hair and locked them there, and only then did she allow their lips to touch, very lightly, before drawing back to examine him again. She felt his breathing quicken, and then his hands tightened on her hips, moving to the small of her back, and he took control from her at last. She surrendered it willingly.

Her mouth parted beneath his, and she pressed herself more firmly against him. The wordless dance of tongue and teeth, lips and breath; the surrender of all thought and care; and the restless, ever-seeking and frustrated brush of fingers against the barriers of clothing . . . perhaps it all lasted less than a minute. But by the time it ended Anna knew that tonight she would not return to her home hiding her longing behind work or a feigned tiredness. She broke the kiss and looked into Matthew's eyes, and saw the same knowledge there.

He took her hand and led her back along the wall until he found a place he could jump down easily inside the outer keep. Then he turned to lift her, and when her feet touched the ground beside his she remained held against him while they both battled with the right and wrong of what they knew would happen next. It was an unequal struggle from the start, and when he began walking towards the dubious shelter of the ancient stone ruin, she followed with no further hesitation.

Once behind the wall, the brisk breeze dropped away, leaving a suddenly awkward silence. Anna wondered if either of them would seek to fill it, but before she had begun to turn her mind to what she might say, Matthew had taken her face in his hands. After a searching but brief look, as if he was worried she might withdraw her willingness after all, he lowered his mouth to hers and she returned the pressure of his lips.

Then followed the clumsy fumbling of fingers on clothing, and the romantic notion of undressing one another was quickly abandoned. Anna wished fervently for darkness; she rarely wore a corset these days, and so had no concern that he believed her more slender than she would prove to be, but neither was she in her first flush of delicate youth. She had at last borne a living child, and nothing would make her regret that, but her own image of the famously beautiful Isabel Penhaligon persisted on taunting her. Then Matthew put his hands gently on her bared shoulders, and she saw him take a short, appreciative breath, and her confidence returned. She raised her head and met his gaze, before letting her eyes explore him properly.

He had filled out since the last time she had seen him partially dressed, and the memory of the feelings that had hit her so unexpectedly, and so hard, flooded back. She gave herself over to the pleasure of touching him at last; the concave belly had given way to a flat, athletic musculature, but the broadness of shoulder was the same, as was the deep swell of his ribcage, and the strong, long-legged stance.

His fingers trailed along her collar bone, leaving little patches of warmth in their wake. She kept her eyes fixed on his chest, seeing his breathing quicken as her own hands dropped to the fastening of his trousers. She could feel the tension in his body, but he made no sound as she pushed the buttons through their worn holes, her own fingers shaking with a new urgency.

When they were finally ready to lie down, Anna glanced at the ground, and only then realised the problem they faced. Or rather, the several problems. The sweetly tense moment was shattered, and she sighed.

Matthew followed her gaze, and gave a snort of laughter. 'We should have thought about this a bit more,' he admitted. It was the first time either had spoken since they had first climbed onto the wall, and his voice should have jarred, but instead it gave Anna a feeling of deep and unexpected warmth.

'We were ... distracted,' she pointed out, and he chuckled. 'Somewhat.' He reached one still-booted foot out and kicked away a couple of stones, one hand holding hers, the other keeping his trousers modestly at full-mast. He looked critically at Anna, and then at the space he had cleared. 'If only you weren't so tall,' he said, earning himself a poke in the ribs. He kicked another stone away. 'There, that should do it.'

'No one could ever accuse you of being overly romantic!' Anna didn't even try to hide her smile. She released Matthew's hand and knelt gingerly, looking away while he lowered his trousers. As a married woman she was no stranger to the male form, but this was different . . . and this was not her husband.

Finn's face floated for an instant before her eyes, as she kept them focused on her skirt, but when Matthew knelt at her side and put his hand over hers, the image vanished and there was only him. He eased her back and lay propped on one elbow beside her, and she experienced a moment of passionate relief that they were not young lovers just starting out; there was no fear attached to this moment. Nothing to spoil it, or to cast a shadow over it.

'Ow!' Matthew's exclamation came so quickly on the heels of that thought that she had burst into giggles before she even thought to ask what was wrong. Then she saw him rubbing his knee, which had found one of the smaller stones hidden in the grass.

'Are you all right?' she asked, through her laughter.

In answer, he gave a low growl and silenced her with a thorough and enthusiastic kiss. Their smiles faded under the warmth of it, but did not disappear, and when Anna felt his hand pulling at her skirt, exposing her to the thigh, she relaxed into the bliss of anticipation and let her head fall back on the grass. His lips drifted down across her throat to her shoulder, and back again, when he entered her, easily and smoothly, laughter was the farthest thing from her mind.

They moved together in a rhythm both familiar and excitingly new; the fascination of learning Matthew's body, and his reactions, was as pleasurable as the sensations he awakened in her. His fingers were rough, but his touch, flatteringly shy at times, became emboldened when he realised she was losing herself in it. She urged him on with soft sounds that seemed to be uttered by someone else, but the bunched material of her skirt was a barrier between them ... if only she'd been brave enough to remove it entirely she would have felt the sweet pressure of his chest on hers, and she knew her pounding heartbeat would pick up the echo of his. Matthew kissed her forehead, his own brow furrowed as his breathing came harder, and she felt the new tension in his shoulders as he braced himself against the ground.

'Anna,' he whispered, and she relaxed her hold on him, giving him the freedom to move to his own rhythm ... he slowed, moving still deeper inside her, before speeding up again and letting go of the tight control he'd been holding. His breath exploded in a low cry, and she answered it, but the greater part of her pleasure was in sharing his; the tingle she felt deep inside woke up and yearned towards him, but it was too late and as he eased himself out of her she felt a flicker of frustrated disappointment.

She tried to keep it from him, but he saw her face and realised, and instead of moving away he cupped her and pressed firmly with the heel of his hand. She caught her breath, and a moment later the sensation she had been chasing flared into life. Matthew smiled, but did not move beyond dropping his lips to her shoulder, and increasing the pressure until Anna shuddered into stillness.

She lay waiting for her heartbeat to slow again, and trying to remember if she'd cried out again, but the moment had been so intense she could remember nothing except the unexpected touch, and then the fierce elation and sweet, pulsing release. Matthew raised his head from her shoulder, and she blinked at him, her vision clearing to show her his eyes, half-closed but still crinkled in a smile, and his hair flopping across his forehead. He looked closer to twenty than to forty at that moment, and on impulse Anna reached up and stroked his jaw, before pulling him down for another kiss. This time their lips did not part, and the chasteness of the touch felt perfect and natural after the passion they had just spent upon each other.

Anna closed her eyes again, and felt Matthew move away to stretch out beside her. They lay in drowsy silence for a few minutes, and she even felt herself drifting away, until he jerked and cursed, and began scrabbling for his clothes.

'Someone's coming!'

Anna gasped and sat upright, glad now that she had kept her skirt on. She pulled her chemise up and thrust her arms through the holes, then seized her blouse from where it lay on the ground, pulling the sleeves the right way out with trembling fingers. 'I can't hear any—' But she broke off as the sound reached her. Voices, wafting on the evening breeze. They sounded neither friendly nor happy, one male and one female, but the absurdity of the situation overcame fear of discovery and disgrace, replacing it with an incongruous desire to laugh.

Matthew caught sight of her expression, and she could see the same instinct in the way his lips pressed together, and his eyes glinted. That made her feel better. She finally worked the last of her buttons closed and took his outstretched hand. He pulled her to her feet, and together they crept to the nearest outer wall, where Matthew peered over.

'It's David Donithorn,' he said in a low voice. 'And that girl who works with Freya at the hotel.'

'Juliet?'

'That's her. Doesn't she know he's married?' He sounded so disapproving, Anna didn't know what to say. She just looked at him with one eyebrow raised, until he realised what he had said, and he opened his mouth to speak, but shut it again as the voices grew louder. When the couple came close enough for their words to sound more clearly, it was apparent Donithorn had worse problems than his marital state.

His voice was sulky, defensive. 'How do I know it ain't Fry's, anyway?'

'I'm near five months,' Juliet said. 'If'n was his it'd be barely four. Unlike you, David Donithorn, my word's good.'

'You're saying I'm a liar now, is that it?'

'Well you haven't told Ginny about us!'

'And if I did, you think she'd care?' The footsteps stopped uncomfortably close by, and Anna exchanged a wide-eyed look with Matthew, who put an unnecessary finger to his lips. Despite everything, she wanted to lift it away and replace it with her mouth, and she looked away before he could see the thought, and its accompanying smile, cross her face. They sat down, still holding hands.

'There's nothing to tell,' Donithorn said, 'and she'd know

that. You bringin' me out here ... did you think I'd go all sentimental just because of where you dish up the news?'

'Well don't you remember how—'

'Don't matter.' Donithorn's voice was grim. 'There's nothing romantic about what we did. Ginny'd know you was no threat.'

'Not even when the child's born with your black hair? Not to mention your foul temper!'

'Threaten just s'much as you like,' Donithorn said, with more than a touch of complacency. 'She's not going to throw away my wage for the sake of a bit of pride. She'd not risk being put out of her home for that.'

'She's got her own money.' But Juliet sounded uncertain again now, and Anna felt an unexpected stab of sympathy for the girl.

'A bal maiden's earnings won't keep her,' Donithorn said flatly. 'You know how my sister Ellen struggles, and she's got the guild behind her. Besides, even if Ginny did throw me out, you think I'd take up with you now?'

'Just a little is all I'm asking. Enough to go away. Bodmin maybe, or even Plymouth. I'd never come back, I swear. You'd never have to see either of us again.'

'I haven't got it to give,' Donithorn said. 'That's just how it is.'

'Just a few pounds!'

'I said I can't! I had to move out of the Trevellicks' place, remember? Cost me near enough everything I had to get me and 'er into Furzy Row.' His voice faded. 'Look, I don't want to hear no more. Do your worst. Tell Ginny. See where that leaves you, but it won't make me no bleddy richer!'

'So that's it?' Juliet was following him, but her tearful anger still carried to where Anna and Matthew sat, breath held. 'You forget everything we did out here, and just go back to your wife, and leave me and *your child* with no support? You're a *coward*, David Donithorn!'

Her cries trailed away, but it was impossible to be sure she had left, and Anna's heart sped up when Matthew let go of her hand and rose to peer over the wall again.

'It's all right,' he said, but in a low voice, as if his words might somehow carry down the hillside after the angry couple. 'Come on.'

Anna stood too, and peered through the gloom in the direction of the pathway towards town. She was dismayed at how quickly the pleasure and, even worse, the fun, had ebbed away.

Matthew frowned. 'Anna? What's wrong?'

She cast about for the right words. 'Do you think that what we did was any better than what they did?'

'How can you say that?' He looked appalled. 'We love each other, don't we?'

'Yes! Yes, of course, but,' she shook her head, 'you're still married, Matthew. In the eyes of the church, and the views of the town—'

'I'm not married.'

Anna wasn't sure she'd heard correctly. Then she gave a little shake of her head; there must still be a good slice of the Catholic in her after all because it still felt wrong. 'Well whether you're married or you're divorced—'

'Not divorced, either.' Matthew looked uncomfortable. 'The truth is Isabel and I were never wed.' He caught at her hand again. 'Please ... Freya would be devastated. I'm only telling you because I want there to be no lies between *us*.'

Anna was certain the dismay must have shown in her face, but Matthew was too distracted to notice. 'It's so long ago, I barely even think about it now,' he went on. 'Freya was baptised as if we had married, everyone thinks we were.' He brightened, and took her hands in his. 'But that means there's no reason why, once a respectable time has passed, you and I shouldn't be a proper family with our two girls.'

His smile wavered slightly when she didn't reply, and he let go of her hands. He flicked the top button of her blouse and cleared his throat. 'Anyway, you'd better put this straight before we go back.'

She glanced down; in her haste she had buttoned herself up crooked, and she focused on correcting it while Matthew kept talking. Nonsense, mostly; he seemed certain that allowing a silence between them would invite a refusal. And of course she must refuse, and right away. It was absolutely out of the question, and it would be wrong to give him false hope by pretending to need time to think about it.

'Yes.' She heard the word fall, burying the torrent of his one-sided conversation with that one quiet syllable.

He held her at arm's length, studying her intently. 'Yes?'

'That's if you were asking me to marry you. Were you?' He nodded, having seemingly run out of words now. 'Then yes,' she repeated, more firmly, and smiled.

She wondered, just for a moment, what she could possibly be thinking, but the tremble in Matthew's fingers, as he released her shoulders and put his hands either side of her face, silenced all the questions that clamoured for her attention. He kissed the tiny furrow between her eyes, and then her lips, and nothing mattered more than this. Nothing at all. It would all somehow fall into place. It must, otherwise she would surely not be permitted this bright, warm, and full-hearted joy, not after all that had happened, and all the lies she had told.

As they began their slow, companionable walk home she opened her mouth once, twice, but in the end she did not speak. Telling him the truth might unburden her heart to some small degree, but if that truth emerged later – God forbid – and people discovered he'd known all along, he would lose everything he had re-built, and this time he would never find it again. The burden must remain hers and Mairead's, but the dark memories of violence and terror would surely fade in the months and years to come. In the meantime there was Matthew Penhaligon and his daughter, and Mairead, and the life the four of them would build together.

Chapter Sixteen

The sun was already beginning a long, slow climb as Freya pulled back the curtain in the kitchen, and the orange glow fell across the table in a broad stripe of warmth. She blinked at the clock on the sideboard and saw she'd slept uncommonly late. Papá had long since left for work, Grandpa would soon be down for his breakfast, and it was nearly time to open the shop already. She wondered for a moment what had caused her to sleep so late, and so deeply, then smiled. She had fallen into bed last night in a state of happy relaxation she couldn't remember feeling since she'd been little. So much worry over the years, with Papá not sure what his future held, but the shop was his now, and he was still working on the boats. He had time to catch a breath, to put some money aside and maybe eventually get himself another boat of his own once the shop started earning its own way.

He'd returned from his evening walk with Anna, calm, cheerful, and optimistic. He hadn't once looked as if he was struggling against the call of the bottle, instead he and Grandpa had talked long and deeply about the future of Penhaligon's Attic, over cups of tea and some biscuits Freya had baked while they had been in Truro. She hadn't yet broached the subject of whether she ought to start offering them for sale, but now it seemed a good time. She would do it tonight.

Later she was putting the finishing touches to a box that had been ordered from them by Teddy Kempton, for his scholarly friend, when Anna poked her head around the open door.

'Good morning to you.'

'And to you.' Freya beckoned her in. 'Not here to buy books, I suppose?'

'Sadly not just now. I came to see if you wanted to come with me to meet Mairead.'

'Meet her?'

'She's been at Porthstennack since sunrise, but she's got work to do. I thought you might enjoy a walk since the weather's so nice. Don't worry, I'll have you back in good time to go to work.'

Freya fought down a rush of sudden panic. 'Thank you, but Grandpa shouldn't be left alone—'

'Rubbish.' Grandpa Robert chose that moment to scuffle into the shop. 'Been perfectly able all m' life, and still am. Besides,' his gruff voice softened, just a little bit, 'I miss seeing that bright-eyed look you always had, maid, when you came back from 'Stennack. One of the things your pa did for the best, helpin' you learn to love it like he do.'

Though warmed by the unexpected note of affection, Freya's heart sank. The re-formed bond between Papá and Grandpa Robert might be real, but it was also fragile and precious. If Grandpa suspected the depth of her fear, and its cause, that bond would be shattered all over again and it might not be mended a second time.

So she nodded, fixed a smile in place, and went into the passage to change into her outdoor shoes. As her trembling fingers failed her again and again she tried to think of some way to avoid the walk without giving away the reason. Her mind picked up and cast away excuse after excuse, and gradually she became aware of the low murmur of easy conversation behind her in the shop, and stopped twisting at the laces. She took a deep breath and scolded herself silently but thoroughly; Grandpa's illness had been real, and his recovery far more difficult, but he had won. With such an example to draw from, surely it was time she faced her own terrors again?

To begin with, everything went well. She and Anna chatted of inconsequential things, how the pub had changed so much since Anna had taken it over, and now even some women were finding it a pleasant place to sup after a long day's work.

'Almost as many as the men, now,' Anna said, with some pride.

'The men and the women in this town have never mixed very well,' Freya observed. 'I can't believe you've managed to get them drinking together.'

'It helps that I've established a new system,' Anna said.

'Once per night a fella can pledge his time against the cost of one drink.'

'His time?'

'He puts a piece of paper into the jar on the bar top, with just his name on. Then he gets a drink, free of charge. Just one. When one of the guild women, or anyone in need, comes in they can draw a name out, and they've got a strong pair of hands to help with the mending of something, or the cleaning of a chimney. Whatever's needed. And a pint here or there isn't costing me too much in profits.'

'And the men are happy to give up what might be hours of their time, for *one* drink?'

Anna winked. 'You'd be amazed what a strong thirst the day before pay day will do to a man's powers of reason.'

Freya flinched. 'I know exactly what it can do.'

Anna looked as if she wanted to bite her own tongue out. 'Of course you do, I'm so sorry.'

'No need to be,' Freya put a hand on her arm. 'I know what you meant. And it helps people, I suppose.'

'It really does.' Anna warmed to her explanation again. 'They're a good bunch, even if they don't like us knowing it. I know at least two who're helping out without putting their names in the jar.'

Freya smiled, and felt her good humour returning. 'A week's wage says Brian Cornish is one of them.'

'And Ern Bolitho, surprisingly. But for the love of God, don't tell him I told you.'

'I won't tell anyone if you won't,'

With their conversation lively and enjoyable once more, they passed the Penworthy memorial almost without Freya noticing, and soon reached the little house where she'd lived until she was eight. She hadn't seen it since the day she and Mama had left, and she stepped off the road and walked over to the gate.

'This is Hawthorn Cottage, where I was born. I loved it here. Someone else rents it now, a lady called Nancy Gilbert and her children.'

'I've often admired the cottage,' Anna said. 'It's very pretty.'

'Very pretty, and very cold. And there's still no indoor plumbing.'

'But you were happy here.'

'I was.'

'But, perhaps a little . . . lonely?'

'Yes, I suppose so. I always wanted brothers and sisters. Some of my friends had so many they'd get under each other's feet all the time, and they'd get so cross. I could never understand why. But being at boarding school was a bit like having a lot of sisters.'

'Mairead has never mentioned any regrets at being an only child.' Anna looked sad for a moment, distant. Her green eyes became shadowed, and Freya was about to ask why but Anna smiled, shaking off her sudden melancholy. 'But that's no indication of whether she has those regrets, after all. I'm willing to bet you never actually mentioned it to your mother either?'

'Lord, no!' To complain of anything at all, let alone something as important as family, was to cause those beautiful dark eyes to swim with tears, and that was too painful to bear. 'Come on, let's go and find Mairead.'

They left the cottage behind and had been walking only

a few more minutes when Freya smelled the first tang of salt. The distant, steady roar of the sea followed, and she slowed, and tried to ignore it. The cry of gulls punctuated the sound, and even with her eyes closed Freya could *see* that great rolling, ravenous beast smashing against the breakwater, fizzing and foaming as it spread over the rocks; she heard again the rushing, heavy gurgling as the water had closed over her head, shutting out everything else.

Through the memory-sounds that filled her ears, she thought she heard someone saying her name ... but she'd thought that before, hadn't she? The cry that had made her climb onto the breakwater, believing someone had found her, only to realise it was the shriek of one of the hungry gulls that flapped along the shore, taking what the tide offered and leaving nothing but despair in return.

Her breath stuck in her throat, and she closed her mouth tight. She swayed, felt the press of the water on her shoulders, the weight of Granny Grace's coat pulling her down, down ... don't breathe, don't breathe ...

Abruptly she opened her eyes again, forcing them, and blinking against the bright sunlight. Anna was looking at her with a frown of concern, and her hand was on Freya's shoulder.

'Are you all right?' Some of the tension lifted at the sound of her voice, so natural and normal, and the memory of the awful, dragging weight of the water receded.

Freya took a deep breath. 'Just a bit of dizziness, I'll be right as a trivet in no time.'

'Oh, I think it was more than that,' Anna said. 'Come on, we're going back.'

'No, really ... ' But the protest was half-hearted, and the

relief at the thought of being safely back in Caernoweth brought tears prickling at the back of her eyes.

'Oh, sweetheart,' Anna gathered her close, and Freya leaned against her, puzzled and angry. It had been *her* decision to shun the beach, hadn't it? To punish it, to deny it her excitement and pleasure because of what *it* had done to *her*? So why, now that she was prepared to forgive, was she struck paralysed and filled with such terror at the thought of facing it again? The unfairness of it was too much, and she hitched a breath, feeling the tears spilling onto her cheeks and dampening Anna's summer blouse.

'I'm sorry.' She pulled back and wiped at her eyes. 'I don't know what's the matter with me.'

'*This* is why you were looking so pale those weeks back.' Anna brushed Freya's hair back, where her tears had stuck fine threads of it to her cheek. 'I heard you had a bad experience at the beach when you were little. It's understandable you'd be frightened to go back.'

'Please don't tell Papá, or anyone else,' Freya pleaded. 'It would upset them so much, and everything is finally going right ...' She looked at Anna, who was blushing faintly through her concerned frown, and tried on a smile. It trembled, but it sat well enough. 'You and Papá are such good friends, and you make him so happy.'

'He makes *me* happy. But just now I'm more worried about you. Let's get you back home. If your grandda asks why you're back so soon we can tell him we met Mairead on the way.'

'You still have to fetch Mairead, and it's too warm to hurry,' Freya said. 'I'll be all right alone. But thank you.'

'Are you sure?'

Freya nodded. She could feel the town at her back like a welcoming hand drawing her up the hill. In town she couldn't hear the water, or smell the salt, and the beach might be twenty miles away. She glanced towards Hawthorn Cottage, and for a moment she wished she still lived there, despite the damp, the cold, and the outdoor privy. Then, with a twinge of sadness, she recognised that what she really wanted was to go back to a time when nothing had truly frightened her.

'I'll come and see you later on,' Anna said. 'Don't worry. I won't tell a soul what's happened here today.'

'Thank you. It's just that Papá ...' she trailed away, but Anna nodded.

'Don't worry,' she repeated. She leaned in and kissed Freya's forehead. The easy familiarity of the gesture almost made Freya cry again, but she swallowed hard instead, and found a smile.

'Enjoy your walk. And thank you again.'

Anna watched Freya walk away. She wondered if the girl knew her hands were still clenched, and her hips rigid beneath the sway of her skirts, and thought probably not, or she would have made attempts to remedy it. To go to such lengths to spare her father's feelings was admirable, and regrettably necessary; he would certainly blame himself, and the difficulty lay in the cold fact that he would be right to do so.

Still, that did not change the warmth that rose in Anna's breast as she turned her thoughts from the daughter to the father. She couldn't deny there had been a faint hope that he would be working ashore today, but when she wound her way through the narrow streets of Porthstennack, and emerged on the road beside the beach, she accepted that it was also a forlorn hope. The beach hummed with activity, but almost all the boats were out, as she should have expected on such a fine June day.

The *Pride of Porthstennack* would have been gone since the early hours. There were a few night catches being sorted and packed into ice for transporting, and those boats were being scrubbed ready for the next trip. Anna kept her eyes moving across the beach, searching for the familiar, stooped figure as Mairead kept up her incessant search for perfection among the shattered shells and chipped pebbles of a working beach. But while her eyes were occupied, her mind and heart were firmly out at sea, with the man who had stolen them.

Since last night's walk, and their coming together with equal shares of laughter and breathless delight, he had settled even deeper into her soul, and she found her fingers curling around her own palm as if it were his. She began to count the hours until she would feel it for real, and there were altogether too many of them. She caught herself, amused, but faintly embarrassed. What was she, a girl in the first flush of womanhood, or a woman in her thirties with a marriage behind her ...? She shook that thought away, and thankfully caught sight of Mairead before it could return and diminish her good humour.

'Come on, *ma mhuirnín*, we've work to do!'

As they came in sight of Hawthorn Cottage, she pondered Freya's childhood, and the small but very real sorrow the girl had revealed. Then she looked at her daughter and wondered, for probably the thousandth time, what it would have been like had her other children survived. Would she have gone on to have Mairead at all?

'Do you ever wish you had brothers and sisters?' she asked, and steeled herself for the reply.

Mairead looked at her, surprised. 'Not at all.' She considered, then shook her head more decisively. 'No, not once. Why?'

Anna relaxed, relieved. 'It's just that Freya was telling me she'd often wished she'd had more company growing up.' She almost added, *apart from her school friends*, but even that had been denied Mairead, so it seemed unfair, and there was nothing to gain by mentioning it.

'I suppose it's unusual for her class, to have just one child in the family,' Mairead said, and Anna had to stop herself from drawing a dismayed breath at this backward step in Mairead's progress. Instead she kept her voice calm.

'You mustn't think like that. We're all the same here.'

'We're not the same as the people back there.' Mairead gestured back towards Porthstennack. 'They're much poorer than the ones in the town. Even Freya and her family are better off.'

'But you mustn't say things like "her class".'

'You always told me class isn't about how much you have, it's a matter of birth. And the Penhaligons were born poor.'

'Actually Grace, Matthew's mother, came from a fairly fortunate family before they lost everything. That's why they don't speak with such broad accents as the other locals.'

'Why is that woman staring at us?'

'Stop that!' Anna put her hand on her daughter's arm and pushed it back down to her side. 'It's rude to point!'

'It's rude to stare, too,' Mairead said bluntly, and Anna couldn't fault her, so she didn't reply. Instead she looked at the woman, who had come out into the yard of Hawthorn Cottage followed by a gaggle of small children. The woman – Mrs Gilbert, Anna remembered – held a washing basket on her hip, but made no move to attend to her task, and instead fixed her eyes on the two women passing her gate. She was too far away for Anna to see her features, but she held herself very straight, and beneath her much-mended dress it was plain she maintained a good figure.

Comparing her own appearance the woman's light golden hair and a long, slender neck, Anna immediately felt dowdy and dark; just a few moments ago she had been basking in the knowledge of Matthew's attraction to her, and the confidence that brought, and she resented the way the woman's frank stare had robbed her of that pleasure. But that was hardly Mrs Gilbert's fault, and so she put a pleasant tone in her voice as she eventually came within hailing distance.

'Good morning. It's nice to meet you. You have a lovely cottage.'

'You'm that Irishwoman.' Even her voice was low, pleasant, and carried well.

'Yes. Anna Garvey, and this is my daughter, Mairead. From the Tinner's Arms.'

'I know,' the woman returned. Her tone gave nothing away, but in her newly disgruntled state Anna found she didn't much care if she disapproved or not. Was it even possible she was feeling a flicker of jealousy that this woman was living in Matthew's old house? She immediately felt guilty; Nancy Gilbert was a widow. How she was making ends meet without a man's wage, and with one, two ... was that *four* children?

When they'd talked about her at the guild meeting she had been a name, someone to be 'seen right', but she hadn't really been a person. Now, here she was with her brood of, seemingly, quite well-behaved children, getting ready to peg out her washing on the very line where Freya and Matthew's clothes had once hung.

'Well, it's nice to meet you,' Anna said, at a loss as to how to behave now. Should she take it upon herself to invite the woman to join the guild? It didn't seem likely she would succeed where others had failed, so maybe it was better to leave it to Ellen, after all.

Mrs Gilbert gave a brief nod, and sought distraction in the activities of her children as they scampered across the yard to the wall on the far side. 'Tory! Don't let Matty climb up, those stones is loose as buggery!'

Anna's heart jolted as Mrs Gilbert said the youngest boy's name, but it was a common one after all. It just seemed quite poignant that this house should, once again, have a Matthew living in it. And the oldest girl, Tory, looked to be around eight years old, just as Freya had been when she'd left.

Anna lifted her hand in a vague wave that went unreturned, and she and Mairead continued walking. It was pointless dwelling on how she might have conducted herself differently; Nancy was clearly on the side of those who were still wary and suspicious of 'that Irishwoman and her daughter'. That portion of the town's population was thankfully diminishing, as more and more people came to know her properly, but Anna had the feeling that Nancy Gilbert would never be one of them.

Chapter Seventeen

Porthstennack Harbour

The day's work was by no means at an end, but the catch was in and to the relief of everyone, not least of all Matthew, it was back to the way it should be. Over the past week or so Matthew had more than once felt the weight of unspoken accusation; as acting skipper, in James's continued and regular absence, he had watched in dismay as the catch had dropped off, and there were days he could almost hear the thoughts of the *Pride*'s crewmen: *bad luck'll follow a man. Once a curse, always a curse.* But today the nets had been dragged in full of whipping tails and fat, arching bodies that were now being sorted by relieved men and women, and the veil of suspicion lifted at last.

Matthew picked his shirt off its usual place on the breakwater, and used it to wipe the sweat from his face before shrugging it over his aching shoulders. He was still looking down, focusing on the buttons and smiling as he remembered

Anna doing the same last night, when he heard someone call his name. James was standing on the shingle, his eyes roving over the *Pride*, now tied up for the day and awaiting cleaning.

James beckoned him over. 'Leave it for now. I need a word.'

Matthew glanced back at the boat, then at James. 'Can't leave her too long, she'll be a bugger to get properly clean if she's sat in the sun too long.'

'Sun's going. A word.'

He spun about and stalked away towards the tide-line, out of the earshot of the others, but Matthew paused at the brusque tone; lately, during their brief meetings, there had been a distinct lessening of the animosity that had characterised their meetings since February. Until now. Frowning, he pulled his shirt straight, and tucked it into his trousers as he crossed the shingle, feeling distinctly shabby next to James's smart appearance.

'Is there something wrong? A problem with the catch? I know the last few days haven't been all we'd have hoped, but today—'

'Nothing like that.' James cleared his throat, and squinted out to sea, deliberately keeping his face away from Matthew. 'Your father's made the shop over to you, I gather?'

Thrown by the question, Matthew could only say, 'Yes.'

'The deed has been signed?'

'Yesterday.'

'Ah. Your birthday.' James nodded. 'That's fitting.' Matthew was touched James had remembered the date, and was about to say so when James went on, 'Look, I know I've not been around a lot, but I intend to remedy that. And I'm sorry, but that means I'm ready to take on my proper duties as skipper.'

'Oh.' Matthew tried not to let his disappointment show. 'I

understand. It was never a permanent arrangement. I'll drop back.'

'You misunderstand me.' At last James turned to him, and Matthew saw tension in the finely sculpted jaw, and wariness in the grey eyes that looked back at him. His muscles tightened, and when he spoke his voice was dull.

'You're putting me off.'

'I'm sure you of all people understand I can't afford to keep anyone there's no room for. And you do have the security of the shop now.' James sounded gruff, regretful, and for a moment Matthew struggled with the urge to beg.

'The shop makes no living.' From somewhere he found a calm voice. 'But I appreciate you giving me this time.'

'What will you do?'

Matthew could feel a pulse jumping in his jaw, and tried not to snap his reply. 'Ask around, I reckon. Brian Cornish might have a place on his crew.'

'He hasn't,' James said. 'I asked him as soon as I knew I was coming back. I've asked all over, in the hopes I could make this easier for you. I'm sorry, Matthew. I really am.'

Matthew took a deep breath, and tried not to think about how it would feel to go to the management at Wheal Furzy, and throw himself at their feet. Just as well he and Anna had agreed to wait a while before announcing their engagement; any notion of the kind of wedding he wanted to give her was sailing over the horizon now.

'Not your fault.' Somehow he kept his voice even. 'I appreciate all you've done.' He backed away, not wanting to look defeated. 'All right if I get on now? Or do you want me to leave right away?'

'Wait! There's something I want to put to you.' James folded his arms, his hands clenched into fists that he shoved beneath his armpits. It was a curiously defensive gesture, and Matthew's eyes narrowed as he retraced the few steps he had taken.

'Go on?'

'A swap.'

'Swap?'

James lowered his hands again, though his hands remained clenched and his voice grew stronger. 'The *Pride*, and my cottage. For Penhaligon's Attic.'

Matthew felt as if he'd stepped off a high ledge. He was aware he must look simple, but so many words were piled up ready to spill out, that he couldn't utter a single one. His mouth worked, but no sounds came from it. James was watching him as if he were a sleeping grizzly bear, liable to erupt into furious wakefulness, and it was at that moment that the truth of everything crashed into place.

'So ... all of this,' Matthew managed at last, '*all* of it ... keeping me on, talking to Pa, making sure he ... oh, you *bastard*.'

'Matthew—'

'Shut up,' Matthew said, his voice bleak, and, to his surprise, James did.

Matthew wondered distantly when the anger would take over, but for now the hollow ache of betrayal was eclipsing everything else. Even his worries for the future. That James had been playing this sneaky little game for the past few months was bad enough, but that he had manipulated Matthew's father to do it made the blood fizz in Matthew's veins. And coming round and round again in the hateful circle of realisations, was the fact that he had been stupid enough to hope that an old and valued friendship might at last be rekindled.

'It's a good offer,' James said, when the silence between them grew too tight to bear. 'You won't get a better one.'

'The shop's not for sale. It's Freya's *future*!' Matthew stared at him, struggling to suppress the fury that had burned away his shock. 'Anyway, what would you do with a second-hand book shop? I've told you it turns no profit. It's my wage from the boats that pays for the upkeep.'

'I'd turn it into an office.' James sounded bizarrely proud. 'I'm setting up my own business. Buildings planning. Conveyancing too, in time. All of it.'

'That's where you've been disappearing off to all these days then, is it? Sneaking off, getting everything all ready for the day when the decision would be mine and not Pa's?'

'It's just the way it worked out,' James protested. 'He was happy to gift the shop to you, and it's taken me this long to get funding to start—'

'You sly little sod!' Matthew shoved at James's shoulder, and the younger man took two stumbling steps back. Matthew had to step back too, to stop himself from following the shove with a solid punch that would have sent James crashing backwards into the foaming tide. 'Every sound that comes out of your mouth . . . ' He'd run out of words again.

Their raised voices had attracted attention, and from the corner of his eye Matthew saw two or three figures approaching. James looked wretched, and as if he wished he hadn't spoken. But he had. And his words were poison.

'Keep your damned offer,' Matthew said in a low, hard voice. 'Roland would be ashamed of you.'

James flushed with his own dull anger. 'Remember you've no job now, Penhaligon. Can you really afford to ignore an offer like this?'

'I'd rather work down the mine than give you my shop.'

'So that's what you'll do, is it?' James shook his head. 'You're prepared to exchange all this,' he waved his hand to encompass their surroundings, 'for the dirt and darkness of Wheal Furzy?'

'Like I said.'

'You won't last a week.'

'So everyone keeps telling me, including your pa. Looks like I'll have to prove you all wrong. I'm going there first thing in the morning.'

'You're a stubborn idiot.' James sounded frustrated now, rather than angry, and Matthew hesitated. *Was* he being stupid? But no. Penhaligon's Attic was Freya's future, he had no right to whisk it away from her for his own selfish sake.

'You heard what happened up at the Wellington Colliery last month?' James went on. 'Hundred and odd dead.'

'That was firedamp. Wheal Furzy's tin, not coal.' But Matthew's blood chilled at the thought of how the terror must have been magnified by the layer upon layer of rock pressing down in the darkness. He shook the image away with an effort. 'Men have worked the mines for hundreds of years, and if it means holding onto my family's business, I'll do it too.'

As the two crew members reached them Matthew and James fell silent and ignored the questioning looks, keeping their taut attention on one another. There was more to be said, and neither was prepared to break away and call it done just yet, but the anger ran too deep in them both for it to become a public battle.

'Y'all right, Skip?' John Rodda spoke to James, but eyed Matthew warily; he'd clearly seen the shove, and remembered Matthew's past troubles all too well. 'Do 'ee need us to step in?'

'No, thank you, John.' James put his hands into his pockets, and Matthew read it as a gesture of confidence. 'I was just informing Mr Penhaligon he is no longer required on the *Pride of Porthstennack*. He's chosen to take it personally.'

Matthew did not address him again. Instead he spoke to his erstwhile crew. 'John, Ern, it's been a pleasure to work alongside you both.' He nodded at them, and, with a last look of contempt at James, he crunched his way back across the shingled beach to the road. The thought of what he was leaving behind him clashed with the happiness he'd found with Anna, and although the joy of one went some small way towards easing the pain of the other, his heart felt tight and heavy in his chest. It wasn't until his feet reached the hard, unyielding surface of the road that he remembered who was in charge of hiring at Wheal Furzy, and that his chances of securing a job there were not nearly as certain as he'd thought.

Wheal Furzy, Caernoweth

The office was cramped and noisy, and the smell climbed into the back of Matthew's throat so he could taste it every time he swallowed. Oil and dust, sour sweat, wet mud ... the combination made his head swim and his stomach twist in revulsion, but he managed to smile as the mine's foreman told him to wait.

'He'll be here d'rectly,' Tobias Able said. 'He's two men short due to sickness, so you'm likely to be startin' today.'

'Suits me well enough,' Matthew said. The words tasted as bad as the air in the office, but even if he'd wanted to he couldn't have bitten them back. Honesty knocked at his conscience. 'You know there's bad blood between him and me?'

Tobias nodded. 'There in't hardly no one who don't. But he's got a team needs fillin', and he's not over-run with healthy lads to do it.' He sized Matthew up, and grunted, 'He'll take you on. Just remember to leave your 'istory at the surface, and don't take it down there with you.'

'I will. Can't speak for David.'

Tobias turned at the sound of boots on the ground outside. 'He knows better'n to carry a grudge below ground.' He picked up his helmet and wedged the candle harder into its holder. 'I'll leave you to business.'

He and David Donithorn passed just outside the door, and then Donithorn was removing his own helmet to reveal a pale stripe across his forehead, where he had sweated away the worst of the dirt.

'What the bloody hell are you doin' here?'

'Came for a job.' Matthew felt his shoulders come up, just slightly, and lifted his chin to reflect it.

'James Fry turned you off, have he?'

'He's taking over the running of the boats.'

Donithorn raised an eyebrow, and gave him a shrewd smile. 'That right? And what in hell makes you think I'd take you on my team?'

'Toby says you've two places to fill.' Matthew flexed his hands. 'I'm a hard worker.'

'You're a drunk.'

Matthew tried not to flinch at the bald statement, but Donithorn was watching him closely so instead he shook his head. 'Was a drunk,' he corrected. 'We both know I've not let a drop pass my lips in eight years or more.'

'You're a danger to others. I won't have you nowhere near this mine.' Donithorn, a good ten years younger than Matthew, nevertheless held Matthew's future in his grimy hands, and it was clear he was enjoying tearing it to pieces.

Matthew kept his voice even, but he leaned forward slightly from the waist. In the small office this put his face quite close to Donithorn's, and their eyes locked. 'You don't run this mine. You might be in charge of hiring and firing, but you can't keep me off the property.'

Donithorn did not draw back. His voice was low, and his bitter tone belied his tight smile. 'Stay, then. But you won't be settin' foot on that man-engine, and you won't be drawin' a wage.'

Matthew's spirits, low to begin with, began a sickening descent. He had held onto a hope that, despite everything, David Donithorn would have matured enough to put their past behind him in the interests of running a full team. Then he felt the old, familiar shame crawling over his skin; maturity was never the issue. Donithorn's grievance was real, and justified.

He chewed at his lip, searching for a calm tone. 'You know I regret what happened.'

'*You* regret it?' Donithorn jerked as if Matthew had slapped him. 'Do you have any notion what you did? How I felt? What it was like to be the person who'd smashed Roland's knee so bad he couldn't work?'

'Of course I do! It was my bloody fault!'

'Yes! But Roland forgave you! Who forgave *me*? No one!' Donithorn's eyes were too bright now. 'I was twelve years old, Penhaligon! Working for Roland was my first job, and after that no one would have me anywhere near their bloody boats! But you?' He gave a choking laugh. 'You, he welcomed back. Christ! I know exactly how James feels.'

'Look—'

'Stop.' Donithorn sounded weary now. 'I know, t'wasn't *your* fault you were his son's friend, and he didn't even know who I was. T'wasn't *your* fault he gave you another chance. But it *was* your fault it happened to begin with.' His expression closed down. 'I ain't givin' you a job. Go home. Sell books.'

For a brief moment, Matthew considered doing just that. He could feel his feet wanting to move towards the door, feel his lungs yearning towards the clear, cool morning air outside. He saw Pa and Freya's faces when he told them he wasn't fit to work at Wheal Furzy; that they would lose their home, and his mother's beloved business ... he even saw himself going to James and pleading for his job back on the *Pride of Porthstennack*. Then he heard himself say:

'I heard Juliet Carne's in the family way.'

Donithorn went still. 'What?'

'Juliet Carne.' He paused, wondering at his own cruelty. But desperation had him in a firm grip now; he needed this job. 'I know you've got her into trouble.'

Donithorn started to shake his head, but Matthew kept his gaze level, and Donithorn read the truth there. He set his jaw and his words came out through clenched teeth. 'Well, Mister know-it-all, I'll tell you what I told her. Ginny won't turn me out on the word of a no-account, cheap girl like that.'

'No. But I heard you admit it,' Matthew said. 'And I'm not a no-account man around here anymore, am I? Much as you like to think it. I'm a business-owner.'

'And yet here you are, beggin' for a job.' Donithorn's grin was tight and humourless.

Matthew matched it. 'I might be struggling, but in the eyes of the town I'm still respectable. More so than ever, in fact. After all, I'm just looking for honest work to feed my family.' He adopted a conversational tone. 'Speaking of family, what do you suppose Juliet will do with her child when it's born?'

'What do you mean?'

'Do you think she's going to be able to feed it? Care for it?'

Donithorn shrugged. 'She'll be all right. She'll go to the Union, over to Truro. They takes kids.'

'The workhouse?' Matthew laughed; it had as strangled a sound as Donithorn's had. Things were becoming darker and more unpleasant by the minute, and his longing for the freshness of the new day, just a few feet away, was stifling. 'Can you imagine Juliet doing that?' He shook his head. 'On the other hand, there's someone else she could turn to, isn't there? Someone far more likely to believe her, and to give her money to go away.'

There was a long pause, while Donithorn's brows drew down and his eyes never left Matthew's. Matthew kept his face expressionless, and hoped his leaping heart wasn't betrayed in the pulse that beat in his temple and throat.

Donithorn spoke slowly. 'Fry. He'd pay to send her off, all right.' He pursed his lips. 'And you're saying that, if *I* don't give you this job, you're going to tell him it's my kid?'

302

'I am.' The time for game-playing was over. Best to say it straight.

'And what if she doesn't go to him? What will you have against me then?'

'Nothing. So if I'm doing a bad job, fire me. If I'm doing a good one, don't cut off your nose to spite your face.'

'And how will I know you won't use this against me another time?'

Matthew shrugged. 'I don't know how to convince you, if that's what you mean. But – drunk or not – I've always been a man of my word. You can't dispute that. And my word's what you'll have.' He saw Donithorn wavering, and pressed home his point. 'If James does believe her, and gives her the money she wants, she'll be away over the horizon and no more trouble to either one of you.'

There was a silence between them, but it was overlaid by the heavy sounds of the mine. Stamping, crushing, and the muted roar of an underground explosion as more ground was cleared. Matthew's gut was tight; the job was within his grasp, but at the same time it would spell the end of his last hope of a miracle that would let him work at sea again.

At last Donithorn nodded, but his voice was no less hate-filled than before. 'We're a four-man team, down to two. Three, now.' He nodded at Matthew, who didn't bother to try and hide his relief. 'Young Tommy will show you where to get your tools and your candles.'

'What are we doing?'

'Breaking ground at the 236 fathom level. I'm in charge, so I position the drill while you boys drive it into the rock. Then we put the powder in the 'ole, and set the fuse.' His brow smoothed out, and a calm look came over his features. 'Let's hope you get well clear before it blows, eh?'

'Is that a threat?'

Donithorn looked surprised that Matthew had addressed it, and glanced over his shoulder at the door in case Toby was nearby. 'No one's ever been hurt or killed on my team, and nor will they, if I've anything to say about it. No, it's not a threat. It's a warning – you're not made for underground, Penhaligon. It's a different world. I just hope you learn fast.'

Chapter Eighteen

18 June, Truro

St Mary's Street was busier than James had seen it in some time. He dodged a group of boys, who had inexplicably chosen to break and run, seemingly by some group consciousness shared only among themselves. For a moment he stared after them, five boys of indeterminate age but boundless energy, and his mind took him back to the days when he and Matthew Penhaligon had been just the same.

Sometimes running had no purpose except as an expression of freedom after schooling, but often they'd channelled it into a quest to catch some of the stray cats that stalked the narrow streets, to hold one aloft in triumph before setting it free in someone's garden. Sometimes one of them would call it a race, naming a finishing point only after the run had already started. But always, as boys, they had been in tune with one another. Now though ... James took a deep breath and pushed it out in a sigh, hoping it would carry the niggling feelings of guilt with it. It didn't.

'Beauty, isn't she?'

James turned to see a well-dressed man, who'd stopped beside him to gaze at the almost-finished cathedral. It was the reason he himself had come to Truro, but he now realised he'd been staring at it without noting any of the stunning gothic architecture, his mind too focused on his own destructive nature to embrace this creative beauty.

His new companion, a narrow-faced man James judged to be in forties, expressed deep approval. 'It's a pity Pearson didn't live to see it through. Still, they made a good job of it. Four types of stone used, they say. Must say I could spend an age studying this one. A lot like Lincoln, isn't it?'

'I've not seen Lincoln,' James confessed. 'Are you an architect?'

'I am, sir. Charles Trubshaw at your service.'

James blinked. 'The Midland hotels?'

'The very same. Manchester and Bradford. I'm down here for a month or so, hoping to see the finished article.' He gestured to the cathedral ahead of them. 'You're in the trade?'

'Recently qualified,' James said, 'but not yet in the business. I studied under Richard Norman Shaw at Bryanston.'

'Ah, Shaw, of course. We met recently in Bradford, in fact, he was there for the city hall extension.'

'So I understand.' James couldn't now take his eyes off the bespectacled, unassuming-looking man, whose name he had heard over and over since his first day of apprenticeship, and in the warmest terms.

'I learned a great deal under his tutelage.' He tried not to sound like a mumbling child, but like a businessman. 'I'm just looking for the right premises to start a business for myself.'

'Well, don't hang around,' Trubshaw advised. 'There's a lot of interest in restoration projects just now.'

'Indeed. I'm hoping to secure the re-build of the old fort at Caernoweth.'

'A fort, eh? Take a lot of work to turn that into something usable, I should think.'

'I believe there's a development company who plan to turn at least part of it into an hotel.' James heard the words spill from his lips and could have kicked himself, but it was too late to take them back now. The thoughts must have shown on his face, because Trubshaw cast him an amused look.

'Well, as I said, don't leave it too long. Where there are investors, there are builders. And plenty of them.' He held out his hand. 'Good luck, lad.'

'It was nice to meet you, Mr Trubshaw.'

With this confirmation of his own thoughts, the softening of James's feelings towards Matthew reversed itself; the stubborn idiot had turned his back on a solution that would have afforded them both a life of contentment, simply because of his personal anger towards the one who'd offered it. Instead he would spend his working days in darkness and danger, and he, James, would be stuck in Porthstennack with a boat he loathed, and a damp, cramped cottage that was collapsing around him.

He watched Trubshaw moving off along St Mary's Street towards the cathedral. If nothing else their meeting had served to persuade him that he had not tried hard enough, so on the journey home he applied his mind to the problem with renewed determination: he couldn't afford to buy a premises, and the only things he had to exchange were the boat and the cottage. Selling them would yield nowhere near the money he'd need to buy, or even rent somewhere, and who else owned a property in town and would consider an exchange?

Anna Garvey? Given the closeness she and Matthew no longer bothered to hide, she would naturally want him to work in the job he loved, and she might consider it since she had little real interest in the Tinner's Arms. James sat upright in the coach, his mind racing. Maybe ... But then he subsided again. Even if Mrs Garvey agreed, and the exchange went through, he would either have to shut the pub down or work from an office within it, and pay someone else to run it. Either way it was out of the question; staff were too expensive, and closing one of the few good ale-houses between Truro and Marazion would cost him even more, including the goodwill of every person he knew. The Tinner's had become a real community meeting place of late, there would be an uproar now if it was taken away. The time to make the offer would have been months ago, when it was still a chilly, damp and cheerless money drain.

By the time he reached Caernoweth, James was becoming increasingly despondent. Perhaps, after all, it had been a mistake to have talked Robert into gifting his son the shop; he might have been easier to persuade if it meant giving Matthew the life he wanted. But it was all conjecture in any case, who knew how the minds of the stubborn and prideful Penhaligons worked? He'd thought he did, once, but they were strangers now.

He stepped down from the coach and, with an inward groan, contemplated the long walk back to Porthstennack in the fading light of the evening. A drink first then. And perhaps the chance to speak to one of the developers who'd begun frequenting the hotel with increasing regularity during the summer months. He even considered capitalising on his two-minute conversation with one of the most famous architects in the land, and thus claiming acquaintanceship with him, so when he heard a voice hissing his name it took a moment for the smile to fade.

'Juliet?'

'I want to talk to you,' she said, obviously misinterpreting his welcoming expression, but relieved by it.

'You're working,' he pointed out, gesturing at her uniform. He looked around, wary in case they'd been seen, but the lobby was empty.

'Everyone's at dinner,' Juliet said dismissively. 'Meet me outside by the stables.'

'What's it about?' James was hard put to conceal his irritation. 'It's been a long day, and I—'

'Please! It's important. I won't keep you five minutes, I promise.'

Without waiting for an answer, she led the way out through the back corridor, and he had no option but to follow. Once tucked away around the side of the huge stable building, he faced her squarely, wishing it was lighter so she could see his impatience and save him the trouble of pointing it out again. She seemed reluctant to begin.

'Well?' he said at last. 'You said it was important.'

'I'm havin' a baby,' she said bluntly.

James stilled, his irritation forgotten. A hundred thoughts galloped through his mind, but all he could manage was, 'Mine?'

He expected her to offer a characteristically snappy response, but her shoulders had slumped the moment the confession was past her lips. She looked at him now, her hand timid on his wrist. 'I'm not asking you to ... to wed me nor nothin', just—'

'Of course I will!' James's voice came out slightly strangled-sounding, and he felt dizzy. He leaned back against the wall, and her hand fell away from his arm. 'When are you due?'

She smoothed her dress so he could see she was showing a more rounded shape than the last time they had met. 'I reckon I'm about four months gone.'

'Of course we should marry.' But his dreams had begun to feather away into nothing at the edges, and it would be no time at all before they disappeared altogether.

But Juliet shook her head. 'I don't want to marry, I want to go away. But I need money. That's all I want from you, not your name, nor your house, nor your life.'

'I have no money to give you.'

'You've got your own business!'

'I have a boat that barely pays its way,' he argued. 'If I had money to throw away on some silly girl and her mistakes, I'd have money to—'

'Silly girl?'

James swore as her boot came down on his foot, and he only just stopped himself from shoving her away. 'I'm sorry. I deserved that.'

'Yes you did.' Juliet slapped his upper arm, and although it didn't hurt through the fabric of his coat, he felt her anger in it. 'It takes two you know, Mr high-and-mighty Fry.'

'I know. I'm sorry,' he said again. 'So will you? Marry me, I mean.'

'You don't want that, no more'n I do.'

He managed a wry smile. 'And here I thought you liked me.'

'I did. I do. But I don't want to be tied to someone who's just doing a duty.'

'Very noble,' he said drily. 'So you'd rather run away?' He sighed. 'Listen. I don't have money to give you now, but that could all change once I get a premises up and running and start taking commissions.'

'And when will that be?'

'Hopefully before October.' He nodded at her slightly rounded belly. 'But it might take a little longer. Look, will you let me do the right thing, or not?'

She scrutinised him in the gathering dark, and he held still, feeling his heart sinking slowly and steadily, the dead weight of a rock. If she refused him he'd be free and clear, and at least he'd have made the offer, but he didn't think she would. Not when it came down to the straight choice open to her.

'All right,' she said at last. 'But we'd better make it soon.'

'People will know soon enough why we're doing it,' he pointed out, trying to keep the resentment out of his voice.

'Maybe so. But I don't want to waddle down the aisle looking like a snowman.'

'You want to marry here in Caernoweth?'

'Why not? It's my home.'

'A minute ago you didn't want to marry at all.'

'I just wanted to be sure you din't feel pressed. It was your choice.'

'My choice is to do what's right. Are you sure it's . . . ?' He couldn't finish, but he didn't need to.

'Yours?' Juliet said, with some contempt. 'Do you think I'd lie over something so important?'

He didn't answer, and there was a silence for a moment, while he considered how everything could change in the space of five minutes. Perhaps he should have just walked straight home after all, and remained in blissful ignorance for one more night, at least.

'So . . . we're engaged, then?'

Was there a touch of impatience in her tone? James looked at her, trying to see her through the new eyes of a future husband. She wasn't as pretty as Lucy Batten – who'd turned him down, in any case, when he'd pushed her just that little bit too far – but she was appealing enough. And she was carrying his child.

'I suppose we are, yes.' He swallowed, feeling the dizziness return, but now it was laced with a strange little flicker of excitement. 'May I . . . ' He mimed touching her stomach, and she dropped the protective hands she'd laid there.

'Hurry, then. I should be gettin' back in.'

'We'll talk properly later. Come to my cottage whenever you like.' He shrugged. 'It'll be yours too soon, I suppose.'

She held out her hand. 'Got a spare key then?'

'No. I'll leave the door unlocked.'

'All right.' When he still hesitated, she seized his hand and placed it firmly on her stomach. Her uniform was thick, and he couldn't feel the warmth of her through it, but he closed his eyes and tried to imagine the shape of the barely formed infant she carried. A son, perhaps, to take away some of the grief of losing Roland – a grief that still surprised him by its depth in quiet moments. Or a daughter, who would look up to him as Freya did to Matthew. He remembered that perfect image of the Penhaligons in their cottage garden; that would be his future now, too. His own family at last.

Freya rubbed her eyes, wincing at the sting of detergent. Her feet ached, her back ached, and her skin felt raw. The extra shifts were welcome, but the fact they were in the laundry was only eased by the enjoyment of working with Juliet. She'd always known she disliked this particular chore, but had only recently learned exactly how much she loathed it. Still, she was better off than her father. Yesterday he had come home early, distant, quiet, and pale. He'd said nothing at first, just stared away into something of his own mind's creation, but eventually, with some persuasion, he'd told her and Grandpa about losing his place on the *Pride*.

The thought of James Fry's offer, explained in tight, deliberately short sentences as if Papá hadn't trusted himself with his emotions, made Freya's own blood tingle with fury. It had been a sneaky, loathsome thing to do, to put him out of a job and then offer the only thing he wanted, in return for the only thing he could not give up. Whatever hope they had held for a reconciliation between the two old friends had been buried in that one gesture, and would never again see the light.

This morning Papá had been up with the lark, and gone to Wheal Furzy before Freya had even stirred awake. When he'd worked on the boats she'd been able to lie still in the comfort of her bed and listen to him moving about downstairs, then the quiet click of the latch as he'd gone out, and his booted feet on the quiet road as he'd strode off to a job he loved ... but now, if he was able to secure work, he would become someone she barely saw. Roland Fry would spin and cry out in his grave if he knew what his son had done.

Freya wasn't aware she was scowling, until she heard Juliet's laugh, and she looked up to see her friend re-tying her apron. 'Where have you been?'

'Outside. Why so fierce-looking? I've not been gone that long!'

'No, I was thinking about Papá,' Freya admitted. 'That mine'll be the death of him.'

'Oh, don't paint it so dark,' Juliet said airily. 'He's only been there one day. David's worked there almost his whole life. And his wife and sister too.'

'I don't mean his actual death.' Freya fished with her tongs in the water, stirring the bedding that lay soaking in its murky depths. 'It's just he loves the sea so much.'

'Not enough to accept James's offer though.'

'Not enough to give up everything his family owns, you mean,' Freya corrected, her voice sharpening. 'We'd have lost everything, including our home.'

'You wouldn't be turned out into the streets, you'd have James's cottage to live in.'

Freya eyed her suspiciously. 'When I was telling you about it earlier, you couldn't have been less interested.'

Juliet shrugged and lifted the lid of the laundry machine closest to her. She wafted the steam away and sniffed. 'This soap smells dreadful.'

'Juliet!'

Juliet let the lid drop again without bundling the bedding into it, and looked at Freya with a secretive little smile playing about her lips. She looked flushed and excited, and Freya's exasperation melted into curiosity.

'Come on, what's to do?'

'I'm gettin' wed!'

Freya was just about to exclaim in pleasure, could feel the short little breath build to do so, but then noticed Juliet's hand had gone, quite likely unbidden, to rest on her lower belly. Her heart sank for her friend, but there was a tired inevitability about it all.

She said, as gently as she could, 'David will never walk away from Ginny, no matter what he's told you.'

'Not him.' Juliet stared at her with a hint of defiance. 'James.'

Freya was silent a moment, while the news unwound itself in her mind and while she battled the instinct to walk away, slam the door, and never speak to Juliet again. Of all the people Juliet might have chosen who would have been pleased and proud to have captured such a wild-spirited bride, why that sly sneak who'd ruined everything? The man who had been back in Caernoweth only a matter of hours before enticing his chambermaid into his bed? A niggling suspicion grew, and she pointed to Juliet's waist.

'Is that *really* his?'

'Of course it is!' Juliet's voice was suitably outraged at the question, but her flush was no longer soft and happy. It was an angry blotch high on her cheeks, and it told a very different story.

'Truly?' Freya kept her voice gentle, and finally Juliet's indignation crumpled.

'I've worked it out from when I first missed. The dates are all wrong.'

'James doesn't know that, I take it?'

'No.' Juliet opened the machine again and began to stuff the soiled bedding into it. 'Don't do nothin' to ruin it for me, Freya. He's a good 'un.'

'Good?'

'His quarrel with your pa has got nothing to do with me,' Juliet pointed out. 'He's going to be a good father, and he'll provide for us all. He'll even be rich, one day.'

Freya looked at her helplessly. 'He's rotten right through! See the way he tricked Grandpa into giving—'

'He never tricked him! You told me yourself, he just put the suggestion there, and everyone was proper happy about it too, at the time!' She sighed. 'He'll be a good father,' she repeated. 'Let us be.'

There was a silence between them, and finally Freya nodded. 'Just be careful.'

'You'll not tell anyone?'

'We're friends. Of course I won't.' She found a smile. 'You can trust me.'

'Good. Because if a bride can't trust her bridesmaid, who can she trust?' Despite her reservations, Freya couldn't help a little smile, and Juliet laughed. 'Just don't look too pretty,' she said in warning tones. 'I'm supposed to be the centre of attention, remember.'

Freya's smile widened, and some of the tension between them eased. 'You will be, never fear.'

She watched Juliet return to her work, and noted the way the smile stayed on her face. Perhaps it would work out well with them; after all, who was she to judge how these two disparate people felt about one another? And, most importantly, Juliet's child would have a decent home.

She surreptitiously put her own hand on her belly, wondering what it must feel like to be growing a new life ... One day, perhaps. When that day came, she was as certain as she could be that it would be with someone worth a hundred David Donithorns, and a thousand James Frys, but when Hugh Batten's face came to the front of her mind she pushed it away.

Chapter Nineteen

Matthew stepped off the man-engine at the upper level of Wheal Furzy, his arms and shoulders aching as they'd never ached before.

'You did all right, for an old 'un,' observed the lad at his back. 'Don't 'ee listen to Donithorn, he's had a bee in his bonnet about you since you started.'

'Thanks,' Matthew said, somewhat drily. He rolled his shoulders, trying to ease the stiffness. 'Good thing too – this'll probably be all I do.'

'Well, 'tis likely,' the boy conceded. 'Though Donithorn won't always be captain, you'd get an easier ride with someone else.'

'So you noticed that too, eh? I did wonder if I'd imagined it.'

Matthew had observed other ground-breaking groups; the tutworker simply held the drill steady and let his two 'boys' wield their hammers, and never a curse or a shout passed between them. In stark contrast, Donithorn's venom had dripped as cold and steady as the water from the rock overhead. Matthew and this lad, Tommy, had put their backs into smashing the drill deep into the rock, and each time it had been Matthew's turn Donithorn had had something to say about the weakness behind the blow.

'The lad's half your age, Pen'aligon, and he's hittin' three times as hard!'

Matthew had known full well this was untrue, but in the thin, flickering light from the single candle he'd been unable to tell if his partner was surprised at the taunts – it was some small comfort to know he had been. When it had been time to put the black gunpowder into the hole they'd made, Matthew half-expected Donithorn to tell him to wait right there while the damn thing blew.

But the shift was over at long last, and warmth and comfort just a wash and a short walk away. Anna would have opened the Tinner's by now, and it would already be filling up, thanks to four months' worth of hard graft, determination and effort. Matthew felt the familiar twist inside as he contemplated walking into the bar. The smell of that pungent air would always make him tremble and doubt himself, but the thought of Anna's calm smile brought with it a welcome strength, and changed the sensation from trepidation into one of anticipation.

At home he splashed water on his face, sloshed much more of it over his chest and armpits, and changed into a clean shirt before going downstairs to the shop. Freya and Mairead had their heads together, as always, and he smiled to see it; they brought out the best in each other, these two, and it was a long time since he'd seen Mairead flicker out of a conversation and disappear into her own little world.

'I'm going to help out at the Tinner's,' he said as he passed through to the front door. Freya and Mairead exchanged a glance that made him roll his eyes. 'She's busy, and Joe Trevellick's got a bad back!'

'So you're just being neighbourly?' Freya asked.

'That's kind of you,' Mairead put in, her voice all soft innocence. 'I'm sure it's appreciated.'

'Girls—'

'Papá, why don't you just come out with it?' Freya said. 'We both know, and we're both pleased!'

Matthew looked from one to the other and threw caution to the winds. 'All right then, we're getting married.' He laughed. 'See, you didn't know *that*, did you?' Then he caught sight of Mairead's face, and he could have kicked himself; it was not his place to break news like this, it was her mother's.

But before he had a chance to say anything further, Freya had thrown her arms around his neck. 'You are perfect for one another! And Mairead and I will be sisters.'

'It won't be for a good while yet,' Matthew said quickly, hoping that would chase away the doubt on Mairead's face. 'And I do understand about your father.'

'I *am* glad.' But she seemed to be making an effort to sound convincing. 'It's just ... a surprise. Will we live here, with you?'

'We haven't talked about that.' In truth he hadn't even thought about it. 'As I said, it's a long way off. We'll have to save a lot of money first.'

Freya laid a hand on his arm. 'It's the best news I've had since Mama told me I was coming back home.'

He patted the back of her hand. 'Good. Now I'd best get off before it gets too busy. I won't be too late back.'

Anna's face, when he walked through the door of the Tinner's, was enough to banish every dark thought that had plagued him from the start of today's shift. She paused in the middle of pouring a threepenny pint of mixed beer for Brian, and sent him one of her bright, warm smiles. Perhaps he hadn't been wrong to tell the two girls, after all, but he'd better warn Anna that he'd done so.

During a lull, he gestured for her to meet him outside, and she called Esther to take over for a minute. Out in the yard, that blasted cat, Arric, wound himself around Matthew's feet and made him stumble into Anna.

She caught at his arm, laughing. 'Steady on, sailor!'

'Anyone would think I'd been drinking your profits.' He frowned at the startled look on her face. 'What is it?'

'I really believe that's the first time I've ever heard you even mention it, never mind joke about it.'

He nodded, and his voice quietened. 'I suppose it's down to you that I can. It makes a difference, knowing you have some faith in me.'

'Of course I have faith in you. I love you.' She smiled, and traced a line down his sleeve to his wrist. 'I've been told it comes with the job.'

'I'm glad to hear that, because I've got a small confession to make.'

She eyed him suspiciously. 'You ate all my bull's eyes?'

'No, but if I'd known you had some, I would've.'

321

'I believe you.' She prodded him in the ribs. 'So, what's the confession?'

He drew her close and cleared his throat. 'I told the girls we planned to marry.'

Anna didn't react as he'd hoped, with a shrug and a philosophical word or two. Instead she stepped out of his embrace, and her face went oddly blank. 'What did Mairead say?'

'She was less pleased than Freya.' He shook his head. 'Anna, I understand, it's not long since she lost her own pa. Can you make her understand I'm not trying to take his place? I've told her it's a way off yet.'

Anna relaxed a little. 'She likes you a great deal, you know. It's not that she'd believe you wanted to replace Finn.'

'Tell her we'll wait until she's ready. As long as it takes.'

'And you'd be happy to do that?' A hint of humour came back into her expression, and he feigned mild panic.

'Oh, God. Um. Is the right answer: no, I'd marry you tonight if you'd let me?'

'Correct!' She slipped her arms around his waist again, and rested her head on his chest. 'Don't take it personally, Matthew. She's had a hard few months, and she's just—'

'I know, she's just beginning to settle in. I thought the same thing.'

'So we'll wait, but we don't have to keep it a secret anymore?'

'If you're ready to tell the world, I am too.'

'Well, the town, at least. I'm even reasonably sure most of them' – she jerked her head towards the pub – 'will be happy for us.'

He laughed. 'Best not to expect too much.'

'Fair point,' she conceded, and stretched on tip-toe to kiss him. He returned the kiss, enjoying the press of her body against his as she abandoned the attempt to keep her own balance. It reminded him of the way she had leaned into him as they stood atop the lower wall at Caernoweth Fort; a gesture of trust, affection and familiarity.

'I'd better get back,' Anna said with obvious reluctance. 'Esther will be leaving soon, to tend to Joe.'

'Poor bloke.' He grinned. 'Go on then. I'll bring the new barrel and fetch the empty.'

Anna went in to take over the bar again, and Matthew went into the store room. He rolled the fresh barrel of ale up through the narrow passage, and Anna, serving Brian Cornish a fresh pint, gestured with her booted foot at the empty.

'That one.'

Matthew saluted, earning himself an arched eyebrow. He was still smiling when he pushed open the door to the store room and dragged the empty barrel inside, and it wasn't until the door slammed shut behind him that he realised he was not alone.

James saw Brian Cornish's figure ambling towards the Tinner's Arms ahead of him, and quickened his pace. Their acquaint-anceship was a decidedly odd thing, grown out of Brian's long friendship with Roland and transferred to his son with no small amount of reservation. But he was a fair-minded man, and, like most working men, too much concerned with making a living to bear ill will. For James's part, the empty space left by

Roland had been in danger of becoming filled with guilt and regret, but Brian, sensing a responsibility to his late friend, had stepped in. They made a familiar sight now, the two of them. Skippers both, although of wildly varying experience.

'First drink's on me,' James said, drawing level.

'Celebratin' something?'

'You'll hear soon enough anyway,' James said, a smile tugging at his lips. 'I'm getting married.'

Brian's face registered mild surprise, but that was all. 'That'll be to Miss Carne, then?'

'How did you know?' James couldn't help feeling a little bit deflated.

Brian tapped his nose, then relented. 'She told young Ellen Scoble she had a fancy for you. I should think she was hoping it would get back to Ellen's brother.'

'Her brother?'

'David Donithorn.'

'Ah.' He'd heard Juliet and Donithorn had been seen together as recently as last year. The lad was married, too – what had she been hoping he would do? He certainly wasn't the type to throw everything away on the strength of a piece of gossip.

'You know what it's like here, once word do get out,' Brian added, as he led the way into the bar.

'Heaven help us when the guild finds out she's having a baby then.' As he spoke the words he felt a lurch of real pleasure.

He'd gone home that night, his mind full of the news, and the more he thought about it, the more solidly the notion settled inside him. And he had thought of very little else ever since. He would be pressed for money for a time, and dreams of renovating the old fort were certainly dashed, thanks to Matthew Penhaligon's stubbornness; by the time James had saved enough to even think about it, any one of a hundred companies would have beaten him to it. Trubshaw had certainly been right about that. But there would be other projects. Some things were more important, the others would wait.

If he kept working hard, he would be able to save enough money to rent somewhere in town. Then, provided he kept up with all the latest learnings in his trade, he would be in a position to compete for those increasingly frequent projects. It would be worth the waiting, now he would have a child to whom it would pass one day. Fry and Son, Architects ... and if it was a girl, well why not Fry and Daughter? There was no reason a girl should not learn as well as a boy.

Anna Garvey served him his beer without comment, and some of his pleasure in the day faded beneath her look of contempt. Brian too, looked uncomfortably caught in the middle, and James suddenly felt worn out by all the pointless bitterness. With this new start, perhaps now was the time to put bygones where they belonged.

'Mrs Garvey,' he said, 'I hope you don't mind my saying, I'm pleased for you and Matt. He's a good bloke, and, well, I've regretted the sour words between us.'

'And deeds.'

'Those too. I don't know if you knew, but we were the best of friends all the way through childhood.'

She nodded. 'That's why it hurt him so much.'

'I know. It just seemed that it was the perfect answer

to everything. I didn't think about how it would look to Matthew.'

'Did you tell him this?'

'I honestly can't remember. We both said a lot.'

'Would you take him back on the boats?'

James frowned. Apologising for a clumsy attempt at making the best of a bad situation was one thing, but he'd be damned if he was prepared to accept all the blame for its failure. 'He would never come back and work for me, you know that as well as I do. Besides, there's no place for him on the *Pride* anymore.'

'So you're still hoping the mine will break him, and he'll come running to you to make that exchange after all?'

'I made that offer in good faith, Mrs Garvey. He refused it, because he's a pig-headed idiot who doesn't care about what he does to everyone around him. That's the end of it.' He picked up his glass and drank deeply, wishing he'd never opened his mouth. A tight-lipped Anna suddenly found something to do at the other end of the bar, and when she'd gone James caught Brian's eye and shook his head, and Brian shrugged and turned away again.

James sighed. What was it about Matthew Penhaligon that brought out the very worst in him? And vice versa? Once again, just when their enmity had looked to be giving way to some kind of truce, one of them had opened his mouth and spat the chewed remnants of the white flag in the other's face.

Matthew's first thought was, *Donithorn*! He heard the scuffle of shoes, and a moment later a pair of hands grabbed his shirt-front, whirled him around, and slammed him against the door.

The breath left his body in a grunt, but as he blinked and his eyes adjusted to the gloom, he picked out the outline of a tall man, roughly his own height, and his fist shot out and clipped his assailant beneath the jaw.

The man stumbled back, and Matthew reached behind him and jerked the door open, letting the late evening sun spill into the store room. The intruder's hand rose to block the glare, and all Matthew could see was a well-dressed man with a neat beard and dark hair.

'Who the bloody hell are you?'

The man straightened, and his hand dropped. 'I might ask you the same question.' Matthew barely had time to register the unmistakable Irish accent, before the stranger's next words cut straight through the dust-filled air between them. 'But instead I think I'm going to ask you exactly what you're doing with my wife.'

'Your *wife*?'

'Her who you were just in a clinch with, right there in your yard. Nice, cosy little chat you were having, and it's interesting to discover I'm apparently dead.' The man's voice turned conversational, but with a brittle edge. 'Still, it's good to know you're not going to rush things, so thank you for that, at least.'

Matthew's mind could not alight on a single one of the questions that clamoured there, and he stared at the man as if the answers would suddenly be forthcoming without any prompting.

At last he found his voice. 'She must have had a good reason to say she was widowed.'

'Oh, I'm positive she has. Sure, wouldn't you like to go and ask her what that reason was?'

Matthew had never wanted anything more. He felt sick, and a churning fury was beginning to creep through him, but he couldn't have said whether it was directed at this man, or at Anna, or even at himself.

He stepped away from the doorway and gestured for the man – Finn, wasn't it? – to go first. 'Come on then,' he said, relieved to hear his voice was steady. 'Let's find out the truth.'

'Truth!' The man laughed, but there was no mirth in it. 'Your woman there wouldn't know the truth if it came to her boxed, and tied up with fancy bloody ribbon.'

The anger exploded at last, and swamped what was left of Matthew's control. He lunged forward and grabbed Finn's jacket, and his free hand swept around in another blow that this time caught the Irishman high on the cheekbone. Both men fell, and somehow Finn managed to twist so that he landed on top, with one knee in Matthew's diaphragm and all his weight behind it.

For a terrifying moment Matthew struggled to breathe, certain he would never be able to do so again; his mouth opened wide in a desperate quest for oxygen, and just when he thought he was going to pass out, his muscles unlocked and the air moved through him again. There was a degree of pain now, with each outward breath, but relief and anger gave him enough strength to push Finn off balance, and to roll to a kneeling position.

He gained his feet before the Irishman, still breathing hard, and trying to ignore the rising nausea. 'Why have you come after her, if you feel like that?' The words came out choppy and broken, and he braced one hand on the door frame, the other trying to massage the pain away.

'You ought to hear it from her,' Finn said. 'Look, I didn't—'

'Shut up.' Matthew straightened, with some difficulty. 'Get on in there then, and let's hear what she's got to say.'

Finn tugged his jacket straight. 'She told me about you, you know.'

Matthew blinked. 'What? When?'

'When she left Ireland.'

'But we've only—'

'Save your lies, you deserve each other.' Finn brushed past him. Matthew followed, taking slow, deep breaths, but grateful in a dark way for the nagging ache; it helped to eclipse the shock, and the dismay that was beginning to unravel inside him. Anna. Sweet and kind, clever and generous . . . and promised to him in marriage. All those things were undoubtedly true, but what else was she?

James tilted his glass for the last of his ale, and set it back on the bar. 'I'm sorry, Brian. I know you'd prefer to see Matt and me on civil terms.'

Brian shrugged. 'None o' my concern. But I'll advise you to be civil to Mrs Garvey at any rate. Your quarrel's with Matthew, it ain't with her.'

James looked along the bar, to where Anna was talking to John Rodda's wife. 'I know.'

'She weren't trying to trip you up, you know. Get you to go against your decision. She weren't beggin' for a job for him.'

'I know!' James sighed. 'She was just . . . asking.'

'She've seen what the mine's doing to her man, that's all. She knows he's not built for underground.'

'All right! Enough.'

'Well then.' Brian took the last of his own drink. 'Let's walk back down to 'Stennack. Bit of air'll do you good.'

He stood, but before either of them could take a step across the floor, the door behind the bar crashed open and a stranger stumbled in, pushed by an unseen hand from beyond. Anna gave a low cry of horror at the sight of him.

Matthew followed, his face pale and furious. 'Anna!'

Anna's eyes were wide, and fixed on the newcomer. James thought he'd never seen anyone look so terrified, and he took a half-step back towards the bar in case violence broke out. Both men looked more than capable of it.

'Matthew,' Anna said, when she could speak, 'find Mairead. Take her away. Now!'

But Matthew just gripped the stranger's shoulder, tight enough to make him wince. 'I bloody knew it. He's hurt you. You go for Mairead, Brian. She's at the shop. Take her somewhere out of this bastard's reach. Everyone else, get out! Now!'

Brian caught at James's sleeve and gestured to the two men,. 'I wouldn't trust either o' they two just now,' he muttered, echoing James's own fears, 'so if you're the man I think you are you'll step up for her should she need you. I'll come back d'rectly.'

The rest of the pub's customers eyed the two men and the woman behind the bar with great interest, as if they were about to perform some kind of play; James had the uncomfortable feeling that the more bloody that play, the more appreciative the audience was apt to be. Matthew's request for them to leave had fallen on deaf ears.

James cleared his throat. 'Perhaps you ought to come through here, Mrs Garvey?'

She ignored him and spoke to Matthew. 'Let him go.'

Matthew threw her an angry look, 'Not until you tell me he's no threat to you.' He tightened his hold and spoke grimly to the stranger. 'Which one was it you hit, your wife or your daughter? Both?'

'I'd never raise a hand to either of them, damn you. Tell him, Anna, for God's sake!' The man was turning pale, and James saw Matthew's fingers had sunk into the muscle at the juncture of his captive's neck and shoulder. He winced in sympathy, and didn't entirely share Matthew's conviction that the man was dangerous.

Anna put a hand on Matthew's arm, and he shrugged it off. A look of pain flickered on her face, but she went on, more quietly now. 'Look, Finn's never hurt either one of us. I give you my word, that's the *truth*!'

'Truth? That'll make a nice change,' Matthew said, and she visibly flinched at the bitterness in his voice.

'Matthew, please!' She looked at Finn, and her face was full of misery and guilt, but not fear. 'He never would. Let him go.'

Doctor Bartholomew's cool voice cut across the bar room. 'You're going to cause some permanent damage to that shoulder, Penhaligon, if you don't ease up.'

'It's no concern of yours,' Matthew flung at him, but James was relieved to see his fingers loosen their grip. His voice changed, lost its hard edge. 'Anna, why ...?' He shook his head, clearly struggling to find the right question, and giving up. He released Finn and stepped away, and James could see it had taken a great deal for him to do so.

Finn massaged his shoulder, scowling. 'She's ruined my career, my life. Everything. And you?' He eyed Matthew with the kind of distaste usually reserved for the leavings of a dog on a man's shoe. 'You have no idea what kind of woman you've taken up with.'

'Then tell me,' Matthew said bleakly, still looking at Anna.

Finn leaned back against the door jamb. 'She's a liar, you've finally learned that much, but when I tell you the rest of it you'll—'

'Stop it, Finn,' Anna whispered. She had gone dead white, and gripped the edge of the bar. 'Please ... I'll do whatever you want.'

'You'll come back with me.'

Anna's shoulders sagged. 'All right. But just me. Mairead will stay here. You'll not contact her.'

Matthew's breath exploded in a curse, and he stared at her. 'You're going? Just like that?'

At last Anna turned to him, and now she just sounded weary. 'I have to.'

Matthew took a step towards her, but halted before he reached her and his hands opened and closed helplessly. 'You promised to *marry* me! Why, when you knew you couldn't?'

'I thought, hoped, maybe ... in time it would be all right.'

'How the hell could it be?' Matthew gestured at Finn. 'And what did you tell him?'

'She took the coward's path,' Finn said, when Anna didn't reply. 'Left a letter to say she was moving away, to some town on the other side of Ireland. With you.'

'No,' Anna said quickly. 'I said I'd met *someone*. I just needed you to be angry enough to let us go. But there was no one. Not then.'

Finn brushed off the details. 'Another lie to add to your list of sins.'

'How did you find me?' Anna's voice was strained.

'Oh I've known since about a week after you left.' Finn gave a short laugh. 'Your solicitor came to the house looking for you; apparently you'd "forgotten", and signed the transfer deed for this bolt-hole with your maiden name. He came to ask you to sign it again in your married name.'

Matthew shook his head. 'You're trying to tell us he didn't notice at the time? You don't expect us to believe it, surely?' He seemed to be clutching at anything that would make a lie of this man's words, anything that would restore his faith in the woman with whom he'd fallen in love. But it was gradually being eroded beneath his fingers.

'Her name is Anna Casey.' Finn shrugged. 'Garvey could easily be mistaken for it, at a glance, and it wasn't until it was dug out again for this transaction that his clerk noticed the discrepancy. Might never have come to light otherwise.'

Matthew folded his arms across his chest as if restraining himself from reaching out and striking Casey; James saw the reddened patch on the Irishman's cheekbone and guessed it wouldn't be the first time.

'This is between man and wife,' he said, keeping his voice calm. 'Matt, why don't you let them talk, maybe they can come to an agreement that means Mrs Garv ... Mrs Casey can stay.'

'I don't care whether she stays or not,' Matthew said, but the pain on his face was clear to everyone, particularly Anna, who was plainly distraught. But not distraught enough to offer an explanation, James noted. Sympathy for her was falling away rapidly, and a quick glance around the room showed the same thoughts passing between the other customers. Mrs Gale, at a table near the window with two of her friends, had a look of quiet triumph on her face, and was giving knowing nods to her companions. Doctor Bartholomew, who James would have expected to be doing the same, instead looked startled, and even a little dismayed. Perhaps Anna had made more of an impression on him than he'd expected.

James's attention was drawn back to the bar as Matthew turned and grasped Finn's jacket, yanking him off the door jamb. He dragged him around and thrust him towards Anna.

She moved aside just in time to avoid a painful collision. 'Matthew, stop it!'

'Go with him!' His eyes were bright and furious, and his breathing fast, and it was only at that moment that James realised he'd misinterpreted that gesture of restraint; instead of hitting out, Matthew seized the nearest bottle off the shelf and tore the cork free. He drank deeply, his hand shaking on the bottle's neck, and when Anna breathed his name in despair he swallowed once more, wiped his mouth with the back of his hand, and said in a low, hoarse voice, 'Just go.'

A moment later he himself had gone, still clutching the bottle, and slammed the door shut behind him. Anna's face was carved from granite, her slender hands clenched, her knuckles white. When she spoke her voice was ice.

'I'll never forgive you for this, Finn Casey.'

'The man's an alcoholic,' Finn said, in wondering tones, ignoring her and staring at the closed door. 'No one but an alcoholic could take rum like that. Oh, my dear girl, what *have* you become mixed up in?'

'He hadn't touched a drop for years,' Anna said bitterly. 'Although why it's any concern of yours I don't know.'

'Are you not going after him?'

'Thanks to you he's made it quite clear he wants nothing more to do with me.'

'Very wise of him,' Finn said. 'I'd have been quite happy if I'd never seen your face again. Although taking my daughter from me was a low, vicious blow. Why did you do it?'

Anna ignored the question. 'Why have you come here now, Finn, since you hate me so much?'

Finn gave her a peculiar, tight smile. 'I'm here because things have moved on since you left. And now it's time to answer for them.'

Chapter Twenty

Matthew's stomach revolted against the onslaught of cheap rum, but he somehow kept the stuff down, swallowing with grim determination, and breathing slowly until the roiling sensation eased. His head grew lighter the faster he walked, and the bottle slipped and slid in his sweaty hand. He just tightened his grip and took another swig.

His mind clamoured with memories. Those wide, ingenuous smiles; her laughter at the dinner table, free and joyful; the impish look she got in her eye when she was teasing him; the softness of her expression when she looked at him, her hands light on his chest; the low, breathy quality her voice took on when they moved closer together . . . how much of it was truth, and how much an act, playing a part in order to settle down here?

And did it matter anyway? For her own twisted purpose, whatever it might be, she had lied. To him and to her husband, and possibly even to her daughter as well as his own.

To the doctor, the guild, her customers, the Trevellicks ... everyone. Damn her! Matthew's breath hitched and he dashed a hand across his eyes; he would not weep for her. He would do his feelings more justice if he were, instead, to weep for Freya – the child didn't deserve parents like the ones she'd been cursed with. Look at him now, so weak. Pathetic.

He swayed under the memory of the day Isabel had taken her away to London. The grief had been like a whip then, too; slicing into him every time he pictured Freya's dark, sorrowful eyes on his, and the last sight of her as the carriage had rounded the corner near the top of the lane. She had returned to him, trusted him, and he'd promised her a different life, but he'd lied. He was as bad as Anna, if not worse.

He had reached the beach now. The sun rode lower in the sky but it was still warm, and the boats in the harbour swarmed with fishermen back from their work at sea and ready to start the next phase in their day. They would work until the light vanished entirely, out here ... His traitorous mind presented him with the image of a different kind of disappearing light, that which he'd experienced as he stepped onto the man-engine and was delivered, layer by layer, down to the 236 fathom level of Wheal Furzy.

The stale darkness engulfed them all just the same, foremen and workmen alike, but most of these men and boys had been working the mine since they'd been old enough to leave school; the tiny, bobbing lights from their candles illuminated sweating, dirt-black faces that knew no different life, and he had closed his mouth against the question that had almost broken free as the light faded: *how do you stand it?*

The roar of the incoming tide splintered the picture, but his skin felt suddenly clammy, and a sweat had broken out along his brow. He looked at the bottle in his hand, and his fingers twitched. He ought to throw it away. He desperately wanted to, for Freya's sake. On the other hand he also wanted to raise it to his lips, and just keep drinking until the pain in his head eclipsed the pain in his heart.

In the end he kept hold of it, and began to walk.

Penhaligon's Attic

Freya had been wrong in her assumption that Mairead and Juliet would get along well. They tolerated one another, but both regarded Freya as their closest friend, and when they were both with her she could feel the subtle tugging from each of them. Mairead's timidity in the face of Juliet's aggressive sexuality had faded, and now she merely looked at her with a mild disapproval, and Juliet still regarded Mairead as something of an interloper. Learning of Juliet's engagement to James had elicited an oddly subdued response, too, and Freya hadn't even told her the full story, so perhaps she had guessed.

However, this evening Juliet's enthusiasm had pushed aside those mutual reservations, and the three girls leaned on the sales counter, poring enviously over some of the picture books Freya had found on the shelves. Many of them depicted weddings in high society, and Juliet's sighs were making Freya smile; it appeared that hard exterior had unexpectedly harboured a heart as romantic as anyone's, which was a pleasant surprise.

'I wonder if I will ever wear anything half so beautiful,' Juliet murmured, trailing her finger over a picture of a stiff-looking bride in a straight white dress.

'I'm sure if you did, you'd look a lot happier about it,' Mairead said.

'Would James buy you such a thing?' Freya asked.

'He's got no money, has he?' Juliet reminded her. 'It don't matter about the dress, anyway, he leaves his house unlocked just for me. I can go there anytime I like. Like he said, it'll be my house soon anyway.' She flicked over the page. 'Why do all these women look so uppity?'

'She doesn't.' Mairead pointed, and Freya and Juliet leaned closer, peering at the portrait of a young woman in a beautiful, white, off-the-shoulder gown. She carried her gloves and bag with a graceful panache, and although she too was unsmiling, there was a lightness in her expression that suggested a smile was not far away.

'That's the queen!' Freya pointed at the caption. 'Just before she married King George. Look, "Princess Victoria May, eighteen-ninety-three".'

'Wasn't she beautiful?' Mairead said softly.

Juliet sniffed. 'When I wed, I'll be wearin' me ma's Sunday best. Imagine her,' she nodded at the book, 'doin' that?' She laughed. 'From what I've seen of *her* mother, it'd go round the queen twice!'

Mairead frowned. 'Don't be mean.' But Freya smiled and shook her head; it was no use pointing out that Juliet only said these things to make people laugh, or to shock them, she'd deny that until the cows came home.

'Well, I ought to go,' Juliet said, regretfully closing the

book. 'James will think I've changed my mind otherwise.' She straightened her blouse and pulled her shoulders back. 'Must be lookin' my best for my fiancé.' She grinned, and gave them a little wave as she left the shop, and Mairead shook her head.

'I don't understand the girl,' she confessed. 'Truly I don't. She says some awful things, but you can't help liking her a little bit.'

'Only a little bit?'

'Well, I *like* her well enough I suppose,' Mairead conceded, 'but I don't trust her one inch.'

'Probably wise.'

'How about you?'

'How about me what?'

Mairead gestured at the closed book. 'What kind would you choose?'

'Me?' Freya gave a short laugh. 'I'd probably have to make one out of the curtains!'

Mairead went over to the window, and draped the long, heavy curtain around her shoulders. 'This style would suit madam beautifully,' she intoned, adopting a deliberately bored-sounding voice. 'Will madam be taking it in the velvet or in the – holy mother of God!'

Freya started, then saw what had caused the sudden exclamation. A figure was standing outside the window, and although it was still light out, it was a moment before she recognised Brian Cornish. Mairead hurriedly unwound the curtain as Mr Cornish pointed at the door, and Freya pulled back the bolt.

'Mr Cornish, what is it? Papá's not here, he's—'

340

'Tid'n your pa I've come to see. It's the young miss.' His voice was tight and rushed, and he looked at Mairead, who paled.

'What . . . is it my mother?'

'She wants me to take you somewhere safe.'

'Safe? What for? Where is she?'

'She's all right. Come with me, miss.'

'You can trust him,' Freya put in, her heart racing 'Mr Cornish, what's happened? Where's Papá?'

'He's with Mrs Garvey. They'm both all right, misses. And James is there to watch out for her too. But you have to come with me.' He gestured to Mairead, who glanced at Freya, still uncertain.

Freya nodded. 'It's all right. I'll find out what's happening. Where will you take her?'

Mr Cornish hesitated. 'Mrs Garvey told me not to tell anyone. Not even her.'

'Then she stays here,' Freya said firmly. 'I can look after her.'

'But—'

'Tell me, or she's not going.'

'Will the two of you stop!' Mairead's voice cracked. 'What's *happened*, Mr Cornish?'

Mr Cornish hissed through his teeth, impatient to get away. 'Someone came to the pub, seems to have had a bit of a fight with your pa,' he added to Freya, 'but I think your ma knows him better, miss. Tall fella.'

Mairead had gone quite white. 'Does he have a beard?' she whispered.

Mr Cornish nodded. 'He do.'

'It's my father.' She turned to Freya, tears gathering in her eyes. 'I'm so, so sorry.'

Freya shook her head, bewildered. Her *father*? There could only be one explanation, and she lowered her voice. 'Did he ... beat you?'

'Seems to be the way of it,' Mr Cornish said grimly.

'No!' Mairead kept her eyes on Freya. 'Father was ... *is*, quite kind.'

Freya's relief was mixed with confusion. 'Then why did you run away? And why did you lie—'

'Miss! Now!'

Mairead drew away from Mr Cornish's grasping hand. 'I'm not leaving Mother alone!'

'She wants you away!' Freya fought to sound calm, but there was a bitter taste in her mouth as she looked at this girl she'd called her friend and even, in her heart, her sister. Papá was all tangled in this now, and she couldn't quash the sick feeling that kept rising. If things became violent ...

'Come with me, Freya?' Mairead begged. She sounded so distraught that Freya almost agreed; perhaps the blame lay solely with Anna, after all. Then she remembered the last time she'd tried to go to the beach, and swallowed hard. She'd be no use to Mairead curled up in a weeping ball in the middle of the lane. Frustration at her own weakness gave her voice a snappish tone.

'No. You go with Mr Cornish. I'll go to the Tinner's instead, and find out what's happening. I'll find you later.' The lie sat uneasily, but there was no help for it. She was more worried about Papá now, and what might be happening at the Tin Streamer's Arms.

She tried to take Mairead's hand, to comfort her, but Mairead removed it quickly and Freya did not try again; the months of lies were layered too heavily on top of the natural affection that had grown between them. It was heart-breaking to think they might never regain it, but Freya couldn't spare time worrying about it, and as she locked the door behind them, the heavy clunk of the key sounded loud and final in the empty street. The severing of a bond that had made them all but sisters.

When they reached the pub they parted company without further words, and Mairead followed Mr Cornish obediently towards Porthstennack. Freya took a deep breath and pushed the door, but it didn't move. A sick feeling of foreboding swept over her ... surely the unexpected arrival of Anna's husband would not warrant the locking of the pub? What could possibly have happened in the scant five minutes since Brian had been sent for Mairead? She stepped back and peered through the window, cupping her hands to block the glare of the evening sun.

All she could see were the backs of several people who'd risen to their feet and now faced where the bar curved around the small room. Something was happening in there, something more than a domestic quarrel. A slow trickle of anger threatened to swell into something far less manageable, and she backed away from the window and ran around to the back yard, and up through the stone-flagged passage.

There was a strong smell of rum by the door, and Freya noticed a generous splash on the floor. She pulled a face, and then her heart skipped a beat; Mr Cornish said it had looked as though there had been some kind of fight, and if Anna's betrayal had driven Papá to drink again, Freya would never forgive her...

Her lips tight, and her heart hardened against both the Garveys, Freya put a hand on the latch, but stopped short of pressing the lever to open it. Instead she listened, frowning. There was an odd kind of quiet on the other side of that door, not the quiet of an empty room, but the suspenseful, expectant hum of a good many people who'd been listening to a tale unfold. A tale Freya had missed most of, by the sounds of it, but resumed as she hesitated.

'Bleating about how it was an accident, makes no difference.' It was a male voice with a heavy Irish accent. Mairead's father. 'The law sees it another way.'

'Why do you think I left?' Anna's voice was tight and controlled. 'Look, I've said I'd come back with you and I'm keeping my word. Just promise me you'll leave Mairead alone.'

'Where are you going?' He snapped it out, and Anna responded in kind.

'To pack!'

Freya's cheek was squashed against the rough wood of the door, and she felt a sudden jolt, and then there was nothing. She stumbled forward, but slim, strong arms broke her fall before she could hit the floor.

'Freya! What in the world are you doing?' Anna clutched at her, and Freya felt the woman's breathing, fast and light. Panicked. For a second she was too stunned to react, then she went rigid and pulled away. She looked around, seeing many stunned faces, but not the one she sought.

'Where's Papá?'

'He... he left. I'm sorry.'

'Has he had a drink?'

'Freya—'

'You've ruined him.' Freya knew her soft voice was fooling no one who heard it. The anger that had been building in her was near to bursting loose now, her chest and throat were choked with it. Their lives, so carefully re-built these past three years, now lay in tatters thanks to this woman, and all she could say was *'I'm sorry'*. Freya swallowed hard, and it hurt. The pub was little more than a quarter full, but everyone's attention was on Anna, including that of a tall, bearded man she'd never seen before. So this was Mairead's poor 'dead' father.

'The last coach leaves at nine,' he said. 'We'll get the onward train from Bodmin in the morning.'

'Finn, promise me you won't—'

'Don't pack a lot, you won't be needing it. The Gardaí will be waiting when we dock.'

'Gardaí?' Freya looked at Anna. 'What's that?'

'The police,' Anna said in a hollow voice. 'There's been ... an incident.'

'Your woman there's been running from the noose,' Finn said grimly, 'and it's found her. That's all.'

Freya felt all the air go out of her in a rush. She felt blindly for the edge of the bar, and let her head fall between her outstretched arms. Her head felt light, her knees weak. 'She can't go back to that.'

'I have to.' Anna's voice was thick with tears. 'I did a ... a terrible thing. Someone died, and now I've to face the consequences.'

Freya could hardly hear her own whisper. 'What happened?'

'It was an accident.'

345

'Tell me!'

'It doesn't matter now.'

'Of course it matters! And what shall I tell Papá?'

Anna paused, and Freya heard her breath catch. 'Tell him there was only truth in the feelings I had – I *have* – for him. And that I understand why he reacted as he did.'

'You love him? That wasn't a lie?'

'No,' Anna said, her voice barely audible. 'My love for the three of you is about the only thing I know to be true.'

'Then stay!' Freya straightened and turned so quickly her head swam. She grabbed at Anna's arm. 'You can't go back there to die! It'd kill Papá too, you know it would!'

'That's not my choice. But Matthew has made his. He's gone.'

'He loves you!'

'No, sweetheart, he doesn't. Not anymore. And I can't blame him for that, now can I?' Anna gently lifted Freya's hand from her arm, and turned to Finn. 'There's nothing for me here, now. You'll get no fight from me.'

'Don't you want to say goodbye to Mairead first?' Freya blurted in desperation. 'I can find her and—'

'No!' Anna paled. 'She mustn't come here.'

'Why not?'

'Because ... it would upset her too much. I'll write and explain everything.'

'How is she?' Finn asked, surprising Freya with his suddenly softened tone. 'I've missed her. What you did was cruel to us both, Anna.'

'Cruel?' Anna whipped around, her fire returning. '*You* kept her away from school, from people her own age! You

346

stopped her from making friends who might have helped her.'

'It was for the best, to keep her out of the public eye. She'd only have been ridiculed, you know that as well as I do.'

'I do not! She's a bright, clever and honest girl, and all you ever saw in her was an embarrassment!'

'I had to have the respect of the community. And you've destroyed that, too!'

The accusations slammed back and forth between them, and soon other voices chimed in, and Freya listened to the din with rising frustration and dismay. Then she glanced at the huge clock on the wall: just after eight o'clock. Less than an hour before the coach left. She grabbed the door handle and wrenched open the door, and before she'd had time to think, she was out of the garden and running down past the Penworthy memorial towards the beach.

Papá was the only one who might talk Anna into staying, and the only place she could think of to look for him was the beach, but what if he hadn't gone there? It wasn't until she reached Hawthorn Cottage that the reality of what she was doing hit her. The distant pounding of the surf cut through the clear evening air, and her feet began to slow even as her heartbeat picked up speed. She put one hand to her chest, and where the other had caught up her skirt to hold it clear of her hurrying feet she could feel it trembling.

She dropped her skirt and lifted her other hand to her stomach, trying to subdue the rising nausea, and as her eyes closed she felt herself swaying. There was salt on her lips ... wasn't there? How could there be? She was a long way yet from the spray of the tide. She licked her lips. Yes, salt. Her clothes felt heavy, her limbs heavier. She could not bring herself to open her eyes and allow the world to right itself, for fear she would instead see only bubbles and roaring water. She was going to fail; Anna would leave to face a grim death in a country that was no longer her home, and Papá would not know anything of it until it was too late ...

She dragged a deep breath; it felt like a sharp finger jabbing beneath her breastbone, but she kept breathing. After a moment she opened her eyes: no bubbles, no water. She took a tiny step towards the beach. Her knees shook, but held her upright. She took another step. And another. She thought about Anna facing trial, and made those hesitant steps carry her onward until finally, and in something of a daze, she reached the outer boundary of Porthstennack. Swallowing the fear that swelled higher the closer she came to the sea, she cut through the alleyways between the fishermen's houses, and then re-joined the main road that wound along the sea front. There was only one place she could think of to look.

Chapter Twenty-One

Porthstennack Harbour

Matthew had wandered the length of the beach, and found a deserted spot by the headland – no one could work here, too many rocks. He sat down heavily, and the tide lapped at his boots and soaked his trousers but he barely noticed. There was a sour taste of vomit in the back of his throat, and he remembered, from his darkest days, that drink-induced dizziness usually eased if he lay flat. He groaned and spat, then stretched out at the water's edge, working his elbows into dips in the pebbles. The ripples washed over him, while the sky spun above, darkening as he watched. The sounds all around were soothing ... the rum coated his thoughts in a welcome, woolly thickness, and he closed his eyes and drifted.

He spluttered awake some time later, when a wave broke over his shirt and soaked him to the chin. Sunset had come and gone, it must be almost half past eight now, and the darkness, while by no means total, had driven the last of the fishermen back to their homes. Or to the Tinner's. Matthew looked at his hand, surprised to see it still clutching the rum bottle, and rolled over to clamber to his feet. He stood swaying for a moment, wondering if he was going to be sick, and when at last he felt his insides settle he crossed the beach and climbed onto the harbour wall, to where the *Pride of Porthstennack* was moored.

He watched her for a moment, rising and falling with the incoming tide, the familiar splash of the water lapping at her bows, her deck cleaned and stocked with freshly mended nets, ready for her next day's work. None of that work had been done by him; he'd been soaking himself, by both tide and bottle, at the time. He didn't even try to quash the rising sense of disgust in himself, but stepped aboard.

The gentle tilting of the deck under his feet felt like coming home. With one hand on the bulwark he walked the length of the trawler, breathing deeply. He still felt woozy-headed; his body was chastising him for his weakness with an undeniable savagery. He bent and placed the bottle on the deck by his feet, unwilling, even now, to cast it into the water.

'Matthew?'

'Christ!' He straightened, and peered through the shadows to see a slender, dark-haired girl with wide eyes and a heart-shaped face. 'Mairead.' He let his breath out in relief. 'I should have realised Brian would bring you here.'

She stepped closer, peering up at him worriedly. 'Is Mother all right? Please tell me!'

'She was when I left her,' Matthew said. Perhaps he should have made more effort not to sound so curt, but there it was.

She knew Anna had been lying, so she was just as much at fault.

'I'm so sorry,' she said. 'Mother told me we must keep it just between ourselves, no matter how much we liked the people here.'

'Well it doesn't matter now,' Matthew said. 'And your father seems determined to take her back to Ireland with him, so that's that.'

'She mustn't!' Mairead clasped his arm. 'Please, you must stop her!'

'You'll be all right.' Then, aware he still sounded scathing, he relented a little. 'Don't worry, we'll look after you. But for pity's sake! Tell me what you were running from if it's not your father. Mairead? Mairead!'

She was staring at him with an unsettling intensity, but when he peered closely through the descending darkness he could see her eyes fluttering. Whatever she was seeing, it wasn't him. His hands clenched into fists of frustration, and he lashed out at the wooden bulwark. The pain pulled him out of his pocket of fury, and he turned back to Mairead and pulled her close. She came willingly enough, but did not return his embrace, and it was a moment before he felt her jerk and step back.

'I'm sorry ...' She snatched a ragged breath. 'I fell into a hole again, didn't I?'

'Is that what you call it?' he said, more gently now; he had surprised himself by the depth of his sorrow for this bewildered child. She needed her mother, but her mother had sent her away. 'Here, sit down.' She did so, a short distance away, still looking terrified and miserable. 'Don't worry, we'll look after you,' he repeated. It was all he could say.

351

They sat in silence on the gently undulating deck. Mairead rested her head on her raised knees and locked her hands around her legs. Matthew tried not to think about Anna, and what might be happening at the pub, but there was nowhere else for his mind to go. No doubt she would be packing her things now, ready to return to her privileged life with her smooth-talking husband. Whatever it was she had done, Finn would be sure to forgive her; who wouldn't?

He suspected he himself would, in time, forgive her lies, even if the fact of them would never cease to hurt. What was this, after all, but simply one lover betraying another? It happened the world over, at every minute of every day. He might never again feel the thundering heartbeat and helpless excitement at the touch of a gaze on his face, or of gentle fingers on his wrist . . . he might never again know what it meant to hear his name on someone's lips and want to press his own to them to keep it there, but in time those feelings would fade. Just as they had when Isabel had gone.

'Matthew?'

He looked up. Mairead was watching him with her usual unnerving intensity. 'Yes?'

'Do *you* know why my father has come here?' Her voice was odd, light, as if she was a breath away from losing control of herself.

'Don't you?'

'No.'

He shook his head. 'I suppose because he must have grown tired of waiting for you both to return.'

She hesitated, then nodded. 'Yes. That must be it.'

'But then why would your mother tell Brian to hide you

away?' His voice rose in renewed frustration. 'For God's sake, Mairead! All these secrets and lies, why?'

Mairead stood, and walked to the other end of the deck. 'I want to tell you,' she said. Matthew stilled, and said nothing. 'But . . . do you *promise* we'll be safe here?'

She sounded so stricken that Matthew's heart contracted and he made a silent promise not to lose his temper again. '*I'll* keep you safe.'

'Father won't find me?'

So she truly was worried about him? He felt himself tensing, dreading what he might hear, but he kept his voice calm. 'Is it something about your father that brought you here?'

'No. Nothing to do with him. But you mustn't be cross with Mother either, she—'

'Papá!'

Matthew lurched to his feet and stumbled to the side of the boat. He stared down the darkened harbour wall towards the beach. 'Freya?'

'Thank God I've found you! You have to stop them!'

'What?' He jumped down, landing on the shingle with a crunch, and his insides rolled sickeningly at the impact.

Freya had stopped midway across the beach and was staring past him at the water, but when he reached her she came back to her senses and seized his sleeve. 'Come with me, stop them!'

'If Anna wants to leave, I can't—'

'But she'll *die*!'

His heart froze, and his muscles would not allow him to move. 'What?' His whisper might have blown away on the late evening breeze if Freya had not stepped closer, this time to grab the wet front of his shirt and tug him forward.

'Something happened, an accident, but if she goes back the police will get her. We must be quick, they're going on the nine o'clock coach!'

Matthew could barely make out her words through her panicked sobbing, but they trickled coldly through the sound of his own crashing heart, and at last he moved. He shoved her hands away from him and began to run, sparing only the briefest moment to turn and shout, 'Get onto the boat and stay there!'

'I can't!' Freya fell to her knees on the shingle, and Matthew skidded to a stop as realisation hit him; he hadn't once seen her here, not since her return. Three years . . . how had he not noticed? The reason for her fear came with that realisation, leaving him breathless with shock and remorse. But before he could say anything Freya had screamed out again, 'Go!'

Blessedly, Matthew heard Mairead's voice drifting down from the *Pride of Porthstennack*. 'Wait there, Freya, I'm coming.'

'Good girl,' Matthew whispered, and faced the hamlet again. He had no pocket watch, and a glance at the night sky told him only that it was clouding over again. He started to run, choosing the shorter route up the sloping shale bank that delivered him, after some desperate scrabbling, on to Paddle Lane. People moved between the houses, none of them paid him any attention. A girl was walking up the path to James's cottage, but she wouldn't find him at home; he was at the Tinner's with all the other nosy town folk, revelling in this new drama. They'd be talking about it for years to come, no doubt.

Matthew pushed himself on, cursing the moment he had tipped the rum bottle and begun a new slide into darkness. His mind might have cleared the moment he'd seen Mairead, but his limbs and innards had not finished punishing him yet.

With the light wind in his face, at least he was spared the miserable heat of nausea.

He reached the pub, and ran through the back yard and up the passageway, but when he burst through into the bar room James simply looked at him, his face pale. 'She's gone, Matt. You're too late.'

'You let him take her?'

James seemed ready to snap back at him, but Matthew twisted to look at the clock. Five minutes before nine. The coach would leave from the Caernoweth Hotel, and was well known for its punctuality ... Ignoring the rising babble of questions he pushed through the crowd to the door, pulled the latch aside, and plunged out into the evening once more.

Twenty yards ahead, just past Penhaligon's Attic, he saw them. A tall, straight-backed figure in smart clothes, and an equally poised woman walking briskly at his side. Finn carried a small case, and Anna held her skirts free of her boots as she strode between the pools of gaslight. It was as if she were the one hurrying them along.

'Hie!' Matthew shouted, and the two stopped and turned. 'Wait!'

Anna shook her head. 'Go back, Matthew.'

'This is the last coach,' Finn pointed out. 'We're not missing it.'

'Just one night,' Matthew panted as he reached them. 'I'll pay for your bed and board at the hotel myself.'

'Why would you do that?'

'Because I want ... I *need* to understand, before I'll let you take her,' Matthew said. 'Freya told me there was an accident. That they're blaming Anna for it.'

Anna's eyes brimmed with hopeless tears. 'They're not blaming me,' she said in a low voice. 'I did it. I killed a man.'

Matthew's mind reeled under the confession, and he struggled to find his voice. 'But ... it *was* an accident?'

'Yes.'

'No matter,' Finn said. 'Even if she doesn't come with me now, we know where she is. I can have the law here in a matter of minutes.' He gestured at the police house near the top of the hill. 'Come on, Anna!'

'Why?' Matthew grabbed at Finn's coat, and pulled him around. Finn jerked away and stumbled, losing his balance and sprawling in the road.

Matthew stood over him, resisting the urge to set to with his booted feet. 'Why have you come here now? Why drag her away, when you know it wasn't deliberate?'

'Because she ...' Finn swallowed what he had been going to say, 'she owes me.'

Anna and Matthew stared at him. 'Owes you?' Matthew said, in a dangerously soft voice. 'Are you telling me this is some kind of revenge? For what?'

'No. Not revenge.' Finn gained his feet, and cradled his left wrist in his right hand. He looked white in the gaslight, and there was real pain on his face, but Matthew shook off the twinge of remorse; there were more deserving recipients of his guilt than this man.

Finn stared towards the hotel, and then carefully released his injured wrist, wincing as he took out his pocket watch. 'We'll never get there in time now.'

'Good.' Matthew let out his breath and turned to Anna. 'Look, whatever's happened, you don't deserve this.'

356

Anna closed her eyes. 'I've no choice. Finn's right. The police would be knocking on my door before breakfast.'

'You can't change what she did,' Finn said, 'and you can't run from it anymore, Anna.'

Matthew whipped around to face him. 'What did you mean by her owing you? Whatever it is, the town will help pay it. She's one of us now. I'll sell the shop—'

'No!' Anna gripped his arm. 'It's Freya's future, you've said so yourself.'

'So it *is* money?'

'In a manner of speaking.' Finn sighed. 'If you want to know everything, I'll tell you. But not out here in the street.'

'Come to the shop then.'

Anna shook her head. 'I don't want your father to hear all this. I've a great fondness for the old man, and I'd hate for him to be taken poorly again.'

Matthew's memory showed him Roland, as he lay dying on his boat, and a chill crept through him. 'No, you're right. We'll clear everyone out of the pub. They wouldn't listen to me but they will to you.'

'What will you tell Robert?' she asked, as they started back towards the Tinner's.

'Nothing. There'll be nothing to tell.'

'I mean, about why I'm not around.'

He gave her a searching look, and repeated, 'There'll be nothing to tell.'

'Matthew—'

'Come on.'

*

The pub was quickly emptied of customers, although several were plainly waiting out in the street in order to keep abreast of developments, and to be the bearers of any news to the rest of the town. Mrs Gale, hitherto one of Anna's most vocal opponents, was quiet, for once, and put up no argument as she was hustled out of the door. She cast a glance over her shoulder at Anna, and looked as if she wanted to say something, but in the end she held her tongue.

James and Doctor Bartholomew hesitated, unwilling to leave her alone with the two men, but Anna nodded. 'I'll be all right.' She glanced at Matthew as she said it, and he was struck by the sadness in her expression. Had she already decided it wasn't worth fighting?

'Before you go, doctor,' Anna said, as Bartholomew took his hat from the stand. 'If you wouldn't mind staying, perhaps you'd be so kind as to look at my hus ... Mr Casey's arm.'

'What happened to it?' The doctor shot a suspicious glance at Matthew, but Finn spoke up.

'It was my fault. I tripped on the pavement and fell.'

Bartholomew clearly didn't believe him, but he said nothing further. He examined Finn's arm, then asked Anna to pass a towel and began to fashion a rough sling. Matthew watched for a moment, but before long his patience snapped.

'All right, now someone'd better tell me what happened.'

'Anna. Tell him.' Finn sounded faint, and his skin was greasy and grey as Doctor Bartholomew lifted the swollen limb and placed it in the sling. 'He's a right to know, if anyone has.'

Anna moved away and folded her arms, cupping her elbows in trembling hands. 'I was out walking alone, on the beach. It was night, and I found myself alone in the company of some young men. They were lost in drink. They became . . . ' She closed her eyes as she struggled to find the right word. 'Not amorous, that's too kind. Insistent.' She looked at Matthew and her eyes were calm again, as if the burden of the secret was eased in its telling. 'When I tried to get away from them they . . . weren't disposed to let me go. There was a struggle. I hit one of them and ran away.'

'Hit one of them!' Finn's incredulity had evidently swamped his discomfort. 'Is that what you'd call it? You left him unconscious and half-drowned!'

'It sounds very much as if she was defending herself,' Bartholomew put in coolly, and three faces swung to him in surprise. He met each set of eyes in turn, lingering longest on Anna's. 'Anyone would have done the same.'

Anna blinked, and Matthew saw the bright film of grateful tears. 'That's true,' she said in a low, thickened voice, 'but I should have gone for help.'

'You were understandably shocked.'

'Why does Anna owe you, Casey?' Matthew said, before the stunned Anna could respond. 'Come on, we know why *she* came, now it's time you told us what's brought you here.'

Finn gestured with his good hand. 'She has been taking the rents from this pub for ten years, and never told me a thing of it.'

'It's her pub, why shouldn't she be paid?'

'I'm her husband. She should have told me.'

'You'd have made me sell it,' Anna said. 'You took everything we had, and poured it into your endless black pit, and this place would have gone after it.'

'It was for *research*!'

359

It had the sound of a tired argument, and Anna brushed it off. 'The pub is the only thing of mine I had left. The only means we had of paying some of *your* bills. I'd probably have told you about it once we were back on an even keel. If we ever were.'

'How will it benefit you if she comes back?' Matthew wanted to know.

'Fergus Cassidy, the boy's father, is a banker,' Finn said. 'He's offered a reward, a substantial one, for information that leads to the arrest of his son's killer.' He watched Anna's expression carefully, and when it didn't change, his eyes narrowed. 'You *knew* who it was, didn't you? That's why you ran away.'

She didn't reply, and Matthew stared at Finn in disbelief. 'You'd have your wife killed for the sake of *money*?'

'She won't be killed!' Finn shifted in his seat, making the doctor sigh and begin re-tying the towel. 'Look, it needn't be so terrible, Anna. You'd come back to Ireland, and I'll tell them you've confessed to striking the Cassidy boy—'

'No!' Matthew slammed his hands on the bar. 'Anna, you can't risk it.'

'Shut up.' Finn spoke calmly and took Anna's hand, and Matthew was alarmed to see she did not draw away; indeed she hardly seemed to notice, it was as if she was being hypnotised. 'With my standing in the community – still intact as it is – and your willingness to confess, they're sure to go easy on you.'

'They won't!' Matthew insisted. 'Anna, you've only got his word that he'll speak for you.'

'Do you think I *want* her to die?' Finn demanded. 'I

have cared for this woman for half my life. Provided for her. Protected her. And *you've* thrown her off at the first sign of trouble!' He stood, and the cloth dropped off his arm again, but this time the doctor only gathered it up and sat quietly.

'The fact remains,' Finn went on, 'she killed a boy, they know she did it, and if I can get her to confess before they find her for themselves, it'll go better for us all.'

'Better for you,' Matthew said, but looking at Anna he felt a growing dismay; she was slipping away before his eyes. 'You can't believe they'll let you off with prison.'

'It doesn't matter.' She turned a haunted look on him. 'I'm guilty. I shouldn't be looking to be let off.'

'But why didn't you tell the truth when it happened?' Finn asked. 'If it actually *was* self-defence?'

'Of course it was! But it would have been my word against Liam Cassidy's when he woke. Besides, even attempted murder carries the death penalty.'

'But it wasn't attempted murder, was it?' Finn said grimly. 'The boy died.'

'He was in a coma when I left. I still had hopes for him.'

'Better for you he did die, then. And carried your name into his grave.'

'No!' Anna went white. 'How can you say that? I never meant to harm him!'

'It doesn't matter now. Fergus Cassidy was all set to invest in my research, until this happened and he withdrew from business altogether. But now he's offered this reward, and that money will make up for everything you've robbed me of these past years.'

'How did you know it was me?'

'I didn't, for sure. Liam's friends described the woman to the police. As soon as they came asking questions, I realised why you'd gone. I already knew where, of course. And now I know the full story.' He took a step closer to Anna, but Matthew jerked him back, heedless of his injured wrist.

'Steady,' Bartholomew barked at him. 'It might be broken!'

'I couldn't care any less if you paid me to,' Matthew said tightly. 'Get out, Casey, and take your filthy accusations with you. She's not coming.'

'I am!' Anna stood. 'Matthew, please – don't make this impossible for us. He's right, I do owe him. And I owe Liam Cassidy's father.'

'You don't!' Matthew took hold of her shoulders and made her look at him. 'The boy was a thug, and a dangerous one. You had no choice! And as for owing him,' he jerked his head towards Finn, 'you owe him no more than I do.'

'We're married!' Finn growled. 'What's hers is mine, it's the *law*!'

Bartholomew gave an undignified snort. 'Did the Married Women's Property Act completely pass you by?'

'She didn't even want to risk being known to be married!' Finn exclaimed. 'Why do you think she was so sly as to sign in her maiden name?'

Matthew stared at him. Finn opened his mouth to say more, but Matthew held up a hand, and, to his surprise, Finn stopped. An idea was forming, but worry, anger, and the conflict of right and wrong in his own heart, were preventing it from taking shape.

'Don't let them leave,' he told the doctor, and went out into the passage. To his surprise it was empty; the townsfolk had more respect for Anna's privacy than he'd given them credit for. He leaned on the wall and closed his eyes, and tried to think past the voices from the bar room that spilled through into the passage.

'Where is Mairead?'

'Hidden. Safe.'

'Does she still have those ... moments?'

'Not so often now. Only when she's deeply upset, or particularly tired.'

Matthew flinched; it certainly hadn't been physical tiredness that had thrown the girl into one of her 'mind holes' on the boat.

'I've been watching her these past months,' Doctor Bartholomew put in. 'I'm sorry, Mrs Garvey, I know it was underhand of me, but something Mrs Gale said sparked my interest. I believe it's a form of epilepsy.'

Finn spoke up. 'I agree,'

'You *knew*?' Anna said. 'All this time?'

Matthew frowned, his idea fluttering to the perimeter of his mind again; Anna sounded lost, and bewildered, and all he could think about now was the fact that nothing he could say would ease it for her.

'Why didn't you tell me, Finn?' she said bleakly. 'We could have found some help for her.'

'There is no help. And once she was diagnosed and it was on paper, as I'd have been obliged to do, she would have been forbidden to get married.' He sounded gentler now that he was talking of his daughter, and it gave Matthew a flicker of hope. 'I don't believe you'd have wanted that for her, any more than I did.'

'He's right,' Bartholomew put in, 'it's against the law for her to marry.'

'But you *knew*,' Anna said again.

Finn sighed. 'She's never had a major seizure as far as I'm aware. But when I noticed those absences, I suspected. So, you see, I wasn't as uncaring or unaware as you thought.'

'No. But you should have told me.'

'What good would it have done?' A pause. 'So, you'll come back, then?'

'Here, doctor, let me do that.' Then, in a quieter voice, she said, 'Yes. I'll come back.'

There was another pause, then Finn spoke again. 'I'm not so sure I trust you, Anna. I find it hard to believe you'd give it all up without a fight.'

'It's a pub, nothing more.'

'I was talking about him. Your miner.'

Matthew held his breath.

'He's made it quite clear he won't have me,' Anna said at last. 'There's nothing here for me now.'

Matthew jerked upright off the wall in dismay. But when he thought over what he'd said since he'd stopped them in the street, he realised she had no reason to believe otherwise. He'd shown friendship and concern, nothing more. Heart pounding, he abandoned thinking through his fledgling idea, and shoved open the door to the bar. Anna had taken the cloth from Bartholomew and was tying a new makeshift sling around her husband's neck.

Matthew addressed Finn. 'Right. You feel Anna owes you for keeping the rents for this place a secret all these years.'

'I know she does.'

'And this banker has withdrawn his offer of support for your research?'

'He never had the chance to make an offer,' Finn pointed out. 'His son was killed, remember? Tends to distract a man when that happens.'

Matthew ignored the sarcasm. 'Anna, you say you feel the need to see justice done. To confess your crime and take your punishment?'

'It's only right.'

'But surely, if Finn hadn't come looking for you, you'd have carried on living here quite happily without confessing anything?'

'I didn't know the boy was dead!' Anna's eyes were filled with hurt surprise but Matthew pressed on, in his reluctant role of devil's advocate.

'Maybe not. But you knew he was badly hurt.'

'I know, I keep telling you I'm ready—'

'Did you kill him deliberately?'

'You know I didn't!'

Matthew softened his voice. 'Then there's no more reason to take the blame, than if you'd known. Look, Finn wants reward money . . .' He took a deep breath, then plunged ahead. 'Why not just let him take the pub instead?'

Finn's face went slack with astonishment, and then sudden interest. He looked speculatively around him, and Matthew's own gaze followed, taking in everything from the rows of bottles and the barrels stacked ready to go out, to the polished tables and chairs, the coloured glass in the lamps, and the pictures made of broken, coloured shells on the walls. The fresh smells of pipe tobacco and ale hung in the air, as a reminder of those who had just been evicted by their landlady. And, tellingly enough, they'd gone with no questions, and no protest. Matthew had not been a regular here for more than eight years, but even he knew the place had changed drastically since Anna had taken over.

'It's a good business now, Casey,' Matthew said. 'A lucrative one. You could either sell it on, or run it yourself. Your choice.'

'Even if he wants it, or if he'll take it,' Anna stammered, 'I don't know if it's … I'll be looking over my shoulder for the rest of my life, in case the Gardaí come for me.'

'We'll tell them you're dead.' But even as he spoke, the enormity of this desperate plan sank home; the level of fraud that this would involve, not to mention that the trust of the whole town would be tested … he shouldn't have said anything, it was hopeless. His spirits plummeted at the knowledge, and he wished he'd kept his ideas to himself.

'Are you completely mad?' Finn demanded, confirming his fears. 'Who would believe something so convenient? Anna, get your things.'

'Wait, Mrs Casey!' Bartholomew looked a little ill, but he went on, with quiet determination, 'They won't come looking for you. Your husband will return to Ireland, in possession of a certificate that says you drowned shortly after your arrival.'

'Drowned?' Anna's voice came out very small, but with a new tremor of hope.

'Can't hang a dead woman,' Bartholomew said, with grim humour, but there was a greasy sheen of sweat on his brow. 'Look, I've never falsified a document in my life, and I never will again, but I'd be prepared to do it now.' He gave an embarrassed shrug. 'I've not given you an easy time of it, I'll admit that. But you've . . . ' he waved his hand at the bar room, 'You've done something here. I don't just mean the pub. What with the guild, and getting the men involved, and giving up your time for people like me, who've treated you really quite shoddily.' He nodded. 'You've helped build a real community. That makes you as much part of this town as your ancestor.'

'Ancestor?' Finn frowned.

Anna ignored him. 'But is this really possible?'

'It's the only way you'll be safe.'

Matthew couldn't say anything at first, and he just breathed out slowly, awed as much by the offer as by the unexpected loyalty that inspired it. Matthew recalled Mrs Gale's odd expression as she'd been ushered out of the pub, too – she might have been vindicated in her belief that Anna had been hiding something, but she would have no wish to see her dragged away to die. He had the feeling the doctor was right; both Caernoweth and Porthstennack would close in around Anna and Mairead, and do whatever must be done to protect them. He felt a twist of pride for them all.

'What do you say, Mr Casey?'

'Say I agree, just for a minute,' Finn cautioned. 'Think about it, Anna, you'll always be known as the boy's killer. You might have been given no choice, but the papers will look for every reason to lay the blame at your door.'

'Let them,' Anna said, and Matthew wondered if she knew she'd stood straighter as she said it. 'My reputation won't affect you, Finn. You'll have done the right thing from the outset. People will respect you for it, not condemn you.'

'What about your family?'

Anna swallowed, and some of the light went out of her eyes. 'Better they think me dead, too. I couldn't bear to see their faces.'

'Once they knew it was a mistake they'd forgive you,' Finn said. 'They love you, Anna.'

'And I love them. They know that.' Her voice stuck, and Matthew wanted to step forward and take her hand, but this was between her and her husband, now.

'You'd lose any of the property you still owned in Ireland,' Finn went on. 'You'd be penniless. Entitled to nothing. It's a poor existence in a place like this, if you've nothing behind you.'

'Then let us live here,' Anna's eagerness returned. 'We'll run the place for you, and pay rent to you out of the profits. That'll make us work hard for you.'

Finn frowned. 'I don't know that my conscience will allow that.'

'Will you give me this chance, or not?' Anna faced him squarely. 'Doctor Bartholomew is right; the choice comes down to a false death here, or a real death in Ireland. So which will you have on your *conscience*, Doctor Casey?'

Finn blinked at her fierce tone, then a reluctant smile crossed his face. 'That's more like the Anna I've known all these years.' He pursed his lips, and looked around again, but Matthew could see his mind was all but made up. 'Mairead will inherit this place. No doubt you've already bequeathed it to her in your will, to stop me getting my hands on it.'

'She'll make it over to you as a deed of gift.'

'And you know this for sure?'

'Oh, yes. I do.' Anna sounded strangely positive now, all

doubt and hesitation had fled from her voice and from her manner. She folded her arms. 'Do I have your word you'll take the certificate back with you, and pass it over to the Gardaí?'

Finn nodded. 'The good doctor here will retain the original, in any case.'

'And you'll be entered into the parish records accordingly,' Bartholomew added. 'You might even still be able to claim the reward, Mr Casey. It'd look doubly self-sacrificing on your part, to have travelled all this way, only to learn of your wife's unfortunate loss at sea.'

'Who knows?' Finn mused. 'Perhaps I'll be a wealthy man again.'

'And you'd be welcome to it,' Anna said. 'I mean it. I wish you nothing but well.'

'Come with me,' Bartholomew said to Finn. 'I'll properly bind your arm, and write out the certificate. You can sleep on my couch tonight. The townspeople are one thing, but we don't want to raise any questions at the hotel.'

Finn inclined his head, and indicated that the doctor should go through the back and wait for him in the passage. When it was just himself, Matthew and Anna left, he took his wife's hand in his good one.

'I know you won't believe this, but I'm sorry. You feeling you couldn't confide in me about any of it came as a shock. I didn't know you were *so* unhappy, I just thought ...' he broke off, and sighed.

'You thought that if you got the backing you could make it all better.' Anna smiled sadly. 'Well, it would have helped a lot of people, right enough, but it wouldn't have mended the fences we'd broken getting there.'

'We'll never know now, will we?' He gave her a searching look. 'I wish you'd let me see Mairead before I go.'

'No.' She withdrew her hand and stepped away from him. 'That's out of the question.'

'But why?'

'I'll get her to write to you once everything's settled at home.'

'Once you know I've kept my word, you mean.' Finn shook his head. 'You need have no fear on that score. I feel for Cassidy's father, but nothing will bring the boy back, and at least this way justice will be seen to have been done.'

He held out his hand to Matthew. 'Good luck with this one,' he said, with a dry and unexpected flash of humour. 'Lord knows you'll need it.'

'I've told you,' Anna said, embarrassed, 'Mr Penhaligon has no wish to continue a relationship with me.'

'Oh yes he bloody does,' Matthew said. 'Mr Penhaligon wishes very much to do just that.'

Anna raised her face to his, her eyes questioning. Matthew was vaguely aware of the door opening and closing as Finn Casey left, and then his arms were around Anna, and he felt her clutching at the back of his waistcoat as if she'd never be prised free.

Her voice was muffled against his chest. 'You said—'

'I know what I said. I was an idiot. I'm sorry.'

She sniffed, and moved back to look at him. 'You were hurt, I can't blame you for that.'

'I love you, Anna. I know I keep forgetting to tell you, and you might have to get used to that, but it will never be any less true for it.'

'I love you too.' She stretched up to kiss the corner of his mouth. 'If you hadn't come back when you did, I'd have been on that coach to Bodmin now.'

'Don't.' He shuddered at how close she'd come to a grisly death at the end of a rope. 'And you've got Freya to thank for that, she's the one who told me what was happening. She's at Porthstennack with Mairead now.' He stepped back and squeezed her hands. 'I won't be long. I'll fetch them back and give them the good news.'

'No!'

He stopped, startled at the sudden panicky note in her voice. 'What?'

'She mustn't come back until Finn has gone.'

'Why not?'

'It's ...' She shook her head, and Matthew's heart sank.

'Anna, there must only be truth between us now. Please.'

Anna stared at her hands, clasped in front of her on the bar top. At last she cleared her throat. 'All right. In the spirit of truth between us now, I'll tell you.' Her brow creased. 'I'm trusting you with everything. Do you understand?'

He didn't know if he could bear to hear what she was going to say, but he nodded. His heart thumped uncomfortably, and he could smell that damned rum on his own breath, but she seemed aware of none of it.

'She can't come back yet, because as soon as she sees Finn she'll tell him the truth. It was her that killed Liam Cassidy.'

Chapter Twenty-Two

Freya stared, stupefied. '*What?*'

Mairead took a deep breath. 'I left someone for dead. It was … shocking.' She glanced around James Fry's little sitting room, as if there were people lurking in the shadows, but James had not yet come home. It was Mairead who'd remembered Juliet saying the house would be unlocked, and who had taken on the role of protector as Freya sat hunched and terrified on the beach.

Now the terror was on Mairead's face instead. 'I have to tell someone,' she whispered. 'I left him for dead, and now Father's come for me. It *must* be why he's here.'

'It's all right, we won't let him take you.' Freya leaned forward to take Mairead's hand. She couldn't yet bring herself to tell the girl that it was so much worse than she thought. That would come, in time, but Mairead was already shaking uncontrollably, and her gaze was skipping and slithering all around the room, finding nothing to focus on.

'Tell me what happened,' Freya said gently, and Mairead finally brought her eyes around to hers. She said nothing for a long moment, but gradually calmed, and then nodded.

'All right. It was a bit after the new year. Mother and Father were having a dinner party, in honour of someone Father hoped would invest in his research. He was so close to a breakthrough, you see, in a particular kind of surgery. Lapa-something. It was supposed to make it safer, somehow, with smaller holes or something. Anyway, there was a German doctor who'd carried out the procedure on a dog, seven or eight years ago, but Father was in the race to perform it on a human subject.'

'So he needed money.'

Mairead nodded. 'He kept giving all these dinner parties we couldn't afford, just in the hopes that one of his guests would be the one to lend it. I wasn't allowed to attend, of course.'

January 1910, Ireland

'You'd only be bored, *ma mhuirnín*.' Mother pressed Mairead's hand, and her own expression made it clear she herself would prefer to be spending the evening in her room. She looked enviously at Mairead's comfortable house-dress, then at her own elegant gown; old, and re-sewn in places, but skilfully enough that hopefully no one would notice.

'What time will you be finished?' Mairead wanted to know. 'I was hoping we could go for a walk later.'

'There'll be no time for that,' Mother said. 'It'll be dark in half an hour and dinner doesn't even start for another two after that.'

Mairead glanced out of her bedroom window, at the gathering shadows. Beyond the road lay the sea, and if she listened hard she'd be able to hear it, but with her door open all she could hear were the voices of guests arriving downstairs. Loud. Annoying. But so necessary for Father's future.

'Will the bank lend enough, do you think?' she asked.

Mother looked startled. 'I'd no idea you knew what this dinner was for.'

'Just that if Father can persuade Mr Cassidy to give him some money, then his research can continue.'

'Well, that's all there is to know, I suppose.'

And if I'm there, Mr Cassidy will be embarrassed, and not want to help. Mairead didn't know what it was about her that Father was ashamed of; she always behaved well, and watched her tongue … although sometimes people were *so* foolish, it was for their own good that she spoke up and put their thinking straight.

It was a long time since she'd fallen through one of the holes in her mind, the ones where she could be talking happily one minute, and the next she'd be looking at the person she was talking to and seeing a puzzled frown, or a discomfited search for her mother to come and rescue them. But even so, tonight was too important to Father to risk it happening again, and so tonight she would stay here and listen to the clink of glasses, and the pompous voices, from a distance.

'If Father gets the money, will I go away to school?' she asked.

'Would you like that?' Mother pushed a lock of hair behind Mairead's ear, and it felt all wrong so Mairead unhooked it again. Now it felt better.

'I don't know. Would people think I'm an idiot there, too? Even though I'm better at mathematics than everyone?'

'You're not an idiot.' Mother's voice had an edge to it, and Mairead was pleased with herself for hearing it, since she didn't usually recognise things like that. She'd been told this was part of the problem; an outspoken comment couldn't be fixed by a warning glare from either parent, because she didn't know what they were trying to say. But why didn't they just come right out and tell her, if they thought she was being rude? Surely it was better to be honest?

'I have to go down now,' Mother said. 'I'll come and see you before I go to bed, and if you're still awake I'll tell you all about dinner, and whether or not Mrs Cassidy's dress fits her any better this time.'

'It won't if she's still fat,' Mairead said, and Mother sighed.

'She's trying to lose weight.'

'She's still fat. And lazy. Not like you. You're beautiful. She probably doesn't like that.'

Mother put the back of her hand to her mouth, but Mairead saw her mouth widen behind it, in guilty amusement. 'You mustn't say such things,' she cautioned, and kissed Mairead's cheek. Mairead could feel her still smiling. 'I'll come and see you after,' she repeated, and then she was gone, down to where the boring people would spend the evening trying to out-talk each other. Poor Mother.

Mairead sat looking at the door for a time, and when she stood she wondered if she'd fallen through a hole again; there was no one here to tell her. She wished the doors and walls could speak; she spent such a lot of time with only them for company, she was sure they'd be able to tell her if she was truly getting better.

It was too hot in here, even for just after Christmas; the house had been overly warmed in honour of the banker Cassidy and his wife – and the other doctors in Father's research team, of course, but mostly for Mr Cassidy, since he was the one with the large purse. Mairead went across to open her window, and her attention was caught by the brightness of the moon. Close to full, it hung low in the sky and cast a silver glow across the beach, touching the tips of the waves that rolled in and broke against the rocks. She stared until her eyes adjusted and it was almost like daylight.

Five minutes later she had donned her coat, picked up her collecting basket and walked quickly down to the front door. She saw no one, although she wasn't trying to be sly about it; it was simply as if the fresh air called her, and she answered. It wasn't until she was halfway along the wet path that she realised she was still wearing her indoor shoes, but it didn't matter, there was no one to admonish her out here. The biting wind felt glorious against her skin, and the smell off the sea quickly banished the cloying combination of scents that permeated the house. The pounding surf was sweeter music than any string quartet her father could hire, and she smiled to hear it.

She shifted the basket more comfortably into the crook of her elbow, and picked her way carefully down the cliff path. The wind was strong enough tonight that the few clouds blew rapidly across the moon and away again, leaving a thin light reflecting on the distant water, and on the pale sand. The beach was deserted, and Mairead stooped to pull off first one shoe and stocking, then, balancing on the damp sand and curling her toes into it, she bared the other foot. The sand was cold, but the freedom of flexing her toes against the chill felt wonderful.

She began her usual, slow walk across the beach towards the opposite headland, pulling at her hair fastenings as she went. The wind got in among the newly freed curls, so much like her mother's, and tugged at them so they whipped around her face. She stopped now and again to pick up a shell, or a pebble that caught the moonlight in some way, but her pleasure tonight was just in the walking.

She reached the low, flat rocks on the other side of the beach and sat down, her feet dangling in the cold pools left behind by the receding tide. Sheltered here, she let her mind roam where it would, and, as usual these days, it took an inquisitive peek into her future. Did she want to go away to school? What would they make of her, the idiot daughter of a respected – and perhaps soon to be famous – surgeon? Apart from a flair for mathematics, what did she have that would earn her a place alongside other students? Even her early governesses had, one by one, given their notice and left, and they had already known what to expect when they'd taken the job.

Mairead suspected that, rather than the given excuse that they could not cope with her behaviour, it was more the case that she knew far more than they did and they risked looking incompetent as a result. It had probably not helped that Mairead's own frustrations had found their outlet in displays of what Mother would call 'unacceptable temper tantrums'. But she had only struck one governess, and that was because the woman had kept shouting at her, with her face right up close to Mairead's, and it was the only way to make her stop. She'd stopped all right; her mouth had dropped open, and her reddened face withdrawn from where it had seemed to press Mairead against the wall, even without touching her. She had also withdrawn from Father's employ.

At last Mother had taken over her schooling, and the tantrums and outbursts almost never happened anymore. Mother said she had simply outgrown them, as a child would, and perhaps she was right. Maybe her life would re-join the correct path, and leave the turmoil of its younger years behind in the past, where it belonged.

A sound drifted across the rocks and halted her thoughts. Voices, throwing casual insults back and forth. Laughter that held a disconcertingly raucous note, and the unmistakable, off-key singing of a young man too far in his cups to care what others thought of his talents. Mairead strained through the darkness, and as the three young men came closer she recognised two of them: the Cassidy brothers, whose father was even now at her home, enjoying her own father's best whisky. The third, the one who seemed determined to entertain them all with his song, was someone she'd never seen before.

They glanced in her direction, but she held as little interest for them as they held for her. She looked back at her feet, at the waving weed that tickled her toes in the water, and listened with irritation as the three boys slipped and slid over the rocks, chuckling, singing, and generally not going away fast enough. The peace was shattered, it was time to go home.

Mairead sighed, and dragged her feet from the water with deep reluctance. She braced one hand on the rocks and made her way carefully back to the sand, where she sat down and used the hem of her skirt to dry her feet so she could put her stockings back on. Absorbed in this, she hadn't realised the voices had fallen silent until she heard a stifled giggle behind her, and she whipped her head around to see the singer's face inches from hers.

'Away with you,' she said crossly. 'You're drunk, the lot of you.'

'You're drunk!' the singer mimicked, in a high-pitched voice. The others laughed.

'And you're not as clever as you think you are,' Mairead said. 'Go on and leave me alone.'

'Go on and leave me alone!'

'Ah, would you just listen to yourself?' Mairead gave up trying to keep her dried foot off the ground, and stamped it instead. Her bare foot on wet sand made a most unsatisfactory hollow thump, and all Mairead got for her trouble was a sharp pain that shot through her ankle and into her shin.

'You think we're drunk?' the younger of the two brothers said. He took a step forward and seized her wrist. 'Sure, should we show you how drunk we are?'

Mairead ripped her arm free. 'I can see that very well. Go home to your playroom.'

The boy's face darkened. 'I'm no child.' His voice was hard, and Mairead's heart slithered, making her feel sick. She backed away, almost tripping over her skirt, but righted herself before she fell.

'Just go home,' she said again, trying not to let the fear travel to her voice. It didn't work, and she heard the singer's awful giggle again. 'I'll not tell anyone you were here. Just leave me alone.'

She flinched backwards as the older brother reached for her arm, and he missed. But that was all Mairead needed; she whirled, grabbed her skirt away from her feet, and ran up the beach as fast as she could. Her ankle throbbed and slowed her a little, but the boys' drinking must have been working against them, and in her favour. Through the intermittent darkness and moonlight she saw she was close to the cliff, but ahead of her a shape moved along its foot; one of the lads had guessed where she would make for and was heading her off.

Mairead veered away again, and found herself running towards the sea with no thought of what she would do when she reached it. Her coat was open, and snapping out behind her, her breath came in painful gasps, and she held her skirt high with one hand, using the other to push the hair out of her eyes as she ran.

She heard footsteps slamming down on the packed wet sand behind her as her flight brought her back into the path of the other two, but thank the Lord she'd been right about them having too much to drink; their laughter fell further behind with every step and then she could hear only her own panicked breathing, and the little cries of desperation as she urged herself faster.

She reached the edge of the sea at the eastern side of the beach, and relief lifted the weight of exhaustion; a quick scramble across these rocks, a few steps across dry sand, and she would be at the next path that wound up the cliff. She risked a glance behind her, and gave a breathless cry of horror; two of the boys had, indeed, succumbed to the alcohol they'd enjoyed, and had fallen back far enough to be out of sight. But the younger Cassidy brother had persisted, and was close enough for her to see the expression on his face, and this time she had no difficulty reading it.

He reached out for her flapping coat, and jerked her to a halt. 'No you don't,' he breathed, stepping closer. Mairead could hardly move, all the fear-induced speed and strength ebbed away, and she dragged in breaths that were not enough. Her heart felt as though it might burst from her chest at any moment, and her throat was too tight to speak; she watched Cassidy with wary eyes, pleading with him silently to let her go, to return to his friends. To have some compassion.

'I know who you are,' he went on, swapping his grip on her coat for one on her shoulder. 'You're Finn Casey's daughter. The simpleton.'

'Leave ... me ... alone,' Mairead managed. She was shivering now, despite the sweat that pooled in the hollow of her throat. Her heart was still pounding, and she felt light-headed, but readied herself to tear away from him the moment his grasp on her shoulder slackened the tiniest bit. She waited.

' ... not running away. Mother of God, you *want* this!'

Mairead blinked, then realised he had already let go of her shoulder and put his hands on the front of her blouse. Terror seized her; *a hole! She had fallen down a mind-hole ...*

Cassidy's fingers wormed their way between the buttons and pulled. The buttons flew off into the darkness, and Mairead felt the cotton give way, exposing her corset cover, and Cassidy grunted in frustration at having more layers to tackle. He pushed at her, and she stumbled over her skirt, but this time she had no chance to catch her balance, and she fell backwards with her top half in the surf. She tried to shuffle away, but Cassidy was too quick for her; he dropped to his knees, straddling her, and pinned her to the sand. The sea rushed in, breaking against Mairead's shoulders, and wetting her to the waist. She found herself wishing it had closed over her head instead.

Cassidy's face came towards hers, and she twisted away, pressing her lips closed, but his fingers found her cheeks and sank into them, bony and hard, and dragged her face back. She squeezed her eyes shut, and prayed for him to kiss her and leave, now he had proved himself to his friends, but even as his tongue forced her lips apart she felt his hand fall away from her bodice, and begin to fumble at the sides of her skirt. She did the only thing she could think of: she bit down hard on his tongue.

He reared back in shock, spitting blood to the side, but the surge of satisfaction was shattered as he brought his free hand around to connect with the side of her face in a hard, stinging slap. The other hand still dragged at her skirt, and when she felt his fingers close on her bare leg, pinching the delicate skin at the top of her thigh, she knew he wouldn't stop. Not now.

'Call me a child?' he panted. 'I'll show you who's a child.'

She let her hands fall away from where they had been pressing against his chest, and instead groped around on the sand at her sides until she found what she was looking for ... She wrapped her right hand around the rock, and brought it up and around in a tight arc. The sensation as it struck the side of his head was both sickening and savagely thrilling, and for a second she thought she might have to do it again, and she was ready, but he groaned and crawled off her, shaking his head like a wounded dog. He tried to stand, but couldn't, and collapsed, face-down in the sand.

Mairead lay there in mute shock, and only came to her senses when another wave swept in, this time washing over her face and making her choke and spit. She rolled over and climbed to her feet, and stumbled away from Cassidy's prone form, over the rocks. Her clothing, wet and heavy, dragged at her as she ran for the cliff, but all her thoughts were ahead, on home and safety. It wasn't until she was halfway up the path that she remembered her basket, still sitting by the rocks on the far side of the beach. The tide would doubtless carry it away, along with her indoor shoes. Mairead stopped, her breath cutting off short again; she had left Cassidy alone down there, unconscious, and on the very edge of the rapidly encroaching sea. She stared towards the beach, but she could see nothing except the moonlight, touching the white tops of the incoming tide.

Terror fought with conscience, and Mairead took another half-step forwards, homewards, then drew her foot back, barely acknowledging the rough grass beneath her feet, or the small pebbles that pressed into her skin. She felt again the stinging, choking sensation of the water rushing up her nose and down her throat. No one should suffer that, no matter what he had done.

With a soft sound of fearful realisation, Mairead turned back down the path to the beach. Even if she could only manage to pull him onto the rocks, that would give him time to wake, or for his friends to find him. If the rock hadn't killed him. Her heart stuttered at the thought, but her feet kept moving, and finally delivered her back onto the dry sand at the foot of the cliff. She moved towards the rocks, but before she had stepped onto them she heard voices above the sound of the rolling surf.

'Look, he's passed out, the stupid wee ossal!' The dubious singer's voice was shrill with mocking delight.

Cassidy's brother grunted; he was likely pulling Cassidy out of harm's way. 'He wasn't drinking, Donal, did ya not notice, or were ya too busy searching for your talent in the bottom of yer cup?'

Mairead wished she could see across to the other side of the rocks, but it didn't matter now. They had found him, and he'd be made safe without the need for her to go near him again; she could all too clearly imagine how it would feel to be pulling him to safety, only to feel his hand grab her arm and hear his voice suddenly spitting promises of vengeance.

'Wake up, Liam!' The older Cassidy boy was sounding less cross than worried now. 'Come on.'

Mairead had begun to walk away, but stopped again. A sick feeling wormed through her, and she swallowed hard.

'Jesus!' It was Donal, this time. 'Look, he's got blood all down him!'

'Where?'

'It's from his head, I think. The sea kept washing it away. Jesus, Rory, what if he's dead?'

Mairead's head swam, and she crouched, sure she was about to faint. She missed some of the words that flew between the panicked boys on the other side of the rocks; the thundering in her own ears was all she could hear. She took a couple of deep breaths, her mind spinning, seeking ways to escape and dismissing them immediately. How could this have happened?

'... breathing, thank God. But we need to get that head looked at.'

'Did he fall, d'you think?'

'Onto what?' Rory's voice was grim. 'No. It was that girl, it must have been.'

'We'll fetch the police on her – this is attempted murder.'

'Did you recognise her?'

Mairead held her breath.

Donal's voice was thankfully dismissive. 'No. Just some whore. Who else'd be out here alone, at this time of night?'

There was another grunt from Rory Cassidy. 'Come on! Help me with him. Wake up, Liam, damn you ... '

Mairead listened for a little while longer, still crouched, still trembling, and not even able to fully embrace the relief that Liam Cassidy was still alive. When she finally crept away to the cliff path again, all she could hear was his voice as he'd dragged her to a halt.

'You're Finn Casey's daughter ... '

* * *

'What did you do?' Freya's mouth was dry.

'I ran home. I changed into my night things and I went to bed. Not that I slept. I pretended to when Mother came in, though. It wasn't until the morning that I heard Liam had been taken to hospital and that he hadn't woken yet. That was when I told Mother what had happened.'

'What did she do?'

'She told me not to worry, and not to tell a soul. She went to the beach and found my basket with my stockings in, and one of my shoes. The other shoe was washed out to sea. Then she went out for the whole day, and when she came back, she said we were leaving first thing the next morning.'

'And you came here.'

Mairead nodded, and wiped a trembling hand over her face. 'Liam Cassidy must have woken, and told the Gardaí who it was that hit him.' She gave a little sob, and bit the back of her hand. 'They'll hang me for this, Freya!'

'No! They won't!' Freya didn't know which was worse, but Mairead deserved to hear the truth now, and so she took a deep breath. 'I'm sorry, but the Cassidy boy is dead ...' She held up a hand as Mairead stared at her in horror. 'Anna has taken the blame on herself. Papá has gone to stop her leaving.'

'No!' Mairead leapt to her feet, and moved towards the door, but Freya caught at her.

'He *will* stop her, I'm sure of it.'

'What was that?'

'What?'

Mairead subsided, and looked fearfully at the kitchen door. 'I thought I heard someone out there.'

Freya listened, but heard nothing. 'You're jumping at shadows. I'm not surprised. Come back and sit with me a while.' She led Mairead back to the lumpy couch, and sat beside her.

'I'll make some tea,' she said eventually. 'Then we'll walk back together. Your father will be gone by then, and Anna will be safe at the Tinner's. Papá will take care of her.'

Mairead nodded, her hands twisting in her lap. 'All right,' she whispered.

Freya patted her shoulder and went into the kitchen. Most of these cottages suffered from the damp conditions, but Roland had always taken good care of his home. It seemed, for all his learning, James was not so diligent; paint was peeling away from the walls on which the plaster was also cracking, and one of the sash cords had snapped, requiring the window to be held in place with a wedge of cloth. Still, at least it was warm.

She slid the heavy kettle across onto the hot plate of the range, and noticed the pantry door was off the latch. Would James mind if she took some bread, or a piece of cake if he had some? She had only taken a couple of steps across the kitchen when the front door opened and she stopped, heart thudding.

James sounded equally startled. 'Who the bloody hell ... oh!' The next time he spoke his voice was gentle. 'Miss Garvey. What are you doing here? No, don't get up, it's all right.'

As James continued to speak Freya slumped in relief; Papá had managed to stop Anna getting on the coach after all, and James actually sounded glad of it.

'I must go to her,' Mairead said, and Freya heard the panic in her voice.

'She doesn't want you to be caught up in it,' James said. Freya peered into the sitting room and saw him sitting next to Mairead. 'Let them talk it out between them,' he said. 'You're more than welcome to stay here for the night.'

A tiny sound came from the pantry, distracting her. Mice, no doubt. When she listened again Mairead was speaking.

'... kind of you, but Freya is going to walk with me.'

'Ah. She's here?'

'In the kitchen.'

A moment later James appeared in the doorway. He looked meaningfully at the two cups on the table, and at the now-boiling kettle, blowing out steam on the hot plate.

'I'm sorry,' Freya said, blushing. 'It's just that Mairead's in shock, and I thought some hot, sweet tea … I'll pay you for what I've used.'

'Actually I was wondering where my cup was.' James gave her a little smile. It made him look much more like the sort of man who might have been friends with Papá once. She had to make herself remember what he'd done, and was annoyed with herself for almost bending under his apparent friendliness.

'You can have mine,' she said instead. 'We won't stay long, we'll be out from under your feet soon enough.'

'You're a good girl, Freya,' James said. 'Look, I know things have been difficult with your pa and me, but none of it is your fault. Or that poor girl's in there.' He gestured with his thumb, over his shoulder. 'If you'll allow me, I'll walk both of you back to town. It's dark, I wouldn't feel right turning you out.'

There was another scrape from the pantry, and Freya was surprised to find herself smiling at James. 'You probably ought to use your time getting rid of those mice,' she said. 'And get that window fixed, Juliet won't be best pleased to move in otherwise. Don't worry about us, we'll be fine now. Thank you.'

'If you're sure.' He frowned at the pantry; clearly he was less used to vermin than the average Porthstennack dweller, but he would get used to it. He would have to.

Freya went back into the sitting room, and found Mairead on her feet ready to go. 'Don't you want your tea?'

Mairead shook her head, and pulled open the front door. 'No, I want our parents. Come on.'

She started down Paddle Lane towards the main Caernoweth road, and Freya hurried to catch up, but flinched at the rush of the tide over the shingled beach, and stopped. Now the urgency to find Papá was no longer driving her on, her courage had once more failed her. She closed her eyes, and told herself the sea was beautiful. It was harsh, and it was dangerous, but it was also wild and exciting, and miles away over its rolling whitecaps lay unknown places she might even visit one day.

The sea was beautiful. It was filled with creatures both familiar and strange. Whole cities were said to lie submerged beneath the grey-green, forever shifting surface. She had found a whole childhood's worth of treasures there herself. The sea ran through her papá's blood and her own; it provided a living for those who respected it; it drew artists and musicians to gaze on it, inspired to create their own beauty; it fed the world.

The sea *was* beautiful ... But she still couldn't look at it.

She took a deep breath, and opened her eyes again, feeling the sting of frustrated tears at the back of her throat. Then she realised Mairead had returned wordlessly to her side, and stood waiting. Freya unclenched the fist she hadn't even known she'd made, and willed her foot to move forwards; it wasn't fair to Mairead to make her wait, not when her mother was just a few minutes' walk away. She wanted to tell her to go on, that she would make her own way, but her muscles would not move, and her voice would not make a sound.

Then, startled, she felt Mairead's warm, strong touch on her fingers. The girls looked at one another in silence, dark brown eyes meeting moss green, and then there were two tremulous smiles, and a slight nod from Mairead that Freya answered with one of her own. She closed her fingers tightly around Mairead's and took a step forward, and one more, and they walked together, hand in hand like sisters, up the winding hill to Caernoweth.

Epilogue

Caernoweth Churchyard

The gravestone had not yet been made, but the marker was a lonely and unsettling sight:

> Anna Casey, laid to rest here.
> B: 3 January 1877.
> D: 7 February 1910.

'It's true, in a sense,' Matthew moved to stand at her side. Anna looked at him, grateful for something to drag her eyes away.

'I know. She's gone, and here I am instead.'

'And thank God for it.'

They stood without talking for a while. Anna was still struggling to make sense of everything that had happened, and she could hardly bring herself to accept that life might settle down now, after all. But it was true. She had Doctor Bartholomew to thank for that, as well as for the forged death certificate; he had forbidden any questioning of Mairead by the police, stating she was still in deep shock after the accident that had claimed her mother. There was nothing to be gained from it anyway, he'd told them, it had simply been one of those tragic incidents with which any coastal area was all too familiar. They had agreed, and there the investigation had ended.

'How will you feel, working for Finn?' Matthew asked, breaking the silence.

Anna frowned, hearing a different question in his voice. 'Do you mean, will we become close again?'

Matthew looked about to deny it, then gave up. 'Will you?'

'Matthew Penhaligon, have you lost your wits? Anyone lucky enough . . . ' She broke off, shook her head, and smiled. 'No, Finn and I will never be close again.'

'Good.' He nodded briskly, as if he'd known the answer but had been compelled to ask the question anyway. A formality completed. He held out his hand. 'Come on, Freya's making tea.'

They left the small churchyard, and she slipped her hand into his, aware that something had made her wait until they were clear of the consecrated ground. 'It's odd,' she said, 'but even though the grave isn't real, it still feels wrong that this isn't a Catholic church.'

'I didn't think you practised now.'

'I don't, but I still have my beliefs. I suppose they never go away.'

'It's going to be hard,' he cautioned, not for the first time. 'I know it was the only way, but you'll lose everything.'

'Not quite everything,' Her smile returned, and she let go

of his hand and took his arm instead. 'Even if the noose wasn't waiting for me back home—'

'Anna!'

She hugged his arm close to her side. 'Sorry. But what I mean is, even if things hadn't gone so horribly wrong, I would still rather be here with you and no property, than back there with that big ugly house and no hope of happiness.'

'And your aunt and uncle? Your cousins?'

'That's the worst of it,' she admitted. 'Knowing they think I'm a murderess.'

'Finn will have told them it wasn't deliberate.'

'I hope so. And I hope they won't shun Mairead through shame.'

Outside the shop again, Anna looked at the name above the sign, then back at Matthew. 'You were prepared to give this place up for me.' Every time she remembered it she felt awed and humbled.

'Well,' he shrugged, 'you were wearing a particularly nice blouse that day.'

Anna laughed. Then she shook her head. 'I still find it unbelievable that the whole town has taken my side.'

'*Most* of the town. There are those who'll resist even your charms.'

She smiled, but he was right. It had been far from a unanimous decision to help her evade the law, but those who had supported her had quieted the protests to a low murmur no one else would hear, and soon even the dissenters would cease to care – they had their own lives to worry about. 'We'll have to hope the Donithorn family keep a tight rein on David,' she pointed out.

'Ellen will see to it. You guild ladies stick together, after all.' Matthew pushed open the door, but Anna stopped, realising something.

'I'm not a widow. I was *never* a widow, so I can't be a member.'

'Then you won't be a member. But you run their meeting house, and they'll thank you for it. Besides, you'll always be Malcolm Penworthy's ancestor. Like the doctor said, this is your town now, as much as anyone's.'

'Do you really think that's the reason people have been so willing to help?' Anna couldn't help the twinge of disappointment.

'And that you're now Anna Penhaligon, of course.' He grinned. 'No, that's not the only reason.' He drew her into his home and closed the door. They stood in the hallway, listening to the girls' chatter from the kitchen, and the deeper, gruffer tones of Robert Penhaligon that underlaid it as he tried to fit in a word edgeways.

'The town loves you,' Matthew went on. 'Brian would never go to the Tinner's again if you weren't there to serve him; the guild would need a new meeting house; Mrs Gale would have to find someone else to make up stories about, and that'd drive her potty; and as for me . . . ' He bent his head and kissed her, and she rested her hands lightly at his waist and kissed him back, swaying towards him until he gathered her close.

'As for you, what?' she asked a little breathlessly, when he released her.

'As for me, I'd have to learn to enjoy properly cooked food again.'

'How dare you!' She slapped his arm, and turned to go into the kitchen, smiling as she heard his laughter follow her down the hall.

When she went into the kitchen, however, she was astonished, and disconcerted, to see Robert sitting in his usual chair, his face thunderous.

'Got a bone to pick with you,' he said, his bushy brows drawing down, and Anna's heart sank.

'Whatever's the matter?'

'I know all about the lies you been tellin'.' He shook his head. 'No, I understand why you 'ad to say um to everyone else. I don't blame you. But ... well, to look at me square, and tell me *such* an untruth, while I'm lyin' helpless in me own bed?'

'I ... d-don't understand,' Anna stammered. 'What untruth now?'

Robert's eyes held hers, and although she wanted desperately to turn to Matthew for support, she found she couldn't look away. Then, as if someone had whipped away a dark, scowling mask, Robert's face wobbled, and he let out a bellow of laughter.

'You in't no bleddy nurse!'

The End